"Either way," Sordaak said, connecting the dots, "they know we are on the road going north."

"That means they probably have a pretty good idea where we are," agreed the paladin.

"If they know of this place—and we have no reason to believe they don't—then that is a valid assumption," the ranger said.

"We were herded here!" Sudden realization struck the caster hard.

"Maybe," Breunne said.

"But why?" asked the cleric.

"That I don't know," replied the ranger. "However, if any of the previous assumptions are correct, then it's reasonable to think that their goal by such a storm is to slow our progress."

"To what end?" Sordaak was still doubtful.

Breunne looked over at the caster. "To allow them to catch up with us."

Sordaak's eyes widened as he quickly stood. "It's a trap!"

ICE HOMME

VANCE PUMPHREY

KELLIS,

I WANT TO THANK YOU SO MUCH

FOR YOUR CONTINUED SUPPORT OF ME
AND MY BOOKS! BOOK IV IN A
COUPLE OF WEEKS!

THANKS FOR READING,

LEAPING WIZARD PRESS

Vance L Pumphrey

Ice Homme

Book Three in the Valdaar's Fist Series

Copyright © 2015 by Vance Pumphrey

Cover Art © 2015 Joe Calkins
Sword Logo Design © 2015 Joe Calkins

Published by Leaping Wizard Press

ISBN-10: 0988740575
ISBN-13: 978-0-9887405-7-0

This book is also available in digital formats.

Discover other titles by the author at
VancePumphrey.com

I'd like to dedicate this book to the purveyors of fantasy known as
TSR and specifically Dungeons & Dragons.
I was initially dragged into the game kicking and screaming.
My first "toon" died only moments after I spent at least a half hour creating him,
and I was hooked.
My second character yet "lives" and will be part of future books.
It goes without saying that once in, I quickly became engrossed and play to this day.

The game became more than that to many, many people—including myself.
After only a few months as a participant, I was transferred by the Navy.
I thought that was the end of my playing days.
Then one night I happened on a group of guys reading three new books:
The Player's Handbook, *The Monster Manual*, and *The Dungeon Master's Guide*.
When I asked them what they were doing,
they replied that they were trying to learn how to play Dungeons & Dragons.
I laughed and told them they would never learn that way,
and they asked me to teach them.
After a few moments hesitation—I had never been a Dungeon Master before—
I asked them if they would let me borrow their books as I had none.
In exchange, I said that I would create a "dungeon" that afternoon
and meet them back there in the common area that evening.
They readily agreed.

That dungeon was just the beginning.
From there my "world" grew to encompass dozens of adventures.
My characters grew in stature and power.
Many of those characters and dungeons can be found within the pages of this
and others of my books—they are the reason I write.
I started these books as a "history" so that I wouldn't forget.
Quickly they became more than that.
Thank you for reading.
And thank you, TSR, for creating a place for many of us
to wander in our minds.

Ice Homme

What has Gone Before

Forged by mortals. ... Enchanted by Drow. ...
Wielded by a God. .... Lost by man...

Or was it?

If you have not read *Dragma's Keep* and *The Library of Antiquity*, then I would suggest you do so! You will not be disappointed.

Ice Homme is the third book in a series called Valdaar's Fist. However, in the event it has been some time since you read the first two books, here is a synopsis of what has gone before.

Sordaak, the sorcerer in this story, pulls together a group to make a raid on Dragma's Keep in book one of the series, coincidently named *Dragma's Keep*. He's after the ancient wizard's fabled staff, *Pendromar, Dragon's Breath,* and his spell books. Sordaak meets up with a rogue, Savinhand, under nefarious conditions and they decide to work together. In the process of escaping from the aforementioned situation, the mage steals a horse, ostensibly with the intention of returning it. The owner of the horse, Thrinndor, a paladin of the Paladinhood of Valdaar, takes exception to such thievery and is intent on exacting appropriate payment from the caster's hide. But smooth talker that he is, Sordaak not only worms his way out of being exacted but also convinces the paladin and his best friend Vorgath, a barbarian dwarf of the Dragaar clan, to join with them.

Together they begin their assault on the Keep, but don't get far before they realize the folly of their ways in making the attempt without some healing power. Lo and behold, what do they find deep in the bowels of this keep? You guessed it! A healer, Cyrillis by name. Not just any healer, either... but a servant of the same god as Thrinndor—Valdaar. There is a minor discrepancy, though... This Valdaar has been dead for many centuries.

Anyway, the companions make their way through the underground labyrinth, battling orcs, sea-monsters, a fire demon and another wizard consorting with assassins. Along the way, they discover that the paladin is a direct descendant of the dead god Valdaar, and are surprised to also learn that Sordaak is a direct descendant of Dragma, a powerful sorcerer that served on Valdaar's High Council. When the paladin tells the story of his master's demise, it is revealed that he is after the immensely powerful sword of his master, *Valdaar's Fist*. With it, he and a person from the line of Dragma (assumed to be Sordaak at this point) and another from the line of Angra-Khan—the High Priest from the god's Council—will attempt to raise the god from his prison in death. In the end it is surmised that Cyrillis must be the third person, but she is orphaned and knows very little of her heritage.

After they fight their way to the treasure room, it is discovered that neither the staff nor the sword is in the booty. However, the powerful greataxe *Flinthgoor, Foe-Cleaver and Death Dealer*—which once belonged to Kreithgaar, Valdaar's mighty General of armies—was there.

Upon exiting the Keep, the companions are beset by Sordaak's mentor, who is also after *Pendromar*. A huge battle ensues, but alas our heroes prevail. But now the mage needs a new mentor, and must go in search of one. The group agrees to meet again in a few weeks' time after getting with their respective trainers.

That's where book two picks up. Vorgath is early to the agreed meeting point, the town of Farreach. He makes friends with a ranger, Breunne, and then manages to upset the locals, getting into a barroom brawl. Big surprise there!

Thrinndor and Cyrillis attempt to squeeze some information about her past out of the local Temple of Set, but the minions don't care for being squeezed so the paladin and healer must fight their way clear. In the process they slay the twin clerics who run the place and burn the temple to the ground. This of course upsets the Minions of Set back at headquarters, and vengeance is promised in the usual manner (not generally pleasant for those involved).

Meanwhile, our rogue learns he has been selected to be one of the contestants in the Rite of Ascension, the process whereby a new leader is chosen for Guild Shardmoor. Savinhand wins the contest, and in order to complete his rise to power he must gather a team and gain access to the Library of Antiquity, which will make him the new administrator for said library.

So, his friends meet him in Shardmoor and they are sent on their way. The companions are led to the secret entrance, only to find out that this is only the beginning of a vast quest during which they are teleported to…where? They have no clue. The only way out of the labyrinth is to finish the quest. Or die.

So the companions again prevail, of course. And of course it is not easy. A hydra, a drow-filled maze, traps out the (never mind where) and a horde of nasty creatures called rakshasa stand in their way. Oh, and a dragon. We mustn't forget the dragon.

The Library contains information that exceeds even what the compatriots had hoped. Cyrillis is indeed of the proper lineage. Thrinndor discovers clues as to the location of *Valdaar's Fist*. Breunne finds in the dragon's lair *Xenotath*, Bow of the First Ranger. And Sordaak goes gaga over the information overload, refusing to sleep while he studied. He had to be dragged out of there kicking and screaming (Vorgath volunteered to do it another way of course, but Thrinndor wouldn't allow it). Savinhand and Cyrillis get their stuff here in Book 3 (tease!).

The companions compare notes and Thrinndor reveals that his prized sword was seen less than four hundred years ago in Ice Homme, headquarters of the Minions of Set. So they decide that is where they must go, at least right after they go rough up some Storm Giants for their outerwear.

That catches you up. So without further ado, here's the third book of Valdaar's Fist, *Ice Homme*.

Chapter One

Road to Mioria

The companions gathered not far from the small cabin they had recently exited. Their drow guides walked a short distance off into a copse of trees. After a few minutes they emerged leading several horses and pack animals laden with supplies.

As the drow turned to go back to the cabin, Vorgath followed them to the door and pulled one aside. Initially there was a heated discussion, but in the end both parties smiled and shook hands.

Goodbyes were again said, and the elves re-entered the small dwelling. The companions were told they should wait a few minutes and then it would be safe for them to enter if they wished.

"What was that about?" asked the paladin as the barbarian approached, whistling a tune and looking pleased with himself.

"What?" Vorgath said.

"That conversation you had with the elf," Thrinndor said.

"None of your damn business!" exclaimed the dwarf as he looked back at the cabin. Curiosity got the better of him, so Vorgath sauntered up to the door and jerked it open. He was not sure what he expected, but it certainly wasn't what he got.

Inside were now the normal contents of an old cabin, one that had been well maintained for the occasional passerby or passersby. There were several bunks and an open hearth for cooking and heating. It was cozy, and were it not late morning, Vorgath would have suggested they stop and rest.

However, the group was anxious to get moving, as was he. He shut the door and affixed the latch. The dwarf shook his head as he joined his friends.

"Well?" asked the paladin.

"Deep subject, shallow mind," replied the barbarian with a grunt.

"Ha, ha." Thrinndor shook his head.

Vorgath looked over his shoulder at the cabin and shrugged. "Just a 'normal' cabin now," he said. "Bunks, hearth, some pots and pans—the usual stuff." He shrugged again.

"What did you expect?" said the paladin as he tightened the cinch for the saddle on the mount he had selected. It wasn't his horse, but this big roan would do, he decided.

"If I knew what to expect," answered the dwarf, "I wouldn't have gone over there in the first place!" He wandered over and checked the pack animals. He nodded his head in satisfaction. These drow sure knew how to travel! There were several small casks of wine, mead, ales and even some water. There was also some fresh meat, bread and a couple of wheels of cheese. They were outfitted for at least a month, assuming they could do some hunting along the way.

After each of the companions had selected a mount, the pack animals were dispersed such that they were evenly distributed among them. The mounts were inspected and found to be in good order.

"The drow are excellent purveyors of horse stock," Breunne said as he eye-balled his mount.

"Indeed," agreed the paladin as he swung into the saddle. The big roan side-stepped skittishly a couple of times and rolled its eyes to get a better look at the human perched on his back, but otherwise it accepted its lot. Thrinndor turned to look at the others who were still standing around. "Ready?"

"Born that way," said the dwarf as he shouldered *Flinthgoor*. "Just don't hurt that old nag by trying to run off and leave me." He flashed a grin at the paladin.

"Worry not, old one," Thrinndor said, returning the smile. "We are in no hurry. I have no intention of harming these excellent mounts." He looked at the others. "Mount up!"

Cyrillis grasped the mane of the black on white speckled mare she had selected and vaulted easily onto her back.

Sordaak walked around the black gelding with three white stockings that had been assigned to him. He was more than a little uneasy, as this big black reminded him of another that had given him quite a ride what seemed like years ago but was actually only...what was it? Three, four months? He sighed. Finally, he looked deep into the eyes of the horse, seeming to warn it, grabbed a handful of mane and tentatively climbed aboard. The big horse's muscles twitched a couple of times, and he rotated his ears back to focus on the pest who dared to ride him. But he did not move. The mage let out a sigh of relief and tossed a nervous smile at the paladin. "Ready."

Breunne leapt atop the compact but powerful-looking stallion he had picked out of the brood, adjusted *Xenotath* to a more comfortable position and nodded his readiness to the party leader.

Thrinndor turned his mount with his heels and started him in the direction toward the same road they had arrived on just a week ago, another instance of time seeming to drag on longer than it actually had. Could it only have been a week? He shook his head mutely. Perhaps a day longer. Certainly no more.

When the party got to the road, Thrinndor pointed his mount north and waited for the rest to catch up. When Vorgath got close enough, the paladin said, "I am not familiar with this region," patting his horse idly on the neck. "What is the correct path?"

"Well, you've got the first turn correct," replied the barbarian. "We follow this road north for about a day. By midday tomorrow we should come across an old road that leads east toward the coast. We'll follow that for about two days." He sniffed the air and looked toward the east, and a concerned look fluttered across his face. "Before we get to the coast we will have to turn north." He cocked an eye and looked up at his friend the paladin. "We don't want to follow the cliffs." He shook his head. "Trust me on this."

"I do," Thrinndor said.

"It's going to snow before dusk tomorrow," the barbarian continued. "It looks like an early winter for the north."

"Great!" muttered the caster under his breath. "I hope they packed some additional clothing in that stuff for us."

"Wait," Cyrillis said her voice dubious, "how do you know it will snow tomorrow?"

Vorgath rolled his eyes. "I can explain it to you in great detail, young lady, but that would take hours!"

"His old bones ache," said the caster with a smug grin plastered on his face.

"Ha, ha," retorted the barbarian. "Just you climb your skinny little ass down off of that flea-bitten excuse for a horse and I'll teach you some respect for your elders!"

The companions got a good laugh over that. "Time is the one thing we seem to have plenty of," the healer hinted, her tone indicating that she still had her doubts.

"Do not get him started," Thrinndor said, still smiling. "He can talk *all day* once you get him on such a subject."

The barbarian scowled at his old friend. "I'll shorten it up for you," he said as he turned back to the cleric. "In part the 'old bones' remark fits." He threw a nasty look at the caster. "Storms ebb and flow on air pressure differences, and 'the joints between old bones' are more susceptible to this pressure difference." Now he gave the mage an I-told-you-so grin. "So, before a storm 'old bones' will notice it first." He took a deep breath before proceeding. "Second, subtle changes in the wind and direction, along with known local tendencies, can also be used to foretell a coming change in the weather."

"I thought you were going to shorten it up?" Sordaak couldn't resist tweaking the dwarf. He smiled at the grimace he received. Besides, he was intrigued at what Vorgath was saying. He'd heard some of this before, but never had it been explained in a manner that satisfied him.

"Last—and this is shortening down the explanation by *a lot*—you can smell an upcoming disturbance—"

"*Bullshit!*" The mage pretended to cough into a closed fist as the barbarian said this.

"Silence, moron," Vorgath said without turning his head. "Discreet aromas may be carried on the wind 'ere a storm strikes. Just a bit ago I tested the air. I was able to catch the faint scent of wet, decaying leaves." He looked over at the nearby trees. "While these leaves are certainly turning and will soon fall, they *are still on the trees*! Hence, the aroma came from elsewhere." He puffed up his chest. "These scents can travel hundreds of miles."

He paused, waiting for another interruption from the caster, but when none was forthcoming, he continued. "While any one of these can foretell an upcoming weather system, it usually takes more than one to forecast anything with any certainty."

"You noted more than one just now?" Asked the healer, her concerns somewhat mollified, even as the doubts remained. She had heard none of this before.

"Oh, yes," replied the dwarf. "When we first emerged from the portal, I noticed an ache in my joints." He scowled at the sorcerer. "I've been in this area many times over the years, during all seasons, and the winds are normally out of the west or northwest." He looked over at the trees. "Right now they are coming out of the east, and they have picked up some even in the couple of hours we have been back out here." He breathed deeply through his prodigious nose, focusing their attention on him. "Lastly, if you breathe deep through your nose, you can detect aromas that may not be from the region you are in. It's better to get a sample of air away from trees, rocks, mountains and anything else that might taint what you are trying to catch scent of."

Without realizing it, Sordaak took in a deep breath; through his nose, of course. He couldn't detect anything!

"It takes years of training," said the barbarian. "Don't fret if you don't detect anything you don't recognize at first. Keep working on it."

"All I recognize is the repugnant aroma of unwashed dwarf!" The sorcerer wrinkled his nose in distaste.

"Shut it!" snapped the dwarf. He discreetly tried to check his underarms. He couldn't smell anything.

Sordaak tried unsuccessfully to stifle a snicker and got a glare from the barbarian for his efforts. "Let's see," said the caster, still chuckling, "we can now add weatherdwarf to your repertoire."

"What?" It was Cyrillis' turn to give the mage a dirty look.

The magicuser held up a fist and then extended his forefinger. "First, our multitalented midget is infallible in his ability to determine direction." Vorgath growled from deep inside his chest as Sordaak held up a second finger. "Second, he is able to determine angles and depths in caverns and other holes in the earth." He smiled as the dwarf's chest again rumbled and held up a third finger. "Third, he can tell the vintage and place of origin for any ale, wine and most other adult beverages." The dwarf took in a breath to again growl, but instead cocked his head to one side and nodded his agreement. "And now," the sorcerer continued, "he can tell us the weather a week in advance with but a whiff with that stupendous schnoz!"

"What do you expect?" Thrinndor asked with as much seriousness as he could muster, which was not much. "He is a thousand years old—he was bound to pick up a few hobbies over the years."

The barbarian turned a couple shades of red and puffed out his chest to protest, but instead burst out laughing. He was quickly joined by the remaining companions.

Breunne, who had been hanging back some, moved in closer as he wiped the mirth from his eyes. "Perhaps I should scout ahead," he said as he turned to peer over a shoulder. "While these parts are not necessarily known for nefarious activity, there have been reports in recent years of wandering packs of wolves and an occasional raid by an orc party."

"I believe that to be prudent," agreed the paladin.

"Bah," said the dwarf, still chortling. "We shouldn't meet up with any resistance until we get off of this main road."

Sordaak held up his hand again, now spreading all five fingers. "And five: Travel guide extraordinaire!"

The laughter began anew.

When Thrinndor finally spoke, he was shaking his head. "Just the same, I would feel better if you were out ahead of the rest of the party."

Still chuckling, the ranger nodded and lightly applied his heels to the flanks of his mount. The two of them bolted ahead of the group and turned off into the trees to the right.

The morning passed with much the same banter being tossed about. It felt good to be moving again, so they chose not to stop for lunch, instead eating in the saddle, except for Vorgath, of course. He made do. He wasn't going to starve, that was for certain. The tricky part was tapping a cask and filling the provided flagons without spilling any, all while on the move. This was one time it was good to have a member of the party on the ground, walking.

Breunne rode out of the trees from their left and joined them. As he rode, he wrapped some venison up between a two chunks of bread. "There are some old tracks in several places from a band of orcs." He took a bite and washed it down with a mouthful of ale before continuing. "I see nothing that is newer than at least three, maybe four, weeks old." He shook his head. "And that bothers me."

"Why?" asked the cleric as she wiped her mouth with a rag she pulled from her sleeve.

"When you see an orc, you know where they are," replied the ranger. "But it's when you *don't* see them—and you know they're around—that you must worry."

A silence fell over the companions broken only by the sound of hooves hitting the occasional rock in the road.

"Very well," said the paladin as he turned to survey the road ahead. There was a slight curve to the right not far in front of them that suddenly made him uneasy. "Do not wander too far ahead then. Stay within the distance of a shout." He turned and locked eyes with the ranger. Breunne nodded. Thrinndor continued. "Keep an eye out for a good defensible place to camp. I want to make camp and be prepared before the sun sets."

Breunne again bobbed his head as he swung easily down from his saddle. "I don't know this mount well enough to trust him." He again locked eyes with his leader. "I'll go on foot from here." He handed his mount's reins to the cleric. "Take good care of him. He's a good animal."

Cyrillis nodded as she accepted the leather. Breunne flashed her a smile, stepped off the road and quickly disappeared into the trees.

The mood of the party became decidedly more somber. The playful banter came to a stop and the men naturally formed a loose ring around the healer, Thrinndor out front with Sordaak and Vorgath trailing behind, one to either side.

As the shadows grew longer, the air became perceptibly cooler. Not quite cold, but certainly less warm than the nice fall day it had been. However, there was no more discussion about the weather. This battle-tested group was wary.

What conversation they did have was subdued, almost whispered. And short. Any who began talking was given the stink-eye from his or her companions. As such, by mid-afternoon, nothing had been said for more than an hour.

Eyes constantly scanned the tree lines, looking for any sign of movement, any hint something was amiss. But by late afternoon the only thing that seemed out of place was that *nothing* was out of place.

The shadows had gotten longer than Thrinndor intended when he spotted the ranger up ahead standing in the middle of the road. As the party approached, he spun on a heel and walked into the trees off the road to the left.

Thrinndor dismounted and followed on foot, leading his roan and two pack mules along a narrow wild animal path between the trees and through some brush. The remaining companions followed suit.

The path twisted and turned several times, leaving the mage with no clue as to direction after the first fifty feet or so. *Damn rangers!* He shook his head as he struggled to keep up as he followed the cleric's pack animals.

Abruptly the brush gave way to a clearing of sorts. In reality it was an area of combined hard packed earth and smooth rock. The clearing was more than a hundred feet across, edged by the brush they had just walked through on the one side, more brush to their left and right and a stone edifice straight ahead. It looked like a sheer cliff, but Sordaak could make out a bit of an overhang that jutted toward them as they walked up to it.

"We can picket the animals over there on that patch of grass," Breunne said, pointing farther down the rock wall almost to the trees to their right. "And we can build a small fire here under the overhang that should not be visible for more than a couple hundred feet in any direction."

Thrinndor nodded his approval as he checked out the overhang. "Very good," he said as he led his animals to the patch of grass, the others following with their mounts and pack mules. There was also small stream that flowed out from under the rock wall that conveniently formed a small pool near the copse of grass.

Very nice, thought the paladin as he idly wondered where they were. This place showed signs of being used frequently, and that bothered him somewhat as he looked around. Well, they would only need it for one the night he reasoned with a shrug. Still, he would have to caution the watches to remain extra alert.

The animals attended to, he walked back to the overhang to find the barbarian already had a fire blazing cheerily in a small pit. The paladin breathed deeply the mountain air and decided his friend was right. He could sense a change coming as well.

Vorgath added a log as his friend walked up. "Uh-huh," he said as he looked up, "I might have been off on my estimation of time until the snow hits." He smiled. "Now I'm not even sure it's going to hold off until morning."

A fleeting look of surprise crossed Thrinndor's eyes. "How did you know I was thinking about the weather?"

"Six," Sordaak said from over where he was setting up his pallet. "Mind reader!"

"Ha!" said the dwarf with a toothy grin. He looked back at the paladin. "I saw you test the air with your nose and then look off to the east." He shrugged as if to show it was nothing more than a logical deduction.

Thrinndor shook his head as he leaned toward the fire. The temperature had dropped several degrees in the short time since they had stopped. "You think we will have snow by morning then?"

It was Vorgath's turn to again shrug. "If not, then shortly thereafter." He looked up at his friend. "As fast as the temperature is dropping this could be a bad one, too."

The paladin made several decisions at once. He turned and looked out toward the clearing. "Where is Breunne?"

"I last saw him down by the horses," replied the cleric.

"Breunne!" Thrinndor raised his voice.

"On my way," came the reply from down by the creek.

The paladin gathered his thoughts as he waited for the ranger to join them. When Breunne walked up, he said, "Thank you."

"Is there a problem?" The ranger looked from the paladin to the barbarian and back.

"Could be," Thrinndor said as he backed his way to the wall so he could address all of them at once. "Vorgath believes, as do I, that the storm is going to hit earlier than we thought." He looked over at the dwarf, still sitting beside the fire. "And that it may be a bad one."

No one said anything at first, although there was some foot shifting going on as they waited for their leader to continue.

"I do not think we will find a better place to wait out the storm than our current location," Thrinndor said. "So we will ride it out here—at least until we are able to determine just how bad it will be." He shifted his weight. "Before the light fails completely, I want Breunne, Vorgath and myself to scour this area. It has been used a lot, and from appearances, not that long ago. I would think that previous occupants may want to return to the shelter this place offers if the weather turns as we think it will.

"Sordaak and Cyrillis," his eyes shifted to take in both of them, "do what you can to make this shelter more...cozy." He smiled. "The winds are only going to get worse, and we will need to protect ourselves, and the fire, from its wrath." The caster and the cleric nodded their agreement.

Their leader looked out at the fading light. "We only have a half hour or so of light remaining, so we must hurry. Be as thorough as you can, but be back here in no more than an hour." He checked and got a nod from each as the party separated.

Breunne went left past the animals. Thrinndor went straight back toward the road, intent on checking the other side. Vorgath worked his way along the rock wall to the right.

Sordaak turned to Cyrillis as they both stood to begin their assigned tasks. "Check the packs and bring any and all blankets or rugs you can find." The healer nodded as she moved to comply. "I'll start cutting branches to provide structure," he added as he picked up a small axe and headed for the trees.

By the time the first of the scouts, Vorgath, returned, Sordaak had a good start on the wall. He had cut and gathered dozens of branches, taking care to select those with as much foliage remaining as possible. He'd heard somewhere that boughs from the dense evergreens worked the best, so he collected as much of that as he could find, using his light spells as necessary once the light from the sun failed. He sent Fahlred scouting for the bushy trees, as well.

Vorgath saw the progress, grunted and selected a much larger axe from among his repertoire and trudged off back the way he had come. He had seen some likely candidates not far away.

By the time Thrinndor returned, the shelter was coming together nicely, so he turned his attention to the animals. He pulled up the stakes and led them in groups over closer to the wall of rock and retied them. He bunched them as much as he could, knowing they would huddle together for warmth once it got cold enough.

By the time he was finished, clouds had blotted out the stars and the wind had picked up. But the wind was coming out of the south, and the temperature seemed to be *rising*! It was getting *warmer*!

"Vorgy," Thrinndor said as he brushed aside the blanket that hung as a door.

"What?" grunted the barbarian as he was weaving branches together in one of the walls.

"How come the wind is out of the south?" the paladin said, his massive arms crossed on his chest. "And why is it getting warmer outside?"

Vorgath quickly stood upright. "What?" he repeated. He lurched forward and pushed his way past the big fighter. "Move," he said as he stepped outside.

Thrinndor made eye contact with the caster, who had noted the entire conversation. It was hard not to; the walled in area was not all that large—maybe ten feet wide by fifteen or twenty in length. Both lifted their right eyebrows, Sordaak stood and then both men followed the dwarf into the darkness on the other side of the blanket.

It took a few moments for their eyes to adjust. Finally the paladin spotted the barbarian standing out in the middle of the clearing. Thrinndor tapped the mage on the shoulder and pointed toward the dwarf. Both men slowly sauntered over that way.

When they got close enough, they could hear the barbarian swearing under his breath in a most colorful manner. After a few moments of this, Thrinndor decided it was time to find out what was bothering his friend. "Vorgath," he said hesitantly, "what is it?"

The dwarf stopped his cursing and turned to stare at his friend. "I may have underestimated this storm."

"What?" Sordaak looked around. The paladin was right. It *was* warmer. "It's getting *warmer* out here!"

"I know that!" snapped the barbarian, exasperated.

Thrinndor and the mage looked at one another. "Make some sense, man!" Sordaak was not sure what was going on, but he was fairly certain he didn't like it.

Vorgath looked from one to the other and took in a deep breath as he looked down at his boots. "Weather systems move on air currents," he said. "Those air currents are made possible by minute changes in air pressure."

Thrinndor's right eyebrow was flirting with his hairline. He'd never heard his friend talk like this.

The dwarf continued. "When a large storm approaches, it rides a lower pressure system. That lower pressure draws air into it before the actual storm arrives."

"What are you talking about?" asked the caster dubiously. Vorgath had mentioned some of this before but he still didn't understand it.

Vorgath threw his arms up in the air. "Don't you see?" he asked, again exasperated. "The larger a storm system, the more air it draws in. This warm air is being sucked in and it has traveled from far away." The magicuser could see something akin to fear in the dwarf's eyes. "That means this storm is a *BAD* one!" He looked up at the paladin. "Maybe *very* bad." He allowed his voice to trail off. When he spoke again, it was in a voice so low that both the caster and the paladin had to lean in to hear it. "It's far too early for such a storm."

"You are sure?" asked the paladin. He knew his friend was prone to exaggeration, but he had never seen him like this. This was really bothering the barbarian.

Vorgath shook his head. "Hell no," he said. "With weather *nothing* is certain." He looked over to where the wind was bending the trees so as to prove the barbarian's point. "But it has been years since I have seen anything like this." He looked back at the paladin. "Many years."

"All righty then," said the magicuser as he turned to head back to the shelter. "Someone wake me when it's over."

Thrinndor watch the mage walk away and shook his head. "Any idea when it will hit?" he said without turning his head.

"How long have the winds been out of the south?" was the barbarian's answer.

"No more than a couple of hours." The paladin turned to face his friend.

"The winds generally do not last long—they will be strongest right before they stop. At which time they will reverse." Vorgath again turned to check out the trees. "The temperature will drop quickly from that point." He thought about it for a few heartbeats. "I think we'll see the winds die before midnight." He again looked around at the paladin. "By morning we'll have snow."

Thrinndor nodded and turned to go back to the shelter.

"Wait," the barbarian stopped him. "We will need to stockpile more wood and whatever else we might need for the next several days."

The fighter stopped and slowly turned back around. "Days?"

Vorgath nodded. "Days." He pointed to the trees. "We will have to work to keep the snow clear of the exit, or risk being trapped."

The warm wind made it hard for the fighter to wrap his brain around what his friend was so adamant about. But he did not doubt the dwarf. "Then we had better gather enough wood for those several days."

The dwarf didn't wait for more. He turned and marched toward the tree line. Thrinndor walked quickly back to the shelter to enlist the aid of the ranger. After a brief explanation of what Vorgath had said, Breunne nodded and followed the paladin back out into the clearing.

Cyrillis redoubled her efforts at sealing all the gaps she could find. Even Sordaak felt the tension in the air and worked at weaving the branches tighter. He could now easily hear the wind whistling through the trees outside. It was getting worse.

Vorgath, Breunne and Thrinndor gathered wood until well after midnight, which is when the winds suddenly went silent. The barbarian again stopped in the middle of the clearing, his eyes working to focus on the black sky to the west.

The paladin saw his friend standing there and walked over to join him. The dwarf appeared to be concentrating, so he did not say anything. While the two of them stood there silently the ranger walked up as well.

Thrinndor held a finger to his lips and shrugged when Breunne looked at him with a question in his eyes. The ranger nodded and then he too stood and waited—for what, he knew not.

Finally the barbarian shook his head, his beard wagging silently across his chest. He looked up at the two men towering over him and said, "It begins." Then he turned and went back out into the ring of trees in search of more wood.

The ranger and the paladin stood there a bit longer, each enjoying the quiet of the night and a break from dragging logs and branches in for firewood.

Breunne looked over at the semi-neatly stacked pile of wood. "That should be enough for several days."

"Not enough," huffed the dwarf as he drug up another large log, depositing it next to the others.

The paladin rolled his eyes as he headed back into the trees, the ranger following closely.

After a couple more hours there was a slight breeze starting to pick up out of the west and the three fighters stood by the wood pile, taking a break from the back-breaking work of gathering wood.

"That is it for me," said the paladin as he stretched his arms. He started toward the entrance to their shelter.

Breunne looked over at the panting barbarian and said, "Me too," as he followed the paladin through the opening.

Vorgath's weary eyes followed the two through the opening, and then he turned to look at the pile of wood they'd gathered. He looked off to the west, catching an unfamiliar scent on the wind. Snow. "I sincerely hope that's enough," he said as he pushed the curtain aside and entered the warmth within.

Chapter Two

Winter Storm Warning

Vorgath woke several times through the night and walked outside to check on the progress of the storm. The wind picked up steadily out of the west until it was a howling morass that threatened to take their shelter apart one branch at a time.

Yet the shelter held. Several times the barbarian stopped to check the craftsmanship of the wall as he assessed the weather. Nice. The healer knew what she was doing, he decided.

Outside the temperature plummeted while the air inside remained warm and cozy. The dwarf threw a small log on the fire and stirred the coals each time he checked outside.

Just before dawn it began to snow. What concerned the barbarian was that the wind did not die down. Instead, it continued to grow in intensity, indicating colder air still was on the way.

Vorgath went to check on the animals, finding the ranger already there, calming and quieting them. As expected, they were huddled together against the rock wall. He was immediately concerned for the outer animals as they were exposed to both the wind and the snow. They were a miserable lot, indeed.

He signaled for the ranger to join him inside the shelter. Together, they quickly made their way back and brushed aside the makeshift curtain and stepped inside. There they found the paladin at the door. He was about to step outside to check on the pair.

"This cold has only just begun," Vorgath said. "The continued strong wind out of the north tells me it will get far colder." The ranger nodded. "If we don't do something for the animals, they'll freeze."

Breunne hesitated. "We must move them." His eyes went to those of the paladin. "We can't protect them where they are."

"But where?" asked the paladin. He had yet to go outside and was thus unable to judge the need for concern.

The ranger took in a deep breath. "With a little work we can augment the protection the trees offer by felling one or two and weaving the branches."

Sordaak sat up rubbing the sleep from his eyes. "But," he croaked, as the dry air had sucked the moisture from this throat. He swallowed a couple of times as the three fighters waited patiently for him to continue. "But, we won't be able to protect them out in the trees!"

"True," answered the ranger. "However, there will be no predators out in this weather. By the time any that seek us are once again out and about, we will be back on the road."

"Those to whom this shelter is native might be out," the paladin said ominously.

The ranger looked over at the big fighter. "I hadn't thought of that," he said. "But we may not have a choice."

"There might be another option." All eyes turned to the cleric. None had seen her rise, nor noticed her moving to warm herself by the fire. She pulled her robe up around her shoulders self-consciously. "We could move the animals further down the wall to where the stream emerges. There we topple some trees against the wall and tie the tops together." She smiled. "They would be protected from the wind *and* snow that way, and have access to water."

The four men traded looks, each trying to find fault with the idea. None was able to do so. "Just where exactly did you find her?" Breunne asked as he shouldered an axe the dwarf handed him, his right eyebrow high on his forehead.

"I'll tell you the story sometime," answered the dwarf as he shouldered one of his older greataxes.

"What little you remember of it," said the paladin as he took the huge axe the barbarian handed him. "You were flat on your back, out cold most of the time!"

"Ha!" snorted the dwarf. "I see the cold has affected your memory, as well!"

The men chuckled softly. "All right," said the paladin, ready to give the orders at last. "Vorgath, Breunne and myself will cut and move the trees into place." He looked over so as to take in the cleric and the mage. "You two get the animals prepared to move. See if you can find any extra blankets. If we can put one on each animal that will help."

Sordaak nodded as he crawled out from under his blankets, scratching his head and yawning as he did so.

"Who's going to climb the trees to tie them?" asked the dwarf. "Here's a hint: It isn't going to be this old dwarf!"

"I will do it." Again all heads swiveled to see if the healer was serious. She lifted her chin defiantly and removed a single coin from a pocket in her tunic. "I wager a plat I can best any of you in any form of climbing." She tossed the coin high and caught it as it spun back down into her palm.

"No, thank you," said a chuckling paladin. "You certainly continue to amaze me, young lady." He glanced over at the other two fighters to verify he spoke for them. "Very well," he continued. "We three will fell the trees and get them into place. Cyrillis will tie them at the top and weave the branches as best she can on her way down. Sordaak will prepare the animals to be moved. Any questions?"

He got shakes of the head in reply.

The fighters went to their packs and pulled out the heavy furs provided to them by the drow. As they donned them, the magicuser said, "Wait! Is it cold out there?"

Vorgath stopped with the coat half on and eyed the caster. "Not yet," he said as he finished pulling on the cloak, took up his greataxe and stepped outside.

A frigid blast came through the opening the moment it was pushed aside, stirring the flames and sending a spray of sparks toward the ceiling.

"Liar," griped the mage as he searched around for his own cloak. "Damn! I hate the cold!" He shivered at the thought and pushed through into the frigid air.

While Sordaak and Cyrillis tended the animals and got them ready to move, the three fighters fought wind, blinding snow and bitter cold to cut halfway through the three trees selected. They were near enough to the rock wall for the trunks to reach it without the tops making it all the way to the ground.

The trick was to get the trees to fall toward the rock wall with the wind whipping them in every direction but the one desired.

It was decided that one of them must climb up the tree and tie a rope to the trunk so that each tree could be pulled in the correct direction.

Breunne was about to make the first climb when Cyrillis walked up, wondering what was taking so long. It was *cold* out here!

Seeing the problem, she grabbed the rope from the ranger and leapt up to grab the lowest branch. Quickly she scaled the tree, going from branch to branch until she was just over halfway. Once there she tied the rope around the trunk as high up as she could reach and threw the remainder of the rope down to the waiting ranger.

Problem solved, the rest of the operation went much faster. Once the third tree was leaning against the wall, Cyrillis again climbed the tree with a coiled rope on her shoulder.

She climbed as high as she dared and cinched the rope to the tree on which she stood. Then she grasped a bough from the nearest other tree and swung across to wrap the rope around its trunk and then leapt to the third tree and repeated the maneuver. Next she pulled the treetops together as tight as she could and wrapped the remainder of the rope around the trunks for security.

Once the trees were tied as best she could, she started down, weaving branches together as she went. Fortunately the trees were evergreen and had dense branches, so not much was required. Her hands were getting numb by the time she had her feet, also freezing, back on the ground.

Vorgath and Thrinndor were dragging up another tree they had cut, but Breunne was nowhere to be seen. So she headed off to see if she could help the sorcerer get the animals into the makeshift shelter.

When she walked up, Sordaak was leading two of the horses, followed by two of the mules along the rock wall, through the snow that was starting to build up to the area they had built. She loosed the pickets of the remaining animals and followed the indentations in the snow, the animals in tow.

When the horses and mules were all inside, she checked to make sure the blankets were secure on each as the paladin and barbarian dragged another tree across the opening. Cyrillis stood back and looked over what they had built. It was an effective corral, and she was sure none of the animals could get out—not that they would want to. Fortunately the downed trees also blocked the bulk of the wind.

After the animals settled down, they again began to move closer together to share body warmth.

Satisfied they had done what they could for the animals, the companions quickly made their way back their own shelter.

Once inside they stripped off their cloaks and gathered around the fire, rubbing their extremities to warm them. Vorgath poked at the fire, which had died down somewhat, and put two small dry branches on the fire, knowing those would burn quicker and, more important, hotter.

The branches quickly flared up and Cyrillis sighed contentedly. "Thank you, sir," she said formally.

The barbarian grunted an unintelligible reply and continued poking the fire.

Outside they could hear the wind howl as it shook the walls of their shelter. "It's going to get *colder*," Vorgath said, staring into the coals of the fire.

"I don't know," said the caster, who was still shivering from his foray out into the cold. "It's pretty damn cold out there now."

"Those winds are bringing down air from the frozen wasteland beyond Ice Homme—beyond even the Northron Wastes." The dwarf looked up and locked eyes with the mage. "It is going to get colder."

"Damn." Sordaak held his hands out to the fire.

The companions fell silent as they listened to the whistling of the wind. Occasionally, a gust would weave its way through the walls, reminding them just how cold it was outside. After one such gust, Vorgath said, "Once the snow piles up, it will block those cracks."

"At least we have that to look forward to," said the spellcaster, sarcasm edging into his voice.

Nonplussed, the barbarian continued. "However, once the snow starts to pile up, we will have to lower the temperature in here."

"What?" blurted out the caster. "Why?"

"Because we don't want the snow blocking the cracks to melt," replied the dwarf without looking up from the coals. "It would get messy in here fast." He looked up as a whisper of the wind blew a tendril of smoke away from the natural chimney they had left open along the rock wall. "We must allow the snow to melt slightly, and then refreeze. That will keep out the wind."

"How cold?" Sordaak asked.

The barbarian finally looked away from the fire. "In here? Or out there?"

The sorcerer thought about it for a minute. "Yes."

Vorgath rolled his eyes. "It won't need to be *that* cold in here," he said. "Wear layers and you'll be fine." He looked over at where a blanket was fluttering slightly from the wind. "Out there..." He hesitated. "I don't know." He looked over at Thrinndor. "This storm is not natural."

Cyrillis licked her lips. "What do you mean?"

"It's too early in the season for this kind of storm," the barbarian stated flatly. "In all my days I have not seen such a storm this early." He looked over at the mage. "This storm was conjured."

"Impossible!" said the caster.

"Is it?" Vorgath asked quietly.

"No." Cyrillis' voice was barely audible above the moaning winds. She looked into the eyes of the caster. "I mean, it *should be* impossible!" She wrung her hands together. "But, a lot we have seen of late *should* have been impossible! Teleportation beyond anything ever seen before! Those drow returning to life in the maze! A dragon protecting a library!" Her face twisted up in uncertainty. "Is it so hard to believe a storm can be conjured?"

Sordaak held her eyes with his. "You have a point," he said. "But to conjure up a storm of this magnitude... I don't know." He shook his head as he pondered. "I *suppose* if you got the storm giants together with the frost giants—bear in mind they don't even like each other—and combined their powers. Add a sorcerer or two who can direct such power, and *maybe* they could stir up such a storm." He looked at the dwarf. "But, why?"

"Huh?" Vorgath said.

"Why?" the sorcerer repeated. "Why would whoever go through all that effort?" He looked around at the paladin. "Make no mistake," he continued, "it would take an *enormous*, coordinated effort."

The curtain parted and Breunne stepped in. "Because someone is aware of our intentions and is trying to stop—or slow—us."

Startled, Thrinndor realized he hadn't noticed the ranger was missing. "Where have you been?"

Breunne's face took on a grim expression as he peeled off his cloak, gloves and hat as he moved closer to the fire. "I encountered some tracks while scouting for suitable wood."

"*WHAT?*" The mage almost shouted the word. "You found tracks in *this weather?*"

The ranger rubbed his hands vigorously, held them close to the fire and nodded. "Yes," he said. "Worse, the tracks clearly could not have been made long before I found them."

"Obviously," agreed the paladin.

"What kind of tracks?" asked the cleric.

"Humanoid," the ranger replied. "Only one set, though." He paused and the tension built. "We are being followed."

"Shit!" spat the caster. "We've only been out of the Library for a day. It must be the drow!"

"Or someone who waited for us while we were inside." The ranger's expression remained grim.

"Shardmoor!" Vorgath joined the conversation.

"Possibly," answered the ranger. "But I believe this person more likely to be a Minion."

"*The Minions of Set?*" blurted out the caster. "*Here?*"

"It's the only logical answer," Breunne said. "The drow have no quarrel with us that I am aware of." His eyes shifted from the mage to the barbarian. "Guild Shardmoor certainly would keep tabs on us if they deemed it necessary. But I don't believe Savinhand or Bealtrive would allow it at present." He turned his eyes upon the cleric and then to the staff, never far from her side. "Who then has reason to want to know our whereabouts?"

"The Minions of Set," answered the paladin, nodding his head. "Then they know where we are."

"Not necessarily," countered the ranger. "Only the high priests are capable of the communication across long distances. If it is indeed a minion or one of their spies, I doubt he has gotten word to his masters of our location as of yet."

"But you think they are responsible for the storm?" Cyrillis asked.

Breunne again looked over at the cleric and took in a sharp breath. "Responsible? Yes. Conjured by them? No."

"Explain." The paladin's brows were knitted together in concentration.

The ranger's eyes shifted from the paladin to the sorcerer as he spoke. "All I have at present is a theory." When no one said anything, he continued. "Spies for the minions found our trail while we were questing for the Library—that would have not been hard." He again looked over at the staff. "While we were inside, I believe they made arrangements to halt or slow our progress while help arrived."

"Hence the storm." Cyrillis nodded.

"Part of that makes sense," agreed the paladin. "Part does not."

All eyes turned to the big fighter as he prepared his thoughts. "I will concede that it would not have been hard to track our movement—even to locate the cabin and wait for us to emerge. We have to assume the minions have a spy within Shardmoor." He paused as he worked on how to word the rest without calling into question the ranger's powers of deduction. "However, this storm was called into being—if indeed it is conjured—the same day as when we emerged." He got nods from both the sorcerer and the barbarian. Bolstered, he continued. "If the one following us is not a minion, how then would word have gotten to whoever is controlling this storm to bring it into being so quickly?" Finished, he crossed his arms on his chest and waited.

All eyes shifted back to Breunne, who nodded as he prepared his thoughts. "Again," he cautioned, "all I have is a theory." The dwarf rolled his eyes but said nothing. "I believe initially there was more than one waiting for us to emerge from the Library. I have seen tracks that preceded us down the road we were on. Tracks of a group in a hurry."

"Why didn't you tell us about them?" asked a wary dwarf.

"Because it is a road, after all," answered the ranger. "I had no reason to believe those tracks were related to our movement, until now." He looked over at the cleric. "While we have been out of the Library for only a day, bear in mind that anyone watching he entrance would have seen activity long before that."

"The drow," Sordaak said.

"Correct," Breunne agreed. "The drow have been preparing for our departure, possibly for several days."

"Damn," muttered the sorcerer, nodding. "It all adds up."

"Except they couldn't know which direction we were going to go." Vorgath crossed his arms on his chest in smug satisfaction.

"Know?" answered the ranger. "True. However, I let it be known those many days ago that I would be traveling to Ice Homme with the staff. They have no reason to believe otherwise. So I think it's a probable assumption on their part that we would continue north."

Thrinndor nodded his agreement, and then his right brow climbed higher. "Wait," he said. "You also told them that you killed all of us, did you not?"

"Yes," Breunne replied, ready for that particular question, anyway. "So either they have figured that I have new companions, or they know I was lying and that all of you yet live."

"Either way," Sordaak said, connecting the dots, "they know we are on the road going north."

"That means they probably have a pretty good idea where we are," agreed the paladin.

"If they know of this place—and we have no reason to believe they don't— then that is a valid assumption," the ranger said.

"We were herded here!" Sudden realization struck the caster hard.

"Maybe," Breunne said.

"But why?" asked the cleric.

"That I don't know," replied the ranger. "However, if any of the previous assumptions are correct, then it's reasonable to think that their goal by such a storm is to slow our progress."

"To what end?" Sordaak was still doubtful.

Breunne looked over at the caster. "To allow them to catch up with us."

Sordaak's eyes widened as he quickly stood. "It's a *trap!*"

"That is a distinct possibility," agreed the ranger.

"We need to get out of here!" The mage's eyes took on a cornered look and darted around wildly.

"Relax," soothed the paladin. "While this weather certainly has us hemmed in, they cannot strike at us, either."

"Right," agreed the ranger, although is voice didn't have the conviction of their leader's.

Calmed somewhat, the sorcerer sat back down. However his eyes maintained the look that he could bolt at any moment.

"To slow us for what purpose?" Cyrillis asked the unasked question.

"Good question," replied the ranger. "The only answer that makes any sense is that the minion army is behind us."

The day passed slowly with the wind continuing to shake the walls of their shelter. Outside the temperature dropped further and the snow piled up.

Periodically, one of the fighters pushed aside the curtain that was the only barricade between the warm air inside and the bitter cold outside air and stepped out do ensure their exit remained clear of the drifting snow and to check on the animals.

Stories were told and retold from a different viewpoint. Plans were discussed and argued over, and contingencies were made.

"We must do the unexpected." Thrinndor was speaking and he had the attention of his companions, seated around the now much smaller fire, their cloaks pulled up around their necks.

"What do you have in mind?" Breunne asked as he chewed on a piece of jerked meat.

"It is not for the faint of heart," the paladin warned. If he hadn't had their attention before, he did now. "We leave tonight under the cover of darkness."

Sordaak fought down the urge to point out the folly of that plan. A large part of him wanted to get out of this trap so bad, it didn't matter to him how cold it was outside.

Momentarily surprised at the lack of resistance, Thrinndor went on. "We disguise our exit by stoking the fire so that it burns far into the day tomorrow and we work hard today to leave plenty of tracks for our adversary to investigate." He knew this next part was going to be where he lost the support of one or more of the party. "We pack up all we can carry and sneak out along the rock wall, leaving the horses and pack animals."

"What?" Sordaak sat bolt upright. "That's crazy!"

"They will die without us," Cyrillis said quietly in contrast.

"They will certainly be tended to once it is discovered we have escaped their trap," answered the paladin. "We must use the fact that the minions really do not know of our plans to detour to the Cliffs to our advantage." He drew nods from the other two fighters at that. "They will assume we will continue north when in fact we will have left the main road. They will have to waste time thinking that we left the road only to conceal our path north."

Now even Cyrillis was nodding her head. The spellcaster was still not so sure. It was *cold* out there!

"Assuming it is the Minion army from Desert Homme that we are trying to avoid, our sojourn to the Cliffs at Mioria should allow them to pass and get ahead of us." Thrinndor hesitated as he pondered what he must reveal next. "It is my belief, based on the assumptions we have made to this point, that an army from Ice Homme is on the move south and it is the High Priest's intention to catch us between the two armies and thus capture their true objective."

"The staff," the cleric finished for him.

"Correct," said the paladin with a nod. "While the Minions certainly desire our demise, that would in no way guarantee the results that is their ultimate goal—and that is to ensure our Lord Valdaar never returns to this land. There are other possible offspring who can take up the torch to complete that goal. There can be no way of knowing how many of us exist." His eyes bored into those of first the cleric and then the mage. "But to remove the artifacts required from the equation, that would accomplish their goal for the foreseeable future."

"The staff," Cyrillis said again, her eyes slowly going over to where it stood against the stone wall of their shelter.

"Yes," the paladin again agreed. "It is my belief they already hold *Valdaar's Fist.*"

Now Sordaak was nodding. "My research led me to believe they also hold *Pendromar, Dragon's Breath.*"

The eyebrow on the right side of the paladin's forehead inched higher. "What leads you to this belief?"

Sordaak raised his eyes to meet those of the paladin. "I was able to trace the last reported sighting of the staff to the Cliffs at Mioria. There a sorcerer known only as Kraafthur wielded it in defense of a small keep against a horde from Ice Homme."

Now it was Thrinndor's turn to nod. "So it all points to Ice Homme," he said. "With a side trip to verify your staff is not at the Cliffs of Mioria."

"Correct," said the caster. "That and to pick up some cloaks that will be an integral part of plan."

Breunne sat up suddenly on the stump on which he was sitting. "We have some items for you to look at," he said as he stood and went to a large bag leaning up against the wall of their enclosure.

"What items?" asked the sorcerer.

"Stuff we took from the hoard of the dragon." The ranger returned with the bag in hand and dumped it unceremoniously at the feet of the caster.

"Really?" asked the caster as he nudged a circlet with the toe of his boot. "You're just now telling me about this?" His eyes were accusing.

"We've been kind of busy," muttered the dwarf as he threw another large branch onto the fire. *Pity they wouldn't need all that wood they had gathered,* he thought absently.

"Granted," Sordaak said as he bent over to pick up two wands that had caught his eye. "Nice," he mumbled as he tucked both away into the folds of his robe. Closing his eyes, he whispered the words to a spell and waved his hands over the pile of items at his feet.

Immediately each piece started to glow various colors, with a couple of the items glowing two or more colors at once.

Sordaak bent over and picked up a ring and inspected it briefly. "This ring holds the symbol of a cat, indicating an increased nimbleness to the wearer." He sat it off to the side. "That we'll hold for the rogue." Next he picked up a pair of bracers. "These are strongly colored with the aura of red and have the markings showing a bear. They should enhance the wellbeing of the wearer by a substantial amount."

"I'll take those!" said the barbarian as he leaned forward and snatched them from the hands of the caster. He began the tedious process of removing his current bracers to make room for them.

Sordaak held the magic window open by remaining in an almost trance-like state. He picked up the circlet he had originally pushed aside with his foot. "This item will enhance the wisdom of its bearer." Seeing a second hue almost hidden behind that of the first, he added, "It also will provide protection from...*undead?*" He shook his head. "Not sure on that one. But it is some sort of protection."

"I will take that," Cyrillis said as she stood to take it from the mage's hands. She looked at the dwarf on her way back to where she was sitting.

"Not like I was going to wear that thing!" Vorgath said, turning his attention back to putting on his new bracers.

"But you would have looked so *cute*!" Thrinndor said with a smile.

"Ha, ha," mocked the dwarf as he cinched up the leather ties binding the bracer to his left arm.

Ignoring the banter, Sordaak selected another ring at his feet. "This ring also has multiple powers—three at least." He focused on the most prominent of the auras. "First, it provides an aura like that of armor to the bearer." He switched his focus to the second visible hue. "Second, it makes the bearer immune to poison." He had to close his eyes to focus on the third color. Surprised, they popped back open. "Third," he said, his voice almost a whisper, "it allows the wearer to breathe underwater as if he or she were on dry land." He slipped the ring on the middle finger on his right hand. "I'll take this one."

Vorgath started to protest but knew the armor component of the ring would be useless to him. It was a ring crafted for those unable to wear any sort of armor. Like a caster. He shrugged indifference.

Next, Sordaak picked up the breastplate, initially more to get it out of his way, but he decided to study it before casting it aside. It too showed to have multiple powers. The first thing he noticed was how light it was—this was no ordinary alloy, he concluded. It was creamy white in color, but when stared at, it was hard to pin down a color. The brightest hue was orange, unusual in and of itself. That color denoted special properties that were not discernible with the standard spell. It was going to require the attention of someone with a higher ranking than he currently held. He *could* tell, however, that it was specifically enchanted to block the attack of an axe. Interesting. "The primary ability of this armor is beyond my ken, but it is indeed beneficial. I am not familiar with the alloy, but it is very light." He lifted it easily to give credence to his words. "There is a secondary enchantment to block the attack of a particular weapon—in this case the axe."

"Let me see that," said the dwarf. Sordaak handed it over. After a brief inspection, the barbarian's eyes widened. "This is an alloy of mithryl that has not been used since the time when gods walked the land." He looked up from the armor to peer into the eyes of the mage. "It is *very* old."

"Yet it appears to have been forged yesterday," replied the mage.

"I think that is a bit large for you," said the paladin playfully.

"Enchanted, it will size itself according to the wearer," replied the mage as he reached for an old pair of boots.

"I know that!" Thrinndor said, noting his scorn was wasted as the magicuser was already studying the boots.

"However," Vorgath continued, "I am satisfied with my current armor and believe this will be more suited to our healer." He got up and offered it to her with a bow.

"Thank you," she said, dipping her head as she accepted the armor. "While my current armor was given to me long ago by a friend, it is dated and much the worse for wear."

"These boots are built for speed," Sordaak said as he set the boots to the side.

Quickly, the ranger reached over and snatched them just as Thrinndor was about to pick them up. "I'll take these," Breunne said with a sardonic smile.

"I am going to have to be a little quicker on the draw," grumbled the paladin.

The mage picked up a robe that had been rolled up into an unrecognizable tube of fabric. It also was glowing a most interesting color, a deep violet. When he shook it open, he noted another color. Green. "Hello," he said quietly. Slowly he re-rolled it and set it by his side. "I'll keep this, as well. I'm the only one that can wear it, but I need to study it more before I do."

There was very heavy cloak, also rolled up. He reached out to pick it up, but instantly dropped it. "Damn," he muttered as he focused his magic sense on it. He grasped it, picked it up, and began to unroll it.

Again there was more than one hue involved. "This is interesting," the caster said as he noted the almost invisible feathers that were sewn into the hem on the fabric.

"What?" asked the dwarf as he leaned forward to hear what the caster was saying.

"See these feathers?" the mage asked, not looking up from the cloak. "They are enchanted to give the bearer the power of flight."

"Really?" the ranger breathed quietly.

"These runes," Sordaak said, pointing to faint symbols that were sewn into the collar, "speak of increased strength to that of the great Roc."

"I'll take that!" said the barbarian as he reached for the cloak.

"Not so fast old one." Thrinndor grasped the wrist of the dwarf. "I could use it as well."

Vorgath glared at the paladin and considered whether an altercation was in order. "Ahem," said the ranger. "I believe I could put that to better use than either of you."

His hand still gripping the wrist of the barbarian, Thrinndor looked over at the ranger and said, "Why?"

"My ability with multiple ranged attacks would tie in nicely with the ability to fly," Breunne said. "Combine that with an increased strength and I would become an even more formidable opponent."

The paladin and the barbarian exchanged looks.

"Besides," Sordaak broke in, "I plan on outfitting you morons with Cloaks of the Storm Giant here in the next couple of days."

"Deal," both fighters said at once. Sordaak threw the cloak to the ranger, who caught it deftly and flung it around his shoulders to test it for proper fit.

"You got the cloak," said the paladin as he held out his right hand toward the ranger, palm up. "I get the boots, then."

Breunne looked at the boots and then the robe. His briefly considered arguing. "Deal," he said as he pick up the boots and tossed them to the paladin.

"I wouldn't test the fly operation of the cloak in here," the mage said smugly. "That might result in a bump or two."

"Got it," Breunne said as he tied the thong at his neck.

The last item still on the floor of the shelter was a pair of spectacles. Sordaak picked them up and casually set them next to the ring he had set aside for Savinhand.

"What are those?" Vorgath noticed the glasses now sitting next to the ring.

"They are enchanted to enhance the ability of a rogue or such person to find and remove traps, and even give him a better chance of avoiding said trap should the attempt to remove it fail." Sordaak grinned.

"Savin," the four others in the room said as one. They looked at one another and laughed.

They wandered to various portions of the shelter to spend time learning the enhancements of their new items and in some cases exchanging older equipment for new.

After a time of this, Thrinndor called the group together at the fire. "I propose we eat a light meal and try to get some sleep." He looked at each of them and got a nod in reply. "I would like to sneak out about two hours past midnight, again following a light meal." More nods. "To that end, I will awaken each of you an hour prior to our departure to help with the meal or to make preparation for departure."

After they had eaten, they each went to their pallets and rolled in with their thoughts. Fahlred was left to keep watch.

Chapter Three

Escape

Sordaak woke with a start, as a hand shook him roughly. "What?" he croaked as he tried to rub the sleep from his eyes.

"Get up, sleepyhead!"

It was a woman's voice. One he'd heard before. The hand shook him again. "I'm awake!" he grumbled as he tried to roll out from under his blanket and also his cloak, which was acting as a blanket at the moment. Where he was came back to him in a rush. "What's the hurry?"

"No hurry," said the paladin from across the shelter. "Unless you want something to eat before we depart in about a half-hour?"

"Whatever!" griped the caster as he stumbled toward the entrance. He pushed aside the curtain and was greeted by an icy blast of air that momentarily took his breath away. "Shit!" he muttered as he gathered his robes about his body as best he could and headed off to the facility set aside for personal ablutions. Fortunately the area was sheltered fairly well and he managed to take care of business quickly.

He ran back to the shelter as fast as he could, shivering uncontrollably when he let the curtain close again behind him. "Damn, it's cold out there!"

By comparison, the air inside the shelter was hot and humid, almost stuffy. "I thought we were going to keep it 'cool' in here?"

"We no longer need to worry about the snow melting, as we will not use this shelter much longer," replied the paladin.

As he got something to eat, Sordaak watched Vorgath set up an elaborate series of sticks, rails and logs that presumably would keep the fire going long after they departed.

Appearances must be kept up, he mulled silently as he chewed on a dry biscuit, which he washed down with some bitter coffee from the pot next to the fire. He briefly wished for some goat's milk to add to the coffee, but that was a luxury they couldn't have out in the wild.

The caster watched sourly as the paladin readied his pack, knowing he needed to work on his as well. "Damn," he muttered as he stood, stretched and then scratched his chest absently. He walked over to his pallet and began to prepare his pack.

In much the same manner, with a few variations based on gender, class and general level of grouchiness, the process was repeated by each member of the party until all were packed and ready to go.

Loath to leave any of the casks of wine or ale behind, Vorgath had tried earlier to consume whatever his skins could not carry. Hence he was one of the grouchier companions.

Thrinndor tried teasing him about it, but the barbarian just glowered at him from under bushy eyebrows—it was amazing how fast those grew back on a dwarf!—until the paladin gave up.

Finally they were ready at the door, wearing all the clothing, robes, jackets and cloaks they had. Mittens and headgear had been provided by the drow, so now it was getting decidedly warm inside the shelter.

Vorgath took one last look at the log contraption he had assembled to steadily feed the fire, and he threw another large log on the existing blaze for good measure. It would burn for at least a full day, perhaps more, he reasoned. He grunted his satisfaction, pushed his way past his companions and stepped outside without saying a word.

The paladin and the ranger looked at one another, shrugged and followed the barbarian out into the bitter cold.

Without speaking—they had all been cautioned against any verbal conversation or anything else that would make a sound—Thrinndor took the lead and led the way down the once well-beaten path along the rock wall toward the shelter they had made for the animals.

Sometime during the night the wind had stopped, but it was snowing steadily, hard enough that their tracks would be erased within an hour, long before daylight. Once past the animal shelter they walked single file, each following in the footsteps of the person in front so that any tracks that were left would look like those of a single individual.

As they passed the horses and mules, Thrinndor heard the mount he had been riding whinny questioningly and stamp a hoof. The stallion was unmistakably the leader of the animals, and it was serving warning to what it had to assume were predators stalking the herd.

The paladin was not worried, knowing the heavy snowfall would muffle any noise they might make and the animals would not be heard more than a few feet away.

Thrinndor wove around trees and avoided snowdrifts, knowing that plowing through some of the three- and four-foot-high drifts would leave a clear mark for much longer than footprints in lesser amounts of snow. Fighting through the drifts would also sap massive amounts of energy, and he knew every bit of that was going to be needed before they stopped. He did not plan to camp until it was again dark—maybe long after dark.

Thusly the companions trudged as silently as possible as close to due west as possible. They eschewed the road, sticking instead to animal trails through the back brush.

Thrinndor set a stiff pace, as much to stay warm as to put the miles behind them. The miles were a benefit, to be sure. By the time the sky began to lighten enough to help the paladin select an easier path, he figured they had traveled at least ten miles.

As he chose a route, he began to search for a large evergreen with sagging boughs, which was pretty much every one of them. He just wanted one large enough.

Finally he spotted a suitable-looking fir not far off of the path he had set. He adjusted his trajectory, making straight for the tree. Once there he ducked around the lowest branches, which sagged to the ground under the weight of the snow piled on top.

As the remaining party filed in, they found an empty patch of ground and flopped down onto the soft pine needles underneath.

"Damn, boss," Sordaak whispered between deep breaths, "you trying to kill us?"

"Contrary," said the paladin with a straight face, "I am trying to ensure body and soul remain together." He smiled. "At least for the time being."

"Very funny," said the caster as he leaned over and pulled a small branch that was poking him in the backside through all the layers.

"Ten minutes," said the paladin, back to all business. "Get a bite to eat and take care of any personal business. I do not plan on stopping again until darkness precludes our further progress."

"Great," muttered the dwarf as he stood and walked away, looking for some privacy.

Personal business taken care of, the party members gathered near the trunk of the immense tree and settled in for a brief respite, each working on a dry biscuit or jerked meat. Vorgath passed around a skin of fortified wine. "For medicinal purposes," he explained with a grin.

"How far to the coast?" Breunne asked as he passed the wine skin to the cleric, who was on his left.

Vorgath grunted and looked up at the branches over his head while he did some mental calculations. "Two days maybe," he said. "At this pace we'll see water before sunset tomorrow."

"Damn," the mage repeated, "I thought it was closer than that."

"It is," replied the dwarf after a long pull from the skin, "as the crow flies. The path pretty boy has taken us on adds several miles."

"Great!" gripped the sorcerer as he flopped back onto the soft needles behind him. "Can't we stay here for a few hours?"

"I do not deem that wise," said the paladin. "I fear our adversaries may have dogs."

"Damn," Sordaak said as he sat back up and struggled to his feet. "We should get a move on, then."

Without another word the party climbed back to their feet. There were, however, lots of groans.

It was still snowing hard as they stepped back out from under the tree. In fact, their previous footprints were mere indentations. In another hour, they would not be visible.

Thrinndor looked over at Vorgath. "You will let me know if I wander off course?" he asked. He normally had a very acute sense of direction and it would not be a problem, but with it snowing so hard, visibility was poor at best, so he was unable to select any landmarks in the distance to stay on track by. Even the normal seeing one's own tracks if one were circling test was not valid with the snowfall being so heavy.

Vorgath looked at his friend and debated in his mind several snide remarks, but chose against any of them. "Of course," he said. "I don't want to be wandering around in this any longer than I have to!" He smiled and pointed in the general direction they had been going. "That way."

The paladin nodded and started off in the indicated direction, again setting a brisk pace. He kept his stride shorter so those behind him who were not as long of leg could remain in his footsteps without struggling too much.

After the first quarter-mile, Sordaak was already puffing mightily as he did his best to match the stride. "Dumb-ass, long-legged galoot!" he muttered under his breath as he slipped, barely catching himself before putting a much larger imprint in the snow. He wondered vaguely where he had picked up the term "galoot," then decided it was not worth the effort to figure out.

All through the day Thrinndor pushed them. Only when the light had failed beyond a useful level did he begin to look for a place to make camp for the evening. Something similar to where they had stopped that morning would suffice, he decided.

It was another mile or so before he found it. The snow had pushed the lower branches all the way to the ground of an evergreen, and even then continued to pile up. It actually resembled a massive version of one of those tents he had seen used by the wandering nomads where the poles were tied at the top. Walking around it, he found a place where they could get through without disturbing too much snow on the branches.

Inside, the party members flopped to the ground wherever they could find a spot without regard to privacy or any other such thought.

"Damn," the magicuser breathed aloud as he glared at his leader. "I was beginning to think you were going to keep going all through the night!"

"I considered it," the paladin replied with a grim smile. He too was tired. "But I figured I would have a mutiny on my hands if I continued much longer."

"You figured correctly," grumbled the ranger as he removed his boots and rubbed his feet. "These new boots fit, well, differently." He peeled off a sock. "Damn," he said. "Blisters. I thought so." He looked accusingly at the paladin.

"Mayhap you should have stayed with your old boots knowing a long trek was in order." The paladin smiled. "Tomorrow we continue until we reach the coast."

Groans escaped the lips of several of the companions. Vorgath began stacking twigs and branches for the beginnings of a fire.

"No," said the paladin with a shake of his head. "We must not."

The barbarian looked at the big fighter as if he'd lost his mind. "Surely you jest," he said. "No one will be able to see the smoke in this—even if it were light out.

"The scent of burning wood can carry for miles even in this weather," Thrinndor said sternly. "We camp dry."

The dwarf glared at his leader, silently deciding whether it was worth a fight. Finally he decided he was too tired. "Very well," Vorgath said. "We camp dry." He pulled out a bag containing his rations and began to eat.

One by one the companions walked to the far side of the clearing under the tree—which was quite large as this particular fir was several hundred feet in height—to take care of their personal business.

After eating, each built a base for their bed from the more than adequate supply of pine needles, rolled out their blankets and turned in. Even the dwarf built a bed to get as far from the frozen ground underneath as possible.

While it was bitterly cold under the boughs of the tree, at least it was dry. After a few minutes of shivering beneath every piece of clothing and every blanket they had brought the companions finally warmed to the point where they could sleep. Exhausted, they slept hard, with the mage's quasit again standing watch.

*

Thrinndor awakened before the first light brightened the slate gray sky. It was pitch black when he opened his eyes, so he opened and closed them several times to see if he could tell any difference. He could not.

However, he was awake. He could tell he had slept several hours and would not be able to go back to sleep. As quietly as he could he rolled over and got to his feet, avoiding where the others had set up for the night.

The paladin shuffled his feet slowly toward where he remembered the exit was, knowing none had lain down between it and him, as he had planned it that way. He was met abruptly by a branch across the face. He had misjudged the location of the opening. He reached out with both hands and by feel worked his way to his left until he found the opening. He pushed aside the bough and stepped through the opening into the cold beyond.

It was still snowing out, but not nearly as hard. The snow on the ground reflected what little moon light made it through the clouds and it was deceptively light out. One could almost believe it was dawn was approaching, but the paladin knew that was not the case. Dawn was still an hour away, at least.

There was now almost two feet of snow on the ground. It was not piling up as fast now, but still it would be enough to cover their trail as long as the snow continued. What was bothering Thrinndor was that if this storm was indeed conjured, it had already lasted longer than it should have. It could not go much longer. He wanted to get moving while the snow held.

Taking a deep breath of the snow-washed air, he turned and bumped into the ranger. "Excuse me," the surprised paladin whispered. He had not heard anyone approach, and that bothered him.

"Sorry," Breunne said as he stepped aside. When Thrinndor didn't immediately respond, the ranger looked past the paladin and said, "It's beautiful, isn't it?"

With Thrinndor's heart rate returning to normal he smiled as he turned to again look at the landscape. "Yes, it is quite beautiful." Then the paladin stepped back inside to the total darkness. He stood at the entrance for a moment, ensuring no one else was trying to get out.

"Rise and shine," he called somewhat softly, not wanting any bent feelings from a harsh awakening. He heard some stirrings from off to his left, but otherwise nothing. "We need to be moving, people." This time he spoke a little louder. There was a muffled groan from off to his right, and then all was again still. "We move out in a half-hour." Now his voice was well above normal volume. "If you want to eat and/ or take care of any personal business, you had better get a move on!"

This time there were more groans and a number of mumbled curses. Satisfied he had everyone's attention, Thrinndor turned to go back outside.

"Where's the coffee?" came the sleepy voice of the sorcerer.

The paladin stopped in the entrance, half in, half out. "No fire. No coffee," he said as he pushed his way through.

Sordaak let out a string of curses. "Who's driving this train, anyway?" he said.

"Train?" Cyrillis asked into the darkness.

"Huh?" replied the caster. He had forgotten where he was.

"You said, 'who's driving this train anyway?'" she repeated. "What is a train?"

"I have no idea," said a puzzled spellcaster, wishing he could take back some of what he'd said. Actually, he wished he could take back *all* of what he'd said. "Sorry about that."

"What?" the cleric asked. She knew why he was apologizing, but wanted him to say it nonetheless.

Mildly irritated at having to explain, the mage said meekly, "My little tirade just then."

"Oh that," the healer said smiling in the darkness. "Think nothing of it. I am getting used to you heathens." Now her smile touched her voice as well.

"Hey," said a groggy barbarian, his voice coming from off to their left, "I resemble that remark!"

The three of them had a brief chuckle as Sordaak waved a hand at a pine cone he clutched tightly under his cloak, causing it to light up brightly. "Watch your eyes," he said as he pulled the cone out slowly so as not to blind anyone.

"Ah," said the cleric. "That is certainly better." Sordaak held up the cone and tied it loosely with a leather thong to a low hanging branch.

"You obviously haven't seen *him*!" The mage pointed over at the barbarian and grinned.

Cyrillis turned her head in the indicated direction. "Oh dear lord!" she exclaimed lightly.

Vorgath looked from one to the other, his eyes bleary. "What?"

The dwarf's hair was all askew, the right side of his moustache was sticking straight out from his face and tangled in his hair were several pine needles and even a pine cone or two.

Sordaak chuckled. "It's a shame we don't have a mirror," he said. "Even you would think yourself comical!"

"Whatever!" groused the dwarf as he spotted the recalcitrant facial hair out of the corner of his eye and smoothed it as best he could. He struggled to his feet and disappeared around the massive trunk of the tree to the other side.

Still grinning, the caster dug around in his pack and pulled out his coffeepot. "Watch this," he said. "I'll get that big grumpy guy back in here really fast!" He proceeded to fill the pot with snow he was able do fish out from under an opening in a lower branch. He then muttered a phrase in what was presumably elven and a fire sprang up from his right index finger.

He arched an eyebrow as he moved the second finger over, where it also caught, and then a third. Soon the fingers on his right hand were blazing brightly as he held it under the pot.

"Does not that hurt?" the cleric asked dubiously. But she could see with her percipience that it did not. Still, it defied reason.

"No," said the caster with a smirk. "Fortunately, we magicians can't harm ourselves with our own spells." His smirk vanished. "Most of the time!" As the snow melted, he looked over at the cleric. "If I could prevail upon you to add more snow as the stuff in the pot melts, I would appreciate it."

Cyrillis moved over and scooped up two handfuls of the requested snow and put it in the pot as asked. It seemed a bit strange to her, but liking the warmth of the fire, she stayed close and even warmed her hands next to it.

"What's going on?" Vorgath asked as he again rounded the base of the tree.

"Shhh!!" hissed the caster. "I don't want boss man back in here before it's ready." He smiled to remove any offense from his words. Noting the water was steaming, he said. "Now if you could reach into that pouch," he pointed at the same pouch that had produced the pot with his nose, "pull out the bag of coffee and add some to the pot."

Cyrillis again did as requested, placing a small handful into the steaming pot. "Now, if you will excuse me," she said lightly as she got to her feet and made the trip to the other side of the tree.

As she came back around the tree trunk Sordaak took notice that her hair was in much less of a mess than it had been before. Funny, the thought, I don't remember it being *a mess before*! But it sure looked different now. Nice different. He didn't remember ever noticing *that* before, either.

Suddenly he looked around quickly and, spotting a flat rock nearby, he set the metal pot down with a clunk. He shook both hands, the right to extinguish the flame spell, the left to cool it. "Damn," he muttered with a smile at the healer who sat down next to him on a large broken branch. "While my flames didn't hurt me any, the bare metal of that pot sure got hot in a hurry!"

"I said no fire!" The branch protecting the entrance pushed aside and Thrinndor stepped in, his face red in anger.

"What fire?" the mage said innocently. He looked over at the cleric. "Do you see a fire?"

"Umm, no," she replied with a shake of her head, trying to suppress a smile.

"I smell coffee," replied the big fighter, certain he was the butt of a joke but not sure how to figure out who was at fault.

"Yes," offered the barbarian as he moved to the pot cup in hand, "there's coffee." He looked up at the paladin as he poured himself a generous portion of the steaming black liquid. "You'd better get some before it gets cold."

Now Thrinndor was certain he was being made fun of. "How did you—" he started, but his voice trailed off as he spotted the mage out of the corner of his eye using a flame on his finger to pre-heat his cup. "Oh, hell!" he griped as he stomped over to his pack. He returned, cup in hand and a smile on his face. "I know when I have been beaten."

"Early and often," Vorgath said with a smirk. "Early and often."

"Do I smell coffee?" The branch once again parted and the ranger stepped in, a disbelieving look on his face.

"Yup," said the caster, pointing with his filled cup. "Better get some before Vorgath goes for seconds."

"Damn straight!" muttered the dwarf. However he was cradling his cup gently with both hands, both to keep the warmth in the cup as long as possible, and to extract that warmth from it.

Quickly Breunne made his way over to his pack and returned with his cup and poured his cup about half full. He held the pot out to the mage and Cyrillis, still seated beside one another on the branch. "Can I refill anyone's cup?"

Everyone's cup was still full, as the coffee within was too hot to drink. "Go ahead and finish it off," the caster said as he looked over at the cleric. "We're good." She nodded.

Those two are mighty cozy, thought the paladin as he took a tentative sip, scalding both his lip and tongue in the process. He bit off a curse for allowing himself to become distracted with the two sitting together, smiling. There was something going on there, but it was hard to believe. Still, that was worth keeping an eye on. As leader of this group he had to watch out for sub-alliances. Those could lead to problems within a party, he knew.

Still, he reasoned with a shrug, that was their business. Something to watch, but their business. He again tested the coffee. It was cooler, or his tongue was still numb from the first taste because it didn't burn him this time.

"Good cup of coffee," said the ranger. "Thanks."

"You're welcome," replied the caster with a nod of his head.

"Not as good as that damn thief," said the barbarian, a smile twisting his lips to remove any harm from his words.

"Agreed," said the sorcerer. "I think he slips something in the pot to settle the grounds better and take the bite out."

Vorgath nodded his agreement as he continued to nurse his cup. "Not sure it could top this for sheer timing, though." He raised his cup to the mage in mute salute with a twinkle in his eye.

The mage too raised his cup and nodded in return. "You're welcome, old friend!"

An amused paladin watched over the rim of his steaming cup. "So," he said, "two months is all it takes to become old friends these days?"

Both the barbarian and the caster turned to stare at their chosen leader. "Yes," they said as one.

"Agreed," said the ranger as he stood, also raising his cup in salute. "*Particularly* in *these days* when adventurers in our chosen lines of work may meet his or her demise on any given such day."

"Here, here!" Vorgath said as he too rose to his feet.

One by one the remaining party members also stood and held their cups aloft before them. "Here, here!" they said in unison and then each drained what remained of their coffee.

Chapter Four

Worg

"We need to be moving," said the paladin as he turned, pushed aside the branch blocking the entrance and stepped outside.

The others stowed their packs, shouldered them and followed their leader out into the bright sunlight beyond the entrance.

Momentarily blinded, Sordaak held his hand up to block the sun. "That's different," he mumbled as he adjusted his pack on his back.

Vorgath looked around quickly and sniffed at the air. "Change is coming," he said as he too rearranged his pack on his shoulders once clear of the confines of the tree.

"How so?" asked Breunne.

The dwarf glared first at the ranger and then at the sun. "It's going to get warmer," he said. "Much warmer."

"Hmmm," said the caster. "I think I could've figured that one out." He still held up his hand to block the intense light. It was also noticeably warmer than it had been when they took refuge under the tree.

Vorgath turned his glare upon the sorcerer, obviously wrestling with whether to pummel the spellcaster with words or simply use his fists. "No," he grated, "*much* warmer." He decided to let the matter drop. "By midmorning most of this snow will be gone and we will be peeling off layers of clothing to cool off!"

"I'd ask just how it was you deduced that," Sordaak said with a shake of his head, "but I'd probably regret it."

The barbarian grinned. "Yup."

"That is going to make travel difficult," Thrinndor said, "or at a minimum messy."

The dwarf turned to look at the paladin. "If we can reach the coast it is mostly rock along the cliffs. Travel will be easier there."

"Let us move out then." The big fighter shouldered his pack started east, again setting a brisk pace.

Vorgath's prediction turned out to be correct. Within a few hours the snow was not much more than a morass of slush and mud. The companions shed layers as the temperature rose.

Soon, however, they were trudging along on solid rock and the sound of waves crashing against something hard reached their ears from somewhere nearby.

The temperature had moderated to that of a standard sunny, pre-winter day. The companions had long since packed away their winter gear, and most were sweating profusely under the noon day sun when they got to the road. There was no sign of the snow from the previous days.

Thrinndor stopped a few feet from the edge of the once well-worn path. Now it was overgrown with patches of weeds and littered with rocks and other debris.

Breunne stepped to the right and checked for any sign of recent use. He found none. Undaunted, he continued his search to the north of their position.

After several minutes he approached the others, who remained where he had left them. The eyes of the ranger met those of the paladin and he shook his head. "None have passed this way in many days, perhaps years."

"It's a branch off of the main road that leads to the abandoned coastal city of Ardaagh." Most were surprised that Sordaak was doing the speaking. Vorgath lifted a brow but said nothing, waiting for more.

The caster sighed and looked over the water that was now clearly visible from where they stood. The road was between them and a lip of rock that was the edge of the shoreline. No beach—just sharp, jagged rocks that were beaten by the waves for countless centuries as far as the eye could see in either direction.

"Ardaagh was the farthest north city on the west coast that served the Isle of Grief—Home to Valdaar's Rest." Sordaak paused his narration and looked over at the paladin. Thrinndor lips were a thin line as he stared out across the water to where the island in question could be barely made out far off the coast. The mage continued. "The coastal city managed to survive for a few centuries after the Isle was declared off-limits by Praxaar following the defeat of his brother, mostly as a service port for those left behind to destroy the old keep. After that a security force watched over the island for a few hundred years operated out of the city, but the city's decline was well underway. Without the Keep on the isle for commerce, Ardaagh was destined to fail.

"After those first few hundred years, interest waned even for those that guarded against a repopulation of the island until none were left to guard." The sorcerer cleared his throat. "For more than a millennium the once thriving port has stood empty."

It was the barbarian's turn to clear his throat. "Not exactly," he said, his right hand partially covering his mouth. All eyes turned to look at Vorgath. He straightened his tunic. "Actually," he continued, "there have been several inhabitants—rather, groups of inhabitants—in that last millennium." He looked over at the sorcerer pointedly. "Orcs, goblins, various bands of were-folk, two separate groups of giants and for a time the abandoned village was home to a dragon."

"A dragon?" Cyrillis' ears were suddenly alert.

"Yes. Theremault, the last of the known blue dragons," replied the barbarian. "But that was several hundred years ago when dragons were not nearly so scarce as they are now."

"If they were not hunted at every appearance," the cleric asserted, "perhaps they would not be so scarce!"

"Dragons are vermin!"

"They are NOT!" Cyrillis' voice was shrill.

"They exist solely to build their vast horde by any means. They kill, maim and destroy as they deem necessary until they themselves are slain." Vorgath pulled himself up to his full height. "That's where I step in."

"You?" sneered the healer. "Not even YOU are old enough to have slain Theremault!"

"*Me?*" snorted the dwarf. "Of course not! I was merely referring to my current status as *Dragonslayer.*"

The paladin, who had been taking a drink from his water skin, spit water all over the ranger. Breunne had the misfortune of being in the wrong place at the wrong time. "*WHAT?*" Thrinndor exclaimed. "*YOU?*"

"Yes," answered the barbarian, meekly. "Me."

"What qualifies you to such a title?" Thrinndor asked.

"I, ummm," stammered the dwarf, "sort of checked, and the title had not been taken." He looked up defiantly. "I spoke with the drow back at the library and I paid the fee to have my name permanently recorded as Vorgath Shieldsunder, Dragonslayer."

"You *what?*" Thrinndor cried. He crossed his arms on his chest and suppressed his smile. "Vorgy," he said, "were you drinking, by chance?"

Suddenly the barbarian was looking down at his feet. "Maybe," he said, his voice barely audible.

The paladin laughed heartily, soon joined by the ranger and cleric. Even Sordaak chuckled some. Finally, Vorgath smiled sheepishly and succumbed to the mirth.

"Wait!" All eyes shifted back to Thrinndor. He in turn looked over at the sorcerer. "How did you know all of this about Ardaagh?"

Sordaak scratched his head, causing his hat to bob about comically. "I did some studying on it back in the Library," he said.

"Why?" asked the cleric.

"Huh?" replied the mage. He was fidgeting nervously now.

"Of all the stuff I know you were working on during your limited time in the Library," Cyrillis said, "why would you spend time on ancient history of an abandoned seaport?"

Sordaak was clearly struggling with something, Breunne decided. His eyes were shifting and his hands were trembling slightly. He was nervous.

Thrinndor decided it might be better to ease up. "If you would prefer not to say..." He let the thought hang there, unfinished.

Sordaak hesitated. "Now is not the time," he said. He glanced quickly at the healer and then looked up at the paladin. "It's not intended to be a secret," he began slowly. "But it will require more than a little explanation." His resolve grew as he spoke. "I will speak of it once Savin has returned."

An uncomfortable silence fell over the group. "Very well," said the paladin. "I am sure you will explain when you feel the time is right."

The sorcerer smiled as he shielded his eyes from the sun. "Yup," he said. "Trust me on this, it's a good thing."

"Trust is earned," began the paladin.

"Not granted," finished the barbarian. He wondered idly what was bothering the caster, but knew him well enough that he would explain in his own time, and not before.

"Which way?" Thrinndor asked suddenly.

Without hesitation the dwarf pointed to his left. "North," he said. "No more than a few miles." He checked the position of the sun. "We'll have no problem making it before sunset."

Breunne looked back to the right. "I'm going to go south and check the main road for signs of travel."

"It is not possible we have been followed, is it?" The look on the healer's face said she did believe it was.

"Possible? Yes," replied the paladin. He raised a hand to block her protest. "But I do not believe it is so." She backed down. "Our pursuers have no reason to believe we came this way." He looked over at the ranger. "They have to be thinking we will have to continue north toward Ice Homme."

"All the same," Breunne said, "I would like to check the road and even circle behind to check our trail." His eyes took on a distant look. "Our enemies—whoever *they* are—are not the only beings to fear out in this wilderness."

Thrinndor hesitated and then nodded.

"I'll not be long," he said as he turned. "I'll catch up to you before you reach the abandoned city." Breunne trotted off into the trees, disappearing quickly among them.

"Savin sure has some interesting friends," said the barbarian as he watched the trees for any movement.

"Us among them," said the caster with a smile and a shake of his head. "Us among them."

"I for one am glad to have him along," Cyrillis said. She too was watching where the ranger had gone.

Thrinndor scratched his head and turned to look down the road the way they were going. "I am as well," he said with a sigh. Without changing his line of sight, he changed the topic. "Vorgy," he said with a hint of concern to his voice, "any idea as to who—or what—is currently taking up residence in the old abandoned city?"

"I thought you'd never ask, o pompous one," the dwarf replied with a smile. The paladin tuned his gaze upon the barbarian, who continued, "At last report there was some crazy old wizard dabbling in the dark arts of returning the dead to life in these parts, and that he was trying to populate the city that way."

"Quozak," Sordaak said, sounding as if he were spitting the name from his mouth in distaste. Which he was. All eyes turned to him. "He was certainly crazy," agreed the mage.

"Your old master?" asked the paladin.

"Mentor," corrected the sorcerer with a flash in his eyes. "That old bastard was *never* my master!"

"Whatever!" quipped the dwarf.

Sordaak turned his icy stare on the impudent barbarian. He held it there until Vorgath shifted uncomfortably. Finally, he shifted his eyes to the paladin. "That 'old wizard' had designs on these artifacts we seek—especially *Pendromar*." He waited to see what effect his words had. Disappointed, he continued. "He fancied himself to be either the one who was going to bring Valdaar back, or stop whoever else who tried."

That got their attention. "What?" Cyrillis and Thrinndor said together.

The magicuser smiled smugly. "You don't think you are the *only* ones to know about this 'secret' quest to bring back a god, do you?"

"No. But…" Cyrillis searched for what she was trying to say.

"He had not the pedigree," the paladin finished for her.

"So say you," Sordaak responded quickly. At their confused looks he continued, "Word has it that those on Valdaar's High Council were fairly, well, promiscuous." When neither offered to interrupt again, he shrugged. "Who is to say there are not others of their lineage wandering the land?" Again they said nothing. "I happen to *know* from extensive research in the matter, however, that Quozak *was not* of the correct bloodline. When I tried to point that out to him, he tried to kill me."

"Really?" asked the cleric? "What happened?"

The sorcerer shrugged. "He was not successful." He smiled. "Obviously." Sordaak looked over at the paladin. "It was the end of our relationship."

"Understandable," approved the big fighter as he stepped out onto the road. "We need to be moving."

Thrinndor took the lead with the healer and mage side-by-side behind him and Vorgath bringing up the rear. They marched in silence for a few miles, enjoying the warmth of the sun on their backs. While it was certainly warmer than the previous couple of days, it was still cool. Winter was rapidly approaching.

As the group approached a bend in the road, Thrinndor stopped and waited for the others to catch up. He turned to face Sordaak and Cyrillis. "Ardaagh is less than a mile away, just around that bend." He pointed ahead unnecessarily and looked up at the sun, now low in the sky. "It is getting late, and I would prefer to have our party at full strength, both in manpower and stamina."

"That goes well with my policy on not dealing with undead during the night hours," agreed the barbarian as he walked up. He dropped the head of *Flinthgoor* to the ground and leaned heavily on the shaft.

"You are sure we will be required to deal with them?" Cyrillis asked. "Can we not just bypass the town? We are on our way to the Cliffs of Mioria, are we not?"

"We are," answered the mage. "However, it is in our best interest to investigate, and possibly eradicate, any inhabitants of said city."

"Whose best interest?" asked the dwarf, suddenly wary. "While I certainly don't mind being part of any eradication involving the less than living, I prefer knowing *why*."

"Yes," agreed the healer, crossing her arms on her chest. "Why would that be good?"

All eyes were now on the spellcaster. He shifted uncomfortably, and then suddenly straightened to his full height. "I said I would explain," he snapped. "And I will." He shifted his glare from one to the other until he had glared equally at each of them. "When the time is right!"

"When the time is right for what?" Breunne asked as he appeared suddenly out of the trees.

"You're as bad as that damn thief!" Sordaak said, his heart rate elevated well above normal.

"He prefers to be called 'rogue,'" replied the ranger with a smile.

"Whatever!" growled the caster.

"He was explaining to us why he cannot explain to us why we must take a detour through the undead-infested Ardaagh and clean it up while we are there." Sarcasm gave the cleric's tone an edge. "Does that about sum it up?"

"Yup. Anyway you're in luck," Sordaak said as he looked down at the wristlet that adorned his left wrist. "That was the signal that our *rogue*," he looked pointedly at the ranger, "is ready to join us." He spun to face the paladin. "If you'll get camp prepared, I'll go get him." Sordaak started to turn away. "When I return, I'll explain to *everyone*, as promised, what all the intrigue is about."

Thrinndor met the eyes of the magician and nodded. "Very well."

Sordaak stepped aside, whipped both hands into the air and vanished, taking his familiar with him.

Breunne looked over at the paladin. "I suppose we're going to have to get used to that."

Thrinndor nodded. "Did you find anything of concern?"

The ranger took in a deep breath. "Yes," he said, "but not what you are thinking." The paladin lifted his right eyebrow. "Wolves."

"Wolves?" repeated the barbarian.

Thrinndor continued to hold the ranger's eyes. "Nothing else?"

"Not in the vicinity," Breunne shook his head. "Several days ago a small army passed along the main road from the sea inland."

"Minions?" asked the paladin.

"Minions," replied the ranger. "Perhaps seventy-five strong."

"Damn!" Vorgath had started off the road but stopped at the news. "They mean business!"

"What about the wolves?" Cyrillis wanted to know.

Breunne looked over at the healer. "There's a large pack roaming the area. Maybe ten in the group, and the tracks are fresh."

Suddenly everyone was checking the trees for any sign of movement.

"What kind of wolves?" Thrinndor asked.

The ranger hesitated. "I don't know for sure," he said. "But they're big—very big."

"Worgs?" Vorgath's tone held a note of concern. Fear would be carrying the concept too far.

"I can't say for sure," replied the ranger. "I have very little experience with them." He licked his lips. "It's certainly possible." As the group turned to leave the road, he continued. "There's more." Everyone again stopped and trained their eyes on Breunne. "One of them is exceptional."

A hush fell over the group. "How so?" asked the paladin.

Again the ranger licked his lips as he hesitated. "One of them is huge," he said.

"Define huge," Vorgath said.

"At least twice the size of the other wolves in the pack."

"Damn," exclaimed the barbarian. "Worgs are big-ass wolves in the first place."

"What is a worg?" Cyrillis asked.

"As our esteemed barbarian so eloquently put it," Sordaak said—he had reappeared with Savinhand while they spoke—"worgs are big-ass wolves of an enchanted nature that are very intelligent and vicious to a fault." He made eye contact with the ranger. "Why are we concerned with worgs?"

"Our esteemed ranger," replied the paladin, "found tracks for a pack of them nearby."

"Actually," countered the ranger, "I didn't exactly say that." He was uncharacteristically wringing his hands. "I said I found tracks for a large pack of very large wolves that *may* be worgs."

"Damn," said the mage with a shake of his head, "it appears my old mentor was a busy little bee."

"Explain," Thrinndor asked.

"Worgs are magical creatures, not natural occurring," replied the caster. "So it appears that Quozak not only worked his craft on the living-impaired, he has also screwed with the natural order of wolves." He shook his head ruefully. "It seems I can't get away from that old fart!"

"We should make camp before it gets too dark," said the rogue.

Thrinndor looked over at the ranger. "Did you happen across a suitable, defensible location for a camp?"

"Sort of," Breunne replied. At the askew glance he got from the paladin, he added, "I know of one from previous forays into the area." Thrinndor nodded. "Follow me," the ranger said as he stepped off of the road to the right, angling toward the water.

While the road at this point was not very high above the water, it was nonetheless higher. The path they took required several switchbacks before the companions reached a rocky beach on which the waves lapped gently.

The ranger led the companions back the way they had come in the failing light before stopping in front of a hollowed-out portion in the rock wall. A blackness beckoned them to enter what promised to be a cavern within.

While Vorgath, Breunne and Thrinndor set about gathering driftwood, Savinhand applied flint to steel and lit a couple of torches to do battle with the gloom.

The cavern was really not much more than a wave and wind-hollowed area in the rock wall, not going back more than ten or fifteen feet before ending in a rough, craggy surface of stones and earth, intermingled with decaying roots from long-dead trees.

As the barbarian got a fire going, Thrinndor walked up and dumped another armload of wood nearby. He stretched and looked around the hollowed-out area. "This will do," he said with a nod.

"No, it won't," said a morose caster. He was sitting on a large log not far from the fire, staring into the flames.

All eyes shifted to him. Without looking up he said, "The worg will know of this place, and will know how to get at us—trapping us inside."

"At least we'll have a place where we can put our backs to a wall," the ranger said. It seemed a good location for defense to him.

"The worg will leap from above," Sordaak said with a shake of his head.

Thrinndor recognized in his friend the need to impart what he knew, but on his terms. "What would you suggest?"

The mage was silent for a few moments, causing Breunne to shift nervously. "What about at the water's edge?"

"They will swim around and attack from all sides," replied the caster, his voice quiet such that they all had to lean in to hear him.

Again the sorcerer fell silent. Now the paladin was getting annoyed, but he tried not to show it. "Perhaps we can rest and rise early, thereby allowing us to prepare to meet them on our terms." He smiled at the thought. *Yes, this idea has merit*, he decided. "The worg will not attack until just before dawn."

"No," said the spellcaster. His eyes had still not left the fire. "They will attack while we sit to eat our evening meal."

"That is not their way," argued the barbarian. "They will try to attack while we sleep."

"Not these worg," refuted the sorcerer.

An uneasiness settled on the group in the silence that followed. There was something the sorcerer was trying hard not to say. Finally, the paladin could wait no more. "How is it you know so much about *these* worg?"

Finally Sordaak looked away from the fire. His eyes slowly made the trip to lock with those of the paladin. "Because I helped train them."

Now the silence was a stunned one. Jaws were agape.

"That changes things," said the ranger, slowly enunciating each word. "How long ago was this?"

Sordaak's eyes regained focus. "Several years," replied the mage as he rotated to look at the ranger. "I was but an apprentice, then."

Savinhand looked around nervously. "So," he said, "they could attack at any time?"

"Yes," said the mage. "But he will wait until the food is being prepared."

"He?" asked the cleric.

Sordaak slowly turned to face her and answer the question. "The alpha male is Dragolith." His tone held a quiet power. "I raised him from a whelp."

"This keeps getting better and better," said the barbarian.

"Maybe we lost them," Cyrillis said hopefully.

Breunne shook his head. "Not a chance," he said. "I found their tracks overlapping ours in several places." His eyes found those of the paladin. "They are following us."

"We must prepare," answered the paladin. He stood before the mage. "How would you do battle with them?"

"I'd avoid them if I could," replied the sorcerer. His eyes fell to his boots. "But we cannot." He looked up and into the paladin's eyes. "We *must* not."

"I doubt that we could if we wanted to," Thrinndor said carefully. "But you are going to have to explain your reasoning ere this night ends."

Sordaak matched the stare of the paladin with one of his own. "Ere this night ends." He nodded as he turned back to the fire.

Breunne thought the mage was slipping back into a trance when he again spoke. "As to how to fight them—him—we must bait them with what they expect, an evening meal. We must be spread out and when they attack, we must hit them from several fronts at once. Confuse them." He paused as he thought. "Hit them with fire, blades, arrows, bursts of sound and lightning, all at once."

Sordaak stood up and moved back out of the firelight. "They will expect us to fight here so that they have limited access, and he will be ready for that." His eyes turned toward the gentle lapping of the waves not far from where they sat. "We must fight them out in the open. I'm thinking over against the water might be where we should set up."

"Good thinking," said the ranger. "They can't attack from water."

"They can, and they will. I forced them to conquer their fear of the big water long ago, but we will be ready for that." He turned back to the paladin. "And this is how we're going to do it." He proceeded to explain.

A half hour later the companions were in their appointed places. Cyrillis was working over the fire, idly stirring the pot hanging from the tripod above it. There was nothing in the pot, but that was not easily discernible unless one was close enough. There were other lumps indistinguishable from the rock hiding just out of range of the fire.

Each of the companions had come to the fire and filled a plate and then settled back into the darkness. Cyrillis carried on a conversation with those just beyond the rim of the firelight.

"Excuse me, miss." The voice came from the direction of the water's edge.

"Yes?" she said as she turned, spoon in hand. *This wolf could talk? Sordaak had said nothing about that.*

Cyrillis could see first one pair of glowing eyes, and as her own eyes adjusted she could see several other sets on either side of that first pair. Without looking she reached out with her un-spooned hand and grasped the familiar shaft of *Kurril*.

"Step away from the fire, please." His voice was almost soothing.

As the healer moved to comply she noted the eyes of the other wolves were in motion, spreading out. Sensing they would soon be spread out too far for what they had planned, she decided the time to act was now.

As Cyrillis dropped the spoon she grasped the rune-covered wood of her staff with both hands and slammed the heel against the stone beneath her feet.

An explosion of sound radiated from the staff, blasting all in its path. The wolves yelped in pain as their hyper-sensitive ears were assaulted by the blast. Several, most in fact, stood in stunned silence, unable to move.

An instant later a wall of flame leapt into being amongst the grouping of wolves, centered upon precisely where the lead dog had been. *Had been!*

Dragolith had vanished!

Several things happened at once.

Breunne rose out of the water where he had been hiding and showered arrows on the remaining dogs, each arrow finding its way home, burying itself to the feathers into the body of its new host.

Vorgath yelled his battle-cry and leapt from the shadows to the right of the fire, *Flinthgoor* held high over his head, poised to strike. He had been instructed to focus on Dragolith, but the lead dog was nowhere to be found. Instead his great-axe rose and fell with machine-like regularity as he waded into the confused morass that had been the wolf pack.

At the signal, Thrinndor drew his flaming sword from its sheath, leaping deftly from the right side of the fire as he did so. His blade also darted and flashed, weaving its particular brand of death wherever it went.

Savinhand had been hiding above the fire, lodged into a niche in the face of the rock. At the signal he jumped silently from his refuge, drawing his short sword and a dagger as he glided to where Dragolith stood facing the cleric. He landed with a thud, not on the back of the massive alpha dog as intended, but on his hands and knees in the sand. The wolf had disappeared! Flames licked at his arms and legs as he rolled hard to his right to engage another of the animals that was rolling in the sand in an effort to put out the flames in its fur.

Sordaak had expected Dragolith to not stay within the jaws of the trap he had so expertly set and immediately sent Fahlred searching for the beast while he launched bolts of lightning and force missiles at those that remained before him.

The mage had no warning when a massive body landed heavily on him and sent him sprawling to the ground. He tumbled hard to his right and surged back to his feet.

A few feet away Dragolith crouched, his eyes burning with hatred. "You should not have come back," the wolf said. "I will finish what you began." the alpha dog said as he sprang at the magicuser.

Sordaak raised his hands and shouted the words to a spell as he prepared to meet the oncoming monster.

Dragolith's sheer mass knocked the sorcerer into the rock wall behind, his massive jaws going for the neck of his former master, intent or ripping the throat from this offending human. Sordaak's hands flashed with electricity as he poured energy through his fingers and tried to wrap them around the dog's neck.

Sordaak felt the wolf shudder in pain as a yelp escaped the throat of the huge beast. Dragolith snarled as he raised up and spun to assess a new threat. The sorcerer caught a glimpse of several arrow shafts protruding from the wolf's back.

The mage used the distraction and the slight separation between himself and the dog to launch another spell, this one a fireball. Normally a larger gap would be preferred, but he needed the power of the blast and the scorching flames of the plasma ball to deal maximum damage.

Dragolith howled in rage and pain, again launching his huge frame at the unprepared magicuser, knocking him to the ground. This time the wolf was able to clamp his tooth laden jaws onto the exposed throat of the caster.

Sordaak closed his eyes as he waited for the inevitable, yet the big dog hesitated. The mage felt the impact of a volley of arrows rack the body of the wolf. Dragolith's jaws bit down hard and the spellcaster blacked out as the searing pain tore through his neck. The last thing he remembered was the crushing weight of the gigantic animal's full heft on his chest.

Cyrillis screamed when she saw the massive animal tearing at Sordaak's throat and the expanding pool of blood that was the result. She flung a gout of flame at the duo from *Kurril* with all their combined might, knowing the wolf's body would shield the mage from most of the damage. Any that got through; she would have to deal with.

Dragolith howled in pain as he looked up at the cleric, the magicuser's blood dripping from his enormous jaws as the hatred that burned within his eyes fixed on her. Cyrillis ignored the glare; she had gotten what she wanted. She hurled her most powerful healing spell at the prone Sordaak, praying as she did that it was in time, and that it would be enough.

As she did, Dragolith sprang at her, certain that the afterlife was all that awaited his former master.

Hearing the scream of their healer, Thrinndor and Vorgath rushed to see what was amiss. They arrived simultaneously, the paladin shoving her aside and stepped in front of her as the big wolf sailed through the air.

The paladin reacted first, his flaming bastard sword slicing deep into the huge front legs of the beast as Dragolith flew toward him. The barbarian went for the less subtle approach. *Flinthgoor* whipped through the air to sink deep in the unprotected side of the wolf.

Dragolith crashed hard to the stone floor of the alcove and immediately rolled back to his feet. Only three of the monster's legs worked, however. One front leg was mostly severed, hanging only by a few tendons as the bone had been cut through. The giant wolf crouched there, ready to wreak his havoc on any that dropped their guard.

Cyrillis bushed past the paladin as he warily moved in for the kill, and rushed to the side of the supine sorcerer. "No!" she moaned as she wrapped an arm under his neck and gently lifted the mage's head into her lap. She could see that he was not breathing.

The wolf looked on with amusement, for the moment ignoring the approaching fighters. "Waste your energy not on he who needs it no more, pretty lady." Dragolith's voice was strained with pain, but he remained clear enough to be heard. He snarled and lunged at the barbarian, who had gotten too close and received a nasty gash on the left forearm for his efforts.

Cyrillis looked up from her work, and through tear impaired vision she was certain the wolf was smiling. "You bastard!" she cried. "Why is it you hate so?"

"I hate not," replied the giant wolf. "My pack must eat, and man-flesh is a delicacy we seldom get these days."

"And not one you will ever taste again," yelled Vorgath as he charged in, his greataxe raised high above his head in preparation for the killing blow.

Dragolith whirled, still unbelievably quick, on his remaining three good legs to meet dwarf's the attack just as three arrows flew in from outside the alcove to strike home in his heavily muscled chest. While not mortal wounds, these arrows distracted him as the paladin also pressed his attack from the side opposite his friend, his blade again flashing in a wide arc that bit deep into the wolf's neck.

From the other side, *Flinthgoor* flashed in the dim light of the fire and plunged into back of the creature, severing his spine. Dragolith released a howl that signaled pain and frustration as he tried to again turn to attack the barbarian.

Another volley of arrows whipped past the ear of the paladin, causing him to flinch slightly as he raised his sword for another blow. Two shiny daggers followed the arrows, all five missiles striking the worg in the side and penetrating deep.

Thrinndor again swung his bastard sword, this time with all his might, two hands on the haft, as he aimed for the same point on the back of the monster's neck as before. Despite the distractions, his aim was true and his blade severed the spine at that point, as well.

Dragolith tried to scream in pain, but all that emerged was a gurgling sound as he lunged forward one last time at the barbarian. His effort bowled over Vorgath, and the giant wolf collapsed on top of the dwarf and did not move.

The alcove fell silent, save for the cleric sobbing softly as she cradled Sordaak's head in her lap.

"A little help!" came the muffled voice of the barbarian.

Thrinndor looked over at Breunne, who had come walking up bow in hand and winked. "You hear something?"

The ranger started to respond but noticed the smile on the paladin's face. "What?" he said, winking in return. "I didn't hear anything."

"Down here you morons!" came the muted shout from beneath the dead body of Dragolith. "Get this oversized fireplace rug off me!"

"There!" Thrinndor said excitedly. "I heard it again!" He made a show of looking around. "Where did it come from, I wonder?"

"I can hear you," bellowed the dwarf, "so I *know* you can hear me! Now get this damned mutt off of me!"

"I think it's coming from under that big wolf!" Savin had walked up and immediately understood what was going on. He grinned at the paladin.

"Shall we?" asked the ranger as he leaned forward and grasped two handfuls of fur. The rogue and the paladin followed suit and did likewise. Together they pulled the dead body of the worg to one side, exposing the dwarf beneath, covered in blood.

"Good lord," exclaimed Thrinndor in mock concern. "I hope at least *some* of that blood is that of our former opponent!"

Vorgath climbed unsteadily to his feet. "Of course it is, you cretin!" he said. "I've only sustained a small scratch for all that whelp's effort." He raised his left arm to show the long, deep gash in his meaty forearm. He shook his head in mock disgust.

Thrinndor was about to reply, but Savinhand raised a hand to ask for silence. The paladin looked to where the rogue was looking and saw for the first time the cleric sitting quietly with the magicuser's head in her lap, rocking gently to and fro.

The barbarian turned to follow their eyes, and all four men walked demurely over to stand next to the healer. Outwardly Sordaak appeared whole, but his eyes remained closed and he appeared to not be breathing.

When Cyrillis did not immediately look up, Thrinndor cleared his throat noisily. The healer raised her head slowly, revealing deep sunk eyes and tracks down both cheeks.

"Is he…" The paladin could not bring himself to finish the sentence—or the thought.

"He is dead," Cyrillis said, her voice barely above a whisper. She looked back down at the serene face of the sorcerer. "I tried, but I was too late to save him." Another tear fell from her chin to join the previous droplets that had formed a pool in Sordaak's left eye socket.

Chapter Five

Smoked!

Thrinndor's shoulders fell and he stumbled backward, tripping over *Kurril*, which the healer had unceremoniously dropped to the ground in her haste to get to Sordaak's side. The paladin managed not to fall, but the kicked staff skittered noisily across the stone floor of the alcove.

Cyrillis looked up with fire in her eyes, ready to blast the big fighter for his clumsiness, but she hesitated. Her eyes opened wide in sudden hope. "Bring me my staff!"

The four men were stunned by the sudden change in the healer so that initially none moved.

"*Bring me my staff!*" she shouted. All four of the men scrambled at once. Savinhand was nearest where the staff had come to a stop, and he reflexively reached down and wrapped both hands around it.

He was quickly reminded of why he did not touch her staff as white hot electricity burned both his hands, forcing him to drop it back to the stone. "Son of a *bitch*!" he howled in pain as he shook his hands trying to cool them.

Ignoring the rogue, Thrinndor bent and hurriedly picked up the staff, having previously wrapped his hands in his cloak to prevent harm to himself, and turned to put it into the outstretched hands of the cleric.

Cyrillis grasped it greedily and gently slid out from under the caster's head, easing him to the stone floor. She brushed his tunic straight and laid the staff onto his chest, lengthwise down his torso. "Give me room," she barked without looking up as she knelt beside the prone mage.

The four men obediently took a step back, Savinhand momentarily forgetting his burned hands as he watched the healer do her work.

When Cyrillis bowed her head and began to pray, Thrinndor did as well. Soon the chanting from both joined as they spoke in the arcane language of their forbearers.

Thrinndor went silent as the voice of the healer changed timbre. Her tone took on an insistent quality as she reached out and touched the staff, causing the runes on it in the vicinity of her touch to glow with an at first faint, and then stronger, light. Without looking up, her right hand went to another point on the staff and it too illuminated in the same silvery light.

Once more her chanting grew stronger as her hand slid down the staff to come to rest on another set of runes, which immediately began to glow, as well. Now three places on the staff were glowing and still the voice of the cleric rose. Cyrillis opened her eyes wide and shouted the final words of her incantation.

The silvery light from the runes she had touched immediately jumped off the staff and swirled about a few inches above the arcane symbols. The three lights combined and spun rapidly above the face of the dead magicuser. With an audible *plop* the lights rose and dove into Sordaak's forehead.

For a moment, nothing happened. Patiently, the healer sat and waited, wondering briefly whether she had gotten the spell correctly. She had never tried this before.

Then the mage's eyes flipped open and his back arched off of the stone floor beneath him such that only his shoulders and buttocks remained in contact with the cold rock.

Cyrillis placed both of her hands on Sordaak's chest and poured more of her healing into his wracked body, knowing that he yet remained on the brink of death.

Slowly the eyes of the sorcerer regained focus and his taut frame relaxed. His eyes searched those of the cleric, who waited for a sign of what to do next. "What..." his voice croaked. The mage swallowed painfully and tried again. "What happened?"

While the healer hesitated unsure how much to reveal at this point, Vorgath had no such qualms. "You were dead," he said.

Cyrillis turned and glared at the barbarian, who backed up a step under the scrutiny. "What?" he said defensively.

The healer's lips formed a thin line as she continued to stare down the dwarf. When she turned back to her patient, her countenance softened and she forced a smile. "How do you feel?" she said.

"Alive," replied the magicuser as he tried to push himself upright. "I think."

"Not so fast," said the cleric, biting her lower lip apprehensively as she spoke.

"I assure you I will indeed live," Sordaak said, wagging his head side to side. "Although only a few moments ago I was being escorted toward a great light when he who was doing the escorting turned me away from the light and told me my time was not yet at an end." He looked at the cleric. "How did you do that?"

"It was not me," she said. "It was the staff. While I was in the library I researched everything I could find on *Kurril*." Her eyes turned to the staff which she held in her left hand. "It has many powers I have yet to tap. The spell we call Raise Dead is one of them. I studied the incantation and was able to use it to return life to you."

"Well," said the sorcerer as he put his hand to his throat and rubbed at it absently, "thank you." He smiled for the first time since his return from wherever he had been headed. He turned his smile upon the barbarian. "Live and learn."

"Die and don't," Vorgath answered, the hint of a smile touching his lips as well.

"How barbaric!" announced the cleric with a huff as she crossed her arms on her chest. Yet the faint beginnings of a smile also touched her lovely lips.

"Yet apt," said the caster as he struggled to rise. Immediately, the ranger and rogue stepped forward to steady him. He scowled at them. "I've got this!"

Breunne arched an eyebrow as he stepped back, remaining ever wary in the event the caster stumbled.

Sordaak again smiled as he managed to gain control of his legs and stop swaying. "Our most illustrious healer did a magnificent job," he said as he turned his smile upon her and offered her a hand to assist her to her feet. "I am indeed much better as a result of her ministrations."

Cyrillis blushed slightly at the compliment and took the proffered hand as she, too, regained her feet. "Thank you," she said. "However, I fear that had I not been so preoccupied I would have noted your fall much earlier and would not have had to resort to such tactics to keep your body and soul as one."

"Think nothing of it!" Sordaak was obviously feeling *much* better. "Your priorities dictated that you keep the meat-shields alive at that moment. I was behind you and not in you field of vision. In retrospect," he added, rubbing idly at his itchy and previously torn out throat, "in future encounters I will have to make a note to place myself in a more appropriate position."

By now the others had gathered and were standing around the mage. He shifted uncomfortably at the attention, not to mention he was still a little uneasy at the thought of having been dead only a few moments before. "Perhaps," Sordaak said, clearing his throat, "we can get on with the evening meal after we get rid of these dead animals." His eyes fell pointedly upon the carcass of Dragolith. "We have much to discuss."

The companions fell about the task of cleaning up their chosen point of refuge quickly. Noticing that the barbarian favored his left arm, Cyrillis stopped him as he walked by. "I thought we had an understanding on this?" she said, her eyes flashing as she focused her gaze upon the blood-soaked bandage on his forearm.

"We did—I mean we do!" Vorgath stammered. "You were busy and I thought it best not to disturb you. It's really not much more than a scratch."

"I will be the judge of that," she said. "Let me see it."

Sheepishly the dwarf held the arm up for her inspection. "See," he said, hope welling up from deep down that the cleric would let it go.

Letting go was not meant to be, however. Without a word Cyrillis untied the knot that held the bandage in place and none to gently unwound the bloody cloth to reveal the deep gash beneath. "Scratch, huh?" she said, her tone laden with disdain. "Why, this cut is almost to the bone!" Her disapproving glare shifted to bore into the eyes of the barbarian. "I have half a mind to leave you to your own devices!" Her lips were a thin line. "But I cannot! If it were to become infected—which it would without attention—you could lose your arm! A lot of good you would be to the party with that enormous greataxe and no way to wield it!"

Vorgath briefly considered arguing with her. Very briefly. "I hadn't realized it was so bad," he said contritely. "Can you please make my arm whole again?"

The healer's eyes searched those of the barbarian for any hint of mockery. Finding none, she closed her eyes and said a short prayer and put both her hands on the dwarf's arm.

As her spell worked its way into his arm, Vorgath watched in wonder as the wound knitted itself together and ceased oozing blood. Relief flooded though his veins. He hadn't realized there was so much pain. That part always amazed him. One moment pain wracked his lower arm, the next he felt like he could do battle with a god! "Thank you," he said like he meant it, because he did.

"You are welcome," Cyrillis answered. "Remember, we are on the same side. You can do your job better if you allow me to do mine."

"Yes, ma'am," replied the dwarf. "You are of course correct." He shook his head ruefully. "Just realize old habits die hard. I'm working on it, and will continue to do so." His eyes sparkled with his smile. "Just mark me down as your most recalcitrant patient!"

"I will do so," the healer replied. "Just mark *me* down as your most stubborn cleric."

Vorgath laughed as he turned to work on the neglected fire, muttering happily under his breath.

Savinhand prepared a meal from a selection of what remained of the supplies. When everyone had eaten, they went about the business of making themselves comfortable around the cheerily popping fire.

"I hope the current denizens of Ardaagh did not hear all that howling and screaming from the battle," Cyrillis said as she cupped a hot flask of tea in her hands. While the bad storm was indeed past, it was well into the fall season and the nights got cool in a hurry when the sun went down. Particularly on cloudless nights such as this one.

"If Vorgath is correct," Breunne said, "and the township is now populated by undead, then we have no fear of that. The sense of hearing is not high up on their abilities."

"Agreed," said the caster as he removed his pipe and looked askance at the dwarf, who was adjusting the position of the rock he had been sitting on closer to the fire.

Settled at last, Vorgath plopped down on his rock and stretched wearily. Out of the corner of his eye he spotted the sorcerer preparing a smoke in his long-stemmed, ornate pipe. The barbarian stopped mid-stretch and reached for his pack.

Seeing the dwarf take the bait, Sordaak smiled and said pleasantly, "Care to join me?"

His hand emerging with is pipe, Vorgath said formally, "I don't mind if I do!" He remained where he was as he pulled out his tobacco pouch. He took considerable care as he packed the bowl of his pipe in layers. He tamped each one down with a special tool he also removed from his pack.

He turned the pipe over several times in his hands, inspecting it from every angle. Satisfied, he put his pouch and tools away and reached over to the fire and pulled out a small twig that was burning from the one end.

Sordaak similarly took extreme care packing his bowl. Seeing the dwarf already pulling hard on the stem of his pipe, the sorcerer called up the necessary magic to light his finger and set about the task of lighting his bowl, too.

After a few minutes work as the others gathered around, both had their pipes ready. "Would you prefer I begin this time?" asked the barbarian around the stem of his pipe, which remained between his teeth.

"Please," the mage said, nodding in deference to the dwarf.

The others leaned forward from their seats in anticipation. Thrinndor threw two more deadwood logs onto the fire to get more light. The dried wood caught immediately, and soon the desired light manifested itself.

Vorgath puffed contentedly on his pipe, each time drawing in more smoke than he let out. Finally ready, he craned his neck backwards, pursed his lips and began blowing the smoke out with a purpose.

A figure began to take shape—a *big* figure. Still the barbarian drew hard on the pipe and blew out smoke. As the smoke coalesced, the size of the figure continued to grow. The shape was no longer big, it was gigantic!

Arms formed, legs took shape, and soon a head could be made out. The figure *was a giant*! Either a stone giant, or possibly a storm giant. Whichever, it was huge. At least ten, maybe twelve feet tall! As the dwarf continued to billow out the smoke, a sword began to take shape in the monster's enormous hands. The sword was also huge, at least six feet in length.

Now the features began to emerge as Vorgath continued to work his craft. Deep-sunk eyes, high cheekbones, thick neck and the typically prominent fore-head attributed to the larger class of giants. A cloak formed and hung loosely from the creatures massive shoulders. Storm giant, Breunne decided. Damn! He loved these contests! The ranger marveled at the detail of the smoke figure.

The giant's head swiveled until his eyes locked onto the sorcerer and the fig-ure turned his body to face Sordaak. The monster extended his right arm toward the mage, palm up and beckoned insolently for the spellcaster to do his best.

Sordaak arched a single brow, that being his only acknowledgement that a giant now stood before him.

The mage began to puff furiously on his pipe until the bowl glowed cherry red in the dim light of the alcove. Sordaak pursed his lips and began to build his answer with smoke of his own. He went back to the pipe for an occasional reload as he worked. Soon it became obvious that his figure was going to be much smaller.

The figure of a man began to show itself as the billowing smoke took shape. Not just a man, his raiment showed him to be a *magicuser*! The tall pointy hat and the swirling robes made that apparent. A magicuser that closely resembled Sordaak, no less!

The giant waited patiently for the figure forming in front of him to take shape. When he saw what it was he faced, the monster threw back his head and laughed.

Without hesitation, the smoke-sorcerer lifted an arm and pointed a finger at the giant. The mage's lips seemed to move and then a small ball of fire jumped from his pointed finger directly at the massive creature's head. The ball exploded in a brilliant flash of light that startled several of the seated companions.

When their eyes adjusted following the blast, the party could see the giant stagger backward under the force of the impact, his eyebrows gone and his hair smoldering.

The creature roared in rage as he raised a hand of his own, pointing a single finger at the sorcerer. Electricity crackled as a bolt of lightning shot forth at the puny human that dared to do battle with him.

The magician rotated the hand he had used to launch the ball of fire such that the open palm presented itself to the giant. When the lightning struck the hand, it seemed to rail against an invisible shield radiating from the open palm. None of the energy got past this shield.

Again the giant roared his displeasure, grasped the sword with both hands and raised it above his head. He took a step toward the smoke-caster, intending to end this duel in one mighty blow.

Without moving his feet, the sorcerer again rotated the outstretched hand, once again pointing a finger at the monstrous figure before him. Again the lips moved silently and a stream of energy went from the mage's finger to strike the giant square in the chest.

The giant's eyes widened in surprise as his forward motion came to an immediate halt mid-stride, his enormous sword still poised high above the magicuser.

As the companions watched, the giant's skin began to take on the look of stone. Soon the stone enveloped the entire being of the creature and it stood still as a statue, unable to move.

Without the expression on the mage's face changing even a small amount, he reached into a pouch at his side and withdrew a tiny hammer. In two nonchalant steps the sorcerer was standing next to the massive left leg of the giant. The caster appeared to search for a specific spot and then raised the hammer in his right hand and tapped lightly twice on the left knee of the monster.

Tink, tink was heard by the companions. On the second *tink*, the massive form of the giant crumbled to dust and showered down upon those companions who happened to be seated nearby.

Surprised, Vorgath's eyes widened as they went from where his giant creation had stood to the smoke-sorcerer. The smoke figure raised its right hand to an open mouth, stifling a yawn. He then extended his arm toward the dwarf as the companions held their breath. The mage rotated his palm upward and beckoned for the dwarf to continue, mimicking the motion of the now dissolved giant.

Vorgath's expression showed his focus as he removed his pipe and checked his bowl, obviously pondering his next move. Deciding there was an adequate supply of tobacco in the bowl, the dwarf again placed the stem between his teeth and he drew deep on his pipe until the bowl began to glow a blood red.

Sordaak took an occasional maintenance puff on his pipe and blew smoke as necessary to keep his smoke magician properly formed.

His concentration complete, the barbarian this time ignored the sorcerer as he once again began to billow forth his smoke. He sent the acrid cloud toward the ceiling, and the paladin assumed he was going to form another bird, or some other such flying creature. Thrinndor was surprised when the large cloud split into three separate blobs of smoke and they slowly settled toward the ground, forming a triangle on all sides of the smoke-sorcerer.

Sordaak lifted an eyebrow as he briefly considered a preemptive strike on at least one of the now forming figures, but decided instead to maintain his stance and see what the dwarf had in mind.

The three blobs rapidly coalesced into dwarven figures, each complete with armor, helms and—of course—a mammoth greataxe. As the smoke-barbarians became more finite, they began to twirl their weapons in unison. Over their heads and around their backs the massive axes spun. The pattern was mesmerizing.

Slowly the smoke-sorcerer turned, trying to keep an eye on each of his opponents. Cyrillis found she was holding her breath. What were the barbarians waiting for?

In a flash the three smoke figures struck as one. They charged in, axes held high. The healer gasped as the charge began. Surely the sorcerer would be overrun! She could almost hear the barbarian war cries as each opened their mouth to shout.

The smoke-sorcerer's right hand shot skyward and he opened his mouth, speaking a soundless word of enchantment.

The smoke-barbarians crashed into an unseen barrier surrounding the smoke-mage and they were thrown back by an invisible force. The fighters landed hard and tumbled immediately back to their feet, weapons at the ready.

The smoke-sorcerer lowered his raised hand and pointed at one of the barbarians. A bolt of lightning flashed from the caster's pointed figure to the fighter, disintegrating him in a literal puff of smoke.

The other two smoke-barbarians sensed an opening and charged in, axes held high.

A blade arced toward the caster, his back still to the charging dwarfs he seemed unaware of the danger. At the last possible instant, the smoke-sorcerer side-stepped the flashing blade and began a tumbling pass, somersaulting and rolling away from his attackers. The barbarians gave chase.

As the smoke-sorcerer tumbled, he cast spells at his adversaries. Force Darts flew from the caster's fingers every time his tumble brought the dwarfs into his line of sight. While the darts did little obvious damage, after a few of them the smoke-barbarians were beginning to slow.

Abruptly the smoke-caster sprang high into the air and did three backflips before landing deftly on his feet, facing the still charging smoke-barbarians. Slowly the mage lifted both hands, palms down. He spread his fingers, touched his thumbs together and pointed them at the fighters.

The barbarians were only a couple of steps away from the mage when the smoke-sorcerer smiled. Gouts of flame shot from his fingertips, engulfing the two fighters. One of the barbarians managed a weak, blind swing with his axe, but the sorcerer easily sidestepped the blade as he kept the flames trained on his opponents.

Vorgath was sweating profusely as he tried to maneuver his apparitions out of the fire, to no avail. The smoke-caster showed no mercy as first one and then the other smoke-barbarians succumbed to the flames and dissolved into the air.

The smoke-sorcerer finally let the spell die as he turned to face the seated dwarf. The smoke figure raised his hands to his face and appeared to blow on his fingers, his eyes never leaving the seated barbarian.

Cyrillis, sensing the end of the competition, began clapping loudly. Thrinndor, Breunne and Savinhand all did the same, with some whistles thrown in for good measure.

Vorgath checked his pipe, shook his head slowly and climbed tiredly to his feet. As he walked toward the still seated magicuser, he waved an irritated hand through the smoke-mage, dissipating the apparition.

"Sore loser!" teased the thief.

"Damn straight," replied the barbarian as he came to a halt in front of the seated caster. Deliberately he put the stem of his pipe in his mouth and clenched it between his teeth. He lowered his hands and slowly began to clap them together as well.

Sordaak breathed a sigh of relief (the dwarf was known to have a temper, after all) as he climbed slowly to his feet to stand in front of the dwarf. He bobbed his head in difference to the dwarf.

Vorgath stopped clapping and stuck his right hand out toward Sordaak. The caster grasped the offered forearm and met the eyes of the dwarf. "Well done," the barbarian said as he released the magicuser's arm. His eyes settled on the caster's pipe. "New pipe?" he asked.

"Yes," replied the mage. "A gift from Rheagamon." Sordaak smiled. "He said—"

"That won't help you next time," said the barbarian tightly. He turned on a heel and strode back to his rock next to the fire and plopped down and began to clean his pipe.

Sordaak also sat back down as he shook his head. He too began to clean his pipe, taking great care as he did so, inspecting every nook and cranny of the instrument.

Thrinndor waited patiently for the caster to finish with his pipe. As Sordaak put the pipe carefully back in its custom-made box and then stored the box in his portable hole, the paladin cleared his throat noisily. All eyes turned to their leader. "I believe our magicuser has some explaining to do."

The sorcerer tensed as he tucked his folded artifact away behind his belt. He let his shoulders droop as he looked up to meet the eyes of the paladin. "Yes," he said, "I guess it's time I do." He stood silently and walked out of the enclosure.

Vorgath and Thrinndor looked at one another and shrugged. Breunne and Cyrillis stood and followed the mage out past the fire. Savin, who had been lounging quietly in the shadows, also climbed wearily to his feet and got in step behind the ranger and cleric.

The barbarian, semi-comfortable on his rock, wanted to argue, but sighed resignedly and noisily stood, stretched and motioned for his longtime friend the paladin to precede him. Thrinndor smiled at the barbarian, stepped around the fire and out through the opening into the dark night beyond.

The paladin paused briefly once outside as he allowed his eyes to adjust to the moonless night. Spotting Savin ahead and to his left—heading for the beach—he waited for the barbarian and motioned for Vorgath to follow him.

Silently Sordaak waited at the water's edge until the dwarf and the big fighter walked up.

"This had better be good," griped Vorgath. There was definitely a bite in the air, and it had been much warmer in the enclosure.

For an answer the sorcerer turned and pointed out over the water.

The dwarf looked where the caster pointed and squinted but could see nothing except inky black darkness, broken only by the usual myriad of stars. "What?" he demanded.

"You look but do not see," replied the sorcerer.

Thrinndor too could see nothing in the darkness. Perhaps the mage's brush with death had affected him adversely. "Maybe you should explain to us just what it is we should be seeing," he said, concern an underlying current in his voice.

"Really?" said the caster. "You, too?" Sordaak shook his head as he looked down at the sand at his feet. "I thought for sure *you* would be able to figure it out."

"Maybe you should explain it to us, trickster," Vorgath said menacingly. The breeze coming off of the water was cold.

Perplexed, the paladin again looked out over the water where the caster had pointed. Something was nagging at the edge of his memory, but it remained just out of reach. Sordaak was watching him carefully.

There! He could see lights dancing on the surface of the water on edge of the range of his vision. But lights to what. Still the thought he was looking for eluded him. What was it? What were the lights?

"I see the lights," said the paladin, "but I do not perceive their significance."

"What lights?" asked the barbarian. "I don't see no lights?"

Sordaak made an exaggerated roll of his eyes. "Oh, for pity's sake!" He pointed out over the water again. "Maybe you're too damn short to see that far!"

"Watch it, trickster!" said the dwarf.

"Can anyone else see the damn lights?" asked the dwarf, plaintively.

"I see them," said the cleric. "But I have no idea what it is I see."

"I also see them," said Breunne.

"As do I," said the rogue.

That something was still nagging at Thrinndor. He could almost see it. "Please tell us what it is we are looking at."

"I still don't see anything!" griped the dwarf.

Sordaak ignored the dwarf. He turned slowly to look out at the lights. "The Isle of Grief," said the caster quietly.

"*What?*" cried the cleric.

There! The nagging thought finally popped into Thrinndor's head. The Isle of Grief was not far off of the coast of Ardaagh.

"I still don't see nothin'!" said the dwarf.

"What *about* the Isle of Grief?" asked the paladin quietly.

Sordaak turned slowly to meet the eyes of the paladin. "I am building a keep there."

Chapter Six

Revelations

Suddenly the companions were all speaking at once. Everyone except for Thrinndor, and of course Sordaak.

"What?"

"Where?"

Sordaak ignored them. His eyes never left the deeply shadowed eyes of the paladin.

"Rebuilding Valdaar's Rest," Thrinndor said. It was not a question. The others stopped talking, deciding they would get more information by just listening.

"Yes and no," replied the mage.

"Please explain." The paladin had not moved.

"Very well, but I can do so back in the warmth of the alcove," said the magicuser. Without waiting for a reply, he turned to head back to the cliff wall.

"Finally!" griped the dwarf. "Someone is making some sense!" Before he turned to follow the caster, Vorgath squinted one last time out over the water. There! Some flickering lights on the edge of his vision, right where the horizon met the sky. Why build a keep out there, he wanted to ask, but his companions had their backs to him and were rapidly receding into the darkness, toward the warmth of the fire. That's where he wanted to be, he reminded himself as he walked quickly to catch up.

Once back in the relative warmth of the alcove, the companions gathered around the fire holding their hands out to garner what warmth they could. Vorgath, still grumbling from the nonsensical trip out into the cold, stirred the fire and added a couple of pieces of driftwood. The dried wood caught quickly, and soon the blaze chased away the chill of the night.

None in the party seemed to want to disturb the sorcerer as he stared into the coals of the fire. Finally, Sordaak felt their patience wearing thin and he began to speak.

"I have a lot to say," he said barely loud enough to be heard over the gentle sounds of the fire, "so please do not interrupt me. All will be explained to your satisfaction ere I am done."

Feeling he could not just let go of the wasted trip outside, Vorgath said, "Just get on with it already!"

The mage turned his tired eyes upon the barbarian. Sordaak was in no mood for idle banter. He stared down the dwarf until Vorgath grabbed a stick and poked some more at the fire.

Satisfied he was not going to be interrupted, the caster again lost his eyes in the blood red embers of the fire. "During my search while an understudy for Quozak—my previous mentor—I discovered what is known now as the Isle of Grief. My curiosity piqued, I began my own search for anything related to the island."

Sordaak paused for a moment when a large *pop* from the fire showered the mage with sparks and startled him. Idly he brushed the few dead ember remnants from his robe as he continued. "It—the island—was placed off limits by the Paladinhood of Praxaar as our leader attested to previous. That ban effectively passed a death sentence on Ardaagh, for it was the major supply port for Valdaar's Rest and the support community that existed on the island." He paused to consider. "But I digress. I discovered in my studies in The Library that the reason Praxaar destroyed his brother's keep and placed the island off limits was because the two combined provided a source of power for the god and his followers—that much you know already."

The mage was silent for a bit as he collected his thoughts, trying to decide how much he should reveal. None of the companions had any thought to interrupt.

"I discovered during my prior research—even before I had access to Antiquity—the plans used to build Valdaar's Rest." There were several sharp intakes of breath, but still none spoke. "More than a year ago I quietly began building on the site of the original keep. For the most part, I will stay true to the original plans. However," the caster turned his eyes upon the paladin, "information I was able to glean from Savin's library showed me several...flaws in the original plans."

"*What?*" escaped Thrinndor's lips before he could clamp down on his emotions.

Sordaak nodded his head, expecting the outburst—actually the paladin's reaction was more diminutive than anticipated. "It is sooth," the magicuser continued. "The entire keep is built around proportions that are designed to enhance the power the god derived from both is people *and* the ground on which it sat. Some of the dimensions used were fractionally off. I have sent the corrections to my engineers."

Again the sorcerer fell silent as he stared into the fire. "I also have sent instructions for them to focus their efforts on the main temple and the outer fortifications." Thrinndor wanted to reach out and shake the words from the caster as he paused again; such was his fervor for what the mage was saying. He knew this to be important…

"For we will need the temple for the ritual required to return Lord Valdaar to this realm." Sordaak held his hands up to silence the questions on the lips of both the healer and the paladin. When he was satisfied they would say nothing, the mage continued. "And the fortifications will be required to protect us from the servants of Praxaar that will surely try to prevent me when they discover what I am doing out there."

Thrinndor opened his mouth again to interrupt, but thought better of it. Instead he nodded his approval of the plan.

"Unfortunately my lead engineer has informed me the progress is slow. His lack of manpower, funds and the proximity of a seaport for supplies combine to throttle his efforts." Sordaak turned to look at the cleric. "Focusing only on the walls and the temple, he tells me I am looking at three to four years for construction to be complete."

Cyrillis' face drooped. "That is too long!" she said forlornly. "We must not delay once we have the Artifacts of Power."

"Agreed," Thrinndor said. "What must be done to hasten the construction?"

Sordaak turned back to the paladin. "One of the reasons we are making this side trip is to make Ardaagh available to us. If we can clean out the undead and secretly—and I mean *secretly*—set up a port of operation, that will aid the cause greatly. But, word *must* not get out what I have begun, else we will be stopped long before we are ready."

"What about manpower and funds?" asked the paladin in the silence that ensued. He knew the sorcerer was leading to something.

Suddenly Sordaak found something interesting down around his feet. "I, of course, have sent all available funds to my construction engineer. My take from the dragon's horde will certainly help, but he informs me that a skirmish with a band of troglodytes that has set up base in the mines where we must get the special black granite for the walls has slowed his progress to almost nonexistent."

"We must go there and assist!" said a resolute healer. "Surely a band of troglodytes would prove no match to us!"

Sordaak did not immediately answer. Instead, he looked over at the paladin. The mage knew the big fighter to be chafing at not pursuing the lead on the *Valdaar's Fist*. Thrinndor's lips were pressed into a thin line, but he did not speak.

"That was my thought, as well," said the spellcaster. "I only learned this yesterday. I can communicate with my lead engineer through Fahlred." Sordaak again looked down at his feet as he fought back several emotions trying to win the day in his head. When he looked up, he locked eyes with the paladin. "I do not wish to speak for Vorpal," he said quietly. "We are chasing a strong lead that I know our leader wishes to check out as quickly as possible."

Thrinndor merely nodded, his lips remaining tight.

"But my engineer informs me that these troglodytes are stronger and smarter than the usual run-of-the-mill trogs. They have thwarted the best efforts of the security force I had established for just such a purpose." The sorcerer shook his head. "It appears they have gleaned additional power from the surrounding rock and even have a wizard among them that wields considerable power." Sordaak snorted in derision at the thought. "I fear my security force is no match for this band of troglodytes."

"How long?" asked the paladin. His tone was grim.

"Three days—no more," said the mage softly, unable to look up to meet the paladin's eyes. Three days was a long time.

Thrinndor did not immediately reply. Cyrillis and Breunne looked at their leader, wondering which way this was going to go. His eyes bored into those of the magicuser. "You are certain this temple is necessary to return Valdaar to this plane?"

Sordaak nodded, a lump in his throat.

"No other temple will suffice?" asked the paladin.

The mage shrugged. "Maybe," he said. "But the power generated by the rocks and the design of my temple will allow us to focus our spells and abilities, thereby increasing the odds of success. Do you want to chance that another temple might not prove sufficient?"

Thrinndor shook his head. Abruptly his shoulders drooped. "Very well," he said finally. "I see no other choice but to rid your isle of these troglodytes." His eyes held those of the caster. "What else?"

All eyes shifted back to Sordaak as he was again studying some imagined speck on his shoes.

He remained quiet for a few heartbeats. "Manpower and funds," he said, not elaborating.

"Funds are easy," Cyrillis said. "My take from the dragon and Dragma's Keep are set aside for the service of Valdaar—what better service than to use those funds in building his temple?" She smiled at Sordaak.

Thrinndor's right eyebrow shot up. "That seems a logical use for my take, as well. I also have a fairly significant amount of coin set aside from previous expeditions that I can have delivered to you once we finish at Ice Homme."

It was obviously what the magicuser had hoped for. He breathed out a deep sigh as his face split in a tentative smile. "Thanks."

Vorgath interrupted. "How much?" He eyed the paladin with a mischievous half-smile on his face.

"Must everything be a competition with you?" replied the paladin, a half-smile playing at his lips, as well.

"How much?" repeated the dwarf.

"250,000—give or take a few," answered the big fighter.

"Gold?" pressed the barbarian.

"Yes, gold," replied the paladin, wondering just where this was going.

"I too have a *small* horde set aside," Vorgath said. His attention shifted to the sorcerer. "I had always planned on building my own keep, some day." He snorted at his own words. "But, what use do I have for a keep?" He shook his head at his own audacity. "I'll settle down when I'm too old to swing *Flinthgoor*!" Now the barbarian smiled at the caster, who waited semi-patiently.

Sordaak licked his lips nervously when the dwarf did not continue. He sensed Vorgath wanted to make him work for it. "How much?"

"1,400,000."

The mage who had been slouching sat bolt upright. "Gold?"

Vorgath smiled. "Plat."

"*What?*" Sordaak fell backward off of the rock he was sitting on.

"Surely you jest?" said Thrinndor, whose right eyebrow had reached new heights.

Vorgath sat upright. "Surely I do *not*!" he said. "I have been at this adventuring thing for more than a hundred years before you were *born*!" His glare begged for the paladin to argue with him. Thrinndor chose not to. "As I have no need for a keep, I have no real need for that much coin, either. I will keep some back for operating expenses." He smiled at the paladin and winked. "But I think I can throw in the bulk of my holdings—say 1,000,000." He paused for a moment. "Plat."

Cyrillis looked at the dwarf in awe. She had never even heard of such amounts! Tears welled up in her eyes as she stood suddenly and ran the few short steps to the barbarian and bent to throw her arms around his neck. "Thank you," she whispered.

"Aw, now," stammered the dwarf, "none of that mushy shit!" He was beaming when the cleric drew back and wiped the moisture from her eyes.

Cyrillis smiled back. "Thank you just the same," she said as she made her way back to the driftwood log she had been sitting on and sat down.

"Yes," said the mage quietly as he crawled his way back up onto his rock. "Thank you, indeed."

"One million plat should pay for any labor force you might need, I should think," said the dwarf with a wink.

The smile left the mage's face and he began to fidget on his rock.

"What?" asked the dwarf. "You need more?"

"No," Sordaak said quickly, "I mean yes!" he corrected himself. His face was a mask of uncertainty as he sat on his rock and said nothing.

"What is it you are trying so hard not to tell us?" asked the paladin.

The sorcerer looked over at the big fighter, and then back to the dwarf. Still his indecision held him and he said nothing.

"Speak up!" griped the dwarf. He was not sure why, but he thought this was going to be something he didn't want to hear.

Abruptly Sordaak's shoulders slumped as he went back to staring at his sandals. "It's not that I can't hire plenty of workers with that kind of coin," he said slowly. "But *what kind* of manpower can I get with it? Knowing I must do so in secret and avoid any possible connections with the followers of Praxaar."

"Go on," said the paladin. He had no idea where this was going.

"Just what do you have in that oversized mind of yours?" said an inherently suspicious Vorgath.

Sordaak sat upright, straightened his shoulders and appeared to pull confidence from the air as his eyes bored into those of the dwarf. "I need—we need—the dwarves of the Dragaar Clan of the Silver Hills if we are to have any hope of completing the keep and temple on time."

"Impossible!" Vorgath shot back.

"Why?" Sordaak said, not backing down. He had expected this would not be easy.

"They will not leave their homes in the mines of the Silver Hills," the barbarian replied easily. He knew his people.

"Why?" pressed the magicuser. He knew Vorgath's people, too. At least he thought he did.

"Simple," answered the dwarf. "They mine the silver, and other precious metals. Sometimes even a few stones worthy of turning into jewelry." If anything, Vorgath had understated what was widely known. Dwarven jewelry, weapons and armor were highly sought after throughout the land.

Sordaak smiled as he reached for his storage device. The companions looked on curiously as he removed it from its place behind his belt, gently unfolded it and set it on his lap. He reached inside and began fumbling around for something.

Savinhand always found it unnerving for the mage to reach into the opening, his arm simply disappeared. Strange.

Finding what he searched for at last, the sorcerer hesitated before withdrawing it. With his arm still inside, he looked over at the dwarf. "What if they were to find something more precious to mine?" he asked as he pulled his arm out of the artifact. Clutched in his hand was a chunk of rock three or four times the size of the average fist. The rock glittered with exposed metal veins and glistened where a couple of blue facets jutted from its irregular surface.

Vorgath, who had taken in a breath to renounce any talk of his people moving, let that breath out slowly in a noisy hiss. "Let me see that," he said softly.

Without getting up, Sordaak carelessly tossed the heavy chunk of rock over to the barbarian, who snatched it out of the air and held it closer to the fire for the better light.

"Is this…?" his voice trembled as it trailed off. He looked up at the sorcerer, wonder in his eyes.

"Platinum," said the caster, nodding as he did. "And those smaller veins on the other side are mithryl." He hesitated slightly before continuing. "There are other metals as of yet to be identified in smaller amounts within that sample."

Vorgath rolled the rock over to inspect the spidery thin veins opposite the much larger veins of platinum. It was his turn to lick his lips nervously. He had never seen this much mithryl in a single sample of rock. "Where did you get this?" The dwarf's eyes never left the rock.

"From the mines beneath the old keep, below where I must build." Sordaak had known the question was coming.

Finally the dwarf pried his eyes from the rock in his hands, avarice still haunting his vision. "What is it you propose?"

"I need the skilled craftsmanship of your stone masons," replied the mage, "and your people need the precious metals imbedded in the rocks that we must use for the walls."

When the barbarian didn't immediately answer, the mage shrugged. "I propose a trade," he said. "The mines on that island—and there are many different mines in several different locations—are rife with various metals and gemstones. I propose that in exchange for building me this temple, and eventually the keep to go with it, I will allow your people exclusive rights to the minerals on the entire island. They can stay there as long as they so desire." Sordaak folded his arms across his chest and waited.

What he got next was not what he had been hoping for. "What gives you the right to bargain for and with this island?" The look in the barbarian's eyes was of pure greed.

Taken aback, the mage stammered. "I, ugh," he said. Abruptly the emotions on his face changed from confusion to anger as he stood and marched over to the dwarf. He snatched his sample rock back from the barbarian and returned to his seat.

A silence fell over the companions. Each waited to see what was going to happen next.

Vorgath's face mottled in rage and it appeared an explosion was imminent. Slowly, however, the barbarians rage subsided and his color returned to normal. Silently he looked at his hands as he tried to figure out what he had done—or lost. "I'm sorry," he said softly. His eyes lifted slowly to look into those of the sorcerer. "You must pardon my actions," he said. "I have never seen such a sample in all my years. My people would…" He didn't finish the sentence as he allowed his eyes to again drop to his hands.

If Sordaak had been taken aback by the dwarf's earlier reaction, he was positively stunned at the apology. After a few moments when nothing else was said, the anger also drained from the mage's face. "I laid claim to the island shortly after verifying it was still uninhabited." He grinned suddenly, "Well, except for the occasional wild animal and obviously a troglodyte or two."

"Or three," Breunne said, joining the conversation at last. "Obviously." He grinned as well.

"I briefly considered filing a formal claim at the deeds and registrar's office in Farreach," the magicuser returned the grin, "but decided that might be counterproductive. The fewer that know what I am up to on the island, the better."

"Agreed," said the paladin. "And good thinking."

"Wait," said the cleric. "You said you began work on rebuilding the keep a year ago." Her face was contorted in confusion. "Yet you only joined our ranks in the attempt to return Valdaar to us a couple of months ago?"

"I figured one of you would eventually catch that," replied the caster with a wink. "I always thought you were the smarter of the two holier-than-thou types." He smiled smugly at the paladin, daring him to argue. When Thrinndor just grinned back at him, the mage continued, "It's the power generated on that island. Since learning of its existence, I've been trying to figure a way to harness that power." He shrugged. "Only following our success in Dragma's Keep did I instruct my chief engineer to shift his efforts from the outer fortifications to include reconstructing the temple."

The magicuser shifted his attention back to the dwarf, who was still sitting quietly studying his hands. "Vorgath, do you think you can convince your people to aid in building the Keep?"

The barbarian slowly raised his eyes to meet those of the mage, his face still ashen from his earlier outburst. "With that sample in hand, you just try to *stop them*," he said quietly.

Sordaak nodded, it was as he had figured. "We *must* prevail upon them to build the temple and the outer walls *before* they succumb to their desires to mine and forge."

"The ore is in the mines where we must cut the stone for the walls, correct?" asked the dwarf, pondering the situation.

"Yes," said the mage. "At least most of it is."

"Well, we must be careful not to give them that information, and not allow them to go wandering," Vorgath said, rubbing his chin as he thought. "As long as they are allowed to work the quarry to cut the stone and mine whatever ore they find in the process, they will be far happier than where they are now." He paused to consider. "But how do we get word to the Silver Hills to get them here?"

"And once here," asked the paladin, "how do we get them to the island?"

"I'll answer Vorgath's question, first," replied the mage. "I have a couple of scrolls," he announced as he turned to face the barbarian. "They will allow me to teleport the two of us to your home and then back once we have secured their support."

"The second question begs an answer from the barbarian," he added. Vorgath raised an eyebrow but did not say anything. "How many of your people can I expect for aid?" When the dwarf opened his mouth to answer, Sordaak held up a hand to preclude him. "Wait. Know that we must leave behind there in the Silver Hills a small force to both protect your homes and to keep up the appearance that the Hills are not deserted. We *must not* allow word to get out about what we are up to."

The barbarian nodded his agreement. "Leaving behind said force of a hundred or so," he held up his hand to block the caster's protest. "There will be at least that many that will not want to relocate, no matter what the prize." A deflated Sordaak nodded solemnly. "That will still allow for a force of," the dwarf made a show of counting on his fingers and in his head. Sordaak found he was holding his breath. "I think I can muster about twenty-four or twenty-five..."

"*What?*" cried the sorcerer. "That's *it?*"

"Hundred," continued the barbarian with a grin.

"Really?" said a shocked Cyrillis. "That many?"

Vorgath merely nodded.

Sordaak sat back down hard. He didn't remember standing. He looked back over at the dwarf. "Twenty-five *hundred?*" The dwarf again nodded. "Holy shit!" said the magicuser, incredulous. "With that many motivated dwarves, I could rebuild the entire complex in a year!"

"You are too kind," replied a beaming dwarf. "While my kin are indeed skilled, they would probably take at least fifteen or sixteen months to build such an edifice." He was certainly enjoying the moment. "When properly motivated."

"Yeah," interrupted the paladin, "meaning plenty of strong drink!"

"That is truly a staple of life," agreed the dwarf, refusing to rise to the bait. Abruptly he turned back to the magicuser. "When did you want to leave?" Once a path is decided, it's very hard to deter a dwarf.

Sordaak's hand reached into his cloak and emerged with two scroll tubes. "I thought you'd never ask!"

"Wait," said the thief, who had been idly wondering just how much of this was going to affect him as leader of Shardmoor. "You never answered that second question." When all eyes turned upon Savinhand, he continued, "How are you going to get twenty-five hundred dwarfs out to your island?"

"Oh, yeah," said the sorcerer. "I truly did not expect such an army." He rubbed his chin in thought. "I have a couple of small supply ships out at the island that can be used to ferry small groups back and forth. I also have one larger vessel that can carry many more, but it is in need of repair. I'll have my chief engineer make that a priority. That will have to do. We can't afford to deal with the raised eyebrows purchasing a larger vessel would cause at this time."

"You are going to need a larger one at some point," said the ranger thoughtfully. "Perhaps you can have your chief engineer make arrangements for one back in Farreach." Sordaak turned to look at Breunne. "Your engineer can certainly get a good deal on such a vessel with winter coming on, and he can make up some sort of story about using it to supply the Minions down in the southern region." He grinned. "That would certainly be a believable story, assuming they came into port as we thought."

"That might work," agreed the mage. "I'll have my chief engineer sail to Farreach with the story he needs to trade in his smaller ship for a much larger one. I like it!"

With that, Sordaak called for his familiar and communicated with him silently for a few minutes and then Fahlred winked back out of existence.

Finished with that, Sordaak walked over to stand by the dwarf. "Ready?" he said. The barbarian nodded as he stood.

The mage turned to Thrinndor. "We should not be long. Depends on how quickly our silver-tongued dwarf here can convince his people they need to march."

"You just let me hold that rock, and we'll have to get out of their way or get marched over the top of!" answered the dwarf as he reached for the sample the magicuser brandished carelessly in his left hand. Vorgath then reached over and picked up his greataxe and said, "Ready."

The sorcerer removed the seal on one of the scrolls and shook the contents out into his hand. He put the other scroll tube back into the folds of his robe. Carefully he unfurled the dry parchment and took a step closer to Vorgath and began to read in a language the dwarf did not understand.

When they winked out of sight, Thrinndor shrugged. "Perhaps we should prepare for a rest period." Suddenly, he smelled the stew Savin had been working on since they had vanquished the wolves. His stomach grumbled, reminding him he had not yet eaten. "*After* we get something to eat!" he added. "I am starving!"

"There's plenty here," said the rogue. "I imagine those two will dine with the dwarves."

"Probably," Breunne said wistfully. "Damn those dwarves sure know how to eat! Makes me wish I had gone with them."

"Not me," replied the paladin as he ladled a large portion of the stew onto his plate. He took a big whiff of the stew and walked over to his log and sat down. "I will take Savin's cooking over a teleport trip any time!"

"I will agree with that," said Cyrillis enthusiastically as she ladled some of the stew onto her plate. "Teleporting around is so unnatural!"

The ranger lifted an eyebrow as he made his way to the fire, plate in hand.

"Oh, no!" said the rogue, feigning damaged feelings. "You can go eat your dried rations!"

"Aw now," said the ranger, "don't be that way!" He smiled innocently. "You know your campfire cooking is without comparison! After all, I taught you everything I know."

"Yeah, well," replied the rogue, "you didn't teach me *everything* I know!" He returned the smile.

"Ouch!" Breunne said. Cyrillis was trying to hide a smile as she put a spoonful into her mouth.

Thrinndor ignored the three of them; he was too worried for the caster and the barbarian. If they did not succeed, the cause could be doomed before they really got started. Silently he said a prayer to Valdaar to aid his friends.

The nervous banter continued as they ate. After they were finished, they got more nervous than playful. Having cleaned up, the companions again gathered in silence around the fire.

After perhaps an hour and still no sign of the duo, Breunne stood, stretched and said, "I'm going to turn in. They'll be back as soon as Sordaak convinces the Dragaar Clan what we all know he will." He smiled as he turned and walked into the darkness.

Savinhand also stood, but he said nothing as he walked over to where he had laid out his blankets.

Cyrillis looked over the top of the fire at the big paladin seated on the other side. Their eyes met and Thrinndor shrugged. "I will tend to the fire," he said. "You must rest."

The cleric thought to argue but changed her mind as he also stood. Quietly she nodded, turned and walked toward her bedroll.

The paladin picked up a stick and began poking at the fire, getting the almost burned through logs to collapse. He picked up some of the greener, heavier wood available and set them up so that they would catch fire and burn slowly.

Satisfied, Thrinndor walked out of the alcove into the still of the night. Reflexively he walked toward the sound of the water. The paladin stood at the water's edge and allowed his eyes to adjust.

Silently he looked across the water at the lights on the island. The longer he looked, the more certain he got that he could see activity out there. Mesmerized, he was still standing there when he realized he was not alone.

Slowly he turned to look into the eyes of the sorcerer. Behind the mage, Thrinndor could see his long-time friend the barbarian. Sordaak, however, held his eyes.

"The dwarves march in the morning," the magicuser said. "They'll be here in three days." He turned and walked toward the alcove.

Vorgath smiled. "The hard part was finding a hundred to stay behind." He too turned and headed for the alcove.

Chapter Seven

Sentries

Sordaak awakened to the crackling of the fire and the smell of bacon sizzling in a frying pan. The companions had talked long into the night—none had been able to sleep. Hence it was now well after sunrise as they rolled out to start the day.

"Overslept a bit today," the paladin said as the mage approached the fire, idly scratching his head.

"It won't matter," said the caster as he filled his cup from the pot sitting up against the coals. "We'll only need a half day to clear out the scum that inhabit Ardaagh."

"You certainly are full of confidence this morning," Cyrillis said over the rim of her cup.

"That's not all he's full of," said the barbarian as he refilled his cup. He smiled at the mage.

"Whatever!" said the mage as he shook his head. "Is it soup, yet?"

"Soup?" asked a confused rogue as he looked down at the bacon he was turning. "For breakfast?"

Sordaak rolled his eyes. "It's a saying!" He got blank stares in return. "OK," he said. "It's possible that saying might be from *the other* reality." He smiled. "Just maybe."

"Almost," replied the rogue leader, also shaking his head.

"Good," Sordaak said. "I'm hungry." He turned his eyes to the healer. "And yes, I am confident it will take us longer to eat and clean up from breakfast than it will for us to rid Ardaagh of the undead infestation that currently resides there." He grinned widely. "Confident enough that I have asked my chief engineer to send a boat for us this afternoon!"

That got Thrinndor's attention. "Well, we will clear a path to the docks first," he said. "Just to make sure your friends are not surprised."

The magicuser considered a scathing rejoinder to the paladin's distrust of his assessment of the town's occupants, but he was feeling too good for that. "That sounds like a good idea." He held his plate out for some bacon.

Savin lifted some forehead hair and obligingly placed a couple of strips of the breakfast meat onto the caster's plate. This day was starting out rather strange... The rogue again shook his head as he ladled some eggs onto the smiling mage's plate.

Sordaak took the two steps necessary to get to the rock he had claimed as his own, humming some mindless tune as he waved his hand over his food to cool it. Things were certainly going his way. Not only did he have the required coin to complete his keep in one-tenth the time he had figured it would take, he had arranged for the best stone workers in the region to build it for him! Ardaagh was soon to be rid of the undead that threatened to shut down his entire operation, and some new nuisance troglodytes were going to be disposed of in the same manner.

He and his companions were only a short distance from one of his major goals—to acquire the cloak from a living Storm Giant. After that, they were headed to where he was now certain was the current holding place of what he sought after most: *Pendromar, Dragon's Breath*, last known to be in the hands of the minions of Set at Ice Homme.

Yes, life was good. He continued humming as he ate; ignoring the strange looks he got from the others in the party.

Thrinndor shook his head. He figured the mage's good mood was due to events of the previous evening, and he wanted to do nothing that might spoil that mood. However, they had a job to do, and he had a sword to find.

"Let us talk about what we will find in this town of undead," the paladin said to get the conversation moving.

Sordaak frowned as he was pulled from his reverie. "What?" he asked. He blinked a couple of times to get the grey matter to change direction. "Oh, Ardaagh," he said with a nod of his head. He resumed smiling. "The town itself is really more protected by a bad reputation and poor location than physical beings."

"Really?" asked the cleric as she was about to put a spoon of eggs into her mouth. "Please explain."

"Happy to do so," replied the caster amiably. "You see, Ardaagh was constructed to service Valdaar's Rest more than anything else. The town is too far north to be of any real use to the shipping lanes to the southern regions, or even Pothgaard for that matter." The mage had done quite a bit of research on the matter, and always loved showing off when he was privy to information that others did not have.

"Once Valdaar's Rest was put off limits by Praxaar's lackeys," the magicuser continued, "the town sort of dried up and was abandoned. To ensure it stayed that way, several High Priests of Praxaar—along with some Sorcerers for assistance—began populating the town and surrounding region with assorted ghouls, ghosts, skeletons, zombies and possibly a few other denizens of the less-than-living variety."

"Undead," spat the dwarf.

"That's what I just said," agreed the mage, still in too good a temperament to complain when interrupted, even if it was to confer the obvious. "Well, that took those servants of Praxaar a long time to complete the task because those that are labeled as 'good' or 'just' aren't supposed to dabble in the *undead*. That is supposedly reserved for us less-than-savory characters." Sordaak scrunched up his face in distaste at the thought of being classified as evil. "But apparently the 'goody-two-shoes' of the land never got the memo, because they created quite a host of the 'evil' undead when it seemed to suit their purpose." He grinned at his hyperbole.

"But, undead cannot reproduce," continued the caster. "Hence, the few times anyone wandered too close to Ardaagh, one or two—sometimes more— were sent back to whence they came and were not replaced. So, while the region got a 'bad' reputation and was therefore steered clear of, the 'citizens' of the town have been depleted over the span of time since they were brought into being in the first place more than a thousand years ago. The outer sentries have been especially decimated. Five-hundred years ago we would have been accosted by undead long before we settled for the night at this wonderful rest stop."

Sordaak smiled and spooned the remaining eggs from his plate to his mouth. He frowned when he discovered they had grown cold with all the talk, but not even that dampened his spirits. "Those worg we faced last night were the last remnants of a vast protection system build around the old seaport. Combine the town's bad reputation as a den of undead with the lack of need for the town itself, and you have a tried-and-true method of keeping people out of the region."

"Until now," said the ranger.

"Until now," agreed the mage. He frowned slightly. "Well, there is one rumor I have been unable to confirm." His words hung ominously.

"What is that?" asked the ranger as he blew on a cup of coffee he had just poured to cool it.

The caster took in a breath and looked askance at the paladin. "It is said— again, I have been unable to corroborate this story—that a Lich Lord is in charge of the undead at the old seaport."

After a few heartbeats of stunned silence, the companions began speaking all at once.

"*What?*" Cyrillis' head snapped around to stare at the magicuser.

"No way!" said a stunned rogue.

"You have got to be kidding!" said the barbarian.

"Really?" said Breunne. "I haven't heard that."

Only Thrinndor was silent. When silence again reigned supreme, the paladin looked at his recently acquired friend who was staring intently into his empty cup. "Where did you hear this?" the big fighter said quietly.

Sordaak looked up slowly to peer into his friends' eyes. "I didn't," he said evenly. "I *read* it."

Thrinndor held up a hand to forestall the hubbub that began anew. "Let him finish." His eyes never left those of the sorcerer.

"Thank you," breathed the caster. His eyes took on a faraway glint, and the paladin feared the mage's mind was wandering to the other existence. Sordaak continued, "Back in The Library of Antiquity, while researching Ardaagh I stumbled upon some peculiar words written by an old sorcerer—a servant of Praxaar, it seems—that had let it be known he had discovered a way to 'live forever'.

The magicuser fell silent for a few moments. The companions knew better than to try to rush the caster when he was speaking thus. "It was written that after this proclamation, the old sorcerer walked into the woods and never returned." Again, Sordaak paused, his eyes still locked on those of the paladin. "Rumors began to emerge that the undead at the seaport had a new commander." Sordaak took in a sharp breath and let it out slowly. "A Lich."

"Bah!" spat the dwarf. "That's it? That's all you've got? There's not enough there to even concern ourselves with."

Sordaak turned slowly until he faced the barbarian. The mage's eyes narrowed as he stared down Vorgath. The dwarf shifted uncomfortably under the penetrating stare of the sorcerer.

"Dragma did the writing," the caster said quietly.

A hush again settled over the companions.

"Why didn't you say so?" said a belligerent Vorgath, his tone accusing the magicuser of withholding important information.

Sordaak, returning his attention to the paladin, said, "Because I'm not sure I believe the stories."

Bothered by the sorcerer's demeanor, Thrinndor asked, "Why?"

"Because, although I searched other tomes from the time period, I was unable to find anything more on the old sorcerer, nor any other mention of this Lich Lord. No one has ever seen him—or at least none that have lived to tell the story."

A vague memory at the back of the paladin's mind was suddenly piqued. "Who was this old sorcerer of which you speak?"

Sordaak licked his lips nervously. "Dahjvest."

Thrinndor nodded slowly, vague memory confirmed. "I too have heard parts of this story," he said. "Dahjvest was a junior member of Praxaar's High Council, a sorcerer of some renown. It was said that he became obsessed with living forever and embraced what was called 'dark sorcery.' He was expelled from the council for his efforts."

The magicuser nodded. "That also was written."

"Wait," Cyrillis said, her tone confused. She turned to the barbarian. "I thought you said Ardaagh was occupied by goblins, giants and various other creatures—even a dragon for a while?"

"It was," replied the barbarian. But he too caught the conflict and turned to the mage, his right eyebrow, now fully grown back as a dwarf's hair grows *fast*, riding high on his forehead.

Knowing what was coming, Sordaak held up his hands. "All of that is true—at least as far as I know," he said. "However, Ardaagh is actually two cities in one. There is the seaport itself down on a peninsula that juts out into the sea. The harbor proper is well protected from the harsh weather that occasionally comes from that direction—an important attribute this far north. There is, or was, a bridge connecting that peninsula to the mainland. The only other route is by land a couple of miles north. The main part of the town is built into various openings in the cliffs and buildings constructed on the small beach area."

Sordaak paused as he arranged what he knew of the town in his head. "The undead—and presumably the Lich, if there is one—occupy the portion of the seaport along the cliffs. The other denizens mentioned occupied the peninsula at various times over the years, except the dragon." All eyes were on the mage. "It was reported that Theremault never actually lived *in* Ardaagh, instead using a massive cavern complex a mile or two inland as his base of operation." He shrugged. "But it was also reported that the dragon was responsible for running off the last of the peninsula's occupants—the aforementioned giants, if it matters—and he has not been seen for several hundred years."

The mage raised a questioning eyebrow of his own as his eyes refocused on the healer. "Did that explain the story to your satisfaction?"

Cyrillis nodded as she sipped her coffee. "Thank you." She smiled with her eyes.

Sordaak shifted uncomfortably on his rock, which was not much of a stretch, as it *was* uncomfortable. "Now I—*we*—need this old seaport and the infrastructure it brings to return the island—and the god it served—to power."

"Very well," said the party leader; it was getting late. "I believe it is time for us to go reclaim this den of iniquity for our lord." He pushed his massive frame to his feet and walked to the water's edge to rinse his utensils.

Without any complaints, the rest of the companions did the same. In short order the camp was broken down, eating implements stowed, the fire put out and sleeping articles rolled and bound.

The party gathered out on the rocky beach area, each liking the warmth of the sun on their skin after the cold night before. When Cyrillis walked up,

Sordaak could not let it rest. "Always waiting on a woman!" he said. When the healer looked up sharply and opened her mouth to lambaste him with a nasty reply, the caster winked at her.

A surprised cleric smiled sweetly and said, "You had better get used to it!" With that she turned and started back down the path that had brought them here from the road above, her backside swaying in a most interesting manner.

Thrinndor's right eyebrow did its own version of calisthenics as he scratched his head, wondering what all that was about. He was starting to get an idea, and was not sure he liked it. Ultimately he shook his head and started after the healer. "Marching formation," he said. It would not do to be surprised, undead ranks decimated or not, especially now that a Lich was reported in the mix.

The trip into the town was uneventful and it was beginning to appear Sordaak had been correct. As the first of the buildings came into sight around a bend in the road, Thrinndor called the party to a halt.

"All right," began the paladin, "as some of us have had little dealings with undead, I would like to discuss what we expect to face and how best to combat them."

"Good idea," replied the magicuser who was still in a good mood. "I believe we have dealt with what remained of the outer defenses last night." Sordaak turned and tried to see past the first couple of buildings, but sighed as he was unable to do so. "There will be a graveyard on this end of town, and there we will encounter what remains of a once vast horde of skeletons."

"Blunt weapons for those," said the barbarian as he undid the thong that tied his massive great club to his belt. He slid the haft of *Flinthgoor* though a hook on his shoulder where the axe would be available if needed.

"Right," said the sorcerer. "There may also be a few ghouls in there as well." When no one said anything, he went on, "Any weapon will work on those guys, so stay with the sharp stuff, if possible." Sordaak tilted his head back in thought. "There are reported to be a few ghosts, but most of those are said to inhabit various buildings in the town. They can't come out into the sunlight."

"Silver or enchanted weapons are required to do damage to those," Breunne said. "Don't let them touch you," he added. "They can cause you to age far beyond your years."

"Don't let them near Vorgy," said the mage. "A couple of hits and he'll be ready for retirement."

"Ha, ha! Very funny," said the barbarian. He smiled at the quip, however.

"I can turn those with my special ability," Cyrillis said. "Better let me try that first."

Sordaak nodded, still smiling at his own joke. "Agreed." After a few moments more thought, he said, "Zombies—more than a few of those will probably remain."

"Any weapon, again," said the rogue. "They are very slow and we should have little problem with them."

Sordaak nodded. "A wall of fire, or two, will certainly get their attention!"

When the caster didn't immediately continue, Thrinndor asked, "What else?"

The magic-used scrunched up his face in thought. "Let me see," he said as he held up a hand and ticked on his fingers as he counted, "Skellies, ghosts, ghouls and zombies." He looked up at the paladin. "I think that should about do it."

"And a Lich," said the barbarian.

"And a Lich," agreed the sorcerer. "Assuming there is indeed a Lich." His tone took on a somber note. "If there is, we're going to need a well-orchestrated attack plan."

"Why is that?" Cyrillis asked.

Sordaak turned to face her. "Because if he's there," he said slowly, "he's going to be a real bad-ass. His spell ability will most certainly exceed mine, if he hasn't forgotten his spells over the thousand or so years he's been stuck here." The mage closed his eyes as he turned slowly to face the barbarian. "This time it's my turn to be the chew toy," he said as he forced a wry smile. Opening his eyes, the sorcerer said, "It will be up to me to get his attention, and up to you to send his boney ass back to the grave from whence he crawled."

Vorgath stared at the caster, his expression grim. After a moment, the barbarian nodded slowly. Abruptly he gripped the greatclub in both hands and whipped it around his head once, gathering speed. He slammed the head of the club to the dirt of the road with such force that the ground shook beneath their feet. "Deal," he said, and then he cracked a smile.

"Well," said the cleric stiffly, "If the undead were not aware of our presence, they most certainly are now!" She smiled sweetly at the barbarian.

"Good," snapped the dwarf. "The day grows long, and I have yet to kill anything!"

"Hold on there, big guy," said the paladin as he clapped a meaty paw on Vorgath's shoulder. "The undead are not going anywhere. I assure you they will await us once we go in."

"Ummm," interrupted the rogue, "I think our illustrious healer was correct."

The companions all turned to look at the thief. Savinhand turned and pointed down the road toward the town. Coming in to their field of vision were several skinny stick figures.

Skeletons.

"Fan out!" shouted the party leader. "Cyrillis and Sordaak behind the four fighter-types." Savinhand turned to melt into the trees. "Do not bother with that, Savin." The rogue turned and lifted an eyebrow. Thrinndor smiled and said, "Skeletons cannot be surprised, so you might as well stand and fight."

Savin paused, shrugged and reached behind his neck and pulled out his quarterstaff. He nodded as he stepped back into line with the barbarian to his right.

Breunne pulled his sword from its sheath at his belt. He saw the paladin staring at him. "I have no blunt weapons," he said. "I have used the flat of this sword to some effect against such as these in the past."

Thrinndor nodded as he pulled a morningstar loose from the thong that held it in place at his side. "Fire does additional damage against these creatures." The skeletons were still several hundred feet away, but they were moving much faster now that they had spotted the party.

"Wall of fire coming up," announced the magicuser. He tucked his scepter under the rope serving as his belt, removed his spell component pouch and calmly shook a few of the leather bag's contents onto the palm of his hand. He started to retie the thong, but he had second thoughts as he searched the internal contents for a few more items. Finding what he was looking for, he retied the sack at his waist.

"Ummm," said the party leader, "today, if you please."

Sordaak looked up at the paladin as he again removed his spell enhancing scepter from his waist—which would also serve nicely as a club should the skeletons get too close—and cocked an eyebrow. Without taking his eyes off of those of Thrinndor to check the approach of their adversary, he pointed his right index finger at the path ahead, and muttered an arcane word.

The spell energy was released and a wall of fire appeared across the path about twenty-five or thirty feet away, just as the lead skeletons, now in a shambling run, stepped into the leading edge of the fire.

Boney jaws parted in silent screams as the undead creatures in front tried to come quickly to a halt. Much confusion ensued as those immediately behind crashed into those in the front ranks. Some were knocked to the ground as still others pushed forward, unable to stop quickly enough.

"Watch this," said an amused spellcaster. He again pointed his finger, whispered the word of command and a familiar flaming ball of energy shot from his finger.

The ball sped in the direction of the very confused skeletons. Reaching the main grouping of the creatures, it exploded in a bright flash and blast of sound that flattened any of the skeletons within a ten-foot radius. Others just beyond the blast zone were knocked askew, and some of those tripped over companions and fell to the ground.

Sordaak raised his index finger to his lips and blew on it. "The rest are yours," he said nonchalantly.

"Not fair!" said Vorgath as he surveyed the damage, trying to figure out the quickest way around the wall of fire. What had started as at least two dozen skeletons was now down to less than ten that still walked. There were others trying to get up, but they were of no concern to the barbarian. Abruptly he shouted a battle cry and charged toward the left side of the flames.

A handful of the creatures stumbled through the obstructing wall and emerged from the other side with tattered remnants of ancient clothing either on fire outright, or at least smoldering. The skeletons ignored their pain and made a rush at the sorcerer.

"Watch those guys," instructed Sordaak. "They're going to be more than a little pissed at me!"

"You think?" said an amused paladin as he moved to intercept the monsters before they could get to the unprotected spellcaster. His morningstar took out the first of skeletons to cross his path with one mighty blow that shattered bone and dislocated joints. The creature half spun as it collapsed in a heap of bones on the ground.

Breunne, seeing Thrinndor and Savinhand had the caster well protected, charged around the right side of the firewall. He slapped at the skeleton who was also trying to get around the barricade with his sword and succeeded in knocking the head off of the creature. Grinning, he whipped the flat of the blade in a backswing that successfully knocked an arm from another of the monsters.

Vorgath was swinging his greatclub in mighty arcs that knocked bones free of their host whenever he connected.

Cyrillis momentarily considered joining the action as she perceived no danger to her companions, but changed her mind when she saw a flicker of movement out of the corner of her eye. Perplexed, she turned to come face-to-face with a stumbling mound of diseased and rotting flesh as the creature reached out for her with an arm that was covered in open sores that oozed a puss-green substance that was probably their blood.

"Zombies!" the cleric screamed as she whipped *Kurril* around to block the monster's attack. In her haste she managed only to brush aside the creature's reaching arm, but she could discern no damage.

Thrinndor spun and quickly assessed the situation. "Trap!" he shouted as he finished off the skeleton in front of him with one swing and dropped the weapon he had been using. "Fall back!" he bellowed as took the two steps necessary to bring him to the healer's side, drawing his flaming bastard sword as he did. "Circle around Sordaak and Cyrillis." His sword crashed down on the still extended arm of the zombie, severing it just above the monster's elbow.

As his companions harkened to his call, the paladin performed a quick assessment of the situation. Several of the putrid smelling zombies were attacking from both sides of the path—at least six or seven on either side. Shit! This was well planned. The companions had spread out and were in the open on the path. Fortunately, the zombies were very slow and had not contacted any of their companions as of yet.

"Cyrillis," the paladin said loudly even though she was only a couple of steps away. "Circle of Protection, please!" He glanced quickly from side to side; they were not *that* slow! "*Hurry!*"

Obediently the healer stood upright from the crouch she had been in, raised both hands to the sky and abruptly brought them together over her head—the staff suspended from her right hand.

A brilliant flash emanated from her hands and as she held the light aloft, a circle of light formed at a radius of about ten feet.

There were several zombies caught within the circle and as one they opened their misshapen mouths and hurled forth a gut-wrenching moan as they stumbled back away from the source of the light. The skin hanging from flayed limbs burned first, followed by the skin on the zombie's faces. Ever quicker they tried to escape the light.

"Regroup *here*!" shouted the party leader. "Cyrillis," he said in a more calm voice as he noted the others heed his words. "Bless us and provide reinforcement of your circle when you are able."

The healer nodded as she shifted her concentration to the staff in her hands. Grasping *Kurril* with both hands she whispered a phrase in the arcane language of the gods. A gong-like noise spread out visibly from her form to encompass each of the companions as they came in range. Instantly each of her friends stood taller, as if more ready than ever to face the challenge that now surrounded them.

The zombies had backed off, except for the two slain outright by the protection spell because they had been unable to escape the harmful effects of the enchantment. The skeletons too had backed off and now maintained a respectful distance outside of the circle the protection provided.

Thrinndor took a brief moment to survey the field. There were still six or seven skeletons and at least a dozen zombies held at bay by the cleric's protection spell.

"All right," the paladin said as he held his shield and sword before him, "Vorgath, Breunne, Savin and myself, step to the edge of the circle and attack only the undead in front of you. Maintain a ring around our spell casters. Cyrillis, you may use any offensive spells as you see fit, but keep an eye on our heath."

"Of course," muttered the healer, knowing Thrinndor had to state the obvious, but it nettled her just the same.

Nonplussed, their leader continued, "Sordaak, blast away to dwindle their numbers, as necessary." The sorcerer nodded as he again raised his right arm, index finger extended. "Ensure you hold back some energy for the Lich," said Thrinndor.

Vorgath stepped forward, more deliberately this time. He had discarded his monstrous club in favor of *Flinthgoor* and waved it menacingly before him.

Breunne, Savinhand and Thrinndor also moved toward the almost imperceptible edge of the circle. Seeing their adversary approach, the undead closest to the circle braved the edge, occasionally getting burned as they got too close.

Sordaak, seeing that the monsters were too spread out for the blast of a fireball to be effective, decided the protection afforded by his wall of fire was again in order. He first cast one of the flaming walls at the edge of the circle in front of him and then turned ninety degrees and repeated the spell. He did this twice more until the circle of protection from the cleric was augmented by his walls of flames.

More moaning ensued from the mounds of rancid flesh and the skeletons either burned to a cinder outright, or backed off from the flames. Pitiful few remained of their original contingent.

Clangs and thuds could be heard as bones were crunched and flesh was severed. Thrinndor, Vorgath, Breunne and Savinhand quickly dispatched the remaining creatures.

Sordaak allowed his walls of flames to wink out one by one and Cyrillis did not renew her spells. Soon the companions were standing in the middle of the path surrounded by dead undead.

"That went well," said the barbarian as he inspected the edge of his greataxe. He'd heard that the hardened bones of enchanted skeletons could do serious damage to a weapon. Apparently not *this* weapon, he snorted to himself derisively.

"Better than the undead expected," agreed the ranger as he surveyed the damage they had wreaked upon the creatures.

"And little or no damage suffered by ourselves," noted the cleric as she planted the edge of her staff into the dirt of the road and leaned on the reassuring sturdiness of the shaft of wood.

"That was *too* easy," Sordaak said as he looked around at the charred and dismembered forms of the undead that surrounded them.

"Agreed," said the paladin as he cast a look up the road they must travel. Something about this coordinated attack bothered him, but he could not place a finger on it.

"What I don't like," Sordaak continued, "is that that attack was orchestrated."

"*What?*" said the ranger.

The mage did not turn to acknowledge the interruption. "Zombies and skeletons do not *have minds* to coordinate such an attack. We were deliberately led along this path and confronted by the bone-bags to get our attention as the zombies circled around behind us." The sorcerer shook his head. "Those creatures are not capable of such an attack."

"What are you saying?" Cyrillis asked.

"Or, trying hard *not to say?*" said the barbarian.

Sordaak turned his disdainful gaze upon the dwarf. "I'm saying that Dahjvest indeed awaits us in Ardaagh."

Chapter Eight

Ardaagh

"It's the only possible explanation," Sordaak said as he crossed his arms on his chest.

"Possibly not the *only* explanation," mused the paladin, "but certainly the most plausible."

The mage begrudgingly nodded his agreement. "We must certainly tread more carefully as we proceed to remove the riff-raff from this town." An ominous silence settled over the grouping. "Dahjvest's presence certainly changes things."

"Other than the obvious," said the ranger, "how so?"

"Well," replied the sorcerer with a sigh, "For one, Liches are more than capable of maintaining the undead force that was thought to have been decimated."

"That explains the thirty-plus skeletons we just sent back to the netherworld," agreed the paladin. "That is the most I have ever heard of as part of one chance encounter."

"Not to mention the two dozen zombies," said Savinhand. The party timbre had certainly turned morose.

"All right," said the spellcaster, forcing his voice to sound cheerful, "so there's a Lich." He shrugged and looked over at the paladin. "That really doesn't change anything." His companions turned to stare at the mage. "We've still got to clear out this town," he said. "We've simply got to be more careful at doing so." He shrugged again.

Thrinndor's right eyebrow twitched a couple of times. "But, a *Lich?*" he said.

Sordaak's shoulders were getting a workout. "We can do this," he said easily.

"If I remember correctly," said the rogue, "these guys," he waved a hand at the further deceased zombies and skeletons scattered about, "are but the welcoming committee."

Sordaak shifted uncomfortably under the scrutiny of the thief. When the sorcerer didn't respond, Savinhand continued, "Something about ghouls, ghosts and 'possibly some other denizens of the less-than-living variety,'" quoted the rogue.

Suddenly there was an interesting rock at the caster's feet that he pushed around with the toe of his leather sandal. "I did say that," agreed Sordaak. "And certainly the maintenance capabilities of Dahjvest could prove troublesome," he added as he looked up defiantly into the eyes of the party leader, "but we will prevail—of that there is no doubt."

The certainty in the sorcerer's voice momentarily took the paladin aback. "Well, ummm." Uncharacteristically, Thrinndor fumbled for words. "That be it as it may," the paladin did not want to sound as if he did not believe in the strength of the party. But a *Lich*? "I am certain you are correct," he said. "However, I have never encountered a Lich, and have indeed only heard secondhand as to their abilities." It was his turn to shift his feet uncomfortably. "What I *have heard* does not please me."

When the paladin did not immediately continue, Breunne stepped in for the rescue. "I too have had no personal dealings with a Lich. And I fear that this *Dahjvest* will prove more troublesome than indicated."

Sordaak puffed up to argue, his face turning red. After a moment of glaring first at the ranger and then the paladin, he allowed his shoulders to slump as he let his breath out noisily. "To be truthful," he began with his eyes now back on his feet, "I too fear that will be the case." His distraught eyes found those of the paladin. "I didn't *know* Dahjvest would be here." His voice pleaded with Thrinndor to understand. "There were only rumors! I assumed them to be way off! Old wives tales meant to keep nosey people from snooping around!" His eyes implored the paladin to understand. "*I didn't KNOW!*"

Uncertain where all these theatrics were coming from or where they were going, Thrinndor merely nodded. "I am certain you did not," he said. "However, it matters not." He set his jaw. "He certainly knows we are here, and we cannot back down now." He shook his head as he turned slowly to set his gaze once again upon the edge of the rundown portion of town they could see. "We must take precautions ere we proceed."

The companions were silent as each also turned to look the direction their leader was looking.

"I suggest we pool what we know about Liches," said the rogue. "Maybe there will be something in that knowledge we can exploit." His tone managed to convey hope as well as doubt.

"Sound advice," Cyrillis said tentatively. "I too have never encountered one, but I know they cannot abide in direct sunlight—*any* bright light is said to cause them harm."

"Very good," Breunne replied with a smile. "It just so happens our mage here keeps some 'portable suns in a stick' in his pocket." The ranger looked from the cleric to the sorcerer. "That should slow him down a bit."

"Enchanted weapons are required to do any sort of harm to such a creature," Savinhand said, getting into the spirit of the conversation. He kept a watchful eye on the edge of the town with no small trepidation, however.

"Generally," said the paladin, "a Lich will only be found within his chambers—which is generally deep underground—"

"Or within a mountain," said Vorgath, as the barbarian turned his gaze upon the snowcapped peak that stood out in stark contrast to the bright blue sky of midday behind the village to the east. The peak was on the southern edge of the mountain range that formed the Cliffs of Mioria to the north.

"Wouldn't that also be where the dragon would be?" asked Breunne. "Were he to still live?"

"Do not tease me so!" said the dwarf with a twinkle in his eye.

"Surely you sated your lust to do battle with a dragon back outside the Library?" Thrinndor suggested with a knowing smile.

"Hardly," replied the barbarian. "I now must have the head of every form of dragon to adorn the walls of my study!"

"What study?" asked a bemused paladin. "You have no study!"

"I'll certainly build one—"

"*Dragon head?*" asked a suddenly very still Cyrillis, her eyes mere slits in her face.

Realizing his mistake, Vorgath cringed under her scrutiny.

"Dragon head?" she said again, her tone quiet, but menacing. "You are collecting dragon heads?"

"What of it?" asked a suddenly belligerent dwarf as he pulled himself up to his full height, which put him about eye level with the cleric's shoulder.

"Did you—" the healer began, but she was interrupted by Breunne.

"Ahem," the ranger said.

"*What?*" snapped both Cyrillis and Vorgath at once.

Taken aback by their vehemence, Breunne simply pointed in the direction of town.

The barbarian, glad for the interruption, spoke first, "*More* skeletons?"

Thrinndor did a double-take. He too had been mesmerized by the confrontation between the cleric and the dwarf. "No," he said. "Well, sort of." Vorgath shot him a nasty look. "Notice the armor," the paladin said as he pointed at the figures lumbering toward them. The creatures were still some distance off, although the gap was closing more rapidly than it had appeared.

"What of it?" said the barbarian with a quick glance out of the corner of his eye at the cleric. Good. She too was preoccupied with the oncoming monsters and appeared to have forgotten about the dragon.

"I will deal with you later," announced the healer as she tuned to face this new threat.

Damn. So much for having forgotten, thought the dwarf.

"Armor and weapons will make these particular skeletons those known as 'skeleton knights,' I think," said the spell-caster. "Very dangerous and extremely hard to destroy."

"Great!" said the paladin grimly. "All right, form a circle around Cyrillis and Sordaak."

"But they're still extremely susceptible to fire," continued the sorcerer as he reached for his component bag. He glanced up at the paladin. "Get on with that protective ring thing. Those guys are about to be really pissed at me." Sordaak winked at the big fighter as he pointed his right index finger at the approaching group and said the trigger word. The usual ball of fire leapt from the end of his finger and sped toward the skeletons.

The ball erupted amidst the lead group, where there appeared to be at last fifteen or twenty of the armor clad figures. A couple of the creatures were knocked to the ground by the blast, but they wasted no time climbing back to their feet, undaunted by the experience. If anything, those affected by the ball of fire hurried more toward their adversaries.

Sordaak was not idle as the monsters approached. Quickly he put up walls of flames at angles that forced the skeletons to funnel into a narrow patch that only one or two at best could get through without getting burnt to a cinder.

Still, some of the creatures fought their way through the walls of flames, while others tried to go around. Much confusion ensued as Vorgath met those funneled to a point with his enchanted greatclub where he wreaked much havoc.

Thrinndor waited at one point for those that tried to get around the wall and pick off any that came through on his side while Breunne did the same for the other side.

Knowing he was not going to be able to surprise this particular foe, and thus much of his attack skill was neutralized, Savinhand stood back with the caster and healer as a last level of protection for them. That turned out to be necessary on several occasions as badly burnt and blazing skeletons did as Sordaak suggested. They were not very pleased with the magicuser, and were determined to get to he who had caused so much pain.

The skeleton knights were not only harder to dispatch, the weapons they wielded (swords, pikes, morningstars, and more) made them more dangerous. Cyrillis alternated her healing skills among the three fighters, but it was Vorgath who required most of her attention. Working at the apex of where Sordaak had set up the walls, he had to deal with the most previously unhurt skellies.

And thus those adversaries wreaked no small harm on him, as well. Still, it was not more than the cleric could keep up with, and soon the ground was again littered the broken forms of more than a dozen of the creatures.

Almost as quickly as the battle had begun, it was over. Vorgath, panting for breath, turned to survey the carnage scattered about him and noticed one of the monsters still writhing on the ground, trying to get up. He whipped his greatclub around in a high overhead arc and brought the business end of said club down on the helm-covered head of the unfortunate monster. The helm provided little or no protection as the club crushed both it and the skull inside. The skeleton knight twitched a couple of times and then moved no more.

The barbarian leaned on the club as it rested on the crushed skull, his battle-lust sated. He was bleeding from several cuts on his arms and torso and he was exhausted.

Cyrillis rolled her eyes and followed a light heal spell with a restorative one. Instantly, Vorgath's back straightened and the twinkle returned to his eyes. "Ten," he said, his face twisted in pleasure.

Again the cleric rolled her eyes as she inspected the others in the party. "Yeah well," she said, concealing a grin of her own, "you should consider using a shield." She knew better than to follow the comment with a look in the barbarian's direction. "Just saying."

"The hell, you say!" snorted the diminutive fighter.

Breunne and Thrinndor both had minor cuts and scrapes, as well—more suited to the standard wrap-and-soothe portion of the healer's ministrations. Cyrillis decided she would conserve on her spell power when possible, as she was unsure how much would be needed later.

The companions grouped around Sordaak and the healer as they assessed the situation, and Cyrillis looked each over with a critical eye.

"I think that about does it for the welcoming committee," the spellcaster said as he looked wearily toward the edge of town. Those walls of fire took some serious energy to maintain.

"Damn, I certainly *hope* so!" Savinhand agreed. He'd had to return four or five of the creatures to their place in the netherworld, and was justifiably winded. "Where do we go from here?"

"Into town." Sordaak pointed the direction for them, in the event anyone had lost track. They hadn't. He looked up at the sun, now high overhead. "The day's not getting any younger!" Privately, he was starting to get a bit worried he had been a bit too zealous in having his chief engineer meet them this afternoon. The Lich was going to be a problem. He was beginning to understand just how much that was true. Sordaak shrugged away the unhappy thought, set his jaw and pushed his way past the paladin, headed for town.

"All right," Thrinndor said as he rushed to get ahead of the sorcerer, "new formation. It looks like this path opens up into a street in town. Vorgath and myself will be up front, spread ten feet or so. Breunne you and Savinhand do the same in the rear with Cyrillis and Sordaak in the middle." He got nods from each of the companions as they settled into their new places. "We will keep it slow for the time being," the paladin continued. "I do not want to be surprised." More nods.

As such they approached the edge of the first buildings moving along at a slow pace, each with his or her head on a swivel, looking for signs of trouble.

Cyrillis spoke as she eyed a broken window of what had been a mercantile. "As we are dealing exclusively with undead," she said, "at the first sign of trouble, gather close and I will cast some area of effect spells that will provide a beneficial effect."

As the lead group got even with the doors of the first buildings—the aforementioned mercantile on one side of the street and a nondescript building on the other—Breunne asked from the back row, "How do we want to do this?" Vorgath and Thrinndor came to a halt as the others approached. "I mean," the ranger continued, "do we want to enter and clear *every* building? Thereby ensuring nothing gets behind us, or do we simply march along and investigate the likely suspects?"

Thrinndor nodded as he looked up and down what appeared to be the main street. "Good question," he said. This dead town was much bigger than he had thought. At first glance it was several times the size of Brasheer. "While at some point each building will have to be searched room by room, we do not have the time for that at present." He got nods from several in the group as each kept their eyes moving. "I feel we must seek out and slay this Lich first, or he will continue to orchestrate attacks against us until we are too weak to deal with him."

"Very astute," came a voice from the doorway of what appeared to be a tavern next to the mercantile. "I have waited many centuries for a suitable adversary to break the boredom. Perhaps the wait is over." The heads of the party spun to see who, or what, spoke.

"I believe we have our first contestant in the *Undead is Right*," whispered Sordaak as he readied a spell.

"What?" asked a bewildered barbarian.

The magicuser shook his head and said, "Never mind! Let's see what we can find out from whatever it was that said that."

Thrinndor nodded as he waved for the others to spread out.

"Wait," whispered Cyrillis, "allow me to cast the spells I spoke of earlier." Thrinndor nodded as she closed her eyes and raised both hands above her head, *Kurril* in her right. She mumbled the words to first one prayer and then another, after which she opened her eyes and nodded.

She knew her companions felt no different than before, but she also knew that the first spell blessed her and her friends, giving them added abilities in battle as well as making them harder to harm by opponents. The second spell provided a protection from most forms of undead within a radius around her. She knew she had to be careful how she used that spell, because killing/sending these undead back to from whence they came was important to her companions, and the cleric didn't want to hinder that part of why they were here. But that spell also gave her a ring in which she could generally work her healing magic unhindered by the creatures should that be required.

"Remember," she said, "I have an ability by which I can destroy some forms of undead with a single word and damage others. I must use it sparingly, however, as I have that ability only five times between rest periods."

Thrinndor nodded and again waved the group into motion. As he set foot on the boardwalk outside the inn, the voice was again heard from within. "This should be fun."

Vorgath growled a deep, rumbling growl. "I agree," he said as side by side he and Thrinndor pushed open the double half-doors, one of which hung by just one hinge and stepped into the cool darkness inside.

It took a moment for their eyes to adjust to the gloom within, and as their vision cleared, neither of the fighters saw who or what had spoken. Thrinndor stepped to the left and Vorgath to the right, allowing Cyrillis and Sordaak to enter.

Inside, the room looked like most any inn or tavern throughout the land. It had a rough-hewn bar that stretched across much of the back of the open space, with a tattered curtain partitioned doorway at the far end, presumably leading to other rooms. There were scattered tables and chairs—all also rough-hewn, but the seats were semi-polished from much use. A thick layer of dust covered everything. Behind the bar were shelves, some of which held bottles, some of those broken.

As Breunne and Savin stepped into the doorway, the doors—suddenly much more sturdy-looking—slammed shut behind them, causing the companions to turn and stare.

"Very good," said the voice behind them. As heads once again turned in unison, they spotted a figure standing behind the bar. This figure appeared to be a youngish human male, perhaps in his early thirties. He was wearing dark robes as would a spellcaster of some sort. "I see you are not as intelligent as I had hoped. You have fallen for this my first trap." The figure shrugged. "So be it. Let's see how you fare against some of my benefactors."

As the figure stopped speaking, the room went completely dark. Even all light from the windows went black.

"What the--?" Vorgath blurted out.

"Sordaak, some light please," Thrinndor said with more calm than he felt. Undead always made him nervous.

"I can't," replied the mage, less calm. Darkness and visions of looming undead made his bones shiver. "The darkness is magical in nature. I will try to dispel that magic, hold on." In his nervousness he fumbled for the correct pouch at his belt. Fortunately he had sorted the pouches for just such a reason and quickly found what he was looking for.

"Today!" Vorgath nearly shouted. He was normally comfortable in the dark, but this wasn't *normal dark*!

Sordaak lifted the proper spell component and quickly said the appropriate trigger word. Nothing! "That didn't work," he said condignly. "The caster of this spell surely has ability that exceeds mine!" *Dahjvest!* "Shit!" *It can't be! He's too close to the sunlight!*

Now the companions could hear a moaning sound approaching. It became quickly apparent it was multiple voices.

"Ghosts!" shouted the cleric. "Gather to my voice," she said, followed by the shuffling of feet. "Let me give it a try."

Breunne felt the approach of the ghosts as he heard Cyrillis slam the heel of her staff to the ground. She shouted a word of power and a bright light erupted from the jewel on *Kurril*, easily illuminating the entire inn and four apparitions as they floated toward her and her companions. "*Be gone!*" the cleric shouted as she again slammed the metal-shod heel of her staff to the wood plank floor.

The ghosts initially threw up their hands to block the light and released a wail that was painful to the companions' ears. The second word caused an unseen wind to drive them away from the group, dissolving them as they flew.

After a moment, normal light from the windows returned to the room and the companions looked at one another in surprise.

"Is anyone harmed?" Cyrillis' sharp tone cracked into the silence that followed, her voice husky from the release of power.

There were several mute shakes of the head. Only Vorgath did not answer. His eyes reflected the fear he had known in the utter blackness as he cowered in a corner by the door.

Thrinndor turned and started to reach out to his friend.

"No, wait!" Cyrillis stopped him. "His fear is not natural. One of the apparitions must have touched him. Allow me." She took a tentative step toward the dwarf, followed by another, all the while ready to pounce should her companion try to bolt.

The fear in the barbarian's eyes was evident to all. Thrinndor motioned subtly for the others to form a boundary behind the cleric should the dwarf suddenly try to flee.

Vorgath watched the approach of the healer with the look in his eyes of one that had seen his own death was found wonting. Cyrillis whispered in soothing tones as she approached. Slowly for fear of spooking the dwarf, she reached out her left hand and put it on his arm. Just as she was about to remove his fear, Vorgath lunged to his feet, shouted "*No!*" and knocked her to the ground as he ran past her.

Right into the waiting arms of the sorcerer. Vorgath had chosen his next adversary well, because Sordaak barely slowed the barbarian who was now at full speed as he was knocked aside. "Shit!" the mage shouted as he sprawled to the floor.

Fortunately, Thrinndor was next to the sorcerer and Sordaak slowed the dwarf enough for the paladin to leap into action. He caught his longtime friend by the arm and spun him around. "I hate to have to do this," he said from between clenched teeth as his right fist made a wide arc and slammed into Vorgath's jaw.

These actions slowed the barbarian enough for Cyrillis to recover and take the two steps necessary to reach the melee. She readied her spell as she approached and wasted no time applying it. She touched the upper arm of the barbarian as he was about to return the blow to the paladin.

Instantly the look of fear on Vorgath's face was replaced with one of confusion. "What the—?" the barbarian said as he stopped his fist just short of the paladin's temple.

Thrinndor stood upright and smiled at his friend. "You were scared," he said.

"Very good," said the voice. The companions turned to see the same figure as before standing behind the bar. Sordaak readied a spell, certain it would have no effect. "Your persistence tells me your purpose," the figure continued. "Let me be the first to inform you that you will not succeed. This port was closed by a god and those that serve him—it will not be reopened by the likes of such as you!"

Spell at the ready, Sordaak shouldered his way past the paladin and barbarian. "Let me be the first to tell *you*, Dahjvest, that this port will be open to trade and traffic ere this day ends."

The tavern was silent for a few moments. "I see that you have done your research." Dahjvest focused on Sordaak. "That is good. You must certainly know that my skill dost exceed yours."

Sordaak shrugged. "And yet we are here," he smiled a crooked smile. "Mayhap it is that we have a few tricks up our sleeves." Fahlred appeared on the caster's shoulder as if summoned, bared his teeth and hissed noisily at Dahjvest.

Dahjvest's eyes opened wide at the sight of Sordaak's familiar. "A quasit? Very nice." He nodded appreciatively. "Mayhap those few tricks will keep your body and soul together for a bit longer, at that." He smiled an evil smile that did not touch his eyes. "At least until I tear them apart with my own hands, devour your souls and use the empty bodies as servants for the next thousand years!" Dahjvest began to laugh at his own pronouncement, quietly at first, but building to a loud cacophony that caused Cyrillis to cover her ears.

Abruptly the laughter stopped and Vorgath stepped forward, his greataxe held before him. "That shit aint funny," he said loudly. However, his words fell on deaf ears—actually, on *no* ears, as Dahjvest was gone. He had vanished! The barbarian quickly looked left and right, but the evil spellcaster was nowhere to be seen.

"Calm yourself, old one," chided the sorcerer gently as he placed a solemn hand on the barbarian's shoulder. "I don't believe he was ever really here. That was a projection—and probably an old one."

"Explain, please," Thrinndor said as he sheathed his sword.

Sordaak nodded as he turned to face the paladin. "Dahjvest is over 2,000 years old," he said. "That person we just witnessed would have been how he looked as a member of Praxaar's council."

"Makes sense," Savin said as he walked up to stand beside the paladin. "Assuming that was Dahjvest, at all."

"It was—of that I am certain," Sordaak replied. "His appearance fits the description written in the log book of those assigned to search for him after his disappearance." Thrinndor nodded. "However," the magicuser continued, "while becoming a Lich can indeed keep body and soul together for an indeterminate number of years or even centuries, it doesn't keep one's body from aging."

Thrinndor's right eyebrow quickly made the ascent up his forehead.

"But," Breunne said into the brief silence that followed, "no human body can survive for 2,000 years!"

"I was waiting for someone to make that connection," Sordaak said. "The body indeed ages, but the mind and spirit do not. They are kept magically intact inside an aging, rotting body. Even with the best of care, the body's skin will wither, die and fall off. Leaving behind only the skeleton and whatever clothes survived the years."

"That doesn't sound pretty," Savinhand said.

"It's not," replied the sorcerer. "The drawings I was able to find—which were few, by the way, showed a skeleton similar to the knights we encountered earlier, but with rotting flesh—for the new converts—and not much more than glowing red eyes in a tattered robe covered pile of bones." His face was grim. "I'm fairly certain Dahjvest will be of the latter variety."

Thrinndor nodded again as he thought. "Very well," he said. "It certainly appears we will have to deal with this Lich." He got nods from the others in the group. "And I now agree with our esteemed caster here," he said as he put his hand on the mage's shoulder, "in that we should search him out sooner rather than later. I feel we will find no rest in this town as long as Dahjvest exists."

"Then let's send his skinny ass to the afterlife," growled Vorgath, "where it should have been for the past 2,000 years!"

"Here, here," agreed the ranger. The others nodded their agreement, as well.

"So," it was Cyrillis that spoke next, "how do we find him?"

Sordaak looked over at where the old/young wizard had stood and shook his head. "Not in here," he said. "Let's go back outside and discuss what needs to be discussed." He took in a deep breath. "While I feel the old wizard's presence is no longer in this place—he should be making preparation for our next encounter with him, I would in his boots—I don't trust the old bastard." With that, he turned and walked toward the door that led back out to the street.

Thrinndor and Vorgath rushed to get in front of him, and prepared to use their combined might to reopen the doors that had slammed shut behind them. No might was required, however, as they opened easily and the pair stepped through.

"You are wiser than I gave you credit for," the voice said from behind them. Sordaak whirled but saw nothing. The voice continued. "You may count on my being ready when you finally make your way to my chambers." Again the voice broke out in laughter.

Back out in the street, the companions gathered closely so they could speak without their voices carrying.

"From what I know of Liches," Sordaak said, "this Dahjvest guy will be holed up in as dark a place as he can find." He looked around briefly to get his bearings. "I don't believe any of these town buildings would suit his purpose." His eyes traveled the short distance to the cliffs that bordered the eastern edge of town. "It's my bet he will be there," he pointed to the cliffs. "Parts of the town were built back into the cliffs, mostly for storage and the like. I think we'll find him in one of those dwellings, probably one that goes back deep into the mountain."

The mage paused as he got nods from the rest of the party. He smiled as he reached up his sleeve and produced what appeared to be a scroll tube. "It just so happens I have a map!"

"What?" Vorgath bellowed.

"Shhh!" Sordaak hissed at the barbarian.

"Where did you get a map?" the grouchy fighter whispered intently.

"That's better," said the caster agreeably. "It's a copy of the last known map of Ardaagh. I had it made for me back in the Library."

"Of course you did," said the barbarian as he crossed his arms on his massive chest.

"I can't help it if some of us were industrious while others slept their possible time in that wonderful wealth of knowledge and understanding away without regard to what they might be missing!"

"Whatever!" grumbled the dwarf. "Anything on the map that might be useful?"

"Of course," Sordaak whispered in return. "Otherwise I would not have produced it just now." Vorgath lifted a brow but remained silent. The mage pried one end off of the scroll tube and shook out the contents. He tucked the tube behind his belt so he could get both hands on the piece of parchment and carefully unrolled the document.

Sordaak held out the map for all to see and the companions leaned in as one to get a better look. The mage frowned and spun the parchment first one way, then another until satisfied. "We're here, I believe," he said as he pointed toward the edge of the map. He slid his finger across the parchment at a diagonal toward the back of the map—away from him. "Here are the cliffs. See how there are indications of tunnels going back into the mountain in several places?" He received several nods—even Vorgath seemed to have forgotten his animosity and was studying the map with great interest.

"Dahjvest will be as far back into the mountain as possible," Sordaak said as he pointed to where one tunnel appeared to go back further than the rest—all the way to the edge of the paper. There were three large rooms or caverns along the way until the tunnel ended in the largest cavern of all. "I believe we'll find the old bugger here," he said, tapping his index finger on that large cavern a couple of times.

"He will have set up defenses in each of these outer chambers," Thrinndor said as he pointed to the three chambers outside of the larger one. "Are there any other ways in?"

Sordaak took in a deep breath, let it out slowly and shook his head. "Not that I can see here," he said. "However, the old fart has had plenty of time to have additional tunnels dug, if he so desired."

Thrinndor nodded his agreement. "Perhaps we should investigate the tunnels to either side of this one you are indicating to see if there are other ways in."

"While the idea has merit," Sordaak said with a shake of his head, "any add-on tunnels will probably be of the secret variety. We could waste valuable time searching for them—and all the while he will almost assuredly already know of our presence and prepare accordingly."

"Will he not do that anyway?" asked Cyrillis, her tone edgy. All this undead was grating on her nerves.

"Sure he will," the sorcerer grinned. "He knows we're here, and he knows where we are. I'd have to say we've put a sizable dent in his defenses, but that is merely speculation at this point." He looked back down at the map and pointed to the entrance he had proposed. "One way or the other we are going to have to fight our way through those three chambers to get to the large one in back. Either going in, or going out. If we pussyfoot around and try to clear all of this," the mage circled his finger around several of the caverns and tunnels built into the cliff area, "we will be exhausted by the time we finally meet up with this guy."

"So, what do you propose?" Thrinndor asked.

Again Sordaak took in a deep breath. "We march right up to the entrance here," he pointed to where the main tunnel went back into the cliff from the inside of a building shaped as a temple, "kick down the doors and deal with whatever to get into this tunnel." Vorgath nodded—he preferred the direct approach. "As we proceed we need to assume that these chambers," he pointed to the first chamber along the path and slid his finger to either side of it to indicate similarly placed chambers on either side of it, "are connected by tunnels, and will contain support crews should an attack be made on the main tunnels."

Now Thrinndor and Breunne also nodded. "As soon as we enter this chamber, we must assume the undead from these side chambers will attempt to flank us as we work to deal with whatever welcoming committee is in this chamber." He again tapped the first of the caverns along the tunnel from the temple. "Savinhand and Breunne will be designated to find a way to block those entrances to keep help from arriving that way."

"And if the 'help' is ghosts?" Breunne asked, his right eyebrow playing with his hairline.

"Then you won't be blocking shit!" hissed the caster. He glared at the ranger. "However, it is doubtful he will have ghosts staged as reinforcements—if for no other reason than they can come and go at will, with no need for doors or passages."

The ranger reluctantly nodded.

"And if the doors are hidden or secret?" Savinhand said as he studied the map, looking for flaws in the plan.

Sordaak had expected that question. "If the doors are not visible as soon as we storm the chamber, I will cast a spell that will show the locations of any secret doors or portals."

Savinhand acknowledged that with a nod.

"We will follow the same plan with each of these three chambers. Vorgath and Thrinndor go in first. I'll fire a sunburst flare into the room over their heads and Breunne and Savinhand will enter next, going left and right around the wall to find the doors that should be there. Cyrillis and I will enter next. She'll blast any undead with her turning ability, and I'll lay down some appropriate area of effect spells to get any remaining baddies attention after ensuring our door-blockers have located whatever it is they are supposed to block."

Now there were nods all around. "Seems like a sound plan," Thrinndor said. He was impressed. "What about the last chamber?"

Sordaak looked back down at the map. "That one we will have to deal with differently," he said softly. He knew what had to be done, but that didn't mean he had to like it. He took in a ragged breath. "That chamber I will be the first to enter."

"What?" Savinhand said louder than he intended, drawing a sharp glance from the mage.

"No way!" hissed the barbarian. "That's my job!"

"Not this time," Sordaak shook his head. "His magical abilities will surely impede you—both of you." His eyes went from Thrinndor to Vorgath. "I must be the chew-toy this time," he continued with a wry smile. "I will go in and hit him with everything I've got—that will get his attention. Once his efforts are focused on me, then the four of you," he swung an arm indicating everyone but Cyrillis, "will bull rush him and knock the un-living shit out of him!"

The group was silent for a minute as they digested this. "What about me?" the healer asked petulantly.

Sordaak turned to look her square in the eye. "Your job is to keep me alive long enough to allow the fighters a chance. With their surrounding and beating on Dahjvest, I'm hoping they will be able to prevent him from continually casting spells." He forced a wry smile. "It's hard to maintain proper concentration with a greatclub shoved up your ass!"

"Damn straight," Vorgath said malevolently. "I'll keep him distracted." He slapped the head of his club for emphasis.

Sordaak's eyes never left those of the cleric. "If I go down, or am unable to cast, the fighters will have no chance." He paused. "You *must* keep me standing long enough for them to reach him and take him out. Understood?"

Cyrillis nodded slowly, and Sordaak thought he saw the beginnings of a tear start to form in the corner of her eyes. He looked away before he could verify that, however. Now was not the time.

Chapter Nine

Oodles of Undead

"**W**ell?" Sordaak asked roughly as he locked eyes with the paladin.

"I believe the plan to be sound," Thrinndor answered. "We may have to adjust as we go along, but as a beginning it should work."

Sordaak nodded as he raised an arm, pointing behind the paladin. "Where we must go is back there then," he said. "We can either go down this road to the intersection and then turn west, or we can see how well protected the alleyways are…"

"Intersection it is," Thrinndor said, glad to be moving. "Same formation as before, please."

Thrinndor and Vorgath took point as before, weapons at the ready. Cyrillis walked uncomfortably close to the caster. Obviously she wanted to talk, but was reluctant to do so. When she finally opened her mouth to speak, Sordaak looked at her and shook his head. The healer bit her lip and nodded.

Decision made, the companions quickly traversed the four hundred feet or so to the intersection. To the right—east—the the companions could see the bridge that led across to the buildings on the sea wall. The bridge looked much the worse for the two millennia it had stood in open defiance to the weather. Thrinndor turned the party to the west, staying as close to the middle of the street as possible. He could see the next street over, and even to the one beyond it, as well. The town appeared to have been laid out fairly well, a fact the map had supported.

Unmolested the party made their way back toward the cliffs and the intersection that went north and south. Thrinndor turned back to the right—north—and immediately they could see the temple that marked their destination.

Thrinndor walked the hundred feet or so required to position the party in front of the temple and halted in the middle of the road and waited for the others to gather around.

"Any last-minute instructions?" Thrinndor asked.

Sordaak hesitated. "How long do those aid spells last?" he asked Cyrillis.

"Just a few minutes," the healer answered. "I do have an ability that allows me to double that time, but at additional spell energy cost. However, that additional energy cost is less than that of casting the spells twice."

Sordaak looked over at Thrinndor, who said, "Very well, double the length, please." Cyrillis nodded. "Once she casts her spells, we must move quickly. It will be as Sordaak said. Vorgath and I will go into the room together and Sordaak will light up any dark chambers. Breunne and Savinhand will seal off any other entrances before joining the melee with Vorgy and myself. Cyrillis will use her turning abilities sparingly, but as required." He looked over at her. "I will call for that when necessary." She nodded. "Sordaak," he said as he looked over at the mage, who lifted a questioning eyebrow, "I believe it prudent to conserve spell energy as much as possible. Let us fighter types deal with the masses so that you will have everything you need for Dahjvest."

The spell-caster nodded. "Wands and scrolls it is," he said as his hand made a flurry of motion, tucking several scrolls and wands behind places on his belt, making them ready for quick action.

"Any questions?" the paladin asked. There were none. "Very well," he said as he again looked over at the cleric. "Cyrillis, if you please."

The cleric nodded as she closed her eyes and raised her hands. This time Thrinndor thought he felt a subtle change in the air.

The paladin squared his shoulders and with Vorgath at his side said, "Let us go see he who dares defy the laws of life and death!" Next he strode purposefully toward the entrance to the temple and without hesitation kicked the double doors right in the center. They burst inward with a loud crash as the two fighters stepped inside.

"You know," Vorgath complained, "kicking doors in is supposed to be *my* job!"

Thrinndor either did not hear the barbarian or chose to ignore him, as what he saw inside those doors required his full and immediate attention. He came to a sudden halt as he surveyed the scene he beheld.

The temple was laid out in the classic style: Rows of benches facing a raised dais with a small podium and an altar. The benches were nearly full of worshipers. There were three priests on the dais, one of them in the robes of a High Priest of Praxaar. He was leaning over a fourth person, this one bound to the altar, a long, thin dagger in his right hand, a smoking sconce in his left.

They were performing the Rite of Sacrifice, with a young woman on the altar in place of the standard goat or lamb. In an instant the paladin realized what was happening. The Priests of Praxaar were sacrificing a servant of Valdaar. They were playing out part of the purge.

"Stop!" Thrinndor yelled as the High Priest lowered the dagger in his hand to place the blade on the throat of the young woman on the altar. The priest did not even look up as he drew the ceremonial blade across the girl's neck, and blood began to pour from the resulting gash.

"*I told you to stop!*" the paladin shouted as fought off whatever it was that had held him in place and transfixed his attention. He sprinted down the aisle toward the dais.

Vorgath raised *Flinthgoor* high over his head, bellowed a battle-cry and followed as fast as his much shorter legs could carry him. He glanced left and right as he ran, daring any of those seated on the benches to try to stop him. None did. In fact, none even acknowledged his presence by a glance in his direction.

Something was amiss, but in his rage he didn't care.

Finally the priest looked up at the fighters running toward him. "May I help you, my son?" the High Priest asked.

"No," Thrinndor bellowed as he raised his sword, "it is I who will help *you!*" He leapt up onto the dais. In one vicious arc he brought the blade of his sword down onto the back of the high priest's neck, who remained slightly bent over, waving the smoking sconce slightly back and forth. "Help you to the afterlife!"

But his blade passed clear through the man's neck, doing no apparent harm. An apparition!

Stunned, Thrinndor did not move as the priest stood erect and looked him in the eye. "While that would no doubt be a desirable result, I do doubt your reasons for doing so and thus cannot allow it."

As Thrinndor watched in horror, the skin on the high priest's once condign face peeled back to reveal a hideous skeletal head with glowing red eyes and bared teeth.

"Slay them!" the apparition shouted. "Slay them *all!*" The doors so recently kicked in now slammed shut, and the previously impassive congregation stood as one, some even taking flight to better get into position to attack.

Thrinndor recovered quickly. "Cyrillis!" he shouted as he squared to face what was once a High Priest of Praxaar.

Vorgath found himself dealing with the other two priests on the dais, and also finding that *Flinthgoor* was ill-suited for the challenge. With regret he cast aside the greataxe and almost immediately had a blade in each hand—a longsword in his right and a long, thin, nasty-looking dagger in his left. He was suddenly glad he had spent time with the drow after their encounter at the Library of Antiquity learning how to fight with two weapons.

Savinhand and Breunne barely made it inside before the doors slammed shut.

As ghosts and ghasts buzzed around her head like flies on a rotting corpse, Cyrillis slammed the heel of *Kurril* to the stone floor and shouted, "*Be gone!*"

Several of the creatures instantly vanished, and still others wailed even louder as they were thrown back by the power of her voice. But there were others that appeared unaffected.

Knowing the mere touch by her staff would also serve to banish these undead, Cyrillis waded in to the melee, *Kurril* flashing first one direction then another, sending these evil creatures to where they rightfully belonged with every contact.

Breunne and Savinhand did as planned and checked for other entrances. The only doors were the ones they came through and a double set behind the dais—presumably the exit. Keeping a watchful eye on these, the pair joined the fracas. With a special rapier he had picked up in Shardmoor for the purpose, Savin dispatched one of the priest/ghosts from behind that was bothering Vorgath. He nodded appreciatively as the blade seemed to perform as advertised. Breunne too had a special weapon known as "ghost-touched," meaning it could harm a ghost as a normal blade did flesh.

Again as quickly as the melee had begun, the companions found themselves alone in the temple, panting with the exertion of keeping up with the fleet apparitions.

Cyrillis leaned on *Kurril* and sent her percipience out toward her friends. The evil that lingered in the place partially blocked her efforts, but she was fairly certain they had escaped without harm. "Is anyone injured?" she asked, her chest heaving.

"Not I," Thrinndor replied between breaths. Part of his abilities as a paladin was that he was immune to some effects of the undead, so that was not surprising.

"Nor I," said the ranger.

Sordaak shook his head, as did the thief. Not hearing from Vorgath, Cyrillis turned her attention on him. He had sheathed the weapons used during battle and was bent over to retrieve *Flinthgoor*. When he straightened and turned to face her, she involuntarily took in a sharp breath. He had aged immeasurably—the ghosts had indeed made contact with him and taken no small portion of his life as a result.

Seeing the cleric rush to his side, the barbarian said stiffly as he leaned on the haft of the monstrous axe in his hands, "I'm all right."

"The hell you are!" snapped the healer as she got to his side.

The questioning glance he threw her way caused her to realize that he had no idea what she was talking about. Rather than tending to him immediately, Cyrillis fumbled around for a small mirror she carried for when a patient resisted her ministrations such as this. Finding it, she handed it to the barbarian.

Still confused, Vorgath took the mirror from her and held it up and looked into it. The dwarf's eyes widened as he caught a glimpse of himself. "Damn," he said. "Starting to show my age."

"Very funny," Cyrillis said as she accepted the mirror back from Vorgath and put it back in its storage place.

"Can you fix me?" asked a dubious barbarian.

The healer took in a deep breath and began chewing on her lower lip as she shook her head. "No," she said demurely, "I'm afraid not."

"That sucks," Vorgath replied, his tone matching hers.

"The aging bestowed upon you is not a spell, per se, but more of an encounter your psyche had with the ghosts," said the cleric.

"Come again?" said the dwarf with a confused look on his face.

"Fear of being touched by the ghosts, and then that fear being realized, allowed the undead monster to force the aging process on your body and mind." Vorgath still looked confused.

"The ghost *scared* you into becoming older," Sordaak said as he walked up.

"That is what I said," replied the cleric sharply as the barbarian's face cleared and began to turn red.

"I know," said the caster amiably as he studied the dwarf as one might an experiment, "but sometimes you have to dumb it down for these barbarians so they—OW!" Vorgath punched him square in the chest. "Was that necessary?"

"Yes," replied the barbarian. "I may have gotten older, but I can still kick your scrawny little ass even when I'm *twice this age!*"

"Ha, ha," said the sorcerer contritely as he rubbed his chest. "I meant no offense—"

"The hell you didn't!" barked the barbarian as he again raised his fist.

"Boys!" Cyrillis stepped between the two men. "We are still in enemy territory!" She looked from one to the other sternly. "Can we please get back to the task at hand?"

Both the caster and the dwarf found something interesting to hold their attention at their feet. Both nodded.

Sordaak looked up, his face pained. "You can't fix him?"

Cyrillis hesitated as she took in a deep breath and shook her head.

"You hesitated," said the spell-caster. "Is there something you are not telling us?"

The healer again began chewing on her lip. Finally, she nodded ever so slightly.

"Explain," Vorgath said, his eyes not leaving the cleric's face.

Cyrillis allowed her shoulders to slump and did not meet the barbarian's eyes. "Essentially, there are three ways to remove what has happened to you: First is not an option: A High Priest could do a full restore on you, which would remove the aging. Second, we could allow the process to naturally work itself out of your system. The aging process will reverse, but that process could take hours to get you back to your normal age, or years."

"Great!" Vorgath said as he began pacing. "And the third?"

"Third," Cyrillis began quietly, "and this is most certainly not an option I agree with, mind you." She looked up and into the eyes of the suddenly still dwarf. "If you were to die, I could raise you and your affliction will be gone—in theory."

"In *theory?*" Vorgath said, his voice telling what he thought of this last option as the rest of the party joined the three at the dais. "I think I'll let the natural un-aging process reverse this curse."

Cyrillis nodded her agreement, relieved that he did not want to die. While she had studied and knew the spell that would bring him back to life, she had only tried it the one time, hence her trepidation. That one time had worked, but...

"But will you be able to function as a front-line fighter?" Sordaak asked as he looked into the much-aged face with no small concern in his voice.

Vorgath growled from deep within as he turned to look at the caster. "If you mean can I continue to adequately perform my duties as meat shield," he said, smiling, "yes, I assure you that I can." The dwarf stuck out his right arm.

Sordaak returned the smile and grasped the exceedingly strong forearm of the dwarf. Yes, that was no idle boast, he decided.

Thrinndor had overheard much of the conversation, but felt it was not his place to interrupt. "Very well," he said. "If all is in order, we should continue our search for Lord Dahjvest."

"I have a suggestion," Cyrillis said. She was again biting her lower lip. All eyes turned to her, and Sordaak had the sinking feeling that she was going to suggest the death/raise thing after all. She turned to face the barbarian and squared her shoulders.

"Your rages are normally an effective boost of your attack skills," she began, gaining confidence as she spoke. "But when raging your defenses are proportionally lessened, making it more difficult for you to evade harm." Vorgath's gaze was unwavering as he measured what it was the cleric was getting at. "Against the ghosts—and possibly other of the undead—the benefits of your gain in offensive prowess seems to be more than nullified by their increased ability to do harm against you."

Vorgath's eyes did not leave those of the healer.

"What she's saying—" Sordaak began.

"I know what she's saying, ass-wipe!" growled the barbarian.

"Oh, OK," the magicuser said quietly, shaking his head.

"That indeed makes sense," acknowledged the dwarf as he nodded his head, slowly. "I will use my rage only sparingly while facing these ghost-farts."

Cyrillis breathed a sigh of relief. "I think that wise," she said.

"Besides," Vorgath continued with a wry smile, "I'll need to save that limited-use ability for that boney, shit-for-brains Dahjvest!"

"Continuing to underestimate the—" Sordaak began.

"Shut-*up*!" Cyrillis, Thrinndor and Vorgath said in unison.

Taken aback by their vehemence, the sorcerer raised an eyebrow but said no more.

"Are we ready?" asked their leader. He got nods from everyone. "Very well," he said, "I believe our next move is through those doors." He pointed at the double doors behind the raised dais.

"Just a thought," Sordaak said tentatively. Eyes went back to him, waiting to see what words of wisdom he would bestow upon them, next. "Perhaps we should check the doors for traps as we move forward."

Thrinndor raised an eyebrow, his only response while he pondered the request. "I believe that to be wise," he said as he stepped up on the raised platform. "Savin, if you please."

"Of course," the rogue said as he stepped around the paladin, sheathing his weapons as he approached the doors.

A cursory glance revealed nothing. Not swayed however, he began a more intense search.

"While we're young!" snapped the barbarian. "Oh shit! Too late!" He grinned at his own jest.

"I am glad you continue to have a good sense of humor," Thrinndor said, "even at your advanced age!"

"Ha, ha!" replied the barbarian, his grin still in place.

"I don't *see* any traps," Savinhand said as he stepped back, idly scratching his head. "However, I have one more trick up my sleeve." He pulled the sleeve back on his right arm, revealing a bracer. He raised the arm and said a word of command. There was an audible release of power and the right door of the two-door set began to glow a pale blue. "As I thought," murmured the rogue, "not the work of a trapsmith, but that of a spellcaster." He turned to face Sordaak. "You're up, o great wise one!"

"I never grow tired of hearing that!" Sordaak chuckled as he stepped up to investigate the doors. He sighed as he removed a wand from its storage place in his cloak. He waved the wand at the door absently and said an arcane word. Without looking, he spun and returned to his place in line. As he walked past the thief, he said, "You really should consider getting one of these," as he returned the wand to its place.

Savinhand shook his head as he again stepped up to examine the doors. "I suspected as much," he said. "These doors are indeed locked." He removed his pick pouch from its place at his belt, untied the thong and unrolled it on the floor. After a careful inspection of the locking mechanism, he selected two picks. Inserting first one and then the other, he worked the two for a couple of seconds, followed by a satisfying click. He tested the doors to verify he had removed the only lock, quickly returned the picks to their place and the pouch to his belt. Just as quickly he stood and returned to his place next to the ranger.

"Ready?" Thrinndor asked needlessly of the barbarian next to him as he stepped up to the door on the left.

Vorgath didn't even grace the question with an answer. Instead, he drew the two-weapon set he had employed earlier as he stepped up to the door on the right.

In unison the pair each raised a leg, kicked the doors open wide and stepped through, weapons at the ready.

Sordaak and Cyrillis quickly moved in behind them, Breunne and Savinhand right behind.

What they found was a long corridor, lit at regular intervals with sconces that hung from the walls. There was no one—or nothing—in the halls but the companions.

"Curious," said the sorcerer as he stepped up to inspect the nearest sconce.

"What?" a couple of the companions asked at once.

"Undead require no light," said the mage without turning his head. "In fact, several types of those living impaired are *harmed* by the light."

"So?" Vorgath asked. He had already taken several steps toward the doors that could be seen not far down the passage. But he had stopped and now watched the sorcerer impatiently.

"So," repeated the magicuser, "why have the passage lit at all if they do not require the light?"

"Why indeed?" the companions heard a familiar voice say as the sconces winked out and the doors slammed shut behind them.

"So that we can be caught unprepared for the darkness," answered Sordaak. "Eyes!" he shouted as he spoke the words to a spell and light retuned to the room as the sconce he had been investigating relit, now much brighter than before.

A moaning reached the ears of the companions. "Wraiths!" Cyrillis shouted. "Ward yourselves!"

"Damn," spat the dwarf. "I *hate* these guys!"

Cyrillis raised *Kurril* above her head and called forth positive energy from the instrument of power. The wraiths noticed and did as she expected and flew toward her.

Seeing this, Thrinndor shouted, "Cyrillis, what are you doing?"

The cleric ignored him and continued as before, summoning more energy. As the first of the many wraiths reached out to touch her, she reversed course and slammed the heel of the staff onto the stone floor, which rang loudly in the enclosed space. Next she released the energy in two shouted words: "*Be gone!*"

Instantly the wraiths nearest her dissolved with an audible *pop*. Those that weren't immediately expelled were blasted away from the group, hitting the walls with discernible thuds.

"Slay them, *now!*" Cyrillis yelled. "They are stunned and have substance for a time!"

The four fighters leapt into action and quickly dispatched the remaining creatures.

Thrinndor looked over at the healer, who was leaning on her staff. "What was that?" he asked.

The cleric straightened. "Wraiths have a natural resistance to the *turning* I perform. That resistance can be negated by close proximity. So I called forth positive energy from *Kurril*, which attracted them to me." She shrugged. "I then applied that unused positive energy to the *turning* and, well, you saw the result."

"I've never seen a wraith take corporal form." Breunne said what most were thinking.

"Nor had I," admitted the cleric. "It must have had something to do with bringing my staff into the ability."

"Ability?" asked Savin.

"Yes," Cyrillis replied. "The *turning* is not a spell. Rather, it is an ability I train for and possess." She looked into the heart of the stone at the head of her staff. "I have yet to learn all that *Kurril* is capable of." She looked up and into the eyes of the caster. "But I am working on it."

Sordaak quickly looked away lest she see into his heart. "Keep working on it, sister," he said gruffly. "I have a feeling we're going to need that."

"As do I," said the paladin as he looked from the hurt expression on the healer's face to what he was sure was feigned indifference on the face of the sorcerer.

But now was not the time to ponder such things, he reasoned as he hustled to get ahead of the magicuser as Sordaak strode toward the doors at the end of the corridor.

Once there, Savinhand approached them without being asked and began his search. Once again he found no traps, but the device on his arm revealed there was magic in use. He stepped aside and Sordaak again removed the traps with his wand.

After unlocking the doors, he moved back to his place and waited for the fighters to perform their duty.

Vorgath and Thrinndor stepped to the doors, looked at one another and performed what was now their usual task: kick the doors wide open so the party could enter unimpeded.

Again they ran into the room with Sordaak and Cyrillis right behind them.

"Sordaak, light!" Thrinndor called unnecessarily as the magicuser was already pulling the appropriate wand from his belt. He pointed the wand toward what he hoped would be a high ceiling and released the requisite energy with the power word.

A small, brightly lit orb sped from the wand high overhead and burst into a brilliant sphere that easily illuminated the large chamber.

If the previous chamber was a temple (and it was) then this one was a... mausoleum? There were what appeared to be sarcophagi lining the walls—some a hundred or so feet apart with several more in the center of the chamber.

As Breunne and Savinhand entered and split right and left, nothing in the chamber had moved save the party members. Sordaak's sphere of light hung more than fifty feet above their heads and seemed to be content to remain there as it had not begun to fall.

"No apparent entrance from this side," Savinhand called from his spot along the right wall.

"Nor here," Breunne called from the left wall. "I do see another set of doors opposite from where we came in, though."

"Very well," said Thrinndor, relaxing slightly, "that is to be expected."

Cyrillis stepped in and to the left to inspect a sarcophagus. "Do not break these," she said uncomfortably. "I do not know what is inside, but whatever it is, I prefer it stay there."

"Agreed," Thrinndor said. "*If* we are attacked, keep your distance from these sarcophagi, as I am told any disturbance outside of one can cause them to spew forth their contents."

Vorgath grumbled something unintelligible but stepped away from the nearest crypt just the same. "That's a whole lot of undead that will be *behind* us once we go through those doors," he said as he pointed to the way they must go.

"I hadn't thought of that," Thrinndor mused as he looked at one of the crypts closer. "Damn! If something comes along behind us and opens these, we will be fighting on two fronts!"

"Shit!" griped the caster. "How many are there?" When no one answered, he said, "Never mind, I'll get it." He counted a few, did some rapid math in his head and said, "Forty-eight! Shit! That's too many to leave behind!"

"And too many to battle at once," Cyrillis said quietly.

No one spoke for a moment as the burning orb sizzled noisily above their heads and finally began its slow descent toward the floor.

"What if we were to break them one at a time," opined Breunne, "with the fighters at the ready to deal with whatever emerges?"

Sordaak looked around. "That would take way too long."

"You have another idea?" Savinhand asked. "Because leaving them unopened is probably a bad idea."

The mage glared at the thief. "Yes," he said. "You and Thrinndor take a sarcophagus, and Breunne and Vorgath take another—that will cut the time in half."

"I like that," the paladin said.

"Not opposite sides of the room, however," said Cyrillis. "I must be able to reach, and heal, each of the pair at *all* times."

Thrinndor again nodded. "Savinhand," he said, "can you fix those doors we came in such that they cannot be opened from the other side, but still allow us to exit quickly if need be?"

Savin shrugged. "Sure," he said as he walked back to inspect them. He closed first one, then the other, inspecting them as he went. "Of course, if they hadn't been *kicked* open, the task would be easier." He grinned at the paladin.

"Duly noted," Thrinndor said.

Once closed, Savinhand drove a pair of spikes into the wood of each door. He then removed some steel cable he had wound around his waist and looped it tightly across the spikes. Complete, he tested it by pulling on the cable. The doors did not budge.

"That should hold them," he grinned.

"Very well," the paladin said. "You and I will start here," he said as he pointed to a sarcophagus directly in front of him, "Vorgy and Breunne over there," he pointed to a second one about thirty-five or forty feet away. "Cyrillis will position herself between us, and we will rotate the same direction." The cleric nodded her approval. He turned to look at Sordaak. "What will you be doing?"

The caster grinned as he walked over and sat with his back to the doors the rogue had sealed and grinned. "I'm going to watch these doors and ensure no one comes in to disturb you guys." The grin left his face. "And I'll be preparing several spells and scrolls for when we meet up with big, ugly bone bag." Quickly he looked toward the ceiling. "Some disrespect intended," he said as if the Lich Lord were listening. He looked back over at the paladin. "Call me if you need me," he said with a wink. After a quick glance at his orb of light, he pulled the wand from its place in his cloak and launched another ball. He then began removing scrolls from their resting place, removing the seals and setting them in order.

"All right," the paladin said as he turned back to the coffin he had selected for himself and the rogue. He looked pointedly at the barbarian, who was warming up with his greatclub. "Remember, one sarcophagus at a time!"

"Yes sir," grinned the barbarian as he stepped in and leveled a broad swing at the appointed stone crate. The lid shattered under the impact of the massive club and crumbled in a shower of stone and dust.

Through the dust stepped a skeleton armed with a club of its own. Instead of attacking the dwarf in front of it, however, the creature turned to its left and tapped on the lid of the sarcophagus next door.

"Oh no you don't!" said the barbarian as he leveled a back-swing at the offending monster. But he was too late! The lid of the second sarcophagus exploded into dust and out stepped another skeleton!

"Beware!" shouted the ranger. "The undead inside appear to be programmed to open the sarcophagi next to it!" He swung at the second skeleton with the flat of his sword as it emerged from the settling dust.

Thrinndor was too busy to answer as the skeleton—this one a skeleton knight—emerged and did as the others had before, head straight for the coffin next door and tapped on it. Upon getting the same result, the skeleton turned its attention on the paladin who struck it hard with the club he had ready.

"Savin," the paladin shouted as he noticed the second skeleton emerge, this one of the normal variety, "stop that one!"

"On it!" the rogue said as he stepped in front of the monster in an effort to stop it from reaching the next coffin. The skeleton ignored the thief and tried to step around him, but Savinhand was ready for that and also stepped that way and hit the creature on the side of its head with his quarterstaff, knocking the skull clean off. However the flying skull bounced once and struck another sarcophagus nowhere near where they were working.

The lid on that sarcophagus immediately exploded in a shower of rock and dust.

"Cyrillis," the thief shouted. "Some help here!" Fortunately, the cleric had been watching what was going on, and jumped into action.

"Got it," she said as she swung *Kurril* and blasted the emerging skeleton into at least a hundred pieces. A quick glance showed that Thrinndor and Savinhand had their station under control, but Vorgath and Breunne were in deep trouble. There were already five skeletons, two of them knights, clear of their coffins, and from the look of things that was only the beginning.

"Sordaak," she shouted. "A little help here!"

The mage looked up from his studies and accurately assessed the situation in a glance. "Shit," he cursed. "Can't you lame-brains do *anything* without me?" Without getting up, he pointed his finger at the now six—would have been eight, but Vorgath had knocked two back to from whence they came—skeletons and wiggled his thumb.

A spray of sticky string shot from the end of his finger and fanned out such that it trapped all six, and the soon to be seven, skeletons in the web. Next he removed a wand from his robe. "Back up," the mage said as he watched Vorgath move in for what he assumed to be an easy kill. The barbarian ignored him, so Sordaak shrugged and said the command word, sending a small ball of flame speeding toward the entangled monsters.

Seeing the ball out of the corner of his eye, Vorgath threw the mage a nasty look as he dove to the stone floor just as the ball hit the web and exploded.

The ultra-sticky web immediately caught fire across its expanse. The dried bones of the skeletons were next, and soon there was a brief explosion of flames that momentarily was brighter than both orbs of light.

"I had this," Vorgath said belligerently as he stood and stepped back from the fire.

Sordaak looked at the barbarian, raised an eyebrow, said "Whatever!" and went back to his studies.

Breunne and Vorgath waited for the fire to die down before continuing. Fortunately, that only took a few seconds.

"Let's try this," Breunne said. "I'll smash open the sarcophagus, and you get between whatever comes out and the next coffin. That way you get first crack at it. I'll step in behind the monster and between the two of us we should be able to handle anything that comes our way."

The barbarian nodded his agreement to the plan and placed himself accordingly. The plan worked, and they had no further trouble.

Thrinndor and Savinhand had already worked out a similar plan and were well on their way to taking care of their side of the chamber.

As such, the two groups plus Cyrillis met at the other doors in just over an hour. The cleric's healing abilities never came in to play, but a couple of times she had had to step in and bash skulls to keep things from getting out of hand.

Savinhand pointed out some discrepancies he had noticed in the back of two of the sarcophagi—not coincidently opposite each other where he and Breunne had been told to look for additional doors.

The backs to these two coffins were false. It was clear there would be a passage behind the door that would allow the party to be flanked.

"Can you secure the doors?" Thrinndor asked.

The rogue nodded. "With some help, anyway." He explained what he had in mind. It was the paladin's turn to nod.

Together Thrinndor, Breunne, Vorgath and Savinhand slid and stacked the heavy sarcophagi as directed, rearranging them such that the massive stone coffins blocked those entrances. He also set a couple of traps in the event the openings were breached.

Satisfied, Savinhand did due diligence on the doors through which they would have to pass, and Thrinndor called Sordaak over. The mage had had to refresh the orbs of light on a couple of occasions, and was thus aware of the group's progress. Nonetheless, the companions could hear the caster before they saw him as he grumbled the entire trip across the chamber.

"Y'all finally done, here?" Sordaak asked when he got close enough, never looking up from the parchment scroll he had open in his hands. When no one answered, he looked up to see why.

"'Y'all'?' Breunne was the first to ask, thereby precluding the others who were about to make the same inquiry.

"What?" the mage asked, absently. "Oh, I believe that is slang for the combined words 'you' and 'all,'" he said with a dismissive wave of his hand and went back to reading the scroll.

Thrinndor considered continuing the conversation but decided that would be pointless. Apparently the others did as well, because no one said anything further. There were a few shrugs, but that was it.

After the rogue and mage did their usual tango involving removing the magical traps, the companions took up their now usual positions.

"On the other side of these doors should be another long corridor, correct?" asked the paladin.

"According to the map," Sordaak answered as he rolled the parchment he had been reading, re-inserted it into the scroll tube and put it a designated slot in his robe. "If the old fart has not extended this cavern series, then we still have one more cavern before getting to where I believe he is hiding."

"All right then," Thrinndor said as he looked over at his friend—he was having trouble getting used to his newly aged appearance—and said, "Shall we see what awaits us?" Without waiting for a reply, both he and Vorgath raised a leg and kicked open the doors.

After the resulting noise from the crash died down, Sordaak said with an edge of sarcasm to his voice, "Are you guys *trying* to wake the dead? Because, if not, we should consider a different approach!" He strode past the paladin, who stood with his mouth agape.

A moment later Thrinndor shook his head and rushed past the magicuser. "Remember your place in the order," the fighter said as he passed.

"*You* need to remember where we are!" Sordaak snapped back. "If Dahjvest didn't know we were knocking at his door, he does now!"

"Wait!" Savinhand called out from his position at the rear. "My trap-sense is reacting to something—or *somethings*—in this passage."

Sordaak froze mid-stride. Slowly and with deliberate effort he stepped back first one step, and then another. "A little warning would have been nice!" the caster said as he passed the thief.

Savinhand turned and watched the sorcerer walk back into the room with the now broken caskets. "What's with him?" he asked as he turned to see the paladin doing the same thing.

"I do not know," replied the paladin. "See what you can find." He squeezed the rogue's shoulder as he walked past. Thrinndor stopped next to Cyrillis but his eyes continued to follow the mage, who stopped a short distance away.

"Do you know what that was about?" the party leader said only loud enough for the healer to hear.

Cyrillis bit her lip and shook her head as her eyes, too, followed Sordaak. Her face was etched with lines of worry, emphasized by the fading light from the last of the orbs. "No," she said softly as she tore her eyes from the mage and tried to penetrate the dark pools that hid the eyes of the paladin. "But I fear for him so," she continued. "His episodes are growing more frequent, and he is always on edge."

Thrinndor turned his head slowly to again seek out the sorcerer in the fading light. Absently he pulled a torch from his pack, removed the protective wax covering and lit it with his flint and stone. He pulled a second torch from his pack and lit it as well, this one he handed to the healer. He smiled at her wanly. "Keep an eye on him," he said. "I am sure this will pass."

Cyrillis accepted the torch and nodded. She tried to return the smile, but it didn't come off very well. Giving up, she returned her attention to the mage, who was fidgeting a short distance away.

"Got it!" Savinhand announced. He looked around and realized no one was paying any attention. Vorgath had plopped himself down and sat with his back to the wall a short distance away, watching the thief work. When no one said anything, Savin said, "Don't everyone thank me at once!"

The barbarian began clapping his hands together slowly. "Well done, lad," he said with a smile as he pushed himself to his feet with a groan.

"Easy does it, old-timer," Thrinndor said as he extended an arm to the dwarf. "Here, let me help you up."

Vorgath slapped the hand away, irritably. "Back off, pretty-boy!" the barbarian growled. "Remember, you ain't seen a day I can't best your best!"

"Whatever!" Sordaak surprised everyone by rejoining them at Savinhand's announcement. "Is it safe?" He looked pointedly at the thief.

"Y-yes," stammered the rogue.

"What was it?" demanded the paladin, wanting to regain control.

"Blades slicing in from both sides, knee-high and placed at regular intervals all the way to that next set of doors," Savin replied, glad to be free of the sorcerer's stare.

Thrinndor seemed to ponder that for a moment. "This adds a new wrinkle," he said. "Savin, you and Vorgath trade places." The rogue nodded, but the dwarf appeared about to argue. "Just until we get past this part," their leader added. The barbarian, obviously satisfied with this, released the deep breath he had taken in to air his feelings about the move and said nothing. The paladin did some of that mental brow wiping and continued, "I want to make sure we do not run afoul of any more traps without warning." Vorgath even nodded at this declaration. It made sense.

There was some shuffling as the two traded places and some discussion as to who carried the torches. Ultimately the task fell to Sordaak and Cyrillis.

Settled in their new positions, the troupe continued down the passage. As he approached the doors, Savinhand whistled softly.

"What?" asked the sorcerer from his place in line.

"Look at these doors!" Savin replied as he rubbed his right hand lightly over surface of the door, which reflected the light from the torches.

Those in the back crowded forward to get a closer look. "What is it?" asked Cyrillis.

"I'm not sure," replied the rogue, "but I believe these doors are gilt in pure gold!"

"Not unlike the doors to that chamber of summoning back in Dragma's Keep," Thrinndor agreed. "See," he said as he pointed at some engravings that covered the door, "even the runes appear similar."

"You mean this is another such chamber?" the cleric asked.

"No. Look here," the mage said as he pointed to a specific set of runes that were set aside. "These say that these are the chambers of the mayor of the city." He pointed to another set on the other door. "Here it says that the keys to the city are maintained herein."

The caster stepped back and folded his arms across his chest. "This ain't no chamber of summoning!"

Thrinndor nodded as he stepped back. "All right, people. Give the rogue some room to work." The companions obediently stepped away as Savinhand began the process of inspecting the doors.

Presently the thief put his hands on his hips and stepped back. Looking over his shoulder he found Sordaak and said, "A little help here, please. My device can only be used three times between rests, and it's depleted."

The magicuser sighed as he got to his feet and walked up to join the rogue. Sordaak absently waved a hand over the doors and the result caused him to step back. "Hello," he said softly.

"What?" Savinhand asked, and then he too stepped back and his whole body broke out in a cold sweat.

Both doors were not the usual blue hue denoting there was magical energy present, but a deep pink, almost red.

Thrinndor, noticing the commotion, stood and walked up to the pair. "What have you found?"

"Well," Sordaak began, scratching the small tuft of hair he was growing on his chin, his eyes never leaving the doors, "we don't exactly know at this point." The mage held up a hand to forestall further questions, which he knew to be coming. "While I have never personally come across this before," he continued as he stepped back in for a closer look, "I believe this color indicates the doors are magically held shut."

"They're not trapped?" the rogue asked.

"I didn't say that," the magicuser mused quietly as he continued his inspection. "They could still be trapped, *also*." He stepped back and did some more scratching at his chin. "Any magic used to hold the doors closed could be masking any other." Sordaak noticed the confused look on the thief's face. "Think of it like an onion," he explained, "one layer of magic covering—and hiding—that of another layer below."

Evidently that explanation worked, because Savinhand nodded and said, "OK, now what?"

That question Sordaak was not ready for. He returned his attention to the doors and said, "I don't know for sure. But if the magic was put on in layers, it will have to be removed in reverse order, or risk triggering whatever protective devices await."

"Assuming there are *other layers*," Savin mused.

"Agreed," said the mage. "But, we must assume that to be the case until proven otherwise."

Thrinndor nodded. "Can you remove these layers?"

"That's the million dollar question," answered the sorcerer.

"Dollar?" Thrinndor gave Sordaak a quizzical look. "What is a 'dollar'?"

The mage did a double-take on the paladin. "It's a—oh, hell! Never mind!" He focused on the doors. "Give me room," he said with a trace of his old, grouchy self.

Obediently the paladin and the rogue took several steps back. Stopping there, they watched the sorcerer with interest. Sordaak removed wands and replaced them several times, shaking his head as he went. The caster repeated his show magic spell several times during the process, presumably to check his progress.

After a few minutes of this, Sordaak put his hands on his hips, turned and walked over to where Thrinndor and Savinhand stood. The mage again shook his head.

"I *think* I got all of them," he said as he turned again to look at the doors.

"You *think*?" asked Thrinndor.

"Yes," said the spell-caster crossly. "I can only remove what I can find." He turned to lock eyes with the paladin. "And I can find no more. I removed the spell holding the doors closed—that was a doozy—and I found and removed at least three magical traps. The last one I almost missed. I believe it would have teleported me, and anyone close, to someplace I didn't want to be." He shuddered suddenly.

"I've checked with the most powerful spells at my disposal, and I can't find anything more on the doors." He again turned to look at the doors. "But..."

A few moments of silence were more than Savinhand could bear. "But what?" he asked.

Sordaak turned to look at the rogue, but Savin had the distinct impression the mage was not looking *at* him, but *through* him. "I don't know!" the sorcerer said at last. "There is no more magic on the doors, of that I am certain. But when I cast my 'detect magic' spell, I sense there is some unresolved issue!" He was again silent for a few moments, and this time neither of the pair sought to break that silence. However, curious as to what was going on, Cyrillis stood and walked over to join them followed by Breunne and eventually Vorgath, although it was apparent he was there more to be not left out than idle curiosity.

Sordaak's eyes widened. "Perhaps Fahlred can find out what is on the other side!"

Breunne was dubious. "I thought you could only send him to places you have been before and can visualize."

"Technically that is true," replied the sorcerer as he summoned his familiar. "However, Fahlred can go where he chooses, and is capable of transmuting *through* the door. If there is nothing but rock on the other side, he'll simply come back."

"It is worth a try," Thrinndor said as Sordaak looked deep into the quasit's eyes.

After a few moments of this Fahlred jumped off of his master's shoulder and landed lithely on the cold, stone floor. He walked over to the doors, put both hands on them and pressed his face against its metal.

Next a low strange sound could be heard as the quasit's head began to disappear *into the door*! Barely perceptible at first, but soon the process quickened.

"That looks like it *hurts*!" Savinhand said as he shrank away from the scene.

"Shhh!" Sordaak hissed. "Don't disturb his concentration."

He needn't have bothered. Fahlred pulled his head back through the door much quicker than the process of inserting it. Once he was clear, he winked out of existence and was back on Sordaak's shoulder before anyone could blink, his long tail wound around the caster's neck several times.

"What the—?" began the barbarian.

But the mage waved him to silence. Fahlred was clearly agitated.

"*What?*" Sordaak said involuntarily. Clearly he did not need to speak aloud, but whatever was being communicated to him forced the words from his mouth. "You *sure?*"

The quasit nodded.

Sordaak turned his incredulous gaze upon his companions. "Fahlred says Theremault waits for us on the other side."

Chapter Ten

Theremault

There was a moment of stunned silence and then suddenly everyone was speaking at once.

"*What?*" Breunne said louder than he had intended.

"The *dragon?*" Vorgath said with a gleam in his eye. It appeared he gained back a few of his years in that instant.

Sordaak merely nodded and turned back to his familiar, again peering into the demon's eyes. "I can now see what he saw," said the mage softly. "It is indeed a blue dragon—a really *big* blue dragon." He closed his eyes and shook his head as he broke the connection. "I can't be sure it's Theremault, but Fahlred *is* sure." The quasit nodded.

"Damn!" muttered the ranger.

"Agreed," said Thrinndor.

"What do we do now?" asked Cyrillis.

"We go whoop some dragon butt!" announced Vorgath as he slapped the haft of *Flinthgoor* with his free hand. He was beaming with anticipation.

"Wait just a minute," said Thrinndor. "We need to verify status before we go charging in on a dragon!" The paladin looked over at Cyrillis, first. "Spell power?"

Cyrillis shifted her gaze and closed her eyes. "About seventy-five percent," she said.

"And you?" he asked the spell-caster.

"About the same," Sordaak said, "give or take." He shrugged.

He checked the fighters, finding them for the most part whole. His eyes lingered on Vorgath. "Don't say it," growled the barbarian. "Don't even *think* it! I'll still be capable of bagging a dragon when I'm a hundred years older than this!" He shook his greataxe for emphasis.

"Very well," said the party leader. "We are about as ready as we can be."

"One note of caution," Breunne said. All eyes turned to him. "Actually two. First, we are here to kill a Lich Lord—if we do battle with this dragon, will we have sufficient strength to do so?"

When the ranger did not immediately continue, Thrinndor prompted him. "And the second?"

"Second," the ranger nodded, "Why would a dragon of Theremault's reported stature be stuck back in these *smaller* caverns when he is said to rule an entire mountain?"

Silence again held the group captive. Finally Cyrillis spoke. "Perhaps the dragon is held servant by Dahjvest?"

"Preposterous!" Sordaak said loudly causing the others to look at him sharply. "While Dahjvest had no small reported skills, he does not have anywhere near the power necessary to corral a dragon!"

"And if he raised it?" Cyrillis was nettled at being dismissed so, and let it show.

The sorcerer opened his mouth to rebut, but apparently thought better of it. "I hadn't thought of that," he said as he scratched his chin. "He would certainly be old enough to have raised the dragon from a hatchling... Interesting."

"Again," Breunne said, "how do you get a dragon into that 'smallish' chamber—assuming the chamber ahead is about the same size as the last?"

"There must be another entrance," explained Vorgath. He crossed his arms as if that settled the matter.

It didn't. "In a chamber a hundred or so feet wide a large dragon would barely have room to spread its wings," replied Breunne, pressing the matter, "let alone take flight."

"Then *what?*" the barbarian was nearly shouting in frustration.

"None of this makes *sense*," said the sorcerer as he turned and looked back at the doors. "A dragon being held in a room too small, in a town full of undead, being controlled by a rejected sorcerer-turned-Lich!" He threw his hands up in the air and spun around to face his friends. "Any ideas?"

"What if we have it backwards?" Thrinndor said. It was his turn to scratch his chin as the companions turned to face him. "What if Theremault is calling the shots and Dahjvest is his puppet?"

That also stunned the crowd into silence.

"It still would not explain the size of the room," the ranger said.

"It would if this chamber has another entrance!" Vorgath repeated. "A larger entrance."

"That is certainly a possibility," said the paladin, "but no one explanation seems to satisfy all sides of this story."

"True, so far..." Sordaak said. Now he was trying to rub the hairs completely off of his chin.

"What have you got cooking up in that way-too-big head of yours?" asked the barbarian.

"Well," Sordaak's eyes regained focus as he looked over at the dwarf, "just a thought I had." He smiled. "What if Theremault is also *undead?*"

"*What?*" three or four of the companions said at once.

Sordaak's smile grew. "Think about it," the mage said. "If the dragon were dead, then it makes perfect sense that he's trapped in a chamber much smaller than he would normally." His smile threatened to connect his ears. "It would also explain his presence here, prisoner to Dahjvest!"

If the previous silences were stunned, this one was cataclysmic. No one spoke for several minutes as each pondered the implications.

Vorgath was first. "Sending a dragon ghost to the afterlife won't count as a kill, will it?" He was certainly deflated.

Thrinndor smiled wanly at his friend and clamped a huge hand on his shoulder. "Afraid not, old friend."

"Damn," muttered the dwarf. Suddenly he looked up, his eyebrows almost knitted together in determination. "Can we at least get on with slaying whatever it is?"

"I believe that would be in order," agreed the paladin as he allowed his hand to drop to his side. He turned back to the sorcerer. "Will an undead dragon still have a breath weapon?"

"Good question," replied the wizard. "As I have never even *heard* of such a creature, I don't feel qualified to answer that question."

"Very well," said the paladin, "we will have to assume he does." A thought came to him suddenly. "Could your familiar tell if the dragon were 'ghostly'? Or perhaps more flesh and blood?"

"As in a zombie-dragon?" Sordaak asked.

Thrinndor nodded.

The mage shook his head. "No, there was not enough light." He quickly raised his hands. "I know! Quasits don't require light. However, if he is to use all aspects of his vision, some light is helpful." The mage cocked his head as he tried to remember what he saw through Fahlred's eyes. "However, the dragon didn't *look* ethereal, so I'll have to go with zombie." He couldn't believe he was even having this conversation. "If that is the case, then I would certainly count on the beast having a breath weapon available."

"What type?" asked Cyrillis. When the others looked at her, she said, "I need to be able to pass out the appropriate resistances, do I not?"

"Most assuredly," Sordaak answered for the group. "Electricity. Lightning."

"Damn!" griped the barbarian, "I *hate* being zapped!" His demeanor suddenly brightened. "If the beast *is* a zombie-dragon, that would qualify as a kill, right? I mean, it's not like it was a ghost!"

"You might be able to make a point for that," replied the paladin, not wanting to be the bearer of bad news twice. "However," Thrinndor continued, "if some other party claims the kill for Theremault, then he cannot have been slain twice."

"Drat!" said the dwarf. "I hadn't thought of that!"

Thrinndor smiled. "What else do we know about blue dragons?" he asked.

"I don't know much about blue dragons," Breunne said, "but a zombie version of whatever living creature it embodies will generally be much slower than the living version."

"True," said the thief. "It is also doubtful a zombie-dragon would be able to take flight, even if there were room in there."

"Also a good point," the party leader said. "Will he retain spell ability, assuming he ever had that?" This question he directed at Sordaak.

"I don't know," the mage replied. "However, as I have never heard of a zombie spell-caster, I would have to say the answer to that would be no. Generally a zombie's minds are mush, and the mind is required to cast spells."

"Makes sense." Thrinndor nodded. "Anything else?" He looked around at each of them.

"Can we just get on with slaying whatever is on the other side of that door?" Vorgath wailed. "Today?"

The paladin grinned. "Can we plan our attack, please?"

Vorgath crossed his arms on his chest and glowered at his leader. "Go ahead," he said. "I'm going in swinging! The rest of you figure out how to work around that!"

"Actually," said the paladin, "that is what I had in mind." He turned to Cyrillis. "Vorgath will go in first and get Theremault's attention. You focus on keeping him standing while the rest of us circle and attack from all sides." He looked over at Sordaak next. "Unless we get in over our heads, you should try to conserve your spell ability for the Lich."

Sordaak nodded but said nothing.

"However, some light on the subject will be required," the paladin continued.

The mage nodded as he reached into his robe and pulled out the required wand.

Thrinndor mulled over the preparations and nodded. "Cyrillis, some resist electricity, if you please."

The healer nodded and did as requested. She also performed a couple of additional spells, explaining that those would make them both harder to hit by the dragon and make it that same dragon easier to hit by the party members.

Preparations complete, the paladin asked, "Ready?" He got nods from everyone. "Very well," he said. "Vorgy and I will open the door as usual. Sordaak will immediately provide us some light, and then the mighty midget will charge in and get the dragon's attention. Vorgath, if you can, turn him one way or the other." The barbarian nodded.

"All right," Thrinndor said. "Here we go."

He and the barbarian kicked at the doors simultaneously, causing them to swing inward and crash into the walls, making an enormous racket. Vorgath followed that with one of his battle yells and charged into the chamber as two orbs sped past him to explode high in the air, bathing the cavern with light.

Vorgath spotted his adversary slightly to the left and adjusted his direction accordingly. The dragon raised up on all fours, let out a thunderous cry of its own and lashed out at the charging dwarf with a volley of lightning bolts.

The barbarian took the first electric strike full in the chest, knocking the wind out of his sails. Still he continued his charge—although with slightly less alacrity. His first blow with *Flinthgoor* caught the dragon unprepared. The blade bit deep, and Theremault screamed in rage.

Out of the corner of his eye Vorgath caught sight of a massive claw coming at his head, and he just had time to throw himself to the stone floor, his greataxe still clutched in his hands and he was thus able to avoid serious injury. Knowing what was coming, the dwarf continued the roll as one of the creature's hind feet thundered down where he had been only a blink of the eye before.

The barbarian regained his feet, still fighting for breath just as the barbed tail of the dragon whipped through the air and caught him between the shoulder blades, knocking him forward. Fortunately his breastplate also had a back; therefore much of the damage was absorbed by the metal of his armor. The dwarf had already begun his next swing, but the blow from the tail caused his aim to be off and he missed badly, falling to his knees.

Knowing better than to stay still, the barbarian pitched forward onto his chest and rolled hard to his right. As he surged to his feet, Vorgath came up swinging. This was fortuitous, because the maw of the dragon was going for the kill. Instead, *Flinthgoor* caught the dragon in the side of the head just below the monster's blazing red eye.

Theremault shrieked in pain and jerked back, almost taking the greataxe with him. Vorgath maintained hold on his weapon, however, and took the opportunity while the monster writhed in pain to swing the blade with all his considerable might at a spot he had seen between two previously damaged scales deep into the chest of the dragon.

Again the dragon bellowed in rage and pain. The barbarian yelled as he planted his foot on a scale to use as leverage to jerk his axe free, "Y'all had better get you some of this before I take this mangy whelp of a dragon down on my own!"

"Mayhap we should let you try!" shouted the paladin in return—in jest only, of course. He, Breunne and Savinhand had already gotten into position and were doing an enormous amount of damage as well. Well, at least the ranger and himself... *Where had that rogue gotten off to?*

Movement seen at the edge of his vision caused him to turn that way to see Savin sprinting up the neck of the monster, his vorpal weapon in his teeth. *Damn, that is one brave thief,* the paladin thought as he slashed away at a spot where more than one scale was missing. Idly he wondered just how Theremault had lost so many scales, because there were several missing that he could see.

In only moments the battle was over. The dragon never really recovered from the initial onslaught, and was obviously hampered by its inability to fly.

Vorgath walked slowly over to where the head lay motionless. As he approached, the eyes popped open and focused on the dwarf only a few feet away. The pain seemed to be gone from the creature's eyes, and only recognition of certain death remained.

The barbarian raised his axe for the blow that would end the creature's existence.

"Stop!" the caster shouted as he ran up behind the dwarf.

"Why?" Vorgath demanded as he turned on the mage, blood-lust still burning within him.

"I would like to talk to him," Sordaak answered. "Then he will be yours, I assure you." The sorcerer watched the raised axe carefully.

Vorgath visibly fought for control. Without saying a word, he stepped back, bowed and waved an arm formally in the direction of the prone dragon.

Sordaak breathed a sigh of relief. "Thank you," he said, returning the bow. Then, before the dwarf could change his mind, the mage took the two steps required to stand before the giant head of the dragon.

Unsure how to begin, Sordaak stared into the eerily unblinking eyes of the beast as he sorted what needed to be said in his mind. He started with, "Can you speak?"

The eyes blinked once and the mouth opened slightly. "Yes," the monster hissed, barely audible.

Sordaak leaned closer. He had the sudden worry that Theremault may be drawing him closer for nefarious purposes. He shuddered deep inside while displaying a calm outward appearance. It would not do to show fear at this juncture. "I need to ask you some questions, if I may."

The dragon stared at the human that stood before him for a few moments, and Sordaak began to worry that the beast had died with its eyes open. "Why should I answer anything you may have to ask?"

Sordaak had been prepared for that question. "Because you have two choices as to which way to die and be remembered," the mage said. "One, you can die a quick death and be remembered as the magnificent dragon you once were with your head displayed proudly on this barbarian's wall in his study."

When Sordaak didn't immediately continue, Theremault said, "Or?"

"Or we can just leave you here to die when your heart finally gives out from the blood loss and have your carcass be picked at by the various carrion crawlers and scavengers until only your bones remain." Sordaak crossed his arms and put on his best "and I don't care which you choose" look.

Theremault again was silent for too long to suit the caster. Just as Sordaak was about to prod the monster to verify life, the dragon spoke. "Allow me to speak with this barbarian." There was a hint of pride in his voice.

Sordaak turned to see the dwarf standing not far off where he watched the proceedings with feigned disinterest. At the mage's lifted eyebrow, the barbarian stepped up to stand beside his friend.

"I am Vorgath," the barbarian said with a formal bow.

Theremault's glowing red orbs shifted to the dwarf, apparently studying him. "Who would I share your wall with?"

Vorgath blinked twice in surprise. "As of now there is only one: Melundiir." He puffed out his chest. "There will certainly be more."

"Certainly," the dragon said, and Sordaak thought he detected a hint of sarcasm buried in that one word. "So it was you that slayed my friend Melundiir." The eyes blinked once, and then again. "I would be honored to share wall space with her."

The dragon's eyes shifted back to the magicuser, dismissing the dwarf. "Ask your questions; I will answer if I can."

Sordaak's eyes softened. "You are obviously not dead," the mage began. "Nor have you *been* dead—we assumed you must be a zombie dragon," he tried to explain.

"Zombie Dragon?" Sordaak was almost sure Theremault was smiling. "I have never heard of such a thing."

"Nor I," admitted the mage. "But we could find no other reasonable explanation as to your presence here."

"*Zombie Dragon?* That was your *reasonable* explanation? I'd love to hear the *less* reasonable versions someday." Theremault chuckled which quickly changed to a fit of coughing. "Oh," he said weekly, "that hurt."

Cyrillis appeared at the sorcerer's elbow. "Is there anything I can do to make your end more comfortable?"

Theremault's eyes shifted to the cleric and refocused. "No, young lady, not anymore." Another fit of coughing. "Two hundred years ago I would have given myself over to one as lovely as you," now Sordaak *knew* the dragon was smiling. "but I am old, and my wounds are mortal. However, your offer honors me."

The dragon's eyes shifted once again to the sorcerer, dismissing the healer.

"You have yet to ask a question," Theremault said weakly.

Sordaak took a deep breath. "How *did* you come to be here?"

The dragon appeared to ponder the question. "I have not long among you," the creature said as Cyrillis bit her lip and stepped reverently away, "so I will give you the short version." Theremault raised his head weakly and coughed twice more, blood now showing on his teeth and lips.

"I was resting peacefully when I was set upon by a group similar to your own," the dragon said, closing his eyes briefly to rest. "We battled long and hard ere they submitted and departed, taking their dead and wounded with them. I know I slew at least one of them, and possibly more." Another fit of coughing interrupted the beast, this time leaving the dragon visibly weaker. When finally the dragon again opened his eyes and spoke, his voice was considerably softer. "Dahjvest came upon me in my battle-weakened state, forced me to my human form and brought me here." The dragon tried to look around, disgusted, but had to settle for rolling his eyes as he was now too weak to raise his head. "Once here, he did what little he could for me to bring back my strength but, at my age, the harm inflicted in battle takes longer to heal and it has been but a short time."

"Why do you serve him?" Sordaak asked.

"He said he would release me if I killed you and your party," Theremault said weakly. "Seemed easy enough at the time. Now it is you who will release me."

Theremault closed his eyes and his labored breathing could easily be heard in the quiet cavern. Sordaak took the opportunity to ask, "What were they after?"

When Theremault again opened his eyes, Sordaak could see the light behind them fading. "The same as you, of course."

Sordaak was stunned. "*What?*"

Theremault tried but failed to nod. "You sorcerers are all alike," the dragon said, his voice softer. "You think that no one knows your secrets. Bah!" Vehemence returned for just that one word.

"What am I after, then?" The wizard had to hear it from the dragon before he would believe it.

"*Pendromar, Dragon's Breath,*" replied the dragon, some semblance of a spark returning to his eyes. Sordaak stumbled backward a step and fell hard on his ass. "I see that I have surprised you," Theremault continued.

"Y-*you?*" the mage stammered as he climbed back to his feet. "You had *Pendromar?*"

"No," Theremault said. "You are not listening. I have but a few moments left, try to keep up." The dragon closed his eyes, and Sordaak feared he had indeed passed. Slowly, and with substantial effort, the dragon raised his eyelids to about half open. "I had the staff briefly several hundred years ago," the dragon said. "It passed to me for safekeeping, but then it was taken from me about four hundred years ago." Sordaak heard Thrinndor's sharp intake of breath behind him, but dared not interrupt at this point. "I tried multiple times to get it back, but was never able to do so."

When Theremault went silent for longer than the mage could stand, Sordaak prompted him. "Who took the staff from you?"

The dragon appeared not to hear. "She did not believe me," the dragon said. Sorrow could be heard through the pain.

"Who?" Sordaak asked gently.

"She who drove her companions so hard, even unto death." The dragon paused for a moment. "Shaarna," he said. "Yes, they named her Shaarna. She *really* wanted that staff!"

Sordaak knew that name but could not immediately remember from where. "Who took the staff from you?" the mage repeated.

"I heard you the first time," Theremault replied. The dragon again paused, closing his eyes. "The Minions of Set at Ice Homme. They have the staff, now," he said without opening them.

Ice Homme! The staff was *so* close! In Sordaak's elation, something the dragon said nagged at a memory. Shaarna?

"Why does this Shaarna want the staff?" Sordaak asked, his eyes suspicious.

"Ah," Theremault said, "finally the right question."

"I don't understand," said the mage.

"Because you talk too much," the dragon said, "and listen too little."

"I'm listening," Sordaak said.

"She requires the staff not to use it for herself," Theremault said, "but to keep *you* from having it." The dragon's voice was barely above a whisper.

"*What?*" Sordaak's knees buckled, but this time he was able to maintain his feet. "None know of our—of *my*—quest for the staff!"

"She does," the dragon said, his voice now so low the mage had to lean closer to hear it.

"She *who?*" an exasperated Sordaak nearly shouted.

"Shaarna," the dragon said. "Your sister."

Chapter Eleven

Dahjvest

"**What?**" This time Sordaak did shout. "What did you say?" the mage raged at the closed eyes of the dragon. "You must be mistaken! I *have* no sister! I have no *siblings*, period!" When Theremault didn't respond, Sordaak stepped forward and placed his hand on the huge head and shook it. "Talk to me!"

Cyrillis grabbed the sorcerer from behind and wrapped her arms around him, hugging his flailing body to hers. "He is gone," she said gently.

"Who's gone?" Sordaak said, confused. "Theremault? No, we were just talking. He *can't* be gone!" Sordaak was gritting his teeth with frustration. "I have more questions!"

"Shhh, shhh," the cleric chided. "You will have to be content with what you have. Theremault is dead." She pushed the sorcerer back and looked into the confusion that clouded his eyes. "He is *dead!*"

"No!" Sordaak moaned as he looked over the cleric's shoulder. Seeing the dragon's sides no longer rising and falling with his labored breathing brought it all home. Theremault was dead.

"Damn!" he cursed himself for letting the dragon ramble so much when he had so many other questions.

"What was that you were yelling about a 'sister'?" Thrinndor asked as he walked up.

"Nothing!" Sordaak said quickly—too quickly. "Aw, hell!" the mage said. "Theremault said that a young woman led a party that fought him for *Pendromar*. He also said she only wanted to have the staff to stop *me* from having it. He also said that she was my sister."

"I thought you said you were an only child?" Breunne said.

"I *am* an only child!" shouted Sordaak.

"You are certain?" Thrinndor asked.

"Yes!" Sordaak answered, again *too* quickly. "I mean, my mother only had one child! My father was said to spread his affections around some," he looked sheepishly at Cyrillis, and then looked away, "but those were merely rumors! And all such rumors were squelched as lies!"

The chamber was silent for a few moments; no one wanted to touch that statement. Sordaak looked up suddenly. "Wait!" he said. "The dragon said that her name was Shaarna! I *knew* a Shaarna when I was but a child. She was about my age. We attended classes together for a time." His eyes grew wide. "But her and her mother moved away after a particularly sticky rumor surfaced about her mother."

"What sort of rumor?" Breunne asked. The companions had all gathered around the sorcerer.

Sordaak looked absently over at the ranger and said, "Her mother was a beautiful woman—a woman without a man, yet with a *daughter*! There are always rumors in such cases, right?"

The fragility of the sorcerer's mind kept anyone from answering. He did, however, get a couple of nods.

"*RIGHT?*" Sordaak shouted. Now he got three acknowledgments of "of course" and two more nods.

"Shit!" the mage said as he turned to look at the now still dragon. "I have a *sister?*" His mind was reeling. "This changes things."

"A half-sister," corrected Thrinndor. "And what does it change?"

Sordaak turned to stare at the paladin. "For one," he began belligerently, "I am *not* the only one remaining who is of the lineage of Dragma." He continued to stare at the big fighter, who remained silent. "And that means I am *not* the only one who can use his staff *AND*," the mage's mind was racing now, "I am *not* the only one who can help raise your dead god!"

"*Our* dead god," corrected the paladin, again. Everyone else in the chamber was a spectator now; no one wanted to interrupt the argument. "You missed one important detail, however."

Sordaak, about to argue further, raised an eyebrow and waited.

"Theremault said that her plan was not to use the staff, but to *keep* you from using it." Sordaak waited, knowing there must be more. "She must therefore be a servant of Praxaar—possibly even a member of the secret sect dedicated to making sure we do not succeed."

"But my father was a servant of Valdaar!" the mage insisted.

"And he spurned her and her mother," Thrinndor said quietly. "It is not uncommon for one spurned so to rebel against those that did the spurning."

Sordaak's eyes went wide. "Of course!" he said. Suddenly his pupils lost focus. "That would explain *so much*!" He shook his head slowly, trying to squelch the memories that came unbidden to his mind.

The paladin moved to stand in front the mage, but the sorcerer didn't acknowledge him. "Sordaak," the big fighter said sternly. Nothing. "*Sordaak!*" he raised his voice. Still nothing. "I hate to have to do this," Thrinndor said quietly. Abruptly he backhanded the caster. "*SORDAAK!*"

Slowly the magicuser's pupils focused on the paladin in front of him. He raised his hand to rub his red cheek. "Ow," he said. "Was that necessary?"

Thrinndor looked around at the others in the party. "Yes," several said as one.

It was Sordaak's turn to look around. "OK," he said, "maybe it was, at that." He smiled and looked up at the paladin. "I think we have some 2,000-year-old bone bag's ass to kick."

As he turned to leave the stunned group he stopped, turned again and looked deep into the eyes of the paladin. "Do not do that again," he said evenly. "Find a different way to bring me back." He turned and walked off.

Thrinndor again looked to his companions. When none of them said anything, he shrugged, spun on his heel and followed the mage.

As Vorgath stood to follow he felt a sharp pain in his mid-back. "Umm," he said, "a little help here." He fell to his knees, struggled for a moment and then his eyes rolled back in his head as he pitched forward onto his face. Sticking out of the back of his armor was a snapped-off barb from the dragon's tail. Blood covered the back of his lower tunic.

"Shit!" Cyrillis exclaimed as she rushed to the dwarf's side. As the others joined her, she said, "Help me get his armor off!"

Breunne and Savinhand knelt and quickly undid the buckles under the barbarian's arms. As they gently lifted, a groan escaped Vorgath's lips.

"Stop!" Cyrillis said. Both men released the edge of the dwarf's back plate and eased back, waiting for further instructions.

The cleric leaned forward and inspected the spike. Approximately a forearm's length jutted out from the armor, and judging by the taper of what was showing, another six inches or so was buried in the dwarf's torso. Cyrillis grabbed the exposed end and tried to work it loose. She got another groan for her efforts. The spike was wedged too tight for her to remove.

"I cannot remove it," she said, frustration edging its way into her voice.

"Move." Concern for his friend made Thrinndor's voice brusque as he roughly pushed the healer aside. He then planted his right foot next to the spike, grasped the exposed end and easily pulled the shard free.

A gasp was ripped from the unconscious Vorgath, his head momentarily raised up with his face twisted in pain. Not another sound was heard from him as his head again hit the cold stone of the floor.

When the paladin stepped back, spike in hand, Cyrillis moved back to the barbarian's side. At a nod from her, both the ranger and the rogue reached in and easily lifted the armor out of the way.

Vorgath's tunic underneath was already soaked in blood from the gaping hole in his back. Cyrillis reached down, grasped the light fabric in her hands and ripped it open. This fully exposed the wound, which now gushed the dwarf's life down his sides, where it pooled on the floor around him.

The healer placed both her hands on the wound and moaned. "There is at least one broken rib here," she said. "I must mend that first—and any internal damage—before I close the wound." She bit her lip as she put her hand into the gaping hole in the dwarf's back.

"Hurry!" Thrinndor said needlessly. He felt the need to do something, however. *Anything!*

Cyrillis ignored the paladin as she raised her eyes to the ceiling and closed them, trusting to her senses when her eyes could not help. Vorgath was sweating profusely and moaned occasionally as the healer worked her magic in his body.

Finding the broken bone, she put it back in place and whispered a prayer as she fused the two pieces together. She did the same for another rib that was only cracked, making it again whole. Finding no other major internal damage, she removed her hand, again placed both hands on the gaping hole and poured her most powerful healing into the dwarf's body.

Instantly the bleeding stopped and the skin knitted together. Seeing there was more to do, Cyrillis repeated the process with a slightly less potent spell.

Vorgath's eyes fluttered open and he was no longer sweating. He looked around briefly, licked his lips and tried to sit up. He stopped with a groan and the cleric reached down to assist him.

"Take it easy," she said. "You have lost a lot of blood, and those two mended bones will be sore for some time."

The barbarian accepted her assistance to stand, his teeth clenched in a grimace. He craned his neck around to look at his back. "Who tore my shirt?" he asked.

Cyrillis put her hands on her hips and bowed until her face was only inches from the dwarf's. "I did," she said, her tone answering his accusation. "I thought we had a deal?" Now it was her turn to sound accusing.

"What?" the barbarian took a step back.

"You were injured—severely—and said nothing about it." The cleric was clearly mad. "Why?" She stood straight, her hands going back to her hips.

Vorgath's face reddened somewhat as he pondered his answer. "Look," he said belligerently, "when I am raging, I feel nothing. A barbarian's rage is designed that way." He softened his tone. "Once the rage wears off, we are in a weaker state until our system recovers. Sometimes we come out of a rage in pain, and are unaware whether it is a new pain, or something that bothers us chronically. I have occasional back pain, and sometimes don't know I've been injured there until I try to do something exceptional."

"Like what?" Cyrillis' tone was scathing. She bent over and picked up the spike that until recently had been stuck in the dwarf's back. It was still covered in blood. "This was stuck in your back!" She indicated how much had been inside him. "Up to *here*!" She was breathing hard with effort *not* to smack the impudent barbarian. "This spike broke one rib, fractured another and stopped this short," she held her thumb and index finger less than an inch apart in front of his nose, "of penetrating your heart!"

Vorgath, taken aback by her vehemence, shrunk away from her fingers. "I guess that explains the twinge I was feeling and that hole in my armor," he said, pointing to his back-plate which lay a few feet away.

"'*Twinge*'?" the cleric's voice rose an octave. Then she noticed his sheepish smile. He winked at her. "Damn you!" she said, fighting back a smile of her own as she spun and stalked away.

The barbarian looked over at the paladin and said, "What? Was it something I said?" He stooped over and retrieved his back-plate. "Damn," he muttered as he set the armor once again on the ground, pulled his great-club from his belt and hammered on the armor until the jagged edges were flattened.

"That'll have to do until we get to town, I'm afraid," Vorgath said as he cast a critical eye on his repair work. He slung the offending armor over his shoulder and fastened the buckles. "All this work is going to cost a lot to repair."

"All the more reason to consider a shield!" Cyrillis said from where she had stopped several paces away.

"Bah!" the barbarian spat. "Shields are for…" He smiled at her. "I guess I've already explained my view on shields."

"A number of times," several of the party said at once, drawing smiles from most of them. They were getting pretty good at it.

"Ha!" Vorgath said with a gleam in his eye. He turned his attention back on the healer. "Well, you just keep on doing your usual great job of keeping me alive, and I'll do the same for you!" He winked at her again.

Cyrillis fought back several sharp replies, settling on, "You are *insufferable*!"

"I know," said the barbarian. "That has to be the reason you love me so." He pursed his lips and blew her a kiss.

"Bah!" she spat back at the dwarf. But she had to turn away to hide her smile.

Sordaak, who had been watching the entire encounter with a raised eyebrow, said sarcastically, "If you two are finished with your love fest, we should finish this before Dahjvest has time to cook up some more undead surprises for us."

The offending pair turned to look at the mage. "Whatever!" they said in unison. Both laughed.

"Lead on, oh fearless ex-leader," the barbarian said with a deep bow and a wave of his arm.

Sordaak spun and led the way toward the doors opposite the ones they had come through, his back ramrod straight.

Still smiling, the others took up station, Vorgath and Thrinndor hustled to get ahead of the sorcerer.

If the previous doors were ornate, then these were plain to a fault. Bare wood—thick wood, mind you—with iron bands and an iron latching mechanism.

"You guys check for side doors?" Sordaak asked as he squatted next to the wall, putting his back against it. It was clear he had some preparations in mind before the upcoming tussle.

Breunne and Savin traded glances and turned to walk to a wall, each in opposite directions. "Damn," muttered the rogue, "harassing a dragon caused that to slip our minds."

Sordaak nodded, he had figured as much. He pulled some scrolls from their respective holders and checked the labels on each, placing them back in an order he would recognize in the heat of battle. Next he pulled out three wands and did the same with them.

Satisfied that he was as prepared as he could be, he summoned Fahlred. After the quasit appeared, the two communicated in their way. The creature seemed to linger for a moment before the sorcerer said gruffly, "Go on."

Fahlred winked out of sight, leaving Sordaak to shake his head. He had instructed the quasit to stay out of the upcoming fray. If his familiar were to die, the loss would in turn harm the magicuser greatly, possibly taking him to the brink of death or beyond. It was a complication he dared not allow. Fahlred had resisted.

Presently the rogue and ranger returned, taking longer than expected.

Savinhand spoke for the pair. "There were indeed doors, and they were initially hidden. Once located, I managed to neutralize those methods of entry into this chamber."

Sordaak absently nodded his approval, grunted and stood. When no one moved, the mage nodded at the doors.

With a start, Savinhand remembered he had not checked the massive doors as yet. He sighed and moved forward, holding a torch close as he inspected each.

"There should be another corridor beyond these doors, correct?" asked the paladin.

"According to the map," the mage said, "that would be so."

Savinhand nodded as he continued his work. Finding nothing, he stepped back and shrugged as he looked over at the paladin. "No traps, no locks, boss," he said.

"We go through these doors nice and quiet," Thrinndor said.

"After all that noise we made?" Cyrillis was dubious.

The paladin looked over at the cleric and smiled. "I know," he said, "But we must go through the motions." With that he reached down, lifted the latch and pulled the doors open.

It was dark beyond, so Savinhand stepped forward with the torch. There was indeed a corridor on the other side, but it was a short one. The flickering light from the torch easily reached the doors no more than thirty or so feet away. A quick glance showed nothing in between.

Vorgath started to step past the rogue, but Savin reached out an arm to stop him. His instincts were twitching. He *never* ignored his instincts. "Wait," Savinhand said. Vorgath rolled his eyes but didn't try to pass. "Could I get some real light, please?" the thief said without turning away from the passageway ahead.

Sordaak looked past the rogue and decided the passage was too small for the orb wand. He arched an eyebrow and lifted his scepter. The mage waved his hand over globe on top and the gem mounted there began to glow. Not satisfied, the sorcerer waved his hand again and the gem's light surged such that the companions had to look away or shield their eyes.

Sordaak held the new light high over his head.

"Thank you," the rogue said as he dropped into a crouch and began to search in earnest. The companions remained quiet as Savin worked.

The thief began to sweat as his eyes continued to come up empty. The alarms in the back of his mind did not let up, however, and neither did he. Savinhand switched sides and started over on the right side of the corridor.

Vorgath considered abusing the rogue with some of his usual banter, but a quick glance showed the paladin was imploring him not to do so with a hairy-eye. The barbarian allowed his shoulders to slump as he exhaled noisily. He then crossed his arms on his chest gruffly.

"Ah," Savin said as he stood, reaching for a whip hung on a hook on his left side.

"What?" asked the barbarian.

Savinhand ignored him as he looked up and down the hallway, paying special attention to the ceiling. Abruptly the rogue took two steps back, raised the whip and commanded, "Stay here."

Next Savin took two quick, giant steps and leapt high into the air, sailing down the hallway. His hand shot out, the whip cracked and the end wrapped around a sconce mounted high above the center of hallway. He used his momentum to swing wide, his feet never touching the floor.

Savinhand released the handle of his whip as he arced toward the far doors. He then landed lightly on the balls of his feet and whirled his arms to keep from falling back.

Savin caught his balance and stepped forward. The companions heard a sigh of relief as the rogue again bent to inspect the walls. "Hold the light a little higher, please," Savin said. Sordaak transferred the scepter to his left hand and obediently raised it back to full height.

A few minutes later, the rogue again switched sides of the corridor and repeated his search. "There you are," Savinhand whispered as he again reached for his tool pouch. His fingers probed the stone around the particular stone he had identified as a target.

Finding what he was looking for, he pressed softly on the edge of that stone. It gave slightly, and when he backed off on the pressure, that stone slide out and away from the wall. "Hello," he said softly as he studied the mechanism.

Presently he removed his trap tool pouch from his belt, unrolled it on the floor in front of him, selected a couple of tools and went to work on the springs and wire he had discovered in the box. A few minutes later there was a distinct '*click*' as the latching mechanism slipped in to place.

"Gotcha!" Savinhand announced as he stood. He waved to his companions. "It's safe to cross now," he said.

Vorgath groaned as he stood, grabbed his backpack, slung it over a shoulder and picked up *Flinthgoor*. "About damn time," he grumped.

The others stood from where they had been resting and crossed the open space between them and the rogue.

"What kind of trap?" Breunne asked as he stopped to stand beside Savinhand.

The rogue pointed back the way they had come. "That whole section of floor was set to open in the middle, dropping whoever was on it into whatever awaits below." He smiled. "I'm fairly certain it wouldn't have been pleasant."

The ranger raised an eyebrow. "I'm fairly certain you are correct."

"Have you checked those doors for traps?" Thrinndor asked.

Savin turned and eyed the doors a few short feet away. "No," he said. "A thief's work is never done."

"Rogue," Cyrillis said with a smile.

Savin looked over at her. "Indeed." He returned her smile.

The doors were identical to the ones they had just come through: Massive wood structures, strapped with bands of iron and a simple iron latching mechanism.

Savinhand began his search on the left door. His senses picked nothing up, but they weren't fool-proof. He *always* trusted those senses when they were alarming, but when they were silent, he trusted them less. He found no traps on the left door and moved over to the right.

Finding nothing of concern there either, he turned his attention to the mechanism. Still nothing. He stepped back and scratched his head. "I find no traps," he said staring at the doors, "and they do not even appear to be locked." He shook his head.

With a sigh, Sordaak stepped forward, handed his make-shift flameless torch to the thief and stretched his palm toward the door. He closed his eyes and moved his hand slowly until both doors had been covered. When he opened his eyes, he peered closely at the wood. He motioned for the rogue to move the light further back so he could see any glow that might be there. The light gone, he again looked the doors over. Nothing! Not even a trace.

"I agree," the sorcerer said. "No traps, no magic and no lock. Strange." He stroked the hairs on his chin.

"Agreed," said the rogue as he stepped back in. "Thus far the doors have been not only trapped, but locked. These are neither."

"Perhaps a dragon is deterrent enough," offered the paladin.

Sordaak turned and slowly his eyes focused on the big fighter. "But the dragon was not here a month ago," the mage said.

"True," Thrinndor said with a shrug. "It must then be surmised that he does not fear whatever might come through that door."

"Or *he* is not behind that door," Breunne said evenly.

Sordaak arched an eyebrow. "Both possibilities," he said. "We won't know until we go through, will we?"

Vorgath raised *Flinthgoor* to the ready position as Thrinndor shrugged again and reached for the latch.

"Wait," Sordaak said.

"Now what?" the barbarian said as he lowered his axe.

"I would like to ensure everyone is aware of their assignments," the mage said, his eyes not leaving the glowering ones of the dwarf.

"Get on with it then," Vorgath said, also not backing down.

Sordaak turned and put his back to the door, facing his companions. He took in a deep breath. "You both," he indicated the barbarian and the paladin, "will open the doors wide and will then step aside. I will launch two or three orbs of light as I move quickly into the chamber—hopefully at that point illuminated. I have several spells, scrolls and wands I'm going to unleash on his boney ass as fast as I can release them, all while I'm moving."

The sorcerer looked over at the paladin. "I plan to step to the right once I am inside to draw any area of effect spells away from you guys. Once I have his undivided attention—and I will get it—then the four of you," Sordaak said waving an arm indicating the four fighter types, "will rush him, surround him and beat the non-living shit out of him." He eyed the barbarian. "Got it?"

"Beat the non-living shit outta him," Vorgath said. "Got it."

Sordaak nodded as he turned his attention to the cleric. "Your job is to keep my narrow ass alive," he said solemnly. "And if you see any additional spooks, bone-bags or any other characters of the less-than-living variety, use that turning power of yours to make them go away." The mage started to turn. "But, most important, you *must* keep me alive and casting spells for the duration." His eyes bored into hers. "If I go down, the meat-shields don't have a chance." He smiled. "Understood?"

Cyrillis returned the smile wanly, not trusting herself to speak. She didn't like this plan, but knew there would be no changing his mind, now.

"Lastly," Sordaak said to her, "Do you have the spell prepared that will ensure I don't get held and the one that gives me true sight, in case he does that blindness or darkness thing again?"

Cyrillis thought for a moment, not exactly sure what spell he had in mind, but she had more than one that should do the trick in both cases. "Yes," she said.

"Very good," the mage said. "If you have adequate spell energy, pass both those spells around to all—including yourself. He might get the bright idea that taking you out of the picture would allow him to have his way with us." He again started to turn and stopped. "Any of those group blessing spells and aids you have, please do those as well."

"We call those 'buffs,'" Cyrillis said with a smile.

Sordaak raised any eyebrow. "Good to know," he said as he finally turned to look at the paladin, who nodded. "Very well, buff away!"

Cyrillis cast the individual spells first and then the group buffs, as those spells had a shorter duration.

Complete, Sordaak took his scepter back from the rogue and added another layer of light to the gem, making it almost impossible to look at.

"Now," he said evenly as he readied a wand and set his jaw.

Thrinndor lifted the latch and both he and the barbarian kicked their respective doors open and stepped aside. Sordaak launched an orb up where he figured the ceiling might be just as several explosions rocked the air around him.

Fireballs! More than one—at least four, maybe five!

Sordaak was knocked back, but Thrinndor and Vorgath held their positions. Instantly he felt the healing power of one of the cleric's spells reduce the pain and that allowed the mage to follow through with his plan. He raised the wand again and released two more of the orbs, cast the wand aside and walked quickly into the chamber. In the blink of an eye, the wand was replaced in his free hand by a scroll, which the mage unrolled with the flick of his wrist. Even as his eyes went to the words written on the parchment, he pointed his scepter at the only moving figure in the room and released a fireball of his own.

The words on the page dissolved into puffs of smoke as Sordaak read them. Complete, he shouted the command word and several orbs shot forth from the end of the scepter, still pointed at the moving figure.

Sordaak heard laughter. "Fireballs? Really? You think to hurt me with so mundane—aaaghhh!" the figure screamed as the first of the new orbs got to him and knocked him to the ground. This orb was followed immediately by three more, all finding their mark, all hammering the Lich Lord into the floor.

Undaunted, Dahjvest leapt to his feet, his raiment in rags and burning in several places. "You impudent scum," the Lich cried as he pointed a finger. But just then a three shaft bolt of lightning cracked through the air and hit his frame square in the chest, knocking him back a couple of steps.

Sordaak was relentless. He held true to his word and released spell after spell, each maximized and enhanced to its fullest potential. A cone of cold was next, followed immediately by a volley of force missiles because they were the quickest spell he could unleash, and then another ball of fire.

The sorcerer, his teeth set against any return spell, stepped after his adversary with every step the Lich fell back. Out of the corner of an eye, he saw Vorgath rush past with his great-axe held high, followed closely by the paladin. There were a couple of other blurs, but Sordaak didn't take time to register them.

Wraiths and maybe a ghost or two flew past his head, but he ignored them. Cyrillis must have been able to hold up her end of the attack, because Sordaak never saw the same one twice.

Cone of cold, force missile, ball of fire, force missile, lightning bolt, force missile, cone of cold, and so on. Seeing the Lich trapped against the back wall, Sordaak dropped a wall of fire right on top of him and blasted Dahjvest with a fireball as he staggered out of the flaming wall.

The Lich Lord screamed in frustration and pain as he fell back into the wall of fire where he dropped to the stone floor and lay still. Thrinndor, Vorgath and Breunne continued to hammer away at the prone figure.

"Stop!" Sordaak shouted as he raced into the melee. With a wave of his hand the wall of fire winked out.

The fighters, breathing hard, looked at the magicuser as if he were daft, but stepped obediently away from the prone figure, barely recognizable as the Lich they had first seen only moments before.

Sordaak knelt at Dahjvest's side and looked into the eye sockets to see if there was any source of animation. At first he saw none, but as he looked deeper, he saw a flicker.

"Dahjvest!" Sordaak shouted. "Come to me!"

"What are you doing?" Thrinndor said, stepping back in, ready to separate the two if necessary.

"Back off," hissed the sorcerer. "Dahjvest," he repeated. "Come to my voice!"

The light in the orbital sockets grew faintly brighter. "Good," Sordaak said. "I have some questions for you."

The Lich's mouth opened slowly on shattered jaw hinges. Sordaak lowered his head so his ear was next to the skinless face. "Go to hell!" Dahjvest whispered with what little strength he could muster.

"Listen to me," shouted the sorcerer as he once again peered into the monster's eyes. "You will tell me what I want to know or I will trap your soul so that you will have to endure this pain *forever!*" Sordaak pulled a scroll from a slot in his tunic.

The lights in the sockets grew momentarily brighter. "You would not dare!"

"Wouldn't I?" Sordaak said evenly as he broke the seal on the scroll tube and removed the rolled up parchment.

"You cannot!" the voice of the Lich was getting stronger.

"I have Dragma's spell books and his treasure of scrolls," Sordaak replied. "I can and I will."

"Noooooo!" Dahjvest screamed with his old ferocity as he tried to rise. Sordaak easily kept him pinned to the floor by a knee in the Lich Lord's chest.

"Yes," the spellcaster said quietly. "Your mind and conscious will forever be bound between life and death. My spells will burn your very soul unto the end of time!"

Dahjvest quit struggling and was silent. "You will not."

Exasperated, but not wanting to show it, Sordaak closed his eyes and summoned Fahlred. The familiar appeared on his master's shoulder as requested and wound his tail loosely around the magicuser's neck. The quasit hissed vehemently when he spotted the Lich.

Dahjvest tried to push back, fear plain in his face. "A quasit? Here?" Disbelief clouded his voice. A voice that was getting stronger.

Concerned, Thrinndor whispered in the mage's ear. "Sordaak, we must finish him before he regains his strength."

Irritated, the mage waved him away.

"Yes," Sordaak replied. "He is my familiar." The Lich said nothing. "Fahlred," the mage said, his eyes narrowing to slits, "reach into his mind and force him to tell me what I want."

"No," Dahjvest said. "You would not."

Sordaak's lips thinned, he nodded and Fahlred began to unwind his tail from around his master's neck. Slowly he began to crawl down the mage's arm. The quasit jumped the last step and perched on the exposed ribcage of the Lich Lord.

"Noooo!" Dahjvest shouted. "Keep him away from me!" He tried to squirm away. Again, the sorcerer was easily able to keep him from moving. "I'll tell you *anything*!"

"I'll bet you will," Sordaak said grimly. "Anything but the truth." He looked at Fahlred, who waited almost eagerly on the chest of the monster. "Fahlred," the mage said, "go ahead. Make him tell me *the truth*!"

The quasit nodded. He then leaned forward and placed both his small hands on the sides of the skull of the once powerful sorcerer.

"Noooooooooooo!" Dahjvest screamed.

"Is this necessary?" Cyrillis asked half-heartedly from where she stood a few feet away. She knew the answer, though.

Sordaak ignored her as Fahlred pressed his hands against the bare bone of the Lich's skull. Slowly but steadily the hands began to sink *through the bone* and into the creature's brain cavity.

"Noooooooooooo!" This time his scream penetrated to the spinal column of each of the companions.

Still the quasit pressed.

Abruptly, the Lich quit struggling and Sordaak feared his familiar had gone too far. But no, the faint light remained in the Lich Lord's eyes.

"Dahjvest," Sordaak said quietly.

"Yes," the Lich said without hesitation.

"Tell me how you brought Theremault here."

"What?" Thrinndor said. "We—"

Sordaak silenced the paladin with a wave of his hand, his eyes never leaving the skinless face of the Lich.

"I came upon him after your sister had beaten him to within inches of death," Dahjvest said calmly. "It was but an easy task to bring him here."

That made sense. Sordaak was testing for truth. "Where is *Pendromar*?"

Dahjvest hesitated, and Sordaak nodded again, this time at his familiar. Fahlred obediently pushed his claws deeper into the brain of the Lich, causing him to scream even louder than before. Sordaak wanted to plug his ears, but dared not move his hands from the monster's shoulders.

"Where is *Pendromar*?" the mage repeated.

"The Minions at Ice Homme have it," the Lich said. His voice was laden with pain but clear for all to hear.

"How did they get it?" Sordaak asked.

"They took it from Theremault four hundred years ago," Dahjvest said.

Sordaak again nodded. He took a deep breath and looked over at the anxious paladin, who hesitated and then returned the nod.

"Where is *Valdaar's Fist*?" Sordaak held his breath.

The Lich tried to shake his head, but Fahlred's claws held his skull tight. "I don't know," Dahjvest whispered.

"You *lie*!" Sordaak shouted. "Fahlred!"

Obediently the elbows and forearms of the quasit flexed slightly and his hands pressed deeper into the skull of the prone Lich.

Dahjvest's neck arched and he screamed with renewed vengeance, hurting the ears of all in the party.

Cyrillis clamped her hands to her ears and turned away. It required a massive effort on her part not to spill the contents of her stomach onto the floor. "Stop this!" she shouted.

Sordaak ignored her. "Where is *Valdaar's Fist*?" he asked again.

Dahjvest appeared to struggle from within.

"Where is *Valdaar's Fist*?"

Thrinndor and Sordaak involuntarily leaned forward as the jaws of the Lich began to open. "Bahamut," Dahjvest's voice was barely above a whisper.

"Louder," Sordaak shouted, unsure he had heard correctly. "Where is *Valdaar's Fist?*"

"Baham—" Dahjvest's voice was even weaker before it stopped altogether mid-word.

"What?" Sordaak shouted. But he noticed the lights in the orb-sockets were gone. "Shit!" he screamed, pounding his fists on the breast bones of the Lich. "He's gone!"

"Bahamut?" Thrinndor said as he stood upright, stunned. "The platinum dragon?"

Chapter Twelve

Treasure

Silence held the moment hostage as the companions let the shock of that pronouncement sink in.

Vorgath was the first to speak. "Did I hear someone mention *dragon?*" His smile was as big as Thrinndor had ever seen it.

"*Platinum* dragon," the paladin corrected, his tone solemn. "That is a whole different animal."

"Platinum, shmatinum," the barbarian said with a dismissive wave of his hand.

"You obviously do not understand," Breunne said to the dwarf. "Bahamut is the Lord of all Dragons."

Sordaak too looked suitably grim as he chimed in. "He maintains a court of the twelve most powerful Gold dragons in this the material plane." He looked at the barbarian. "*Each* of those dragons is far superior to either of the two we have already faced in both spell ability and strength."

"*Twelve* dragons?" Vorgath's eyes were literally sparkling with excitement.

"Technically thirteen," Cyrillis said, her eyes mirroring the concern of the smarter companions in the group.

"*Thirteen* dragons?" The dwarf was positively giddy.

"You are not listening, o mental one," Sordaak chided. "We are currently no match for even *one* of those dragons, let alone all of them!"

The barbarian's face slid to a scowl very rapidly. "So," he said pointedly at the paladin, "you're going to give up on the sword, then?"

"I did not say that," Thrinndor said defensively.

"What exactly *are* you saying, then?" Vorgath crossed his arms on his massive chest and waited.

"I…um…" the paladin stammered. Quickly he looked over at the magicuser. "Sordaak," he said, "help me out, here."

"Oh, no," said the mage with a shake of his head. "I'm not getting into this one. You're on your own, pal."

"Thanks," Thrinndor muttered under his breath. He turned back to his old friend. "Look, *if* the sword is in the hands of the Lord of Dragons, then I must have it."

"*We* must have it," Cyrillis corrected.

Thrinndor ignored the interruption. "However," he continued evenly, "I am not given to suicide. Going up against Bahamut and his court is not an option. We must find another way."

It had already been a long day and Sordaak decided he had had enough. "Perhaps we can look into those options once we obtain *Pendromar*. But for now we must keep moving," the mage said. "I'm not sure how long we've been in here, but if my chief engineer is not already at the docks, he soon will be."

"It is mid-afternoon," the dwarf said evenly, his eyes still not leaving those of the paladin.

"Ummm." Savinhand clearly wanted everyone's attention. "What about some treasure?" He got blank stares in return. The thief rolled his eyes. "Certainly during the past two millennia Dahjvest collected an item or two that might be worth taking a look at?" At least some of the eyes staring at him blinked. "And maybe some coin?"

That got Vorgath's attention. "Of course he would," the barbarian was excited again. He looked around quickly, but the mage's light orbs were just about spent and he couldn't even see the walls of the chamber they were in.

Sordaak noticed the dwarf's distress, walked over and picked up the previously discarded wand and fired off another orb, this one straight overhead.

Immediately the chamber lit up such that they could see all around. The chamber was again large, but not quite as big as the previous version; Maybe sixty feet across. The companions stood roughly in its center.

To the left of the doors they had come through Sordaak saw several sets of bookshelves, forming a small library or study. Just past that was a bed-chamber. Did a Lich require sleep? Sordaak couldn't answer that and made a mental note to look it up when he again had time. Someday...

Opposite the doors was another smaller set of doors, these ornately carved and covered in runes. No small amount of metal was used in the doors' construction, he noted. Looked like gold.

The side of the chamber opposite the sleeping area seemed to be given over to a workshop of sorts. A *Lich's* workshop. There were baskets and bins filled with various body parts and several tables, some with partially constructed human forms on them. It was a Zombie manufacturing shop.

Seeing this, Cyrillis quickly looked away.

Sordaak decided there must be some sort of ventilation, because the smell was nowhere near as bad as expected.

Without being asked, Savinhand walked over to the doors and began to inspect them.

Cyrillis turned her attention to assessing the party's health and was pleasantly surprised to note that none of her companions was significantly injured. Sordaak was low on spell energy, but rest would cure that. Since her ability to restore some of his energy and turning undead were tied together in that they used the same energy from her, and since she had been abusing the undead at every juncture, she was down to one use remaining. She decided to hold on to that one in the event it was needed.

The few minor scratches and bruises she noted were mostly from previous encounters and did not require her attention. Which was just as well, as she was also dangerously low on spell energy. A rest period would certainly be welcome.

Cyrillis sighed as she sensed it was not to be and followed the magicuser over to watch Savinhand in action.

The rogue whistled. "Wow," he said. "This is going to take a while." He turned to look at the mage.

Sordaak raised an eyebrow but said nothing.

"I see at least three traps," Savin said, "and possibly a fourth. That does not include any of the magical variety, either." He shook his head. "Whoever did these was pretty good, too."

Sordaak nodded as he sat down and put his face in his hands. The battle with Dahjvest had taken more out of him than he had realized. He pulled back and looked at his hands, noting they were trembling. *Damn*, the mage cursed idly, *I don't remember most of what happened.* A weakness washed over him, and he put his face back in his hands.

Cyrillis looked over at the sorcerer with concern. Knowing she could do nothing for him made her chew her lip in frustration.

Several minutes later, Savinhand stepped back from the doors and said, "Ta-da!" When no one said anything, he turned to see what was going on. Seeing the supine caster, the thief looked over at the healer. "Is he OK?"

Cyrillis nodded, and Sordaak answered without looking up. "Yes, I'll be fine. I'm going to need to rest soon, however." The mage groaned as he pushed himself unsteadily to his feet.

The cleric stepped over to help him up, but Sordaak brushed her hands aside and scowled at her. "I can do this," he said.

Frustrated at her inability to help, Cyrillis turned away and missed the apologetic glance the magicuser gave her.

"I've disarmed all the traps that are non-magical in nature," the rogue said. "I was even able to remove some of that explosive powder you showed me back in Dragma's Keep."

"Bat shit." Sordaak tried to smile, but it came off more as a grimace.

"Right," said the rogue with a smile. "I found a total of four traps, but there could be more."

"I'll check," said the mage as he removed a wand and squared his shoulders. He pointed the crooked stick at the doors and said the trigger word. A blast of flames shot from the wand, surprising everyone, including Sordaak.

The sorcerer took a quick step back and looked closer at the wand in his hand. "Damn!" he spat. "I *must* be tired!" He put the wand back in its place in his robes and removed another. This time he made a great show of checking the wand first. "Who woulda thought the word of activation would be the same for both?" he asked sheepishly as he repeated the word. This time the correct spray of glittering dust came out of the wand.

Sordaak moved closer to the doors to inspect the result, idly brushing away the soot his flames had left behind. Muttering under his breath, he noted that there was indeed one more trap. "What the—"

When he didn't say anything else, Savinhand moved in to look over the mage's shoulder. "What?"

Sordaak hadn't heard him move up and was startled slightly at the sound of his voice. "I told you not to do that!" the sorcerer hissed.

"Sorry." Savin stifled a smile.

Turning back to the door, Sordaak said, "There is another trap here, but it is not a spell I recognize. I'm not sure if I can remove it."

"Can't you just do that dispel thing to make it go away?" the thief asked.

"Yes and no," Sordaak answered. Savinhand's right eyebrow headed north. "I'm sure you know this already, but I'll explain for the benefit of the uninitiated back there," he jerked a thumb to where the companions waited.

"Today!" Vorgath griped.

"There are two types of magical traps," the mage continued. "First, there is the type that a sorcerer or wizard places on a portal more to keep it closed, or at least, others from passing though. We've come across a few of those." Savinhand nodded. "My dispel spell can usually make those go away."

Sordaak paused while he considered what to say next. "The second type is the one you described earlier—spell components left behind in such a manner that if the door/portal is opened or possibly even disturbed, the spell will go off. Which in this case is probably a fireball. The dispel spell is less successful in removing that type of trap."

Again the thief nodded and wondered where this was headed.

"There are some items here that show up as magical in nature," Sordaak continued, "and they are probably components to a spell—or spells—but I don't have a clue as to what they are or what spell will be triggered by their disturbance. We must assume that since I don't know the components that it is a powerful spell." The mage went silent as he pondered the situation and studied the components.

Abruptly the mage looked over at the rogue. "Are they locked?"

"Yes," replied the thief. "I didn't want to disturb anything that might be lurking there by attempting to unlock them."

Sordaak looked back at the doors. "I believe you have sufficient clearance to unlock them." He pointed to a spot in the middle of the door on the left. "Just don't get anywhere near that point."

Savinhand studied the point in question. Seeing nothing, he shrugged, removed his tool pouch and went to work on the locks. He had trusted the eccentric magic-user many times to this point, and there was no reason to stop now.

There was an audible *click* and then the rogue stepped back with a satisfied smile.

Sordaak nodded. "Now I think we'll have to figure out a way to open the doors from a safe distance."

It was Savinhand's turn to nod, and he had just begun to look for a solution when the barbarian got to his feet.

"Oh, for crying out loud!" Vorgath said as he stomped toward the doors.

As the dwarf's meaty hand reached for the opening mechanism, Sordaak said, "I wouldn't do that," as he took a quick step back. Savin stepped back, too.

Vorgath didn't even look back as he lifted the mechanism and pulled on the door. It opened easily. The barbarian turned to flash a knowing smile at the mage and rogue, but then his eyes went wide and rolled back in his head as he slumped to the ground.

"Vorgath!" Cyrillis shouted as she rushed to the barbarian's side and knelt there. He had hit the floor awkwardly and the healer had to roll the dwarf over onto his back. She put her face down next to his. "He is not breathing!"

"That's because he's dead," Sordaak said matter-of-factly.

The cleric turned to scowl at the mage as the paladin walked up. "How is it you know this?" Thrinndor asked.

"Because I finally remember what spell components those were, and I believe Vorgath was hit by a powerful spell we sorcs call 'Finger of Death.'"

"Shit!" Cyrillis spat. "Help me get his breast plate off."

Savinhand quickly knelt and in a matter of seconds had the buckles undone and together he and the cleric lifted it clear of the dwarf. He tossed it aside where it clattered noisily to the stone floor a few feet away.

"Can you revive him?" the paladin asked, suddenly worried.

The cleric shook her head. "That requires a lot of energy, and keeping Sordaak and you guys alive was taxing." She looked back down to the prone barbarian. "I do not have enough energy!" Her voice was a wail.

"What about the pneumonic potions you always carry?" Sordaak asked.

Cyrillis turned to stare at the mage, her face contorted in confusion. Her eyes widened in surprise. "I do not know," she said. "There *may* be one left." Quickly she slung the pack off her back and dumped the contents unceremoniously onto the dwarf's chest.

The healer began to sort through them when she picked one up. "Where did that come from?" she asked. Quickly she tore the foil seal off of the vial, pressed it to her lips and emptied the contents into her mouth. She closed her eyes to steady herself. The potion had been considerably more potent than those she normally purchased.

Opening her eyes, she swept the remaining potions off of the dwarf's chest, placed both her hands on his chest and closed her eyes to pray. Suddenly Cyrillis' eyes flipped open and she pressed on the prone barbarian with her hands and released the spell energy.

Vorgath's back arched and his eyes were suddenly wide open as his lungs noisily drew air into his oxygen-starved body.

Cyrillis, her hand still on the barbarian's chest, pressed him back to the floor and poured her most potent healing spell into him. She knew the Raise Dead spell she had just used would only bring Vorgath back from death, leaving them precariously on the brink of the afterlife.

The dwarf's countenance eased and he tried to sit up. The cleric refused him. "Remain as you are for a few minutes until we are certain your heart beats true," she said.

Vorgath did as commanded, but he opened his mouth to speak. "I was with Kreithgaar." His voice held both reverence and amazement.

"Valdaar's General of the Armies?" Thrinndor asked.

The barbarian nodded. "Yes," he said, "he congratulated me on finding *Flinthgoor.*" His eyes were moist with remembrance.

Thrinndor walked over and extended his hand to aid the dwarf in regaining his feet. Vorgath looked questioningly at the healer. Cyrillis hesitated and then nodded. The barbarian grasped the paladin's hand and together they eased the dwarf to his feet.

Once upright, the paladin wrapped both arms around his friend and refused to let him go. Vorgath initially held back, and then too wrapped his arms around the paladin and returned the embrace.

After a moment of this, Vorgath pushed away and stood looking around belligerently, daring anyone to say anything. None did. The barbarian spotted his armor a short distance away, retrieved it and buckled it back into place.

Once that was complete, Cyrillis put a hand on the dwarf's shoulder and turned him so that she could look into his eyes. At first Vorgath avoided her gaze, but the cleric was persistent until he had no choice but to meet her eyes.

"You are a fool," she said. And then she turned to walk away.

"It was all part of the plan," Vorgath smiled as he held her eyes, refusing to let her turn away. He shrugged easily. "You said that death was the only way to get rid of that age curse I was under." His smile broadened. "I feel *much* better now!"

"You could have *died!*" she said, her tone soft.

"I *did* die." Vorgath's tone matched hers as the smile left his face. "And you, our most magnanimous healer, brought me back." Again his eyes were moist as he continued. "Thank you." He reached out with both arms and wrapped them around the cleric in a heartfelt embrace.

Cyrillis fought him at first, and then gave in and returned the hug.

When she pushed back her eyes again found his. "Do not do that again!" her voice was stern.

"Yes ma'am," the dwarf said, nodding his head. "I'm cured of the find the traps the hard way thing." He smiled. "Damn wizards are getting too powerful for that shit anymore!" He released the healer and turned back to the paladin.

"While you're giving out hugs," Sordaak said wryly, "can I get one?" He put his arms out and wiggled his fingers enticingly.

The barbarian slapped the caster's hand away and released a string of curses that would have the most hardened sailor blushing.

Sordaak smiled. "Yup," he said. "Meat shield number one feels better!"

Everyone broke into a bout of laughter, effectively washing away the stress that had built up throughout the day.

When the mirth died down, Vorgath looked back at his friend, "Can we get on with finding out what the old bone-bag left us?"

"Show some respect!" Sordaak said sternly. "*Mister* old bone-bag lived— sort of—for nearly two thousand years!" The mage walked over and kicked the remains of the Lich in the head. "He's earned some respect!" The mage then reached down and slid a ring off of the decrepit skeleton. He also retrieved an interesting-looking amulet from his neck. Lastly, he took a crown from Dahjvest's head he hadn't noticed before and put it on his own head.

Sordaak felt a surge of energy and almost yanked the crown back off. Almost. The surge of energy felt...*good!* He was not sure just what effects the crown had, but they were not harmful. Immediately the crown went invisible again. *Interesting.*

"Whatever," said the barbarian. "If you're done looting *mister* bone-bag, maybe we could see what else he has left for us?"

"But of course," Sordaak said formally as he rejoined the group.

"I'll go through first," Savinhand said, "if you don't mind. It will allow me to use my trap sense to see if anything else lurks."

"You've got my blessing," Vorgath said as he swept an arm formally toward the doors, the right one of which remained ajar.

Savinhand smiled as he stepped to the door. Seeing that it was dark inside, he asked for and received the mage's scepter, the gem on which still shone brightly.

Sensing no traps, he stuck his head and his makeshift lantern through the opening between the doors. He let out a long, low whistle. "Wow," he repeated as he pushed the door open wider.

"What?" asked the barbarian, avarice retaking control over his demeanor.

"*Mister* bone-bag has indeed been busy collecting stuff over the last two millennia," Savin said as he stepped into the room.

Vorgath followed immediately, only because he couldn't figure out a way to push his way past the thief without being overly rude—not that that would normally stop him. But given recent events, he thought it prudent to not push…

Yet. If that skinny rogue didn't get a move on, he was making no guarantees. Or apologies.

The chamber was much smaller, oblong in shape and maybe fifteen feet by twenty feet. There was a gilded throne toward the back away from the doors— that was the only piece of furniture in the place. Everywhere one looked the floor was littered with coins, gems and pieces of jewelry. There was an occasional weapon interspersed with some pieces of armor and a couple of shields. There were even some opulent robes and other garments hanging from the regularly spaced sconces along the walls.

Deciding it would be prudent to be able to see what one needed to, Savin made his way to the first sconce and after a little work with his flint and stone, lit it. He removed the sconce from the holder mounted to the wall and walked around the chamber, lighting the rest of them.

"Thank you," Cyrillis said absently as he passed her. She was preoccupied with one of the robes hanging on the wall.

Once they were all lit, Savinhand began searching through the various items to see if any could be of use. Seeing there were too many to do it one at a time, he elected to collect everything that wasn't an individual gem or coin and take it to the entrance. There he piled the items to be gone through when they had time.

Vorgath was busy raking the coins into piles according to their metal. Gold here, silver there, platinum next to him. What little copper he found was mostly kicked aside.

Sordaak joined Cyrillis and together they looked over the robes, cloaks and other garments, each hoping to find one that could replace the battle-worn items they currently wore.

Thrinndor's mind wandered as he helped Savin gather the artifacts of interest. He finally knew where to look for his god's blade, but getting it was certainly not going to be easy—maybe not even possible.

There were a couple of swords that interested him, but he wanted to ensure everyone had a fair chance at what loot there was. And he wanted to be sure if an item was of use that the correct person got it for the maximum aid of the party.

In the past—with other groups—that had always been the hard part of being the party leader. Some wanted a particular item just because they knew it was valuable and could be sold for a large amount of coin, not because they could actually use he item. Greed always confounded the paladin.

A few moments later the companions congregated at the pile of artifacts Thrinndor and Savinhand had gathered. It had been determined that the coin would be left behind. Either they would collect it later, or the dwarfs from Clan Dragaar would gather it and take it out to the island. There was little chance of the coin being disturbed while Ardaagh remained for the most part occupied by undead.

One by one the items were scrutinized for their craftsmanship, magical properties and usefulness to individuals in the party. Some items were claimed right away, while others were tossed into the pile of coin to be issued to the armies as they were built. And there *would* be armies, Thrinndor thought idly. Yes, Praxaar must be made to pay.

Chapter Thirteen

Shipwrecked

Wearily the companions gathered near the door. As they stepped back out of the treasure chamber, Savinhand closed the doors and was about to lock them. He looked over at Sordaak for instructions.

Sordaak shrugged and said, "I doubt anyone will come here before the town is cleared of its undead infestation. What remains inside should be safe until my chief engineer can retrieve it and add it to the coin we have on the island already."

"About the remaining undead," Thrinndor said thoughtfully. The companions turned to face him. "Perhaps it is in the best interest of time to leave them for now." That drew a few raised eyebrows. "This is a fairly large town and it would not surprise me to find that more than a few of Dahjvest's minions remain." Now he got some nods. "It could take days or even weeks to clear the town." He looked over at Sordaak. "Not many of the towns buildings will be required for what we have in mind—it might even serve our interests to leave some of the outer buildings 'protected' by their current denizens."

"I like that idea," Sordaak said. "A path will need to be cleared to allow supply wagons and their support staff through, and maybe a few buildings down by the wharves." The mage turned to look at Vorgath. "Maybe we can let the dwarfs of The Silver Hills take care of any that need to be cleared."

Vorgath hesitated and then nodded. "While it has been some time since they've seen action," he said, "I'm sure they can handle a few spooks, skellies and/or whatever undead nasties that need to be returned to the netherworld."

"That's the spirit!" Sordaak said with a grin.

"Ha, ha," Vorgath said. "Very funny."

"I thought you'd like that," the mage said.

"Very well," Thrinndor said, also smiling, "your chief engineer should be at the pier by now. I believe it is time we go meet him."

"Agreed," said Sordaak.

"No rest for the weary," Cyrillis said as she fell into her place in line.

"Lock the doors?" Savinhand asked.

"No," Sordaak said, "Clan Dragaar might not have a locksmith capable of opening them."

Vorgath raised *Flinthgoor* and said, "Locksmith not required!"

Sordaak smiled and said, "Yes, but these doors might still serve a purpose at some future point."

The dwarf returned the smile and said no more. Savinhand shrugged, shook his head and put away his tools.

As they emerged into the street, the companions noted it had begun to rain. Not hard, but a cold, steady and soaking rain. Each grumbled as they pulled rain gear from their packs.

Once the over-clothes were donned, Thrinndor led the party back down the road to where they had seen the bridge. Once at the foot of the dilapidated structure he stopped and surveyed the situation. The bridge spanned the narrowest point of the waterway, but was still at least three or four hundred feet in length, and more than twenty feet above the water at its highest point.

What remained of the bridge was not in good shape, except for the stone ramparts—those seemed to have withstood the tests of time. The wooden structure, however, showed its age. The center span sagged badly and entire sections of boards were either rotten or missing altogether.

"You said there is no other way across?" Breunne asked as he tested the first set of boards with his weight. The ancient wood protested loudly, but held.

"There is," replied the spell-caster as he looked off into the distance to the north. "But it is several miles walk to get around this waterway." He looked at the relic of a bridge and spat a curse as his eyes fell upon the sagging center section.

"Wait," Cyrillis said, "could not your chief engineer bring his ship in to one of these piers? Why should we have to cross this, this *bridge*?"

"You know," Sordaak said, "that's a good point." He looked up and down the waterfront. It was obvious there were not any ships tied up, nearby. "However, I don't see anything—or anyone—here." He looked at the sun, which had settled toward the horizon. It was now early evening, and it would be dark within an hour. "They must have tied up on one of the outer piers."

"Agreed," Thrinndor said. "Very well, we will have to cross." He eyed the bridge dubiously. "We will spread out so as not to put too much weight on any one section and we will bind ourselves to one another."

The paladin looked over at Savinhand, who pulled a length of rope from his waist and shook it clear of tangles. The ranger did the same and in short order the companions were tied together with about fifteen feet between each of them.

Savin stepped up onto the first board, which again groaned. "I'll go first," he said as he started walking slowly up the span toward the first stanchion. "Watch where I step," he said as he tested his weight on each board before proceeding, "and step only where I do."

His next step broke through, but he caught himself on the rope rail.

"I'll not step there," the barbarian said from the back of the line.

Savinhand ignored the quip as he focused on finding a safe place to put his feet. He quickly discovered that the lighter-colored wood was rotten and would not hold his weight. The darker color was usually dark because it was wet, which meant it was retaining water because it was also rotten.

Seeking the more dense wood became easier as the rogue adjusted to this information, and he picked his way carefully. Savin heard Vorgath curse loudly as he broke through on more than one occasion. His bulk combined with his armor and weapon cache made him heavier than any of his companions.

Thus it was almost dark when the party finally set foot on solid ground on the other side. Vorgath had fallen through four times, and Thrinndor had threatened to cut him loose if he did so again. The barbarian's response involved behavior deemed generally unacceptable involving one's own family members.

"I don't like this," Sordaak said as he untied himself and the companions did likewise. There was no sign of his chief engineer. Actually, there was no sign of *anyone*. "My men should have been here by now."

"Nor do I," agreed the paladin. "Perhaps they have tied up on the outer banks."

The spell-caster looked at the paladin absently and nodded. "Perhaps…"

Without waiting for further discussion, Thrinndor chose an alleyway between buildings—mostly warehouses, from the look of them—and set out toward what should be the outer piers.

Without incident the party made it to one of these piers. There was no one waiting for them there, either.

"This is not good," Sordaak said unnecessarily when the paladin looked at him with a raised brow. The mage summoned Fahlred, who appeared on the sorcerer's shoulder, the two communicated briefly and then the quasit disappeared.

"What now?" Vorgath demanded.

"Now we wait," the mage said, his eyes trying in vain to see across the distance to the island. He brushed some debris from the edge of the pier on which they had walked out on and sat down, his leg's dangling.

Sordaak closed his eyes and tried to communicate with Fahlred. It was no good—the distance was too great. So the mage sat and waited, his eyes closed.

The others milled about, some checking out nearby buildings and others sitting near the mage.

After a few minutes, Fahlred again appeared on his master's shoulder. He was clearly agitated as the two spoke without words.

"Shit!" Sordaak spat as he got to his feet. Cyrillis and Thrinndor did the same.

"What is it?" the paladin asked.

The sorcerer looked up into the dark pools that hid the big fighter's eyes in the growing darkness. "They are not there, either," Sordaak said, his lips a grim line on his face.

"Who are not where?" Vorgath asked as he walked up on the three.

Without turning to acknowledge the barbarian, the mage said, "My chief engineer and his crew are not in their chambers. In fact, it appears the entire island compound is deserted." Sordaak scratched his head idly as he thought. "There are no bodies, no sign of a struggle—nothing!"

"So, where are they then?" Cyrillis asked.

"I don't know," Sordaak groaned. "They are all under a tight schedule and the crews should either be working at the construction site, or sleeping in their quarters." The mage turned to look into the eyes of his familiar, and the quasit winked out.

"Where did you send him this time?" Thrinndor asked.

"To investigate," Sordaak answered. "Discreetly." He looked around the pier. The remaining companions had walked up, and now their party was complete. "I suggest we look around to see if we can find a boat—some sort of transportation out to the island."

"You can't just teleport us out there?" Savinhand asked.

"No," Sordaak shook his head. "I don't have near enough spell energy left for that."

"But," Vorgath protested, "Cyrillis has—"

"What happens if I get there and they are waiting for me?" Sordaak said sternly. "I am in no condition to defend myself."

"Sordaak is correct," Thrinndor said, coming to the aid of the caster as the barbarian took in another breath to protest. "Perhaps his engineer is just late. We must wait for them here." Cyrillis and Breunne nodded. "Perhaps we can settle in for the night and maybe get some rest in the event a battle is what awaits us."

Sordaak nodded and silently thanked the paladin for the backup. "Did any of you happen to find a boat?" he asked, his eyes shifting to Breunne.

"I didn't," responded the ranger.

"Me either," Vorgath said with a shrug. "But I wasn't looking for one."

Savinhand was silent, his eyes showing he was uncomfortable with his answer. "I found a *very* old boat," he said finally. "It's inside that boat house there." He turned and pointed at some rotting, closed doors that extended over a finger of the water that ran next to the pier they stood on.

"*In the water?*" Cyrillis asked.

"No," Savin said. "The boat was lifted from the water long ago and is suspended by a series of ropes and planks."

"What kind of shape is it in?" Breunne asked.

The rogue shrugged. "It was not something I was looking to check," he said. "But that's beside the point." Sordaak raised an eyebrow. "Just a moment ago you said that we couldn't go to the island in the shape we are in." The mage blinked at the thief but said nothing. "Why would going out there on a boat be any different?"

"Ah," the mage said, understanding finally the rogue's hesitation. "You are, of course, correct. However, as it is more than twenty miles out to the island, the trip would take three or four hours to make." The rogue blinked twice but said nothing. "If Cyrillis and I could be allowed to rest during that time while you non-wiggle-finger types took turn on the sails and/or oars, *we* might get there somewhat refreshed."

Vorgath answered testily. "By '*we*' you mean, of course, you wiggle-finger types?"

"Of course," Sordaak said, smiling into the darkness.

Vorgath blinked twice and then turned and stomped away, grumbling as he went.

"My," Cyrillis said, stifling a smile, "I believe our barbarian is a bit grouchy."

"Damn straight," Vorgath said as he jumped off the wooden pier onto the old boardwalk that ran perpendicular to it and the others that lined the waterfront.

"I think we should take a look at this boat," Sordaak said as he turned and followed the dwarf.

Thrinndor looked over at Breunne, who shrugged and followed the magicuser. The three of them followed together with Cyrillis bringing up the rear.

Savin hurried to get ahead of the barbarian, pulling a bulls-eye lantern from his pack as he went. He lit it from the torch the paladin carried. He still got to the door first—mostly because Vorgath waited for him there with folded arms. He didn't have a torch.

Savinhand pushed the door open with his left hand and went inside, the dwarf close behind him. "Watch the steps," the rogue said as he started up the three steps that led to a large platform running the full length inside of the building.

Spotting torch holders placed irregularly along the wall, Savin pulled two torches from his pack, removed the protective wrapping, lit them from his lantern and placed them in the holders.

Vorgath saw that the platform continued along the back of the building, and he quickly made his way there and crossed to the other side. Another platform waited for him there, as well. He placed his torch in one of the holders on that side, removed two more from his pack and lit them from the one he had put on the wall. Then he walked down to the next holder and deposited one of those there.

As the room lit up from the light of the torches, the barbarian walked over to check out the craft, with Savinhand and Breunne doing the same from the other platform. Thrinndor walked around to join with the barbarian, his boots ringing noisily on the old wood of the platform.

"You want to go *how far* in this wreck?" Vorgath asked as he got his first up-close look.

"No more than twenty-five or thirty miles," Sordaak said from his place on the platform, where he was talking quietly with the cleric. He was trying to find out from the healer how long it would take for her to regain some portion of her spell power.

"Four hours of prayer, meditation and some rest," Cyrillis answered. "I believe I can provide adequate coverage for a small battle with that." She wrinkled her brow. "Eight hours would be preferred, however."

Sordaak sighed heavily. "I hear you," the caster said. "Four hours should do it for me, as well."

The mage walked over to stand next to the ranger. "Well," Sordaak said as he assessed the boat with a dubious eye, knowing he had no idea what he was looking at, "will she get us there?"

"If you mean by 'she' this collection of rotting planks and decrepit rigging," Breunne reached up and pulled on a rope and it snapped easily in a small cloud of dust, "no."

"Aw," said the caster as he leapt over the gunwale and landed lightly on his feet on the cross-plank obviously used as a seat, "why such a purveyor of gloom and doom?"

The ranger stopped, turned and glared at the caster. "Because this relic of sailing long past has not been in the water for at least a thousand years! Probably more," he said wryly. "When a boat is removed from the water, the wood tends to shrink up, leaving cracks at the seams," the ranger explained patiently. "It is doubtful this boat would even float, let alone sail." He looked around furtively. Spotting what he was looking for, he went to a hinged box in the bow and opened it. Reaching inside he lifted out what had been the once white sheet of a sail. The dry, rotten material turned to dust as he tried to lift it clear. The ranger raised an eyebrow as he turned to look back at the mage.

Sordaak blinked twice. "Where's your sense of adventure?" the sorcerer said as he leaned over and picked up one end of an old oar. There were several others next to in the storage rack nearby.

"Let me get this straight," Vorgath said. "You want the four of us to *row* you thirty miles out to this island of yours while you *sleep?*"

Sordaak made a show of placing his hand on his chin and looking up toward the ceiling in thought. Finally, the mage looked back down and focused on the barbarian. "Rest, he corrected with a smile. "And yep, that pretty much sums it up."

Vorgath turned and looked at the paladin. "You know," he said, "I was starting to like that skinny little shit." He shook his head distraughtly. "And then he goes and pulls something like this."

Thrinndor looked over at his longtime friend. "He is right, you know," the paladin said, amusement in his eyes.

Vorgath looked at his friend belligerently. Finally he said, "Yes, I know," griped the barbarian. "But that don't mean I gotta like it!"

Thrinndor tried to hide his smile as he turned to look at the rope-and-pulley system that was used to lift the boat out of the water. He tested the thick ropes, and unlike the rigging on the boat itself, these seemed to be in pretty good shape.

"All right spell-slinger," the paladin said, "please get your skinny butt off of the boat so we can lower it into the water." He leveled a "move it" glare at the mage.

Sordaak obediently stood and climbed back out of the boat.

After figuring out how the lifting system worked, Thrinndor got the fighter-types at the four ropes required to lift the vessel. Sordaak and Cyrillis had instructions to remove the support boards once the boat was off of them.

"Ready?" the party leader asked as he set his feet. "Take up slack," Thrinndor ordered as he pulled on his rope until it got tight. The others did the same. "On my mark: One, two, *three!*" he said as he heaved on his line.

The joists over their heads groaned as they absorbed the weight of the small vessel, and the pulleys squealed as wheels turned that hadn't moved in many centuries.

Ever so slightly the boat moved. The wood planks underneath flexed such that the vessel stayed in contact with the hull of the boat.

"One, two, *three!*" Thrinndor repeated. Again the men heaved, and again the beams overhead creaked and the pulleys complained. The boat raised another inch, still maintaining contact with the planks.

Sordaak and Cyrillis attacked the planks anyway, to no avail. They were unable to budge them.

"One more time," the paladin said. "One, two, *three!*"

Again the men hauled on their respective ropes. The beams overhead complained some more, but this time they sounded different. Then Thrinndor heard the old wood begin to splinter.

"Get out!" the paladin shouted.

Sordaak hesitated, not sure what the screaming was about. Then he heard it, too. A quick glance underneath showed the cleric bent over, still beneath the boat, furtively trying to slide a support beam off of the side rails. "Cyrillis!" She looked up, a question on her lips. "*Get back!*" the mage screamed.

The look on her face showed she was confused and not sure why the mage was yelling at her. He heard the paladin yell one more time to release the ropes and get clear. Cyrillis looked around and started to move, but Sordaak knew somehow she was not moving fast enough.

In one move the sorcerer brought his right hand up, palm outward. Next he shouted the words to his spell and watched as the cleric was knocked backward by the force of his magiks. Sordaak saw the pained expression on her face as she slammed in to the wall.

It was the last thing he saw before everything went black. Sordaak vaguely remembered hearing her scream his name, but her voice was mostly drowned out by splintering crash as the ceiling beams gave way, bringing the roof down in a thunderous roar.

Released by the four fighters, the boat landed heavily back onto the support beams. Then when the added weight of the roof landed on the vessel, the support beams splintered, sending the whole mess cascading into the water, where it landed with tremendous splash, sending water up and over the platforms, drenching the companions where they lay next to the base of the wall.

Fortunately the wave of water put out the torches, or the companions would have had to deal with a rapidly moving fire as the ancient wood would have caught and burned quickly.

"Head count!" Thrinndor shouted into the eerie silence that followed. The darkness was almost absolute.

"Vorgath," the barbarian called from somewhere to the paladin's left.

"Breunne," the ranger called from across the platform.

"Savinhand." The thief's voice was weak, and there was pain in it.

"Cyrillis," the cleric said weakly from the wall where she had been knocked to, pain also apparent in her voice.

Silence.

"Sordaak?" The paladin asked into the inky blackness as he stood, coughing when his lungs sucked in the centuries of dust that had been on any flat surface. His eyes began to adjust as the light from the clouds above reflected through where the roof had once been.

Silence.

"*SORDAAK!*" Cyrillis shrieked.

Silence.

"*NO!*" Cyrillis howled as she tried to stand. However, waves of pain washed over her from her left ankle, forcing the healer to again sit. A moan of pain escaped her lips as she reached for the ankle only to find it pinned under a massive piece of wood; one of the joists from the ceiling was resting on her lower leg. She could tell with her senses that it was broken, possibly in more places than one.

"Shit!" she cursed in frustration as she realize she was not going to be able to help locate Sordaak. "I need help here," she said as she cursed herself for not getting clear at the first sign, or sound, of trouble.

"Me, too," Savinhand said. His voice was even weaker than before. He knew he was in a bad way with one of the collapsed beams lying across his midsection. Attempts to move it by himself had already caused him to momentarily black out with pain.

"Light!" Thrinndor called. "Give me some light!" He was afraid to move for fear of falling into the water. He knew that once there he would be of no use to anyone.

"Just a minute," Vorgath said from where he had landed prior to the ceiling coming down.

In frustration, Thrinndor almost said that they didn't have a minute, but he bit his tongue instead. Quicker than he thought possible, the barbarian had retrieved a torch from his pack and got it going with his flint and stone kit.

As the now dust-filled boathouse lit up from about twenty feet away, Thrinndor did his best to assess the situation. He was immediately glad he had followed his instincts and stood his ground. The platform immediately in front and to his right had been taken out by a piece of the roof.

"Come to me," Thrinndor said.

"Keep your pants on," the dwarf grumbled. He was already picking his way across fallen beams and missing planks on what had been the floor.

Another light flickered into being as Breunne also managed to get a torch from his pack lit, as well. Thrinndor heard him curse as he found something.

When the light got close enough, the paladin began picking his way back to the wall and then across the parts of the platform that looked safe enough. Fortunately the rear wall and most of the platform remained intact. He sprinted across that expanse of decking until where saw Cyrillis struggling to free her pinned ankle and cursing in frustration.

He got to her side just as Breunne did. They worked together and managed to lift the old wood beam off of her leg.

Thrinndor knelt at her side and began to probe the ankle gently. Cyrillis bit her lip, groaned and shook her head. "Go help Savinhand," she said through clenched teeth. "I will tend to this."

Thrinndor looked at her badly damaged ankle and knew instantly she would have trouble setting the bones herself, but he also knew she would live. His first duty was to find the others.

"And find Sordaak," Cyrillis called after the retreating figures. The paladin nodded without turning.

Vorgath, seeing the ranger and paladin had the cleric's situation under control, began searching for the rogue. "Damn thief," Vorgath spat as he waved the torch furtively trying to find his friend, "always having to save his narrow ass."

"Rogue." The dwarf heard a pain-wracked chuckle from just ahead and to his left. The barbarian looked harder as he got close and saw an arm sticking out from under the splintered end of a ceiling joist. Vorgath held the torch on the other side and immediately saw the thief's plight: Another portion of the same joist was lying across his midriff. He was being crushed beneath it. How the rogue was still conscious, let alone alive, was beyond the dwarf's comprehension.

"I'm going to need some help over here," Vorgath shouted as he jammed the torch he held into a nearby crack, holding it in place. The barbarian, hesitant to apply any additional weight to the beam that lay across his friend, searched for a way around as he heard footsteps approach from behind. Seeing no other way he said, "Sorry pal," and vaulted as lightly as he could over to the other side, but that required some hand pressure on that beam.

He heard a gasp of pain from Savinhand, but Vorgath ignored that as he searched for and found a piece of the beam where he could get a good grip for lifting. "Grab hold over there," he bellowed and pointed as the ranger and paladin came into view.

Breunne stood the torch in the angle between two beams, ensuring it would not fall over nor get too close to any of the dry wood. He then knelt opposite where Thrinndor was already bent over and grasped for a hand-hold.

Thrinndor gave a quick count. "One, two, *three*!"

Together the three groaned and cursed as they strained to lift this much larger piece of the roof. They only managed to raise it a few inches, however. "Breunne, pull him out!" Thrinndor hissed through clenched teeth.

The ranger hesitated; he wanted to ask the paladin if he was sure he had the beam, but realized there was no other way. They were not able to raise it any higher, and clearly a now unconscious Savin was not going to crawl out on his own.

"*Now!*" Thrinndor groaned, sweat running freely down his face in rivulets.

Cautiously, Breunne eased his effort, hearing a gasp escape the lips of the big fighter across from him as he fought to maintain the height they had gained. Seeing the paladin was going to hold, he quickly dropped to his knees, grasped the shoulders of the prone rogue and dragged him clear of the beam.

"Clear," Breunne said. "Release at the same time. *Now!*"

At the command, Vorgath and Thrinndor released the beam and it crashed to the decking of the platform, sending another cloud of dust into the air that nearly blinded them.

Both men dropped to their knees and gulped in the air, dust-filled or not. Thrinndor struggled to get clear of the dust, knowing his ministrations were needed immediately on the rogue.

The paladin, still wheezing from the effort and coughing at the same time from the bad atmosphere, knelt at Savin's side and reached into him with his health sense. His was not as fine-tuned as a cleric's, but it usually sufficed.

Both lower ribs had snapped and there was some internal organ damage, possibly some laceration of the stomach walls. But it appeared the spinal column was intact. Thank Valdaar, Thrinndor thought as he poured his healing ability into his friend. The paladin couldn't do as the cleric had done and set his rib bones back into place; he had to trust the healing power of his god to strengthen the muscles and return the bones to their correct location.

They did. Knowing he yet had another use of his ability if needed, he checked with his senses again. No, the rogue would live; the bones had indeed knitted back together and his internal organs appeared healed.

Thrinndor said to Vorgath, "Stay with him. Let me know if his condition worsens."

The barbarian nodded his compliance as Breunne and the paladin stood and made their way back over to the cleric, the ranger retrieving his torch on the way.

Cyrillis was not where they had left her!

"Cyrillis!" Thrinndor shouted.

"Here!" The paladin thought he could hear the cleric sobbing as she tried to speak. "Help me!" she pleaded.

Breunne and Thrinndor quickly exchanged glances and ran toward the sound of her voice, ignoring the creaks and groans of the severely damaged platform beneath their feet.

The two got to the edge of the deck but didn't see Cyrillis. "Where are you?" Thrinndor called out, his head on a swivel.

"Down here," Cyrillis said between sobs.

The ranger and the paladin looked down toward the water and could faintly make out her form sitting by the water's edge. A closer look revealed there was a head in her lap.

Sordaak. "He is dead," she cried, her voice a wail in the night air.

Thrinndor jumped down the ten or so feet to the edge of the water, ignoring any danger to himself.

As he stood upright Breunne landed deftly next to him, holding his spluttering torch high so as to illuminate the area.

Quickly the paladin assessed the situation. Sordaak was lying in the cleric's lap, a shard of bloody wood sticking out of his chest. It was obvious the mage had fallen from the platform and impaled himself on a sliver of wood sticking out of the sand next to the water.

"This is my fault!" Cyrillis sobbed. "I do not have enough power to bring him back! And I have lost my potion bag!" She looked down at the prone magicuser. "He is dead because he saved me." Her voice trailed off as a tear fell from her nose onto Sordaak's cheek.

"Find her bag," Thrinndor said to the ranger as he took the two steps necessary to reach the cleric and the mage quickly. Breunne obediently took off as the paladin dropped to his knees beside the two. He roughly pulled the sorcerer from her arms and rolled him over, mindful not to disturb the sliver of wood protruding from his chest.

Thrinndor closed his eyes and bowed his head. When he opened his eyes, his hands flashed toward the large chunk of wood that protruded from the magicuser's back, grasped it and yanked it free.

Since the spell-caster's heart was not beating—it had probably been damaged by the sliver of wood—very little blood came from the gaping hole in his skin.

Thrinndor knew he had very little time with which to work, but he also knew that Sordaak had not been this way long. If he could repair the heart, perhaps the healer could get it started again.

"What are you doing?" Cyrillis asked, confused.

"Pray!" The paladin yelled as he rolled the sorcerer over onto his back. He then closed his eyes and raised his face toward the clouds above. Thrinndor silently said a prayer to Valdaar as he placed both his massive hands on Sordaak's chest and reached inside the mage's body with his senses.

Cyrillis, finally grasping what the paladin was doing, did as she was told and raised a brief prayer to Valdaar. When she tried to get to her knees, she gasped in pain when the bones in her useless ankle grated against one another. Biting down hard on her lip, she ignored the pain and placed her hands on the sorcerer next to the paladin's.

Together they worked, both seeing that the shard of wood had indeed pierced the sorcerer's heart and had damaged the muscles around it. Seeing through his mind's eye that the healer was also working with him, he allowed her more acute senses to repair the heart itself. His more clumsy efforts he applied to the muscles around it. He applied the second of his healing abilities slowly as he worked.

All this must have taken longer than he thought, because he heard the ranger land next to him along with the sound of vials clinking together when they were jostled in a bag.

"Here," Breunne said softly. He was certain one or both already knew of his presence, and he didn't want to disturb what they were doing—*whatever* it was they were doing. He opened the bag and poured its contents out in the sand next to the cleric and stepped back, waiting should his limited healing abilities be needed.

The ranger heard some shuffling in the sand and turned to see Vorgath walk up. He supported the rogue as they both made their way over to stand silently and watch the paladin and cleric work.

Cyrillis abruptly sat back, her weight going to her hands. "I can do no more," she said wearily through clenched teeth. She was ashen from exhaustion. It was only then that Breunne noticed her ankle remained at an odd angle to her leg. She had not healed herself!

"Your leg," the ranger gasped.

The healer opened her eyes in surprise; she had not heard the three join them. She glanced at her ankle. "I will live," she said, her moist eyes going to the sorcerer. Doubt still clouded her face when she finally spotted the array of potion bottles lying next to her.

"Thank you," she breathed tiredly as she began to quickly sort through them, casting aside those she deemed useless. Finally finding what she was looking for, she ripped the seal off in one desperate move, raised the bottle to her lips and quaffed the contents.

Cyrillis waited a moment for the potion to take effect. When she opened her eyes, they went wide in despair. She flung the vial with all her remaining strength away from her. The companions heard it break into many pieces as it slammed into something hard not far away.

"Shit!" she screamed.

"What is it?" Thrinndor asked as he too leaned back, exhausted from what he had been doing.

"It was not enough!" Cyrillis yelled. "The potion gave me more energy, but not near enough to use the Raise Dead spell!"

"That was your last potion?" Thrinndor asked, already knowing the answer.

Cyrillis merely nodded as the tears once again came freely. Abruptly she opened her eyes, raised herself to her knees and pulled the prone sorcerer's body to her until Sordaak's head again rested in her lap. She whispered a prayer and the holes in the mage's chest and back mended together, leaving no trace of the damage done.

"Leave us," she commanded. When no one moved, she shouted, "*Now!*"

Thrinndor got to his feet wearily and silently motioned for the others to do as she had said. Together the men walked solemnly from the beach area, none of them sure what was to come next.

Alone, Cyrillis closed her eyes and again bowed her head. Two more tears, one from each eye, made their way down her nose to drip onto the face of the magicuser.

"Hear me O Valdaar," she said softly. "Hear my plea. This one is vital to our mission, and his life has been cut short. Return him to us so that we may fulfill our destiny and return you to the land." She paused as she choked up. "He willingly gave his life to preserve mine, and that is proof that he is worthy." Cyrillis again hesitated as she bit her lip. "It is proof that he is worthy of your service, and proof he is worthy of my love."

The cleric fell silent as yet another tear fell from her eye, followed the path of its predecessors and dripped from her nose and into the open right eye of the caster.

Chapter Fourteen

Seamanship

"What did you say?" Sordaak asked weakly.

Startled, Cyrillis' eyes fluttered open and she almost dumped the magicuser from her lap and onto the sand. But the movement caused a sharp, stabbing pain in her ankle drew a gasp from her lips. She rocked back to a sitting position and held still.

"You're hurt," Sordaak said as he tried to rise.

The cleric pushed him back down, "You must rest," she said, shaking her head. He fought to rise again, more determined this time, but Cyrillis threw her arms around his neck and drew him close.

The cleric's tear-reddened eyes looked into those of her patient and she said softly, "You were dead." Her lip quivered as tears again welled up in her eyes. "I feared that my hesitation had killed you. Forever."

Sordaak closed his eyes and leaned the rest of the way in, placing his lips on hers. Cyrillis clutched his neck tightly, holding him there as she returned the kiss with all the pent-up emotion she had inside.

"Ahem," the two heard, "We thought we heard Sordaak's voice."

Quickly the two separated, both trying to hide what had just happened.

"Obviously we did," Vorgath said, amused. "But it must have been hard to speak with his face pressed against Cyrillis' as it was."

Quickly Sordaak jumped to his feet, but immediately he collapsed back down to his knees when the space around him started to spin. He had lost too much blood and stood too fast.

Cyrillis immediately surged to her knees, again forgetting her own injury in her haste to tend to the sorcerer. "I told you that you must first rest," she admonished.

Sordaak shook his head. "It is you who requires help," he said as his vision cleared. He then reached out and pushed her back to a sitting position, making sure not to twist her ankle any further. "Heal yourself," he said sternly.

It was Cyrillis' turn to shake her head. "I cannot," she said, the pain easing somewhat. "I have nothing left." Abruptly she raised her still tear-stained cheeks to the sky. "Would it have been too much to ask to heal my ankle while you were at it?" She tried to force a smile on her lips at her own temerity.

"What?" Sordaak was confused.

Seeing that he had no idea what had happened, the cleric put a soothing palm on Sordaak's face. "You were dead," she said for the second time. "Valdaar brought you back to me." She smiled, and then her face went blank. "Us, he brought you back to us," she corrected as her face turned bright red.

"Well, umm," Sordaak said, his face also turning red. Suddenly he turned to face the four fighter-types who hadn't moved since discovering the caster alive— among other things. "Can't one of you mental midgets do something for her ankle?" His voice switched between embarrassment and exasperation. "Do I have to do everything around here?"

Thrinndor and Breunne looked at one another, shrugged and stepped forward. They helped ease the cleric's back to the sand so that she was lying with her legs stretched out.

The paladin looked up and his countenance became sorrowful. "I am afraid I do not have your impeccable bedside manner," he said. "This is going to hurt." Cyrillis nodded as she again bit her lip. The paladin looked over at Breunne. "Hold her."

Sordaak stepped in and said quickly, "I'll do it." He again turned red, but knelt behind the healer and wrapped his arms around her chest, pinning the healer's arms to her side.

Thrinndor looked at the ranger and smiled. "Hold him."

Breunne returned the smile and positioned himself behind the magicuser.

"That will not be necessary," Sordaak said stiffly. "I know my place here."

Thrinndor raised an eyebrow and nodded at the ranger. Breunne stepped back but stayed close should he be needed.

"Anyone have some wine to give her?" Sordaak asked.

He got shakes of the head from everyone except Vorgath, who rolled his eyes and stepped forward as he removed the wineskin from his belt. He untied the thong and held it out to the cleric. Quickly he snatched it back, put it to his lips and took a long pull. Then he again held it out to Cyrillis, wiping his mouth with the back of his hand. "The rest is yours, little lady," he said formally.

Cyrillis accepted the skin and dipped her head, returning the bow. "Thank you, kind sir," she said with a wan smile. She pressed the skin to her lips and took a long pull. Her face flushed as she took in a deep breath from the strength of the wine. But she lifted the leather pouch to her lips again and drank deep.

When she dropped the now almost empty skin to her lap—top up so the remainder would not drain out—then she looked at the paladin and hesitated only slightly before nodding her head.

Sordaak tightened his hold on her as Thrinndor put his hands above and below the obvious break. The paladin took in a deep breath and reached into the ankle with his senses. The break looked clean enough to be allowed to heal properly, but there was another place farther up her leg where the bone was also fractured. The bones appeared to not have been displaced, but that spot was going to be a problem, he thought.

Thrinndor let his breath out slowly as he pulled on the cleric's broken ankle and slowly moved the bones back into their proper alignment, using his senses to verify his work as he went.

A moan escaped Cyrillis' lips, causing Sordaak to squeeze even tighter. The mage buried his face in the healer's golden hair, unable to watch what the paladin was doing.

The bones back in alignment, Thrinndor again drew in a deep breath as he began pushing the bones back together. Cyrillis bit off a scream, her eyes rolled back in their sockets, and her head lolled over to rest on the top of Sordaak's shoulder. She didn't move.

Thrinndor ignored her plight as he continued to focus on the task. He was almost out of energy, but knew he had to finish this. The bones now back together and he closed his eyes and whispered the words to the most powerful spell of healing that he knew. He had no more of the paladin's ability to lay-on hands, at least not until he rested. Thrinndor released the spell and guided its healing power with his senses. He repeated that process, again pouring his healing energy into the damaged ankle.

That was it. It was all he could do. He had no more spell energy remaining. Tiredly, he opened his eyes and found Breunne. "Can you use a healing spell here?" the paladin said as he pointed to the other fracture."

The ranger nodded as he stepped around the caster-cleric combo and knelt next to Thrinndor. "I'm afraid it's not much," Breunne said with apology.

"It will be enough," the paladin returned. "Just a minor fracture."

The ranger nodded as he began to whisper the words to his spell in a different language than the holy-types used. His spell energy came from the earth, and it was an ability a ranger learned to use in harmony with nature. He released his spell at the point indicated by the paladin, hoping he was in the right place; he didn't have the health-sense the holy-types had, either.

"Again, if you have the energy," Thrinndor said.

Breunne nodded. "Only one more, though," he said.

"That will be sufficient," the paladin said.

The ranger again whispered the words to his spell and released the energy high up on the cleric's ankle.

"Thank you," Thrinndor said. "That will do." He shifted his eyes to look upon Cyrillis' face. "Now she must rest."

Sordaak released his hold on the healer, lowered her gently back to the sand and said, "As must we all."

Vorgath cleared his throat, gaining the attention of those that remained conscious. "Do we still want to try to row out to the island?" he said as he pointed over at the boat.

The boat was riding easily in the water within the boathouse. There was some minor damage in a couple of places on the sides of the vessel where a beam had come down on it, and a section of the roof was lying across the bow. But all in all, the boat seemed to have come through the ordeal better than the party. The barbarian sloshed his way over to the near side and peered inside, holding the torch above his head. "No water leaking in," he announced as he turned to look at the paladin.

"I don't know that I have the energy to row a boat that big twenty-five or thirty miles," the paladin said dubiously.

Breunne looked at the barbarian who nodded. "I think that the dwarf and I can get us there," the ranger said, his tone displaying confidence he was not all that sure he felt.

"And I think I can rig a makeshift sail from some our bedding and maybe our rain gear," Vorgath said as he looked up through where the roof and been. The stars were plainly visible overhead. The rain had stopped.

Thrinndor looked at Sordaak, who was struggling to regain his feet. Savinhand stumbled over and offered the mage a hand. Gratefully, Sordaak accepted the help and got shakily to his feet. "Thanks," he murmured as he brushed the sand from his robe, noting the hole in the chest where the shard had poked through. "Damn," he muttered, "I'm gonna have to get this robe repaired." He looked up at the paladin. "It's a disgrace!"

Thrinndor stared at the mage as if he had taken leave of his senses.

"What?" Sordaak asked. "Did I miss something?"

The paladin shook his head. "Is it still important that we leave for the island tonight?" Thrinndor asked and pointed over at the boat. "In that?"

"Hell, yes," Sordaak said, straightening to his full height. "More important now than ever."

The paladin stared at the mage, afraid to ask. "Why is that?"

"Because Fahlred has informed me that my people were attacked and those that remain alive are being held prisoner," Sordaak said as he folded his arms on his chest.

"Why did you not just say so!" snapped the big fighter.

The companions worked together to get the boat ready and they put to sea without fanfare. Soon the sounds of the oars hitting water and waves lapping gently against the hull lulled Sordaak and Cyrillis to sleep. The mage had briefly considered offering to share body warmth with the cleric as they tried to get comfortable, but he quickly discarded that idea as not appropriate under the circumstances.

Cyrillis had awakened after only a few minutes of being out. She had tenuously tested her ankle and found she could walk on it. There was still some pain, however, and she walked with a slight limp, which she did her best to hide. She would be able to fix that when she had rested, she knew.

Savinhand, also still recovering from his encounter with the roof beams, was appointed to keep the boat on course. He protested, of course, but the other three men ignored him.

Thrinndor and Breunne took first turns on the oars as Vorgath gathered all the flat material he could and began sewing them together, using a small thin dagger Cyrillis had provided, and some thin rope the rogue had produced. It took time, but soon he had a crude sail that could capture at least a small portion of the prevailing winds that fortunately blew out to sea this time of year.

Savinhand volunteered (was voted) to hang the sail as he was by far the lightest and most nimble of the four men, and stood the best chance of not falling the twenty or so feet to the cold water below. He easily climbed the mast and had no problems maintaining his footing on the narrow piece of wood where he lashed the top of the makeshift sail to the one cross arm that had withstood the roof falling down.

The rogue shimmied back down he mast and tied the now flapping lower ends of the sail to the sides of the boat and went back to relieve the barbarian at the tiller.

The wind caught the sail, and the men held their breath as the seams strained to hold. The mast creaked noisily as power was applied to it, but it held. As did the sails, and soon Breunne and Thrinndor were able to pull the oars back inside as the wind took over pushing the vessel across the sea.

"You all rest," Savinhand said as he made a minor correction to their course. "I've got this."

Thrinndor nodded, he was too tired to argue. "Wake me after two hours," he said. "You must rest also." He looked up at the sail and over the side to gauge their speed. It was slow, but they were moving. "I estimate we will need at least six hours to go the twenty-five or so miles," he said. "And that is only if the wind holds and does not change direction."

Savin nodded as he focused on trying to keep the wind on the same quarter of the vessel. If he drifted off course and they missed the island...that would be bad.

Was it only two nights before that Sordaak had first showed them the fires of his crews working around the clock, constructing his keep on the island? Only two nights? It seemed like many more. Try as he might, he could see no such lights now. Certainly on so clear a night he would be able to see them? *If* they were there...

Savin lashed the tiller in place and found he had to get up and walk around periodically to remain awake. After what had seemed an eternity, Vorgath came back to relieve him.

"Let the blowhard sleep," the barbarian whispered as he pointed over to the snoring paladin. "I'll take the next watch." Savinhand nodded as the barbarian yawned, stretched and settled in at the tiller. "Any idea where we are?" Vorgath said as he looked up at the sail. It was holding he was pleased to see.

Savinhand shrugged. "I've kept the wind coming out of that quarter," he said pointing astern. "As long as it has not shifted direction on us, we should be headed straight for the island."

"Very well," the dwarf said. "I've got this. Now get some rest."

"I had it, you got it," Savinhand said wearily as he stood and stumbled over to where the barbarian had been sleeping.

Vorgath grunted in acknowledgement of the age-old phrase used in the passing of the watch.

Savin searched briefly for a blanket, then remembered all available such luxuries were now lashed to the mast. The rogue glanced overhead at the muted sound of the sail flapping in the breeze. He then shrugged and curled up as best he could for warmth on the bench and was instantly asleep.

*

Sordaak fought his way out of the exhausted slumber in which he had been entrenched. He tried in vain to remember where he was, and why opening his eyes resulted in no increase in light to his pupils. Then he switched the available brainpower to wondering what it was that had awakened him in the first place. That question was answered when a none-too-gentle hand shook him again.

"Shhh," a muted voice urged the sorcerer's silence as he groaned and tried to sit up.

"What?" Sordaak hissed from between chapped lips.

"Come with me," the dwarf said, sotto-voice. "I need your help." With that, Vorgath turned and made his way back to the stern of their little vessel, his feet sloshing in water as he went.

Sordaak lifted a curious eyebrow and then both brows knitted together as he put first one foot and then the other into the cold water sloshing around in the keel of the boat. He was glad to find dry boards to put his feet on as he neared the dwarf.

"What's up?" the sorcerer asked, scratching his head and yawning deeply. "And why is there water in the boat?" Another itch begged for attention, so he shifted his hand accordingly.

"This tub is leaking." The dwarf rolled his eyes. "And your island is close," He said, still whispering. "I need to know where would be a good place to put ashore."

"Why not use the pier?" the magicuser answered as he tried to spot the aforementioned land. "What island?" he asked, unable to see anything ahead.

Vorgath made a show of rolling his eyes, again. "Eggheads!" he said derisively. "Your eyes deceive you. Close them and listen."

"While I'm sure that exercise has merit," Sordaak said pointedly, "if you would but answer my question, this would go faster."

The barbarian glared at the mage.

It was Sordaak's turn to roll his eyes. "Very well," he said as he scrunched his eyes shut. "Now what?"

"*Listen!*" the barbarian insisted.

The sorcerer shrugged and did as requested. He could hear the waves lapping quietly against the hull, the creak of the rigging overhead and even the slosh of the water in the bilge of their craft. But nothing else.

He opened one eye and raised that brow inquisitively.

Exhibiting extreme patience unusual for a barbarian, Vorgath merely grumbled rather than discussing the mage's close relatives in rude detail. "You're not *listening!* Try again," he said. "This time ignore the sounds you know."

"Is this necessary?" Sordaak asked, one eye still closed.

The barbarian didn't entertain that question with an answer. He merely glared at the mage and waited.

With a sigh that succinctly showed what the mage thought of this particular lesson, Sordaak closed the one eye again and did as told. He reasoned that unless he humored the barbarian, they might be here until morning.

This time he closed his mind to the familiar sounds. First the waves lapping against the hull; next the groans of the sail and rigging; and finally the slosh of the water in the bilge. They were going to have to do something about that if they're out here much longer, he thought idly as that sound was extinguished.

Quietly he waited for the sound the barbarian wanted him to hear. Sordaak was surprised to find he was holding his breath. The mage was about to give up and inform the dwarf he was an idiot when he heard the faint sound of waves crashing against something. He wasn't sure; this was not a usual pastime for him. Maybe rocks? Maybe just rolling ashore on a sandy beach?

Sordaak wasn't sure what the sound was, but it wasn't coming from their little boat. He raised the same eye inquisitively at the barbarian. "OK," he said, "I can make out the faint crashing of waves into...something."

Vorgath smiled. "Very good." Somehow he didn't quite come off as condescending. Sordaak frowned.

"Actually what you're hearing is the waves both hitting some rocks *and* washing up onto a sandy beach." He was clearly proud of his observation, and getting the mage to do so, as well.

"Whatever!" the sorcerer grumbled. "Can we get back to my first question?" When Vorgath didn't immediately answer, he asked, "Why not use the pier?"

The barbarian shook his head slowly. "You're not thinking that thought through," the dwarf said. "Your fires are out in whatever development you have set up on your island." He allowed that to sink in. "Which could mean that either we're expected, or we're not. Either way, it seems wise to not fall into any trap that might await us."

Sordaak thought about that and nodded slowly. "Makes sense," he said. "There is a beach a mile or so to the west of—and more importantly out of sight of—the base encampment. I believe that would be a good point to approach from."

Vorgath nodded. "Now you're thinking," he said as he pushed the tiller over hard. The craft turned slowly and the makeshift sail began to flap as it lost the wind. At the mage's questioning look he added, "I think we are very close to that point, already. Hold this," he told the sorcerer as he shifted the tiller amidships.

Sordaak did as told while the barbarian reached over and loosened one line holding the sail boom in place and shifted it to the other side of the boat. Once in place on a small bollard, he pulled on it until the mast turned and the sail again filled with the slight breeze.

Satisfied, the dwarf again tied the rope, fixing the sail in place. The mage handed control of the tiller back to the dwarf after he returned to his seat.

"Go up to the bow and watch for rocks," Vorgath said. "If you see one, raise an arm and point either to port or starboard, indicating a direction I should steer."

"Port?" Sordaak said, confused. "Starboard?"

The barbarian rolled his eyes. "Left and right for you landlubbers!"

"Whatever!" Sordaak as he turned to head toward the bow. "Like you dwarves are a seagoing race!"

Vorgath started to lambaste the sorcerer with stories involving months at sea, but decided they didn't have time. The shore should be approaching rapidly. "Get to the bow!" he growled. "We'll discuss seamanship—or the lack thereof— at another time!"

Sordaak shrugged and hiked up the hem of his robe and cloak to keep it clear of the water that was sloshing around now at least ankle-deep in the bottom their boat. He shrugged again as he jumped from bench to bench in an effort to keep his sandals out of the water as well.

The mage almost made it to the bow. Almost. He mistimed his last jump and landed awkwardly on the front bench. He wind-milled his arms in an effort to regain his balance but, it was not to be. With a yelp Sordaak tumbled backward and landed with a tremendous splash in the cold, nasty water between the benches.

"Shit!" The sorcerer sat up, water running down his face from his wet hair. He felt around in the water next to him until his right hand came up with his hat. Disgustedly he wrung the water from it and put it back on his head as he got back to his feet.

Sordaak raised his right leg to put his foot onto the step so he could get himself out of the water just as a splintering crash came from in front of him. Their boat came to a sudden halt, and the magicuser was pitched forward, over the bench where he again landed with a splash as all the water in the boat surged forward.

"Shit!" Sordaak yelled again as he came up spluttering. He quickly climbed to his hands and knees, and then scrambled to stand as he looked over the side of the boat. Below he could see that the hull of their vessel was sitting precariously atop a jagged rock. Feeling water rushing at his feet, the sorcerer looked down and saw a huge hole in the bottom with a portion of the rock sticking through. The water was coming in at an alarming rate.

Sordaak held up his right arm and shouted, "Port!"

"A little late now, dumbass," Vorgath said as he ran up to assess the situation. A quick glance showed that the shore was still a hundred yards off. "Looks like we're all going to get a little wet!"

The boat shifted, and Sordaak could feel the hull grating across the rock as the wave action tried to move their craft toward shore. Suddenly the boat was again free, and it wallowed between waves, now sideways with respect to the shore. The mage looked down and saw that water was pouring in through the now completely open hole in the bow.

"We're sinking!" Sordaak shouted.

"Quiet!" Vorgath hissed. "We don't want to alert anyone ashore as to our presence!" He glared briefly at the mage. "Now wake everyone up—quietly—and have them gather their belongings." He turned toward the stern. "I'm going to see if I can get this tub closer before she sinks."

"I am awake," Thrinndor said. The boat striking the rock had awakened him. He looked around to see what he could do to help.

"Me, too," Breunne said. "How can I help?"

"Get to the bow and watch for more rocks!" Vorgath said as he reached the tiller. He pushed it hard over, trying to get the bow once again pointed toward shore.

If the old boat had been sluggish in her response before, now she was positively lethargic. The additional weight of the water in her bilges was dragging her down, literally. The barbarian could tell the boat had settled into the surf quite a bit in the past few minutes.

They were sinking. Vorgath cast a worried look toward shore and could see they were almost no closer now than when they had hit the rock. They weren't going to make it.

"Gather your stuff," the dwarf said gruffly. He looked around in vain to see if anyone else was taking an interest in their activities. He didn't see anyone, but he knew that voices could carry for miles over water on a calm night. "We're not going to make it." Now he had everyone's attention.

Grimly the paladin nodded agreement. "Only take what you can carry and still swim."

"Swim?" There was alarm in Sordaak's voice. "*Swim?* I don't swim!"

"Well," Vorgath said sardonically, "I'm not carrying your dumb ass to shore, so now's a pretty good time to learn!"

Sordaak wasn't laughing, and Thrinndor could see from the panicked look in the caster's eyes that learning how at this point was not foremost on his mind.

"Here," Breunne said as he tossed a pair of boots onto the bench next to the sorcerer. "Put those on."

Sordaak looked down at the boots skeptically, but only tightened his grip more firmly onto the side of the boat. He shook his head.

The ranger rolled his eyes. He briefly considered a snippy reply, but the look in the magicuser's eyes stopped him. The boat hadn't moved noticeably closer to the shore, and even the smaller waves now sometimes washed over the sides. "Those are the boots I got back from Melundiir's treasure," he said quickly. "They give the wearer the ability to fly."

Sordaak stared blankly at the ranger and then his eyes brightened. Quickly he kicked off his sandals pulled the boots onto his bare feet. "Trigger word?" the mage asked as he stood on the bench. The water was already lapping at the wood where his feet were.

Breunne raised an eyebrow. "Fly," he said simply. He was already too busy preparing to go in the water to worry about the spell-caster anymore.

"Fly!" Sordaak said as he raised his arm and pointed at the inky black sky. Immediately he launched straight up. All eyes were on the mage as he flew skyward.

The sorcerer's cries were clearly heard as he somersaulted a couple of times, flew sideways and generally showed no control over his direction. A loud *thud* was heard as Sordaak smacked head-first into the mast of their vessel. He fell the ten feet or so after that and landed with a splash into the water sloshing around in the boat.

Cyrillis exclaimed something unintelligible and waded to the fallen mage's side as quick as she could get there. She found him face-down in the water. She rolled him over and all could see a large knot already forming on the right side of the caster's forehead.

"I probably should have mentioned that those boots take some practice to master," Breunne said from his place in the bow of the boat.

Cyrillis glared at him until he went back to what he had been doing.

"That must've hurt," Vorgath observed from over the cleric's shoulder. "He'll live," he added as he reached down and grabbed the mage by the gathered robe at his shoulders and easily lifted him clear of the cleric's arms.

"Hey!" she protested as the barbarian walked over to the side of the boat, dragging the mage behind him.

"There's no time," Vorgath said as the others leapt over the side. The dwarf's eyes found the healers. "An unconscious scared non-swimmer will fight a lot less than a conscious one." He looked down at the water lapping at his feet. "I suggest you get away from here, fast. When this boat goes down, she will try to drag anything nearby with her." He then turned, picked up the caster and jumped into the dark water. Surfacing, he paddled quickly, creating some distance between himself and the boat. He dragged Sordaak behind him, ensuring he kept the mage's face above the water.

Still of a mind to protest, Cyrillis stood, but she took one look at the waves washing over the sides of the vessel and changed her mind. She dove head-first into the water and swam over next to the spell-caster. However, she made no further protests as Vorgath began making his way toward the sound of the waves crashing onto the beach somewhere ahead of them.

Cyrillis turned back just as the boat sank beneath the waves and she felt the tug of the water towards it as the vessel disappeared from sight. She shook her head. Who had ever heard of such a thing?

The companions swam/paddled/struggled their way toward shore. The water was cold enough that when they finally got there, they found themselves shivering in a breeze during the cool hours just prior to sunrise.

Thrinndor looked around, noting the sky beginning to show light to the east. "This way," he said as he walked up the beach away from the water and toward some trees that would offer slight shelter from the growing breeze.

Vorgath reached down to pick up the magicuser, but Cyrillis stopped him. "I will take it from here," she said sternly.

The barbarian shrugged and followed the paladin. "He's all yours," he said. "I'm tired of dragging his boney ass all over."

The healer knelt at Sordaak's side and checked the knot on his head and made sure he was still breathing. He was. Next she placed her right hand on the bump, closed her eyes and said a short prayer.

The spellcaster moaned as his eyes fluttered open. "What in the name of the Seven Hells hit me?" he groaned.

"You were flying—" Cyrillis began.

Sordaak cut her off. "Damn," he said as he once again closed his eyes. "Now I remember!" He moved his hands, and finding sand between his fingers, he quickly opened his eyes. "How did I get here?"

"Vorgath bade me not to awaken you," she bit her lip furtively. "He brought you ashore." She could see it was in his eyes to question her further, but a soft call from the trees saved her.

"You two coming?" The hushed voice sounded like Savinhand, but Sordaak couldn't be sure.

The mage groaned again as he fought to sit up. He accepted the healer's hand and climbed unsteadily to his feet. Sordaak looked around to see if he could recognize where they were, but was unable to do so. His eyes settled on the top of the mast, now barely visible sticking out of the water about two or three hundred feet from shore in the growing light of dawn.

He turned to see the rogue standing among some trees. Savinhand, seeing he had their attention at last, waved, turned and walked into the brush, indicating they should follow.

Sordaak looked over at Cyrillis, who still held his hand from helping him to his feet, shrugged and walked toward where the thief had disappeared, his hand not letting go of the cleric's.

Chapter Fifteen

Valdaar's Rest

Sordaak was thoroughly chilled from his damp clothing and the cool autumn air by the time he found where the paladin had decided to stop so the party could gather themselves.

Vorgath was busy preparing a small fire under a rock overhang that jutted out from the side of a tall hill that marked the edge of a rough ridge of hills ringing the island. Farther inland, Sordaak could see the smoking crest of Kalishnoor—the semi-dormant volcano that made making this island his new home an adventure.

Having piled the wood, the barbarian fumbled around in his pack for his steel and flint.

The mage mumbled the words to his fire spell as he walked quickly to the prepared ring. A burst of flame popped into life on the end of his index finger as he knelt and applied that finger to the shaved wood and kindling. He blew on the dried leaves and twigs, and they quickly caught, spreading rapidly to the other small sticks and eventually to the larger ones.

Vorgath raised his eyebrow as he put his implements of fire back into their wrapping and stored them in his bag.

"What are our plans?" Sordaak said abruptly as he turned to face the paladin, the mage's hands extended toward the growing blaze.

Somewhat taken aback by the sorcerer's question, Thrinndor had to think for a moment before answering. "They have not changed," he said finally. "First we will dry our clothing and prepare a quick meal. Refreshed, we will march the short distance to your encampment to see if we can determine what happened there."

Sordaak nodded as he turned his back to the fire and wiggled his way closer until he felt the fiery warmth through his robe. He sighed, signaling his satisfaction. That became an uneasy frown as the others crowded their way in, each trying to chase away the chill that had settled into their bones. It seemed like days since they had had the warmth of a fire.

Breunne watched the proceedings with amusement. "I'm going to have a look around whilst you warm yourselves."

"I'll join you," Savinhand said, also amused by the tussle happening around the small fire. The ranger glanced over at the rogue, and Savin continued, "Pick a direction, and I'll go the other way."

Breunne nodded and disappeared into the brush to the north of their little camp. The thief did a double-take and smiled. *Damn ranger could make himself almost as scarce as I can.*

Almost. Savin also disappeared into the brush—leaving no trace that he had ever stood in the small clearing.

"Do not wander far," Thrinndor said to the emptiness. No one answered, but he hadn't expected one.

"How long we gonna stay here, boss?" Sordaak asked the paladin.

Thrinndor looked around, trying to gauge how long until it was full light. "Just long enough to dry out and get a warm bite to eat," he answered.

"Ummm," the mage said as he dug through his pack. "Eat what, exactly?"

Thrinndor raised an eyebrow and checked his pack as well. He pulled out a wrapped package that had once contained dried biscuits. Water ran out of it when he pried back the layers. He dumped the mush inside onto the ground and reached in again.

Now Cyrillis and Vorgath got into the act, each sorting through soggy packs.

When the companions had pooled what remained of their meager supply of rations, they had just two small portions of salted meat, a handful of jerked venison and three especially well-wrapped biscuits from the barbarian's pack.

Cyrillis picked up the small pot from the rogues belongings, tested some water from her water-skin and, finding it satisfactory, emptied the skin into the pot. This she placed on the hook the paladin had rigged and began shaving what was left of the meat into the water.

Vorgath sighed as he got to his feet. He wandered into the brush, obviously looking for something that could be added to the mixture. Thrinndor followed, and they separated to cover more ground.

They found a few tubers and some herbs. Cyrillis added them to the pot and added more water so the stew wouldn't get too thick. By the time she was ready to pronounce the breakfast ready, the sun was up and the two scouts had returned.

As the companions ate what was the last of their food supplies, Breunne and Savinhand explained that they had found Sordaak's encampment empty.

They had found no bodies, just tracks leading inland from the camp. The assumption was that Sordaak's construction crew were being held prisoner somewhere on the island.

"Damn!" the mage spat. "This is getting complicated!" He had other plans—ones that didn't allow for traipsing all over his island looking for his builders. "We don't have time for this!"

Breunne spoke next. "It should be a simple matter to follow the trail, kill the usurpers and free the hostages."

Sordaak shook his head. "I doubt it'll be as simple as all that," he said, eyeing the pot and wondering if anything remained inside. With a shrug he set his plate aside. "While the construction crew I hired were not exactly fighters and adventurers, they were not strangers to battle, either." The companions waited for him to finish. "I had thirty of the best stone-masons and engineers available working two shifts—and they were well armed..."

"Thirty?" Vorgath asked, distracted.

"Yes thirty," the sorcerer answered tersely.

"This must be a larger force of troglodytes than we thought," Thrinndor said, speaking the obvious.

"Exactly," Sordaak said, exasperated. "We don't have *time* to deal with an army of trogs!" He glared at the paladin in frustration. "*Pendromar* is at Ice Homme," he said. "I can *feel* its presence! We must not tarry here!"

The paladin stood, walked the short distance over to stand before the sorcerer and placed his hand on Sordaak's shoulder. "We will not," he said with sympathetic eyes. "However, *Pendromar* has been at Ice Homme for many hundreds of years. It will wait a few days more, if necessary." He smiled at this man who had become his friend.

Sordaak looked away. "I know," he said demurely. "We have come so far." The mage took in a ragged breath and sat up straight. "Very well," he said sternly. "I guess we have it to do!" The sorcerer stood and looked around at his companions. "Let's go kick some troglodyte butt!"

"I may have a better idea," Cyrillis said from her perch next to the fire. All eyes turned to her. She cleared her throat and squared her shoulders. "If these troglodytes have indeed taken your men prisoner," she began, "then it is possible they are looking to barter."

Sordaak started to protest, but Thrinndor spoke first. "An interesting thought," he mused. "Perhaps they merely want something."

The mage looked from one to the other as if they had gone daft. "Like *what*?"

The paladin thought about it and shrugged. "I do not know," he said. "But the few troglodytes I have encountered were not especially aggressive—although I have heard they can be in large numbers."

"Agreed," Breunne continued the thought. "They tend to operate from a 'home base' of sorts, and are known to be extremely protective of that home."

"Hmmm," Cyrillis said. "That might explain this assault on your encampment." All eyes again turned to her. "They may simply see your men as a threat to their home."

Sordaak blinked twice, unsure of where this was going. "So, what is it you suggest?"

Cyrillis shrugged. "I suggest that instead of going in with blazing wands and weapons swinging, we try a more subtle approach."

Thrinndor nodded. "It stands to reason that if their numbers are large enough to have taken your men prisoner, they could have simply slain them and been done with it."

Sordaak's head was on a swivel as he followed the conversation.

"It also might be the quickest resolution to the dilemma," Savinhand said. "If you are indeed in a hurry."

"I'm liking the 'wands blazing and weapons swinging' option," Vorgath interrupted. "If it's up for a vote."

"It's not," Sordaak said dismissively. He had made his mind up at the "quickest" comment. "We will try diplomacy, first." He smiled at the cleric. "That was a good observation, and a better recommendation."

"Indeed," the paladin said as the healer blushed slightly at the attention she was getting.

The barbarian grumbled as the companions broke camp quickly, Sordaak remaining near the fire as long as it burned. The sun hadn't entirely taken the chill out of the air, and he felt winter was not going to be long in coming.

Vorgath confirmed his suspicions. "Going to get cold tonight," he said as he studied a cloud formation on the western horizon. "Might snow," he added as he tested the air. The breeze definitely had a bite to it. It was cooler now than it had been all through the night.

"Storms can be rough on this island," Sordaak said as he too inspected the clouds. "Especially winter storms."

"We had best be moving, then," Thrinndor said as he walked up to stand behind the two. He looked over at Savinhand. "Lead the way, please."

The companions neared the encampment before the sun reached noon. The clouds continued to build, and the winds began to mount. There was definitely the scent of snow in the air. Even Sordaak could taste it. Damn!

The encampment was built near the docks at the back end of a well-sheltered harbor. There were three large sailing ships tied up at the docks. The fighter-types verified all were empty while Sordaak and Cyrillis walked the short distance to where the construction had been going on.

"No, NO, NO!" Sordaak shouted when he got near enough to see the progress.

"What?" Cyrillis said, alarmed.

Without answering, the mage hustled over to the tall tower used by the chief engineer to oversee the construction and began taking the steps two at a time to the top.

Cyrillis followed.

Slightly winded from the exertion—the tower was some one hundred feet tall—Sordaak fumbled around for the correct drawing. Finding it, he spread it on the tilted table placed before the enormous window for the purpose. Initially he held the curled top corners in place until Cyrillis came up behind him and placed the leather thongs mounted to the table with weights on the ends over the large parchment sheets, holding the corners in place.

"Thank you," the mage murmured as this freed his hands to slide across the drawing, stopping at significant points. He continued to shake his head as he looked through the window at the construction now far below. "Son of a *bitch*!" he shouted as he slammed his open hand onto the table.

"What?"

Sordaak looked over at the healer, apparently noticing her for the first time. "My chief engineer had specific instructions to work on the temple, *first*!" he said, again looking down at the drawing. He pointed to a series of lines along the edges of the paper. "Yet the construction below is obviously part of the external wall system!" Looking up, he pointed far back into compound. "There!" he said. "They were supposed to be building *there*!" There were some stakes in the ground where a structure had been marked out, but no construction had begun.

"Perhaps they were trying to build the walls to fortify the holdings against the attacks," Thrinndor said.

Sordaak had not seen nor heard the remaining companions join him and the cleric. Looking around on the parapet, he could see that all six were present.

"That may be," the sorcerer said testily, "but he had specific instructions to contact me before making any changes in my plans!"

"Perhaps he tried," Cyrillis said tentatively. "We have been rather out of touch for the past couple of months."

Sordaak turned to glare at the cleric and was about to rail at her when abruptly his shoulders slumped. "You are of course correct," he said quietly. Thrinndor raised an eyebrow in mild surprise. "I might have been remiss in checking in with him."

"Why the temple first?" Breunne asked as he peered over the mage's shoulder at the drawing.

Sordaak looked over at the ranger, confusion showing in his eyes at the question. He realized these, his best friends, knew little of his plans. However, now was not the time for an explanation. "The temple is necessary for the ceremony required to return a dead god to life."

That got their attention. A stunned silence followed.

"What?" Cyrillis said, more sharply than intended.

"How do you know this?" Thrinndor asked.

Sordaak waited for the hubbub to die down. "I learned this while studying in the Library of Antiquity." He turned and headed for the stairs. "You are going to have to trust me on this," he said as he began his descent, "because we don't have time to talk about it now." The sorcerer's head disappeared below floor level as he spiraled his way back to ground level.

Thrinndor looked around the small chamber at the top of the tower. His eyes settled on those of the cleric. "He is correct," he said. "We have no choice but to trust him."

"I know," Cyrillis replied. "I do." She shouldered her way past the paladin and followed the magicuser down the steps.

The paladin's right eyebrow twitched and then settled back in place. The cleric's actions of late regarding the spell-caster were no longer a surprise to him. He was, however, at a loss as to just how that relationship had burgeoned in the first place. He shrugged and followed her down the steps.

Back on the ground, the companions gathered at the base of what was shaping up to be an external wall of the new keep.

"What now?" Vorgath asked.

"Now we go rescue the builders," Thrinndor said.

"It will be a short trip if we don't find something to eat," griped the barbarian. As if on cue, his stomach rumbled loudly. "See?" he said.

Sordaak arched an eyebrow and scratched at the itchy growth on his cheeks. He was used to being clean-shaven, but they seldom had time to take care of personal things such as shaving. Without saying anything, he turned and headed back toward the encampment.

Thrinndor looked at the others, shrugged and followed. Silently the rest of the party did the same.

Sordaak wound his way through the empty buildings housing the sleeping quarters to a long, low building that he knew housed the place where his workers came to eat.

"We checked in there," Vorgath said. "They cleaned out the kitchen and pantries."

The mage ignored the dwarf and went through the door anyway. Again the others followed.

Sordaak made his way between the tables and pushed his way through the curtain into the food preparation area. He continued through there until he came to a large door that stood slightly ajar.

"It's empty," Vorgath protested as the mage pulled the heavy door open.

Sordaak turned his expressionless eyes onto the barbarian, and disappeared inside.

The small chamber was clearly a pantry, with shelves lining the walls. As there was no window, it was dark inside. The mage cast a light spell on bowl he found on the shelf, causing it to illuminate brightly. With this in hand, he stepped into the chamber and began looking around on the floor.

The barbarian opened his mouth to again express his doubts, but decided there seemed to be a method to the mage's madness. He clamped his jaws together and crossed his arms on his chest.

After kicking aside some rugs covering the wood plank floor in places, the mage reached down and grasped a pull-ring he had exposed. He arched his back but nothing happened.

Vorgath, sensing the caster's distress, pushed his way past the rogue, who was scratching his head, lightly pushed the mage aside, grasped the ring and pulled. A large portion of the floor creaked open. The dwarf lifted the hatch which swung on hidden—but noisy—hinges and allowed the section of floor to prop up against the shelving behind it.

Sordaak looked over at the barbarian and mouthed the words "thank you" and shined his light down into the dark, rectangular hole in the floor. "I think you will find everything we need to continue down there," he said as he handed the bowl over to the paladin and walked back out the way he had come in.

"Damn magicusers are always *so* secretive!" Vorgath grumbled as he knelt and swung his way onto the ladder, climbing down with the ease of much practice on said device. "Toss me that light," he said as the paladin knelt to also get access to the ladder. Thrinndor obliged and tossed the bowl down to the waiting hands of the barbarian.

Cyrillis looked down at the dwarf, who was inspecting various goods on multiple shelves. She bit her lip and allowed her eyes to go to the door Sordaak had recently gone through. Breunne waved for her to go next down the ladder, but she shook her head and hurried after the caster.

The ranger smiled, shook his head and dropped easily down the ladder.

Savinhand scratched his head and looked from the opening in the floor to the door Cyrillis and Sordaak had departed through and back. Curiosity as to the mage's destination won out, and he followed in the footsteps of the cleric.

Outside, he spotted the cleric as she rounded a corner into the alley that led back to the walls of the keep. He followed quietly, not wanting to get in the way of whatever she had in mind.

Sordaak walked through what was clearly going to be the main gate of the keep without looking to either side and kept going. He passed where several markers had been placed into the bedrock, indicating places were walls and doors to several buildings were to be placed.

Finally, he stopped some four or five hundred feet from the opening in the outer gates. He stood staring at the outline clearly marked for the walls he knew were going to be for the temple.

Cyrillis walked up slowly and stopped next to him. After a moment of silence, she reached out and gingerly took the mage's hand in hers.

Sordaak, his reverie broken, looked into the clear blue eyes of the cleric and smiled.

Cyrillis smiled in return and asked, "What is this place?"

"It will be the temple where we return your god—our god—to this plane," he said gently. "They should have worked on these walls, first." He looked back at the layout. "My men could have easily defended themselves here if they had but followed my direction." He was silent for a moment. "But, the workers fear this place."

"Fear?" the healer asked, mildly alarmed as she looked around. "Why?"

Sensing nothing personal of import was about to happen, Savinhand walked up to join them in time to hear the mage say, "This place is wrought with power of some sort." Sordaak shook his head, his uneasiness palpable. "Close your eyes," he said, talking to Cyrillis. She did. "Now reach out with your senses." She complied with that as well. "There." He breathed in deeply. "Do you feel it?"

The cleric's eyes sprang open in astonishment. "Yes," she exclaimed. "There is an *immense* power here!" Her eyes were excited. "I cannot tell what that power is, but its presence is unmistakable!"

"I did some research on that," the sorcerer began. "That power is one of the reasons Praxaar ordered the island placed off-limits after the victory over his brother." Sordaak's eyes traveled back toward the markers for the walls that would be the temple. "I believe that the power comes from the very ground beneath our feet."

"I have never heard of such a thing," Cyrillis said, her voice wondrous. This did not come off as doubt.

"I found references to such places during my studies. They are said to be conduits to the very center of all that lives and breathes. Each place of power is said to have its own characteristics—one of pure good, one of pure evil, another of supreme neutrality and two others that support Chaos and Law."

After he was silent for a moment, Cyrillis asked, "Which is this?"

Sordaak's shoulder slumped and he said quietly, "I don't know." Again he lapsed into silence. Abruptly, he looked up and into the eyes of the healer. "But, as this was Valdaar's home for thousands of years, surely it must have been beneficial to him, right?"

Cyrillis bit her lip and nodded. She squeezed the hand in hers and said. "Surely it must be so!" But the alignment of the power source bothered her. "The power cannot be evil," she said, her voice tentative. "I could never serve a god dedicated to evil!" Now her tone was defiant. "It has been said the Praxaar is good, and Valdaar evil, but I do not believe—*cannot* believe—such a thing!"

Sordaak squeezed her hand in return and pulled at her, turning the cleric such that she faced him. He reached up with his free hand and brushed away the tear that had formed there. "It is my belief the lines between good and evil are not so easily defined," he said as he looked into her eyes. "There is good and evil in every person. One that suppresses the evil will tend toward good, and vice versa." Cyrillis sniffed and nodded slowly, not convinced.

"Still," Sordaak continued as he turned back to his would-be temple, "if the power in this place is indeed one of those about which I read, we will need to determine which place that is."

"It is the Source of Law," Thrinndor said.

Startled, Sordaak turned to look at the paladin. In his desire to explain, he had not seen nor heard the others approach—again, and that bothered him. He was too easily distracted of late, and he was beginning to understand why. He looked at Cyrillis out of the corner of his eye; she was focused on the paladin for the moment.

"Really?" she asked. "How is it you know this?"

Thrinndor shrugged. "It is part of the knowledge passed along to me via the Paladinhood." The paladin shifted his gaze to the magicuser and lifted his right eyebrow slightly. "You are correct in your assumption that this 'conduit', as you called it, is why Valdaar built his retreat here."

"It also explains why this place makes me so uneasy." Sordaak looked around, his manner unsettled. His words caused the paladin's eyebrow to inch minutely higher. "While I am in the process of changing my ways, my ties to Chaos are not so easily brushed aside." He shuddered involuntarily. "It also explains why I can't get Fahlred to appear."

Thrinndor was about to question him further, but the mage continued before he could. "He is a creature born into Chaos. My change of heart has been disquieting to him. Had I waited to make the call until now, it would not have been him that answered."

"Yet he continues to serve you?" the ranger asked, curiosity getting the better of him.

Sordaak looked at Breunne, his eyes cold and unyielding. "He does. We are bound." He shrugged as he looked toward the volcano in the distance. "For life. Fahlred doesn't agree with what he deems as 'my choice,' but he understands—perhaps better than I—and will serve until one of us is no longer able to do so."

Breunne nodded but said no more.

"The Source of Law?" Cyrillis was obviously fixated on this. Her eyes had never left the paladin.

"Yes," their leader said. His eyes took on a faraway look, and Sordaak could see that he was about to leap into one of his dissertations.

"We don't have time for that now," the mage interrupted as Thrinndor opened his mouth. "We must be moving."

The paladin's eyebrow rose again. "Very well." He turned his attention to the ranger. "Breunne, if you would be so kind as to lead the way."

"Hmmff," the barbarian sniffed. "Any moron could follow the trail those trogs left!"

"Agreed," Breunne said as he turned and walked from the clearing. "But could any moron determine the number we follow? Or if and when any of those followed abruptly leave the grouping? Or how old the trail is?" His voice trailed off as he separated from the group.

Unconvinced, Vorgath opened his mouth to protest. "Not now," Thrinndor requested gently. "Remember, it is one of the reasons we have him along." He winked at his old friend.

The barbarian was about to protest further anyway but broke it off with another "hmmff" and fell into line.

Chapter Sixteen

Gri`Puth

The ranger led the party unmolested—much to Vorgath's chagrin—along a path that took them first inland and then toward the shore. They wound along that shore as what should have been an afternoon sun began its decent toward the horizon. The thick clouds easily obscured this sun, and no warmth escaped their shroud to the ground below. The temperature had continued to drop as the wind likewise gained in strength. The party members found themselves leaning into this wind as they trudged more or less north into the teeth of that wind.

The tracks of those who had gone before them were indeed easily followed, and it was obvious even to Sordaak that there had been no attempt to disguise the trail. Then at late afternoon the path again made its way inland, and soon the party was working through broken hills and ravines. As the sun disappeared toward the horizon the mage's stomach began to growl and he was about to recommend a brief halt when the path did that for him.

Suddenly the party stood before an enormous cave opening at the end of one of the ravines. The mage hadn't noticed that they had walked up to the base of a large mountain and stood before a very high cliff face. The blackness of the cavern opening beckoned.

"Now what?" asked the rogue, who appeared from behind a rock face even the paladin had missed.

Thrinndor's eyes narrowed in annoyance as he stared down the thief. "Your prowess at hiding and surprising is, I believe, beyond compare. However, one of these days it will also possibly get you killed!"

"Until then," Savinhand said with a smirk as he detached himself from the shadow and approached the entrance, "what is your bidding?"

The paladin's gaze followed the rogue leader and he briefly considered continuing his previous conversation path. Abruptly he let out a sigh and muttered, "Damn rogues!"

Sordaak chuckled as he walked up to stand beside the paladin. His eyes measured the opening in the cliff face. Thirty, maybe forty feet wide, by more than twenty feet in height. He could discern no narrowing of the passage inside, either, but it was getting dark fast.

"We will pause for refreshment before entering." Thrinndor stepped into the cavern opening and slung his now much heavier pack off his shoulder and set it easily on the ground.

The others followed and did likewise. Out of the swirling winds, the cavern felt much warmer.

Vorgath spotted a small rock fire ring not far from where they stood and without a word scouted around for something to burn. He was not disappointed when he came across a neatly piled stack of wood along one wall.

The paladin glanced at Breunne and Savinhand and nodded silently toward the blackness that loomed farther back in the cliff face. The two looked at one another, shrugged and walked back into the opening. "Do not go far," Thrinndor commanded. He picked up his pack and moved closer to the fire ring, followed by the others.

There were some burned-out remnants of a previous fire in the ring, and Sordaak used his finger to reignite a piece of the wood that still showed a not-charred end. By the time the barbarian returned with an armload of twigs and branches, the mage had the beginnings of a small blaze going.

Vorgath took over from there and soon had a fire cheerily going in the ring. Now that all vestiges of light from the sun had disappeared, the temperature began to drop rapidly and the remaining companions gathered around the fire. Cyrillis began to dig through the packs, trying to decide what was to be for dinner. Ultimately, she settled on a variation of what they had had for breakfast: stew. She set a large loaf of bread on a rock next to the fire to warm as she set up the implements for cooking from the rogue's pack.

Just as she was about to add water to the pot which was now hanging above the fire, Savinhand appeared at her elbow. "I'll take it from here, if you like."

Cyrillis considered declining but knew it would be purely for the sake of vanity, and also knew that would not sit well with her. Besides, she really liked the rogue's cooking. "Very well." She smiled as she stepped aside. A quick glance toward the mage showed him to be deep in conversation with the paladin, so she decided to watch and see how Savin prepared such fabulous meals.

Savinhand returned the smile as he pulled his pack closer and rummaged around inside. He removed several packets, which he sat on a nearby rock, and then added water to the pot. Next he searched through the bags of foodstuffs and set aside several larger wrapped packages. Selecting one, he opened it, pulled a wicked-looking dagger from his belt, rinsed it and held it near the fire to further the cleansing process. Holding the contents of the package in his left hand, he deftly shaved portions of some dried meat into the pot. He put a small piece in his mouth, sampling the spices used during the curing process. He nodded his begrudging agreement and shaved more of the meat into the hot water.

One by one he selected a package he had set aside and repeated the process, adding carrots, tubers, and a couple of other items Cyrillis didn't recognize to the mixture. Next he added small portions—pinches, really—from the special packages he had removed from his personal bag.

Soon a pleasant aroma began to emerge from the pot as the rogue stirred it continually. Savin turned to smile at his student as he reached for yet another pouch. He winked at her and held his finger to his lips as he removed the cork from the pouch with his teeth and added some of the contents to the mixture.

Cyrillis stepped closer to see what he was doing. Wine! Savin had added a small portion of wine to the stew! That must be his secret ingredient! The rogue winked at her again knowingly as he put the cork back into the bag and set it aside. He then went back to stirring the mixture without saying a word.

After a few moments he lifted the spoon to his lips and sampled his creation. The rogue turned his head to the side as he obviously pondered what he beheld. Shaking his head he reached for one of his pouches and added another couple of pinches of the contents.

Savin stirred again for a while as the stew came to a boil. He rotated the fork holding the pot slightly to the side, reducing the amount of heat on his concoction. He sampled his stew again, this time drawing a nod as he dipped the spoon back in, retrieved some more contents and offered the spoon to Cyrillis.

"Careful, it's hot."

The cleric, not realizing how hungry she had become just smelling Savin's creation, grabbed at the spoon greedily and blew on the contents to cool it. Finally, unable to wait any longer, she put the spoon to her lips and slurped with abandon.

Wow! That was hot! And *good!* She nodded her approval as she handed the spoon back. "You are an amazing cook! I must learn from you how you make these marvelous meals!"

Pleased, Savinhand blushed lightly. "It's nothing special. Knowing which spices complement another is the key. Getting the correct combination is all-important, and takes some practice."

"I am sure that it does," Cyrillis said appreciatively. "I would still like to learn, just the same."

The rogue nodded. "I will take you with me to the general store the next the next time we are in town. Most good proprietors keep a good supply of the proper ingredients." He winked at her again. "And if you know how to ask, sometimes they will allow you to shop their secret stash." Savin smiled.

"Oh, I would like that!"

"Like what?" Sordaak had come up behind her.

The cleric turned and smiled as her eyes touched those of the mage. "Savinhand has promised to teach me how to make these wonderful meals!"

"I'll be the judge of that!" The magicuser stepped around her, nimbly snatched the spoon from the unsuspecting rogue's hand and dipped it into the mixture. He lifted a spoonful to his lips put it in his mouth.

"Careful! That's hot!" Savin was too late.

Sordaak quickly opened his mouth and fanned its contents with his left hand. Finally he was able to swallow. "Damn! That's *hot*!" He dipped the spoon into the pot again. "But damn it's *good*!" he said as he lifted another spoonful to his lips. This time, however, he paused to blow on it.

"Dinner is served!" Savin announced. The others gathered around, picking up bowls as they got in line.

"Careful, it's hot!" Sordaak smacked his lips as he stirred the concoction in his bowl while blowing on it.

The remainder of the meal was consumed in silence as each got as close to the fire as possible and held the hot bowls of stew to both cool the meal and thaw their fingers.

There was some light conversation around the fire as Savin cleaned up his cooking implements. Suddenly the rogue hissed a warning as he set his pot down and disappeared into the shadows.

In an instant only Thrinndor remained within the ring of light surrounding the fire. There was a sound of steel sliding across leather as he pulled his flaming sword from his belt. The flames on the blade surged to life. "What is it you want?"

There was the sound of bare feet sliding across the rock.

"You must put down weapons and come with us," a voice said from just outside the reach of the fire light. Whatever 'it' was spoke in broken common.

"I do not think that is going to happen."

There was a moment of silence, followed by some whispered arguing in a tongue the paladin did not recognize. The reptilian hissing led him to believe the troglodytes had found them, though.

"We are many," the voice persisted.

"We are powerful. Many of you will die."

Again there was more arguing.

"All of you die," the voice said. There was not much conviction in this decree.

"Perhaps, but I will take many of you to the afterlife before I go," the paladin said slowly. "You will die first." He pointed his flaming sword in the direction of the voice.

Now the arguing was no longer whispered. Thrinndor could tell the one who had been speaking for their group was decidedly not happy. The big fighter smiled.

Abruptly there was a *poof* and the cavern got suddenly very dark as the fire went out.

Breunne shouted from somewhere behind the paladin. "Beware! Troglodytes can see in the dark!"

"Sordaak!" Thrinndor shouted as he took two steps to his right to distance himself from where he had stood. There was a faint rustle to the paladin's left, and without warning the cavern filled with brilliant light.

"Aiyee!" shouted the voice that had spoken. "My eyes!"

"Stop!" Thrinndor shouted as he spotted Vorgath running toward a band of the creatures, his axe held high over his head.

The barbarian obediently skidded to a halt, mere feet from the first of the creatures. He held his axe in the ready position.

"You!" Thrinndor pointed at the creature—they were indeed troglodytes, he noted—he was fairly certain that had done the talking. "Come here." The creature hesitated, still shielding its eyes, trying to hide from the blinding light. "I said, come *here*!" the paladin shouted in his best commanding tone.

Whimpering, the creature looked around for support from his comrades. The two nearest ones pushed the pitiful creature toward the paladin. Some support!

"*NOW!*"

Slowly, the troglodyte shuffled its feet, moving closer to the paladin. He stopped a few feet short and shifted uncomfortably under the scrutiny of the much bigger fighter.

"Where are my people?" Thrinndor demanded without preamble.

"What people?"

"Do not pretend ignorance with me! Your people came to the surface and took many men from the harbor. Where are they?"

"Not pretend," argued the troglodyte. "Not know."

Vorgath had come up behind the scared creature. "Let me at him," the barbarian said. "I'll make him talk!" He raised his greataxe over his head, poised to strike.

The troglodyte turned quickly and raised an arm to ward off the coming blow.

"No," said Thrinndor. "I think I will let our sorcerer burn the skin from his bones. Slowly." The paladin laughed an evil laugh. "Sordaak!"

"Yes, boss?" The mage stepped up to stand beside his leader.

"You want your people back? Make him talk."

"My pleasure." Sordaak narrowed his eyes as he called flames to both hands and stepped forward.

The troglodyte's eyes nearly popped from his head as he took a step back, away from the approaching mage. "*NO!*" he screamed. "I not *know*! I promise." The creature's eyes never left Sordaak's hands.

"He speaks the truth." This was a new voice. A different—bigger— troglodyte separated himself from the pack standing at the back of the cavern in relative darkness. This one's common was also much better. There was some sort of apparatus on his head. "He was not involved in the capture of your men. And he does not know where they are being kept."

Thrinndor turned his attention to the newcomer. "Who are you?"

"I am King Gri`Puth."

"*King?*" snorted the barbarian. "King of *what?*"

Gri`Puth pointed at Vorgath with what appeared to be some sort of jewel-encrusted scepter. "He mocks me. This one must die."

"Just try it, asshole."

Gri`Puth turned to face Thrinndor, who put on his best diplomatic smile. "Pay him no mind. Vorgath hasn't killed anything in days, and that always makes him a bit cranky." The barbarian growled from deep within his chest to emphasize the point.

The dark, reptilian eyes of the self-professed king went from one to the other. "Why did you take our men?"

"They were intruding into my domain. I will return them to you, but you must all depart this island immediately."

"I am afraid that is not possible." Thrinndor shook his head.

"Then you and your men must die."

"I'll see to it that you precede us into the afterlife," grumbled the barbarian as he raised his greataxe.

Thrinndor couldn't tell, but he was pretty sure King Gri`Puth shifted uncomfortably. Certainly he could see the chief troglodyte begin to edge away from the dwarf.

It was Sordaak's turn to smile; he had long since extinguished the flames on his hands. The mage glanced at the paladin, who nodded his assent for the sorcerer to proceed. "Perhaps we can come to an understanding."

King Gri`Puth turned to face the mage. He appeared grateful at the change in how the conversation had been going. "I'm listening."

"How many of you are there?"

The king straightened and squared his shoulders. "We number an army of more than two hundred." That got Vorgath's attention. "And our main village has at least that number more mates and children."

Sordaak had not expected an entire colony of troglodytes. This complicated matters. He swallowed hard. "Very good," he lied. "Perhaps we can be of use to one another."

"I will listen to your proposition, but I can think of no possible benefit to my people in this."

Sordaak nodded slowly. He decided to play from a position of power. "I have a force of more than two *thousand* coming to aid in construction of my keep." Now this got the king's attention. "But they are not fighting men." Vorgath made to protest, but the mage silenced him with a glare. "I propose that we co-exist on this island, with your people providing a security force so that mine can focus on construction."

King Gri`Puth appeared to mull this proposal over. "Why should we 'co-exist' when we can wipe you out and keep the island for ourselves, as it has been?"

Sordaak had been expecting the question. "Because if we war, you will lose most—if not all—of your people." He allowed that to sink in. "And, even if you were to prevail, others will follow us, seeking the source of power—and they will be less likely to be willing to make a deal." The mage folded his arms across his chest smugly, knowing what he said to be true.

Gri`Puth hissed some, nodded some, and hissed some more. Clearly he did not like his options. "What do we get in return for providing this 'security force'?"

"You would be allowed to remain on the island, maintain and even grow your colony, and we will share technology with you to better your way of life."

"Who says our way of life requires bettering?"

"Whose does not?" countered the mage. "We have large ships that can bring in much food for the coming winter. We will have many men to build the walls to keep out that same winter. And," Sordaak had held back the one thing he knew the troglodytes coveted, "we can pay you." He loosened the thong attaching a small sack of coins at his belt and jerked it free. This he tossed the short distance to the king. The contents of the bag jingled as Gri`Puth snatched it out of the air and peered inside.

"Is this?"

"Platinum pieces," Sordaak confirmed.

"We have a deal," the king said as he strode forward and extended his arm. The sorcerer grasped forearms with the creature, inwardly breathing a sigh of relief. That had gone much better than he had feared.

"My men?"

King Gri`Puth waved his hand dismissively as he walked back over to where his people waited uneasily. "We will feed and care for them until this storm passes. Then they will be returned to the construction site." The troglodyte leader turned and his reptilian eyes seemed to lock with those of Sordaak. "You have my word."

"Very well," Sordaak said, rather pleased with himself.

"You are welcome to join us," the king continued. "It is much warmer below."

Sordaak bowed at the waist. "Thank you for that offer. But we must depart at first light, so I believe we will remain here."

The troglodyte king looked past Sordaak into the inky blackness behind him. Outside the winds howled, and the mage could see a few flakes of snow swirl in through the opening. "I wouldn't recommend attempting to leave the island until this storm passes." The king sniffed at the winds. "This storm is a bad one."

Sordaak appeared to ponder the thought. Cyrillis appeared at his elbow in the fading light from the orb as it spluttered. "Perhaps we should avail ourselves of their hospitality until the storm passes." She had no desire to get back onto another boat in the tossing seas.

Still Sordaak hesitated. "How far to this encampment of yours?"

"Not far—just a few minutes' walk this direction," Gri`Puth waved an arm behind where his people stood.

The sorcerer looked over at the paladin, who nodded. Sordaak's shoulders slumped. "Very well. Lead the way."

The companions quickly packed their things and were soon ready to move. Without a word, King Gri`Puth led them deeper into the mountain. Vorgath and Cyrillis each carried a torch, lighting the path for their friends. The troglodytes eschewed the lights, moving quickly ahead to get out of their ring of influence.

Ever deeper into the mountain they trudged. After what Sordaak felt to be twenty or thirty minutes, he felt they must be nearing the northern edge of the island. While the natural cavern had twisted and turned occasionally, he was certain the predominant direction was north. They rounded a bend and the mage could see a faint glow ahead.

Abruptly the tunnel walls opened into a vast cavern several hundred feet in length and breadth. The glow came from the ceiling of the immense chamber— a pale yellowish-orange light that seemed to filter down from the roof itself. This light provided enough illumination that the barbarian and healer were able to douse their torches.

Indeed, as the companion's eyes adjusted to the gloom, they found that they could see quite well. There were many structures interspersed throughout the complex, some small, some quite large. They walked past several curious children who stood and stared openly at the humans as they passed. Most had never seen man before.

Gri`Puth led them along a wide bath between structures, veering to the left, until they came upon a huge, locked door. At a nod from the king, one of the two guards removed a key from around his neck and used it to open the padlock. He slid the bolt back, grasped the pull ring and swung the door open.

A group of men waited on the other side; obviously they were poised to attack. "Wait," Sordaak commanded, stopping them.

"Sordaak?" one of the men spoke. The mage recognized him as his chief engineer. "They've captured you, as well?"

"Hardly," snorted the barbarian as he stepped past the sorcerer. "We're here to get your worthless asses back to work!"

"Vorgath!" Cyrillis chided as she also pushed past Sordaak. "Is anyone hurt?"

"No, ma'am," said the original. "We've been treated relatively well, for what that's worth."

The companions were shown to the guest quarters, and the prisoners were released to do as they please. There was even an apology of sorts from the troglodyte king.

Chapter Seventeen

Ice Storm

The storm raged for two days. When finally the companions emerged from the complex of caverns and tunnels they found an island turned white under a blanket of snow. In the mouth of the cave each donned such winter gear as they carried, bolstered by skins and furs given to them by their new allies.

Fighting their way through deep snow and even deeper drifts, the companions and Sordaak's original crew made their way back to the compound. Once there, they found it too was buried beneath a thick blanket of snow.

Sordaak left explicit instructions as to what was to be constructed next, how the dwarves were to be deployed and other mundane instructions, including what to do with the additional capital now available.

At dawn of the fourth day since arriving on the island, the companions met at one of the piers in the harbor and boarded the smallest of the three transport vessels there. Still, it was a craft much larger—and in considerably better shape—than the one that brought them to the island. Sordaak glanced off to the north and could just make out the mast of the ship sticking out of the water. He shook his head as memories of that night came flooding back, and then he stepped aboard.

The trip north was uneventful. While cold, the crystal blue skies were breathtaking in their brilliance.

The companions gathered around a firepot in the stern of the vessel as Sordaak explained his plan. "In order to harvest a cloak from a Storm Giant, that giant must be *alive*—"

"Aw, come on! Really?" This bit of news clearly upset the barbarian.

"Yes, really. If the giant is dead, the cloak loses all magical properties and is then useless."

"It is my understanding," Thrinndor interrupted, "that the cloak is bestowed upon the male or female giant upon reaching adulthood." Sordaak nodded. "And the cloak is held in place by an unbroken band of pure Mithryl that cannot be removed." He raised an eyebrow. "You mentioned once before that you had a plan for removing these. I believe if we are to risk life and limb in an attempt to capture *live* Storm Giants, perhaps you should explain just how it is you plan on doing so."

"As you wish." Sordaak stood and walked over to the paladin, bracing himself against the slight pitching of the vessel as it wallowed between swells. "Hold out your right hand, please." Thrinndor did as asked. The spell-caster inspected the single ring on the big fighter's hand, removed a black pearl from the pouch at his waist and began to chant.

The companions could feel the power in the air build, and then Sordaak reached out with his right hand with the pearl pinched between his index finger and thumb. This he touched lightly to the ring on Thrinndor's finger. A spark came from the contact and a hum filled the air. The companions watched astonished as the ring began to *grow*!

As it swelled in size, Sordaak easily slid the ring from the paladin's finger and, still in contact with the pearl, put it on his own finger. The ring was far too big, but as they continued to watch, it began to shrink! After a moment or two, it was the proper size for the mage's finger.

"Thank you," Sordaak said as he turned and walked back to his seat and sat down.

"Wait! That ring was given to me by my mother! It is a priceless family heirloom."

"Yes, thank you." Sordaak eyed the ring appreciatively. "Although a bit mundane, it does seem to go well with my other rings."

"Give it back."

"I'm afraid that is impossible." The air suddenly went very still as the companions waited for the explosion that was sure to come. "Once sized for the new host, the process is irreversible."

"*WHAT?*" Thrinndor stood menacingly.

The spell-caster looked up at him innocently. "Just kidding!" He smiled. "Of course I can reverse the process. However, with a battle looming, surely you would prefer I not waste spell energy on—"

"Give it back!"

"Yes, of course. If you insist." As the paladin stood glowering, Sordaak again reached into his pouch, removed another pearl and repeated the enchantment. In a couple blinks of the eye, the ring was back with its proper owner.

"Thank you," Thrinndor said as he returned to his seat.

"If you two are finished messing around," Breunne said from his place at the rail, "you should probably see this."

Thrinndor stood quickly and made his way to the rail, Vorgath and Sordaak right behind him.

Without waiting for their questions, the ranger pointed to the north where a mass of dark clouds was building. Lightning flashes could be seen in the morass of roiling darkness.

"Son of a bitch!" Sordaak slammed his hand on the rail. All eyes drifted to him. "They've been alerted we're coming."

Thrinndor looked dubious. "How can you be so sure?"

The mage glared at his leader. "I know that frequent storms happen this time of year in this place," his face grim, the turned to stare at the mass of rapidly approaching clouds, "but this is no ordinary storm." He turned to look into the barbarian's eyes. "There was no warning." Vorgath confirmed this with a shake of his head. "This storm is not natural."

"Natural or not," Savinhand checked the rigging with a critical eye, "we don't want to get caught up in it." He ran back to the tiller and pushed it hard over, trying to turn the vessel toward land. Slowly the small ship turned, and even Cyrillis could tell they were not going to make it.

Breunne rushed to the lines, trimming the sails to get better fill. Their speed picked up, but it was clear to all it would not be enough.

An idea came to Thrinndor. "Calling these storms requires a spell, does it not?" Sordaak merely nodded, his face grim as he watched the oncoming storm. "Can you not dispel the energy, or something?"

The mage shook his head. "It doesn't work like that," he said through clenched teeth. "One, I would have to know the spell, which I don't, and two, I would have to at least match—preferably exceed—the spell casting ability of the caster. While my prowess continues to grow, I cannot match abilities with an adult Storm Giant—or, even worse—a group of Storm Giants combining their powers to create a storm such as this." Already their vessel was feeling the effects of the choppy swells that preceded the actual storm. Their sails sagged as the winds died. "The calm before the storm," he said prophetically.

Thrinndor glanced toward shore, still almost a mile away. "How could they have known?"

"Damn Trogs!" Vorgath spat.

"No," Sordaak answered. "They had neither the knowledge of our plans nor the ability to alert them so quickly."

The paladin turned his eyes to the sorcerer. "Who then?"

"I don't know." Sordaak pondered the question. "None we left behind on the island knew of our plans to visit Mioria." He scratched his head idly as he thought aloud. "Yet somehow the giants knew to watch for our approach by boat." He turned slowly to look at the rogue who stood at the tiller. "Only two possibilities, as I see it. First, the Drow in the service of the Library knew of our plans."

Savinhand grimaced, but nodded his agreement. It chafed to think those that supposedly served him might have a spy in their midst.

"Second?" Vorgath asked as the winds began to pick up. Winds that held the taste of ice.

"Second," Sordaak's eyes never left those of the rogue, "I believe that there are one or two from Shardmoor that may have overheard our plans."

Savinhand, his eyes locked with those of the magicuser, again nodded, his lips a thin line as those loyal to him were having their loyalties called into question.

"There is a third possibility." All eyes shifted to the barbarian and waited for him to finish the thought. He shrugged. "One of us is a spy."

Sordaak raised his hands for silence at the uproar that caused. After a few moments he got it. "While that is indeed a possibility, I don't believe that to be the case."

"Nor do I." Cyrillis stood by Sordaak, her chin thrust out, daring any to argue further.

"So, it's either the drow or scum from Shardmoor." Vorgath turned his eyes back to Savinhand.

The wind was beginning to howl, and the air had an unnatural taint to it, much like the storm that struck them as they departed the Library.

Thrinndor looked aloft at the rigging struggling to hold the sails against the ferocity of the wind. "It matters not at this point," he said grimly. "If we do not get this ship to shore soon, we might not have to worry about who is warning our enemies."

Vorgath nodded. "There is another option." He had to shout to make himself heard over the winds shrieking through the lines over their heads. "We can turn and try to run with the storm."

"No!" Sordaak shook his head violently. "That's what they want! If the storm holds together, that could blow us *days* to the south! And that's assuming this ship can withstand the battering for that long!"

Thrinndor hesitated. Neither option had a reasonable chance of success. The shore was closer now, less than a half-mile, but their speed in that direction was slowing dramatically in the onslaught.

And then the ice hit. Stinging ice pellets that started as rain high in the clouds, freezing into small hail stones that sliced at the skin when driven by the wind.

"Take cover!" Thrinndor shouted as he made his way to the lines holding the sails. He eased them further lest they be carried away in by the ever increasing velocity of the winds. He felt the ice cut into his skin of his face. He paused to tie a cloth around his head, leaving only a slit that allowed him to see.

Realizing he no longer heard the flap of the sails overhead, he looked up to see why. Fearing the worst, it was worse yet. The ice had not shredded the sails as he thought, but the pellets stuck to the cloth and froze in place. As he watched, the sails continued to increase in mass. Soon they would be too heavy for the mast and it would snap under the additional weight.

Their little ship was doomed.

In a last-ditch effort, he drew his sword and slashed at the lines holding the sails. He almost made it.

Almost.

As he hacked at the last frozen line, there was a splintering crash behind him and the mast toppled over the side, carried away by the weight and wind. Thrinndor watched as the lines that had held the mast in place twisted under the strain as the sail filled with water, acting as an anchor and turning their little vessel into the wind.

With renewed vigor the paladin attacked the lines that kept the mast tied to the ship. Unless he could cut them all, they were doomed. Breunne and Savinhand leapt to his aid—Vorgath was nowhere to be seen. Briefly Thrinndor worried that his friend had been carried overboard when the mast gave and he cast about wildly for the dwarf. A frozen line whipped past his face, forcing the paladin to return his attention to what he had been doing.

Together the three men managed to cut the myriad lines that had held the mast in place, and they briefly watched it float away.

Although it was midday, the darkness was almost total, save for the occasional flashes from a bolt of lightning. The ice pellets were now clinging to every exposed part of the ship, and the vessel wallowed heavily between the huge waves, each threatening to inundate the boat and take it to the bottom.

Yet somehow she hung on. Land was no longer visible, and the paladin was not even sure which direction to look. Suddenly an idea sprang into his head. Sword in hand he rushed to the bow of the vessel.

He almost screamed in frustration as he saw his objective covered in ice. "Help me!" he shouted as he attacked the windlass that had the anchor rope wrapped around it.

Sensing their leader at least had a plan, Breunne and Savinhand worked to clear the ice from the anchor rope and its mechanism. Fighting freezing rain, ice pellets, gale force winds and blowing snow, the three appeared to be losing ground until a flash of flames engulfed the windlass, melting the remaining chunks of ice.

Initially, Thrinndor was too startled by the flames to take action. He looked over at Sordaak, who was readying another round, when he realized what had happened. The second burst of flames freed the mechanism and the paladin knocked loose the latch holding the windlass in place. When nothing happened, the three men each grasped a spike and threw all their weight into the turnstile.

Finally it broke free and the weight of the anchor caused the turnstile to spin out of control.

"Do not allow it to play out completely!" Sordaak shouted over the din of the storm.

As the massive rope neared the end, Thrinndor slammed home the latch. Savinhand was prepared with spikes in the event the latch failed. But the huge turnstile came to an abrupt halt, and the three men ensured it stayed that way with iron spikes.

Soon the ice from the storm recoated the mechanism and they no longer had to worry whether it would hold. The bow of the ship would break off before the windlass gave way.

Thrinndor hoped.

The big fighter rushed over to put his hands on the anchor rope. He wanted to see if he could feel the anchor dragging across the bottom. The thought crossed his mind that the water may be deeper here than the length of rope they had played out. He said a quick prayer, asking for that not to be true.

As it turned out, he needn't have bothered holding the rope. The anchor hung up on something down below, and the rope screamed as it stretched and popped, slowing and then stopping the vessel from its headlong run before the wind.

Satisfied the capstan was going to hold, Thrinndor motioned for the others to get below as he too stumbled toward the ladder that led to the small cabin.

As he dropped down the ladder, Breunne started to shut the door. "No!" Thrinndor called out. "If that door shuts, the ice will block it and we will be trapped down here!"

"Right!" Breunne dropped back down the ladder and joined his wretched companions as the gathered around the fire pot, trying to glean what warmth they could as the storm raged over their heads.

"Where is Vorgath?" Cyrillis' voice held a hint of panic.

Thrinndor's shoulders slumped. "I know not. He was with me as we tried to cut the sails free. But I did not see him after the mast snapped."

No one wanted to say the obvious. All knew that none could survive long in the water in this storm. The companions huddled in silence as the storm's fury waged a battle with their little ship.

The shrieking of the storm seemed to abate for a moment and then there was a thud as something landed at the bottom of the ladder.

"Vorgath!" Cyrillis screamed as she caught sight of the dwarf lying on the deck not far away.

"Rumors of my demise have been greatly exaggerated," the barbarian said through clenched teeth. Vorgath's eyes rolled back into his head and he said no more. The dwarf's beard was a frozen mass of ice and snow and his hair was pretty much the same. His cloak and armor were solid sheets of ice, and his limbs were frozen to the point where movement looked impossible. Yet, there he lay.

"Get him over to the fire!" Thrinndor leapt into action, grasped the dwarf's closest arm and half-lifted, half-drug him over to the fire pot. Cyrillis brushed the ice from his face as she poured her most potent healing magic into Vorgath's prone body. The paladin used one of his healing abilities as well.

Color came back into the dwarf's face, yet he still did not move. Sordaak stepped in with his hands ablaze, and holding them near the barbarian's face and torso, quickly melting the ice away.

Cyrillis brushed off the chunks that remained and they wrapped his unconscious body in a blanket and set him as near the fire pot as possible.

Thrinndor cast a worried look at the healer. Cyrillis shook her head and shrugged. "He yet lives. We have made his body whole, but he has been through a lot. We will have to wait and see." Her voice trailed off. "His will to live is strong."

The paladin nodded and kept his eyes glued to his friend lest he wake and need something.

For several hours more the storm raged outside their little island of warmth. A couple of times the hull shuddered under the weight of the ice and Thrinndor feared the boat would capsize. But, she did not.

Vorgath stirred after a couple of hours and sat up. The paladin helped him to a seat next to the fire pot. "What happened to you?"

Vorgath cast a sidelong look at his friend. "I was trying to help cut the sails free. When the mast snapped I was in the wrong place and was knocked overboard. I would have probably been lost had not a rope from the rigging wrapped around my ankle and kept me from drifting too far. I tried calling out for help, but I knew I couldn't be heard over the roar of the storm. So, I hand-over-handed my way back to the ship. I almost lost my grip when the anchor caught." Vorgath shook his head as his mind went back to that moment. "My fingers were frozen in the shape of the rope, but I had wrapped the rope around my waist for just such an occasion." He paused for a few moments. "By the time I was able to pull myself aboard, you all were down here in the warmth and I decided I would join you." He smiled.

"You should be more careful, old one." Thrinndor's eyes twinkled with the moisture resulting from almost losing his best friend.

Vorgath took in a deep breath to argue, but instead he released that breath with a sigh. "I agree."

The paladin's right eyebrow shot up, but he decided to let the comment pass. Besides, it was right about then that the winds began to subside.

Vorgath looked toward the low ceiling above their heads. "Damn Storm Giants must've finally gotten tired!"

"Or they figure they have killed us," Sordaak said somberly, also looking at the wooden planks above their heads.

"Damn near did." Vorgath wasn't smiling. He surged to his feet. "But it takes a lot more than some blowhard giants to finish off *this* dwarf!" He shuffled toward the ladder leading to the deck.

Thrinndor chuckled as he got to his feet and followed his friend.

Topside, Vorgath let out a low whistle. "Damn, that's a lot of ice!"

"Agreed," Thrinndor said as Breunne and then Savinhand appeared next to him.

It was still dark, but this time it was because the sun was gone, and tonight there were no moons. There were places where the stars could be seen through breaks in the clouds.

The weight of all the ice caused their vessel to sit much lower in the water than it previously did.

"Is the anchor still holding?" Breunne asked as he headed to the bow. He could see the line was taut as it entered the water. "I'll take that as a yes." He walked back to join the others.

Sordaak poked his head up through the hatch. "Any idea where we are?"

All eyes turned to Vorgath. He shook his head. "Don't look at me! I need a point, or points, of reference. The shore should not be far away to the west, but I can't tell where on that shore we would be. Maybe when we get some sunlight I'll know more."

"Damn. I could send Fahlred to the island and have them send a boat to look for us, but without a point of reference, that would be pointless."

"Not to mention that if the Storm Giants spot that ship, we might have a repeat of today," Savinhand said. "That would suck."

Sordaak was about to reply when Vorgath held up a hand asking for silence. All eyes again returned to him as he cocked his head to one side.

"What is it?" Thrinndor asked, his voice laden with concern.

"Shhh!" Vorgath insisted. "*Listen!*"

As there was little or no wind to make any noise through what little rigging was left and the surface of the water was almost glass-like in its calmness, there was little to hear. The silence was almost eerie after the pounding of the storm.

However, as their ears attuned to the lack of sound, a faint one could be heard—the sound of waves washing ashore. The swells were light and spaced far apart, but they were there.

"How far off?" Sordaak whispered.

"I don't know," Vorgath said as he squinted his eyes toward the source of the sound. Nothing! The dark of the night was almost complete, and he could see nothing.

"I have an idea," Breunne said as he pulled his cloak tighter and tied it about his waist with a piece of rope. The companions watched with interest as he said a command word and he leapt into the air, where he stayed. He was flying! "If I shout out, do the same because I may have trouble finding you again in this darkness."

"What if the fly spell doesn't last long enough for a return trip?" Sordaak asked ominously.

Breunne merely smiled. "I guess we had better all hope that it does!" With that, he turned and sped off toward the sounds they had heard.

Sordaak watched where the ranger had disappeared, but his eyes could see nothing in the darkness. "Say a prayer for him, please."

"In progress," Cyrillis replied.

"Me, too," Thrinndor answered.

Sordaak nodded, his eyes continuing to try to penetrate the dark. An idea occurred to him, and he silently summoned Fahlred. His quasit appeared instantly, and the sorcerer communed with him telepathically. The creature nodded, turning the limpid pools that were its eyes in the direction his master indicated.

Almost instantly Sordaak, seeing through the eyes of his familiar, could make out the infrared signature that was the ranger nearing the shore. He should have thought of this sooner! He could clearly see the shore about two or three hundred yards aft and a bit to starboard.

In the midst of his concentration he heard Thrinndor say quietly. "If Breunne calls out for assistance, do not return the call loudly. If the anchor indeed held, we are not far from where we would have been spotted by the giants in the first place. Sound carries very well on such a still night."

He got several nods in reply.

"He made it," Sordaak whispered as he saw the ranger land on the shore and begin scouting about. "He's looking around for something… Wait, he must have found it because he's on his way back." The mage never opened his eyes, instead seeing through Fahlred.

The companions all heard a faint shout. Thrinndor returned the shout in the same manner. He then reached out and began tapping the side of the boat with the pommel of his sword every few seconds.

Sordaak watched as the ranger quickly covered the distance and landed among them out of seeming thin air.

"Very nicely done," Breunne said, his feet back on the solidness of the boat. "Whoever thought of the tapping on the hull is wise. From what I can tell we are not more than a couple of miles south of where we were when the storm hit us."

"How far to shore?" Vorgath asked.

Breunne hesitated. "Hard to say as I was flying in complete darkness most of the time. However, I don't think more than a quarter-mile. Probably less.

"Close enough to make it in the rowboat?" Thrinndor asked.

All eyes turned to the small boat astern meant to ferry those who needed to get ashore when the larger vessel was anchored off shore.

"That itty-bitty thing?" Vorgath asked.

"With six of us and our supplies, that dinghy would be seriously overloaded. However, I can use the boots to fly over one more time—but that will be it for them until I rest. That should help."

"We will cut the anchor rope as we depart," Thrinndor said. "Hopefully the boat will drift south before the sun comes up, and any nearby giants none the wiser that we were able to weather the storm."

"I too can fly," said the sorcerer, "using my fly spell." He got several disbelieving looks and he hurried on, "I have MUCH more experience using the spell than I did with those stupid boots!"

"We will fly together, then," Breunne said.

Vorgath and Thrinndor had to remove the stiff tarp from the little boat, move it over to the side and lowered it with ropes to the water. Vorgath climbed down the rope ladder to the boat and caught the supplies tossed to him by the others. He then broke out the oars and readied them as the others made their way down the ladder.

"I'll cut the anchor rope and then fly ashore," Breunne said, getting a nod from the paladin in return.

Vorgath couldn't let it go, however. "Anything to get out of rowing!"

"Yup," grinned the ranger as he tossed down the lines that had held the small dinghy in place and then disappeared toward the stern. Vorgath and Thrinndor worked the oars while Savinhand made his way unsteadily to the bow of their little vessel. The damn boat rocked too much for his liking, but there was no help for it. The boat was built for three, maybe four, people and provisions for six!

Still, the barbarian and paladin used easy, quiet strokes to push them toward shore, and soon enough the sound of the sea lapping gently on the rocks could easily be made out as they approached the shore.

Breunne and Sordaak met them there. The ranger caught the rope thrown to him and pulled the little boat up onto a sandy section of beach.

Once ashore, the four men minus Sordaak picked the boat up and carried it into some brush, hiding it there.

"We were lucky," Breunne said quietly as the companions gathered under the boughs of a large tree.

"How so?" Sordaak asked.

"Because I found where at least six giants had waited for some time—presumably the Storm Giants who tried to kill us, or at least to send us far out to sea."

"Really?" The Thrinndor asked. "Six? I had not realized there were that many adult Storm Giants left in all the land."

"Me, either," Vorgath agreed.

"That makes no sense," Sordaak said suddenly. The others waited for him to continue. "If there are at least six Storm Giants—and since they rarely travel without their women and children we must assume there are even more—why would they go through all the trouble to raise that storm and risk our surviving? If they know we are coming for them, and we assume they do, then why not just wait and kill us then? Surely six Storm Giants would be confident in their ability to take on the six of us?"

The companions were silent as each contemplated the question.

"They've probably heard of our recent encounters, and don't want to face us directly!" Vorgath seemed rather proud of that assessment.

Sordaak rolled his eyes. "More likely they were asked to only delay us."

"Delay us for what?"

The sorcerer looked at the paladin. "Who else knows we're coming?"

Thrinndor pondered the question for a moment. His eyes went wide. "Ice Homme?"

Sordaak nodded.

"But, they believe we are all dead, do they not?" Cyrillis protested.

"That's what we *wanted* them to believe," countered the mage. "We've never had a way to verify that."

Thrinndor nodded. "I fear you are correct. We must now assume they not only know we yet live, but that they also know where we are."

Chapter Eighteen

Best Laid Plans...

"That changes things a bit," Breunne said.

"Yeah," Savinhand interrupted, his tone dry, "like maybe there are no spies, after all?"

Sordaak looked at the rogue and blinked a couple of times. "Possibly." When he turned back to the paladin, his voice was even. "If they know where we are, they may even now be marching toward us."

Thrinndor nodded. "It is a possibility."

"How do we make sure?"

"Excuse me?"

The sorcerer chose not to answer that obvious question—yet. "I believe it's time for a change in plans." Sordaak rubbed his chin thoughtfully. Thrinndor lifted an eyebrow but said nothing. "It's a safe bet the Storm Giants are in league with the Minions. That would mean those Minions know where we are, and—at a minimum—know which direction we are headed.

"If, as I suspect, the mobilized army of said Minions from the south have been camped somewhere near Farreach—"

"They are," Savinhand interrupted again. Sordaak raised an inquisitive brow. The rogue shrugged. "A little birdy told me that prior to leaving the Library."

"Do we know how many?"

"Seventy-five...ish."

"Then it is also probably a safe bet they have mobilized and are headed this way." This drew a grim nod from the paladin. "The University at Ice Homme has at least that number, maybe more at their disposal." Another nod. "They will also certainly march—but will not leave their home unprotected. Let's say they march fifty, leaving behind a like number."

The companions made themselves as comfortable as they could without a fire after deciding one was not worth the risk. First light was not far off, and staying out of sight for the time being seemed prudent.

"In summary," Sordaak said, enjoying the display of his mental prowess, "We have seventy-five pissed-off minions marching from the south, another fifty or so similarly pissed-off minions marching from the north and at least a half-dozen Storm Giants in this neighborhood, all with malicious intent crowding their minds." He looked from one to another. The mage's eyes had adjusted enough to show faces, but no detail. "Did I miss anything?"

"Yes," Vorgath replied. He said no more, but when Sordaak only stared back, the dwarf rolled his eyes. "Clan Dragaar?"

Sordaak blinked twice, and then a third time, thinking fast. "The *dwarves!*" He sat bolt upright. "Of *course!*" He slapped his knee. "When are they due in Ardaagh?"

Now it was Vorgath's turn to pause and think. "The day after tomorrow, or the one after that, I believe."

"Sounds about right." Sordaak was again thinking hard. "We need to stop them."

"What?" several of the companions said at once.

The mage held up his hands. "I don't want the dwarves fighting the minions."

The barbarian bristled. "I'm fairly certain fifteen-hundred of my kin can handle a group of minions one-tenth that size!"

"What?" Sordaak was momentarily confused; he had been working on a different part of the problem. "No, of course they could!" he said. "But these Minions will be supported by at least two—and possibly three or more—High Lords of Set. They will not go down without exacting a steep price from your people." His voice got quiet. "A price I—we—can't afford to pay. We'll need every one of those dwarves if we are to finish the temple in time."

"In time for what?" Thrinndor asked.

"What?" Sordaak's head spun around to look into the dark visage of the paladin.

"You said, 'if we are to finish the temple in time.' In time for what?"

The mage blinked rapidly several times, having revealed more than intended. Sordaak allowed his shoulders to slump. His eyes fell to the ground in front of him, and he didn't look up as he spoke softly. "There is indeed a time limit on the Soul Trap spell used to hold Valdaar's life force in stasis."

"*WHAT?*" several voices said at the same time.

Sordaak shifted uncomfortably under their gaze. "I spent time researching the spell Lord Dragma used while at the Library. I had to be sure we were not merely chasing a fantasy—one that could have no happy ending." He paused. "While he was not sure, Dragma wrote that he didn't believe the special—powerful—variant he used would hold up for more than two millennia."

There was some nervous shifting in the silence that followed. "What happens then?" Cyrillis asked, unable to bear the silence.

Sordaak still did not look up. "There is a degradation of the spirit trapped. Eventually there would not be enough left to recover."

"No!" Cyrillis' voice was a low moan.

"How long has he been trapped?" Breunne asked.

Thrinndor's voice matched the tone of the conversation. "According to the legends passed to me, last year would have completed two thousand years."

"*NO!*" Cyrillis repeated, louder this time.

Sordaak wanted to ease her fears—*had* to ease her fears. "Yet you still feel his presence, do you not?" His tone was both hopeful and forceful. She nodded. The mage imagined more than saw the tears coursing down her cheeks, yet he was sure they were there. "It is he that grants you your powers, and you have not felt a diminishment. So, therefore we still have time."

She nodded again. "Yet, we must *hurry!*"

"I too feel the need to not tarry, and I have felt it longer," Thrinndor said. "It is my belief that there is no coincidence these events are coming together, now. *We* are coming together, now. Gathering the pieces to raise our lord has been attempted twice in the years since his banishment. It is in my heart this must be the last time."

If the mood was somber before, now there was a fog of despair clouding the air.

Sordaak got to his feet and stood before Cyrillis. He helped her rise and realized it was getting light as he could now see her tears. He gently brushed them away. "We *will* succeed," he said.

The cleric smiled and nodded. "Yes, we will."

"Shall we discuss these 'change in plans'?" Vorgath was itching to see some action.

Sordaak lowered his eyes to the ground and took a deep breath. "How do your people feel about the Minions of Set?"

The barbarian blinked a couple of times, digesting the question. "For the most part, Clan Dragaar will go along with 'to each their own.'"

"And if these Minions are intent on keeping your people from the mines on Valdaar's Rest?"

"Just how do these few *minions* propose to keep fifteen hundred dwarves from their appointed task?"

Sordaak leveled a stare at the barbarian. "Because their intent is to prevent us from rebuilding Valdaar's Rest and thus returning him to the land."

"So?"

"If the Minions are successful, the forces of Praxaar will again shut down the island, and not even an army of dwarves will be sufficient to reopen the mines."

Sordaak and Vorgath maintained their locked eyes for a bit.

"Then the Minions are history," Vorgath said evenly. "But you said you didn't want my people fighting the Minions."

"I don't, and they won't—at least not right away."

"Make some sense, man!" Vorgath had just about had enough of this double-talk.

Sordaak smiled his knowing smile. He looked first at Thrinndor. "With your permission?" The paladin nodded. "We will have to act fast. If these groups of minions—it's hard to call fifty and seventy-five 'armies'—are indeed on the move, their intent is to catch us in their trap." He smiled at the dwarf. "It is my intent to reverse the tables, and catch them in ours."

The light was growing fast. It looked like it was going to be a clear, cloudless day.

"Get on with it!" Vorgath was not sure he liked the sound of where this was going.

"First we must neutralize the giants," Sordaak said. "We will have to be careful and catch them by surprise. Right now the six Breunne discovered are probably hanging around to make sure they were successful. If he can track them—"

"Easy."

"—then maybe we can surprise them and make our job a bit easier. After that, we take on the first of whichever minion groups shows up, and the second one after that."

The companions sat in stunned silence for a moment.

Vorgath was the first to speak. "Let's see if I have this straight. You don't want fifteen-hundred dwarves to do battle with a small army of Minions so that we—six—can? But only after we do battle with between six and ten Storm Giants?"

Sordaak nodded vigorously. "Very good! I see you were listening!"

"Have you taken leave of your senses?"

"Nope. Feeling just fine, thank you." The mage looked around at the group. "I suggest a quick, dry breakfast and then we can get started."

The barbarian looked over at his friend the paladin. "I think he was under water too long the other night."

"Perhaps," Thrinndor agreed. His eyes never left the mage. "You do realize that if one of us were to fall in any of these battles you describe so easily, there would be no need for the temple."

"Of course," Sordaak said amiably. "I have supreme confidence in our abilities and our healer." He smiled at Cyrillis, who tried to return the smile, but all she could manage was a half-grin/half-grimace. "As a single entity, none of the aforementioned groups should pose much of a threat to us." He allowed a scowl to cross his face. "However, if allowed to join forces and prepare, this could get ugly. Fast."

"What about the High Lords of Set?" Thrinndor was not yet convinced.

"You let me worry about them." Sordaak's face took on a smug look. "I'll handle them. And once they are 'handled', the Minions will be in complete disarray and relatively easy to dispose of."

"What about Dragaar Clan?" Vorgath asked. "You said something about the dwarves fighting, just not right away."

"Correct," Sordaak said, turning back to the barbarian. "It is my intent once I take out the High Lords of whichever group we encounter, to lead the remains of that group toward the other group, dispose of the High Lords from that second group and lead what remains toward Ardaagh."

"Now I know he's slipped a disc in his brain," Vorgath said, shaking his head.

Unfazed, the sorcerer continued. "By then the Dwarves will be near Ardaagh, so we alert them and have them set up an ambush. Leaderless, the Minions should be easy to wipe out with little or no fight." He crossed his arms on his chest and put on his best smug expression.

Again there was silence.

This time it was Thrinndor who spoke first. "A viable plan, I think, assuming we can *easily* get past that first part—killing six Storm Giants." He shook his head.

"When we find them," Sordaak said, remaining on a roll, "we will set up a trap for them, as well." He eyed the leader with a haughty stare. "I said nothing about killing them." The paladin's right eyebrow shot up. "In fact, we must take care during the encounter to make sure three are captured alive."

"Can't we kill those six and take the cloaks from those that wait for them at Mioria?" It was Savinhand who asked the obvious question.

"We can't be *sure* that there will be others waiting back at Mioria," Sordaak said as if he were lecturing in a class. "While we may *assume* that, we can't bank on finding the remaining giants there to gain the cloaks we will need to complete our task." The mage smiled at the rogue. "Good thought, though. We'll have to take them from the first group of giants we encounter, thereby ensuring we get our cloaks. If we slip up and kill too many or the first group," the sorcerer threw a hairy eye at the barbarian, "only then will we modify our plans to encompass those giants that remain at Mioria."

There was more silence as each of the companions digested the information. "Any more questions?" Sordaak got several head shakes. "Good. I'm starved. Let's grab a bite to eat and go whoop some giant butt."

"That's usually my line," grumbled the dwarf. "But for some reason I'm not sure I'm feeling it right now."

"You'll feel better after you've had something to eat," the mage said cheerily. He began rummaging through the food bag he carried.

The troupe ate in silence, each contemplating the plan—or at least what Sordaak perceived as a plan.

Breunne scratched his head idly as he munched on a dried biscuit stuffed with some jerked venison, all washed down with water from a skin he normally hand slung at his back. "While I am not exactly thrilled with the plan as stated, try as I might, I find no flaw in it."

"Thank you," Sordaak said formally.

"I see a flaw," griped the barbarian. "Each part of the plan requires complete success with the preceding part. One slip-up and we have a royal pile of shit on our hands."

"Don't slip up!" Sordaak said as he, too, washed down his breakfast with water and stood. "You are correct, O ancient one. One misstep and we'll be scrambling to recover. As we approach each encounter, I'll pass out specific duties to each of you. If those duties are performed to the abilities I know you possess, this will go off without a hitch. By the end of the day tomorrow—or the day after, latest—we will be knocking on the gates at Ice Homme!" Vorgath started to speak, but the sorcerer rushed on before he could. "That's a different plan—one I'll share with you upon completion of the current plans."

"We'll burn that bridge while we're crossing it," Savin muttered under his breath.

Sordaak decided to let that comment go. He was feeling too good to contaminate his thoughts with such negativity.

Having finished repacking his stuff, Breunne stood. "Wait here and prepare. I'll go locate their camp, and come back for you. I doubt the giants moved far off."

"You got that right, little man!" A deep voice boomed in the still morning air, followed by the thud of a club bigger than the barbarian knocking Vorgath from his perch on a rock. The dwarf flew more than fifty feet and landed in deep brush.

The clearing the party had occupied was suddenly overrun with giants! One brandished a sword that had to be ten feet long, which he swung hard at the paladin. Thrinndor's sword leapt to his hand as if by mere thought, and just barely in time to parry the blow.

The giant's attack was well-coordinated, with each of the six having selected a different target. Breunne was momentarily stunned by their appearance; he should have been able to hear any approach by these brutes. And then he was really stunned by a glancing blow from another club. He had seen it coming at the last second but was unable to completely mitigate the blow. He rolled a couple of times, working to get feeling back in his left arm and shoulder.

Cyrillis raised *Kurril* and received a ringing in both arms for her efforts. Although the staff kept the sword from cleaving her head, the force of the blow knocked her to the ground, her arms numb. She rolled to her right, narrowly avoiding another slash that sank deep into the moist ground where she had been only a second before. Seeing the tree they had taken refuge under a short distance away, she continued rolling until under the protective boughs.

There, she surged to her feet, said a quick prayer to restore feeling to her limbs and spun to assess the rest of her team. The heavy boughs of the tree saved her life as the giant had followed her and swung again. Seeing none of her companions were in immediate danger, she swung *Kurril* with both hands and all the strength she could muster. The staff clanged off of the giant's knee and he roared in pain as a blinding flash erupted at the point of impact.

The giant assigned to Savinhand moved in but was dumbfounded to find the rogue not where he had been. The giant roared his displeasure and poked around in the brush with his club.

Sordaak's personal tormentor was fortunately a little slow, giving the sorcerer time enough to prepare and cast a spell. Unfortunately the spell he had on the tip of his tongue was a web. While that spell can certainly slow a critter down, it also served to piss them off greatly. And a pissed-off giant—especially a pissed-off Storm Giant—had way more than adequate strength to easily shred the substance generated by the spell. However, that gave the sorcerer enough time to come up with something better. Fireball. Way better.

Vorgath sat up, disentangled himself from the brush, stood and pulled his breastplate back into place. It had gotten rearranged, and dented.

That pissed him off. Vorgath howled in rage as he pulled *Flinthgoor* from the hook on his back. Just then the giant who sent him on this little journey pushed aside a tree between where he was and where he had been. Had the barbarian not been in the midst of a rage, he might have wondered how he got past the tree in the first place.

In one fluid motion the dwarf whipped the great-axe from his back and embedded it into the upper right thigh of the immense humanoid. Now it was the giant's turn to howl. The giant swung his club again, but this time the barbarian was ready for him. Vorgath ducked under the blow, dislodging his axe as he rolled. Surging back to his feet he planted *Flinthgoor* deep into the giant's other leg.

The backswing from the monster's club this time connected, again sending the dwarf reeling. However, as the giant was no longer able to put his legs into the swing, the barbarian found the blow merely annoying and charged back in.

Vorgath could see the giant was slowed by the previous wounds. The barbarian decided to press his advantage. Brushing aside another feeble swing, the barbarian aimed for the same spot on the giant's upper thigh he had hit first. His great-axe again bit deep, this time nearly severing the leg at the point of impact.

The monster toppled forward and Vorgath buried *Flinthgoor* deep into the giant's back. Still, the creature struggled to rise. Vorgath put his foot on the giant's back and ripped his axe free. With all his might, he swung his blade, this time aiming for the exposed neck.

Vorgath shook his head as he looked down at the severed head. "I hope that damn mage wasn't counting on this one to get a cloak." He then shouldered his weapon and headed for the action he could hear back in the clearing. "OK, who needs help?"

Savinhand had melted into his surroundings with practiced ease at the first hint of trouble. His vorpal in his right hand and a specially enchanted rapier in his left, he circled the clearing to get behind the giant doing his best to eliminate Cyrillis. The thief knew he couldn't reach high enough for the enchantment of the vorpal to do its work on the creature, so he opted instead for an exposed arm as the giant drew back his sword.

While the sword indeed bit deep, Savin was disappointed momentarily when the arm was not severed. At the same time he stabbed hard with the rapier, trying to penetrate the exposed muscles along the giant's ribs and thereby into the monster's heart. Evidently he missed, because the giant hammered backward at this unseen threat and succeeded in grazing the rogue's head with an elbow, knocking Savinhand to the ground where he stumbled backward a few steps.

The thief caught himself and shook his head. Looking up, he realized he had attracted the monster's attention. The massive sword the giant had been hammering away at the cleric with was now whistling through the air at him. Savin threw himself to the ground and rolled directly at the giant. Springing to his feet under the creature, he stabbed with both blades at the unprotected groin of the giant. Except the groin area *was* protected. The giant was wearing some sort of a codpiece. Both swords deflected harmlessly away from the groin, with only the rapier doing minor damage to the upper thigh.

The giant laughed and reached for the rogue, intending to pick up the puny human and sling him to the ground or against some nearby rocks. However, Savin ducked between the giant's legs, slashing at both Achilles' tendons as he swept past. One of his blades hit their mark and the rogue knew he had crippled the monster. Still, the giant was a formidable opponent, proving so as he again put both hands on his enormous sword and nearly decapitated the rogue with a swing he hadn't seen coming. Savin had been momentarily distracted with the giant Sordaak was dealing with. Or rather *should* be dealing with. Instead, the mage and the giant were conversing like old buddies.

His attention back on the giant trying to kill him, Savin circled the creature warily, keeping out of reach of the massive sword and looking for an opening. Several lunges, parries and slashes later found the giant bleeding from multiple cuts and slowing even more. The Storm Giant tried several lightning bolts, but Savin was easily able to dodge them, and they crackled by harmlessly each time.

Finally the monster fell to its knees in exhaustion and Savinhand used his vorpal to end the giant's life, beheading the monster in a single blow.

Thrinndor recovered enough in time to dodge another potentially life-ending blow from the two-handed great-sword of the giant. The creature roared in frustration, removed a hand from his sword and used it to point at the paladin. A bolt of lightning shot from the giant's finger. But Thrinndor had recognized the motion and guessed what was coming. He dove to his right just as the bolt blasted by, most of the energy being wasted on a tree. The paladin didn't even look down at his side where he'd been singed by the spell, knowing the damage was slight.

The giant roared again and stepped after this pesky human, intent on cleaving him in two with his blade. Thrinndor nimbly dodged the swing and parried with one of his own. Although his flaming sword bit deep in the creature's upper arm, the paladin knew the damage done was slight.

The giant recovered incredibly quickly, faster than Thrinndor was prepared for, and the massive blade from the monster bit deep into the paladin's back, slashing through the protective armor there. White-hot pain crippled Thrinndor, and he knew he was in trouble without some help. He stumbled and went to his knees as the giant shouted triumphantly and raised his blade for the killing blow.

Several things then happened at once: Cyrillis threw a healing spell at the paladin, a bolt of lightning hit the offending giant square in the chest, and three arrows hit the monster in the back, each penetrating deep.

The giant screamed in rage and pain as he spun to deal with these new threats. However, there was no one there to deal with! Breunne was some distance off, his attention again on the giant in front of him.

The heal spell restored the paladin, and he surged to his feet, swinging his flaming bastard sword with both hands as he spun. Thrinndor slashed at the exposed back of the giant, cutting a deep gash across the monster's lower back from side-to-side.

Mortally wounded, the giant screamed again and turned to deal with the paladin. But Thrinndor easily fended off the feeble swing of the creature and repeated his slash, this time across the giant's lower abdomen, spilling his guts onto the ground at his feet. The giant looked down at his entrails in confusion and then looked up at the paladin, who held his blade at the ready to fend off further attacks.

The giant then pitched forward onto his knees, and then his eyes rolled back in his head and he pitched forward again, this time his face landing in the dirt at Thrinndor's feet.

Breunne had faced the charge of his giant with his sword in his right hand, his left still useless from the blow he had received. Because the giant used a massive club, the ranger was able to dodge most of the blows while exacting some measure of damage on the monster when he got close enough. Slowly he felt life come back into his left arm, and he was able to use it to fend off blows as necessary. At one point as he circled his opponent, he saw the paladin go down to his knees and could see the giant preparing to finish him off. Breunne dove to the ground, rolling several times as he unslung *Xenotath*. Without bothering to stand he loosed a volley of arrows at the giant, knowing they would find their mark.

This distraction proved costly, however, as the giant he had been fighting pointed his finger and launched a lightning bolt that caught the ranger square in the back. Breunne was knocked forward onto his face, where he lay for a moment, stunned. He felt the ground tremble beneath him as the giant rushed in to press his advantage.

At the last possible second the ranger mustered enough strength to roll aside as the great-club the giant wielded hammered into the ground where he had been only a moment before. Breunne lashed out with both feet at the right knee of the giant. It felt like he had kicked a tree trunk! However, this action had the desired effect of buckling that leg and causing the giant to fall to the ground beside the ranger.

Breunne was first back to his feet and he lashed out with a leather booted foot at the giant's head. His aim was true and the monster shook his head under the force of the blow and spat out a tooth.

The giant smiled showing that this was not the first tooth he had lost and lunged at the ranger. Normally Breunne would have had no trouble avoiding the onrushing monster, but recent injuries and the unexpected quickness of the giant worked against him. The giant got his massive arms around the ranger and began to squeeze.

Breunne hammered away at the back of the giant's head with the pommel of his sword he had somehow managed to maintain his grip on to no avail. The giant continued to squeeze, and the ranger could hear his ribs cracking and he knew that without help he was going to die. He tried to throw himself backward, but the giant anticipated this and lifted him clear of the ground. His vision went black as the pounding in his ears signaled the life was about to be crushed out of him.

Suddenly, the giant released him and the ranger dropped to his hands and knees, his air-starved lungs gasping to pull enough of the life sustaining substance back into his body to survive. The gasping caused a grating in his chest from at least one broken rib, but he ignored that as he gulped in the cool morning air. Slowly his vision came back to normal as his breathing became less strained.

Vorgath surged back into the clearing, startling the giant that had been looking for the missing rogue. The barbarian took one lightning bolt full in the chest as he charged in, his great-axe raised high. In his rage he didn't even notice. A few strokes later he had dispatched this giant pretty much as he had the first—by cutting off the monster's head after taking out his legs.

His rage diminishing, he looked around from more foes and spotted the one that had Breunne in a bear hug. Vorgath charged in and buried *Flinthgoor* deep in the giant's back. He must've severed something important, because the giant could no longer move as the great-axe flashed once more, again taking the head off of an offending giant. Three for three! He *really* liked fighting giants! It was a skill he had worked at over the years, and now that work was paying off.

As Vorgath reached down to assist the ranger to his feet, he looked around to see if there were any more critters that needed his particular brand of attention. He was feeling pretty good about himself, and whistled tunelessly as he helped the ranger to his feet. Together they walked back toward the clearing, Breunne leaning on the barbarian for support.

There, he and Breunne joined the healer, rogue and paladin as they stood staring at Sordaak in disbelief. Sordaak had apparently heated some water and was serving tea with the remaining giant—the remaining *smiling* giant!

Chapter Nineteen

Mioria

Vorgath poked the paladin. "What gives?"

Thrinndor shook aside the reverie he had been experiencing and said, "I have no idea. I just got here."

Sordaak, noticing the gathering crowd at last, waved for them to have a seat. "Come on over, meet Stormheart, leader of the giant clan you just decimated." He smiled and picked up the teapot. "Have some tea."

"Decimated?" Savinhand spoke first. "And he's OK with that?"

"He is for now," Sordaak answered. "He's my *special* friend."

"Ah," said Breunne, "you have charmed him." He also noted for the first time that the sorcerer was wearing the giant's cloak.

"That's right. And as long as I keep him this way, he won't attack."

"Man, is he going to be pissed when the spell wears off!" Vorgath observed. "You want us to kill him before it does?" He brandished *Flinthgoor* menacingly.

"Is that necessary?" Cyrillis' tone left no doubt she didn't think that it was.

The mage pondered the question as he eyed his new friend suspiciously. "It might not be." Sordaak rubbed the hairs on his chin. "If we can get him away from the carnage and mayhem the dwarf wrought"—at this, Vorgath flexed his mighty arms, a huge grin on his face—"I might be able to keep him under spell longer, and eventually win him over to our side."

The magicuser stood, followed immediately by the giant—too quickly for the barbarian's liking. He raised his greataxe to strike. But it soon became obvious there was no malice in the giant.

"Our side?" Savin asked. "Which side is *he* on?" The companions plus one left the clearing, following a slight path that led north.

"Why, he and his kind are aligned with the Minions, of course. We've been having a nice chat, and he's told me all about them. He's also told me—rather reluctantly, I might add—about his family, and how they all have a really nice cave complex up in the cliffs of Mioria."

Sordaak kept his tone conversational as he changed the subject. "As long as we don't make any sudden moves Stormheart would deem threatening, I can keep him charmed indefinitely. I think we can use that to our advantage when we get to his home." He winked at the paladin.

"How many more of his kind are there?" Vorgath asked, not sure he liked the direction this *friendship* was going.

"He says he has a mate and two children. Plus, there are two other mates, each with a child."

Thrinndor did the math. "That is *seven more giants!*"

"Very good! I see that someone paid attention to his studies."

"Is it your plan to simply walk into their home, then?"

"Plan?" Sordaak shook his head. "Who said I have a plan?"

"Great!" Vorgath griped. "Why should this time be any different?"

"Ha, ha! I'll have plenty of time to work on one as their home is almost a full day's walk to the north."

"Is that a giant's days walk, or ours?" Cyrillis asked, noting the she had to hurry to keep up with the seemingly easy gait of the giant.

"Huh? Oh," the mage was also feeling the effects of walking faster to match steps with his friend, "we'll have to assume he meant at his pace."

Vorgath grumbled unintelligible under his breath. With his shorter legs, he was almost at a full jog to keep up.

Thrinndor and Breunne appeared to be the only two who did not have to rush their stride, but even both of them would be hard pressed to maintain this pace the rest of the day.

"Did he say whether or not the Minions have been alerted to our presence?" Thrinndor asked.

"Yes and yes," answered the sorcerer. "But Ice Homme is three or four days' hard march to the north and west, and the encampment at Farreach is at least that far south. So we have a few days."

"We may yet have to modify your earlier plan, then," the paladin observed.

"Agreed." Sordaak waved a hand behind his back, indicating they should discuss their plans no more. Evidently he did not feel all *that* comfortable in his ability to maintain his current friendship.

Cyrillis tended to the few minor aches, pains and scratches as they walked. Breunne took a little more effort, but a single heal spell mended even his two broken ribs. She verified they mended properly before moving on to the next fighter.

In silence the companions struggled to keep up until they stopped for a brief lunch. Even then conversation was kept to a minimum, and nothing was discussed as to plans. Every so often Sordaak refreshed the enchantment, thereby ensuring enduring friendship.

By the time the sun was low on the horizon, signaling that the end of day was near, the companions were beginning to wonder if either the giant had underestimated the time to get back to his home, or whether they were possibly slowing him down. The latter seemed more likely.

However, they had been climbing steadily for a couple of hours, so Sordaak knew they were approaching the cliffs from above.

Abruptly the giant turned and stepped into a previously unseen crease. The mage could see that the narrow crevice led down.

"Wait," the mage called out to his friend. Stormheart stopped immediately, waiting for further instructions. "Wait there." The giant nodded.

Sordaak took two steps toward his friends and demanded silence from them with his hands. "Let me speak," he whispered. "No arguments." He glared at the dwarf. "When we get to the entrance to their complex, I'm going to go in alone with him," he jerked his thumb over his shoulder. Several took in breaths to protest. "No discussion! If we all go in at once, we will frighten his family and we'll have a fight on our hands. If we have to fight, we'll lose the reason we are here." He pulled his new cloak around so they could see it for emphasis.

"It is my intention to allow him to try to reason with them. Once I think it safe for you to come in, I'll send Fahlred for you." He looked around at the giant. "However, I doubt this is the entrance. So, continue to follow. I'll signal where I want you to stop and wait."

He got grim nods from most of the men in the group. He purposefully did not make eye contact with the cleric. Before anything else could be said, he turned on a heel. "All right. Let's go."

Stormheart obediently led off down through the cut, Sordaak right behind him and the others following the sorcerer. As suspected, after a steep winding path that led along the cliff face, the companions found themselves standing in front of a semi-hidden cave opening.

Without hesitation, Stormheart walked inside. Sordaak pointed to Thrinndor and then to the narrow ledge outside the cave entrance. "If I'm not back in an hour, send in a posse." The paladin nodded his understanding and held up his hand for the others to stop.

Cyrillis ignored the hand and walked up to Sordaak as he turned to follow the giant. Quickly she stepped in front of the magicuser, forcing him to come to a halt. She didn't say anything, instead looking into the sorcerer's eyes.

Sordaak quickly looked away and tried to step around her. "Not now," he muttered.

"Now," she replied as she quickly moved to block him.

"I don't have time for this," the mage whispered intently, still not meeting her eyes.

"Make time," she insisted, putting a hand on his chest.

Sordaak rolled his eyes, but finally met hers. "What?"

Cyrillis held his eyes. "Be careful." Her gaze lingered a moment longer, then she leaned in, kissed him on the cheek and walked back out to the ledge.

Sordaak hesitated and then walked quickly to catch up with his newfound friend lest that friendship sour with distance. He needn't have worried—Stormheart waited patiently for him around the next bend.

Back on the ledge, Vorgath sat own and made himself comfortable, which is to say he pulled off his helm and used it as a pillow. He was snoring within moments.

Thrinndor and Breunne squatted against the wall of the cliff and conversed quietly as they each munched on a piece of jerked meat and a biscuit.

Savinhand walked over to join them, leaving Cyrillis to her own thoughts. She removed a biscuit from her pack, sat cross-legged facing the cavern opening and took small bites, washing the dry bread down with an occasional mouthful of water from her water skin.

As the allotted hour approached, Thrinndor gathered the remaining companions, waking Vorgath so they could plan. The paladin was about to make assignments when Sordaak walked out of the opening to join them.

Initially the mage simply squatted on his heels next to the paladin. The companions seemed content to wait for Sordaak to speak, and finally he did. "We have some new friends. However, that friendship is tenuous, at best. Stormheart isn't charmed anymore, and he's pretty distraught at the loss of his companions. However, I've convinced him and his family that working for me—us—will be an upgrade over the minions."

"What about our cloaks?" Vorgath asked.

"Good question," Sordaak said. "You may have noticed I am no longer wearing mine. It turns out the cloaks are made for the young and given to them when they reach adulthood." He hesitated. "My taking Stormheart's while he yet lived raised quite a stir, and I returned it to him as a gesture of good faith." He again paused; clearly he had some unpleasant news to give.

"I thought those cloaks are necessary to your plans?"

"They are," Sordaak insisted. "However, I—we—can do without them for now." The mage took in a ragged breath. "I've convinced the giants to make cloaks for us. Taking them from these giants will write their death sentence."

"What?" Vorgath stood. "I thought that *was* the plan, to take their cloaks and kill them! They're giants! They can't be trusted!"

Clearly annoyed, Sordaak looked up at the barbarian. "Sit down." When Vorgath didn't immediately comply, Sordaak said, "I said, sit *down*!" The mage locked eyes with the dwarf.

With a huff, the barbarian did as told.

"Thank you," Sordaak said. "These are the last of the Storm Giants in the land. They can be of enormous use in the security on the island—"

"You made the Troglodytes responsible for that!"

"And they will remain responsible for the security for the *northern* approach to the island. I have other plans for these giants. They will make a cloak for each of us that requires one in return for sparing their lives and our providing safe haven on Valdaar's Rest."

The barbarian growled deep in his chest, but said nothing.

"OK, I'm going to lead you guys into the cavern, but there must be no visible weapons." He looked over at the barbarian. "Nor any overt gestures—*at all!*"

Vorgath frowned, but said nothing. He placed *Flinthgoor* on the hook at his neck, but left the broad head of the axe exposed. Sordaak could see there were still bloodstains on the weapon—Storm Giant blood—but the mage chose not to make an issue of it.

The mage turned and started into the cave opening. "Remember, Stormheart is no longer enchanted to be our friend. He is a bit on edge, and his family and the other giants even more so. So, *please* watch what you say, and how you say it."

Cyrillis moved quickly up to walk next to the magicuser, grasping his hand in hers. She smiled up at him when he looked over, unsure exactly what to do. "Nice work," she whispered.

Sordaak nodded, his lips a thin line as he briefly considered pulling his hand back. This was getting complicated, he thought, and he didn't need complications right now.

The companions wound their way through the caverns, occasionally passing branch openings to their right and/or left. Their way was lit for them by sconces irregularly placed along the rough-hewn walls.

Abruptly they rounded a bend and the corridor opened up into a much larger cavern. The space was much better lit—almost to the point of being too bright. There was an enormous table in the center of the chamber, with equally enormous chairs around it. Seated in several of the chairs were giants—presumably the females and children of the species. There were seven giants in attendance, there should have been eight, Thrinndor realized. He looked around, noticing Stormheart was not in attendance.

Thrinndor studied the occupants of the room. Only a different breastplate enabled him to tell the difference between the female giants and their male counterpart. They were all hairless, about the same height, and bore the same unyielding expression on their faces.

The seated giants all stood as their leader entered the chamber, showing each to be ten feet or so tall. The children were obviously of varying ages, with the smallest being approximately the same height as the paladin.

Thrinndor strode purposefully toward Stormheart and extended his right hand in greeting. The leader of the giants eyed the hand momentarily, and then extended his own and the two grasped forearms. The giant's eyes widened as the paladin returned the squeeze the giant applied to his arm. Thrinndor's strength was certainly no match for that of a Storm Giant, but his might far surpassed that of most men.

"I am Thrinndor, leader of this small band of adventurers known as Vorpal." He smiled at the giant. "Well met."

"Well met," the giant leader replied formally. "I am Stormheart, leader of all you see here—-the last of our kind in the land." The giant was well spoken, his mastery of the common tongue excellent. Thrinndor thought he detected anger in the giant's words, and maybe sorrow, but certainly no malice.

The paladin continued his grip, looking deep into the eyes of the giant. "It is my sincere hope that we can assist you in remedying that situation. I would like to work with you to ensure your kind continues to walk the land. Eradication of a species hurts us all. Each kind brings something to this great land that no other can." Thrinndor smiled. "May you and your kind live long and do well on Valdaar's Rest."

The giant's eyes widened slightly, as clearly these were not the words he was expecting. "Thank you," he said. "Under the 'protection' of Ice Homme our numbers have steadily diminished until those that you see here are all that is left. It will be good to serve those that truly have our best interest at heart."

"Rest assured that it will be so." Thrinndor released his grip.

The giant nodded as he, too, released his. "Indeed we are well met, then. It is unfortunate that we could not have met *before* the encounter south of here." Stormheart's wry smile showed the true regret he was feeling. The giant turned and looked at the other giants who remained standing. "We will be honored to serve those such as you."

Thrinndor bowed slightly at the waist. "It is we who are honored by your service."

Stormheart returned the bow. "You must be weary." He smiled. "I fear I set a hard pace, today."

"That you did." Thrinndor returned the smile. "We are indeed in need of rest. If you have a chamber where we may prepare a meal and lay our heads, it would be appreciated."

"Forgive my manners," the giant leader said as he turned to the female giants. "Marna, a meal if you please. *Quickly!*"

"At once," the nearest of the giants said, bowing slightly before she turned and ushered the others out of the chamber.

Stormheart turned back to the paladin, a beaming smile on his face. "Come, sit," he said as he waved the companions toward the table. "My *wives*," the giant put an emphasis on the plural, "will have a meal for us shortly."

The troupe approached the chairs dubiously, seeing they were going to have to climb into them. "Forgive my manners, again," Stormheart laughed, "we do not often get visitors of the shorter variety." He smiled as he produced from along the wall a portable step that greatly helped.

As the companions settled in, Marna came back in to the chamber carrying a cask under each arm. These she sat unceremoniously on the table with a thud and hammered a tap home in each with practiced ease. Behind her was another of the adult giants carrying a double handful of large flasks. She set those on the table as well—also with corresponding thuds—and eyed the companions expectantly.

"My apologies that I can only offer a choice of either spring wine or summer ale. The grain crop was late this year, so the mead is not ready." Stormheart smiled his commiseration.

"That will do just fine," Vorgath said. "I've heard that your summer ale is the stuff about which legends are made, and truly look forward to sampling some." He held his flagon out.

Stormheart smiled and bowed slightly at the compliment. "You honor me with your words." He took the barbarian's cup and filled it from the flask on his left. As he slid it back along the table to the waiting dwarf, he added, "I would advise caution there, little man, as our drink can be a bit strong."

The flagon raised half-way to his lips, Vorgath stopped, raised an eyebrow and said, "Bah! If you've never had dwarven barely ale, you don't know what strong is!" With that he raised the cup to his lips and took a large swig. He slammed the mug back down on the stone table and said, "Damn! That is *good!* Some of the best ale I have ever had." Vorgath stood in his chair, clamped his arm across his chest and held it out toward the giant. "I salute you." Vorgath returned to his seat and took another healthy swig from his cup.

"You again honor me with your words," Stormheart said as he dipped his head slightly. "Can I interest anyone else?"

The remaining companions stated their preference, and by the time Stormheart had filled each cup (Vorgath's twice), the giant women were bringing in the food.

Steaming platters of mutton, potatoes, vegetables, fruits and other delicacies (at least for the companions who had been living on what they could carry for what seemed liked months) suddenly lined the center of the table. The companions dug in with gusto as if they hadn't eaten in days.

Even Savinhand tried some of everything, and he chased down the female giants who brought the food to find out how a particular dish had been prepared or what spices had been used.

Within an hour the companions had each eaten their fill and most were feeling no pain, under the influence of whichever of the strong drink had been chosen.

Vorgath was feeling the least pain of all. He was now in deep conversation with Stormheart, sharing tales of battles long past—both of his people and his own.

The carryings on continued for many hours, until most of the companions—and some of the giants—no longer remembered or cared what had occurred or been discussed.

*

Sordaak woke to the usual pounding headache only to discover he was not alone in his bed. Amid no small complaints from his pounding head he rolled over to find that warm lump next to him was Cyrillis.

He took in a sharp breath as he verified he was still fully clothed, as was she. Next some mental brow-wiping was in progress as he noticed the lump beginning to stir, obviously awakened by his movement.

The cleric pushed the hair out of her face, looked around and tried to place her surroundings. She spotted Sordaak sitting up in bed next to her and smiled the smile of unknowing bliss.

However, as the mage watched, her expression changed from one of immense satisfaction, to one of concern and finally to one of pure horror. She sat bolt upright in the bed, checked her clothing situation and scowled. "What the hell happened last night?"

Sordaak did his best to return the smile; however, he was not sure what he portrayed. "I wish I knew."

That was obviously not the right answer as Cyrillis' face mottled in fury and she lashed out with a right hand in a ringing slap that spun the mage's head around. "Owww!"

"What in the name of the Seven Hells happened last night?"

Sordaak turned back to face her but now doubted any words would suffice. Instead he shrugged, saying nothing.

This did not seem to help. Before he had time to react, Cyrillis again slapped the mage as she spluttered to speak. "I am *reserved!*" was all she could get out in her rage.

Sordaak had had just about all of this he could take. His head hurt, his cheek was burning from the recent abuse and he had *no idea* what had happened! Except that whatever it was, it was all his fault!

His silence did not seem to help the cleric come to the conclusion she was after, and she drew back her hand to slap again. However, this time Sordaak was prepared and caught the hand on the way in with his left. "Now look here," he said, his tongue thick and his mouth dry, "if you slap me one more time, I'm going to forget my proper upbringing and hit you back!" He glared at the cleric. "You understand me?"

Suddenly ashamed for her actions, Cyrillis yanked her hand free and used it to clutch the blanket over her body. Sordaak didn't understand the move, as she was still fully clothed—a fact that seemed to have escaped her.

Cyrillis nodded.

"And, while we're on the subject, reserved for *who?*"

Taken aback by the question, the cleric didn't immediately answer. Instead, tears welled up in her eyes and she bowed her head. "I do not know." Her voice was so quiet that the mage wasn't sure he'd imagined it.

"What?"

Cyrillis looked up with a tear-streaked face. "I do not *know*!" She sniffed as she fought back more tears. "I was told from birth that I am not for any man, but I must save myself." She sniffed again. "I was told that when the time was right I would know." Her eyes begged Sordaak to understand.

The mage reached out with both arms, wrapped them around the cleric and drew her close. "I do," he said. "Please understand that I have no intention of intervening in whatever destiny awaits you." He pushed her back so he could look into her eyes. "But know this, I am here for *you*! I will not harm you, nor will I allow others to do the same as long as I live." His eyes bored into hers. "But this slapping me every time I get close has got to stop!"

Cyrillis sniffed again, leaned in and put her head on the mage's chest. "I know," she said, her voice a whisper. "Please understand my confusion. I do not know who or what anymore. My feelings are so…not understandable anymore."

Sordaak wrapped his arms around her and held her tight until he could feel her tension ease. "I'm here for you," he repeated.

"I know," she said, her voice muffled.

"For what it's worth, I'm fairly certain nothing happened between us." Cyrillis pushed away from the magicuser and looked up into his hazel eyes. "For one, we're both still fully clothed." The cleric seemed to note that for the first time. "And two, even in your semi-inebriated state, I doubt any man can make advances on you without incurring the wrath of that." Sordaak pointed at *Kurril*, standing in a corner not an arm's reach away.

Cyrillis sniffed again and smiled. She seemed almost disappointed. "We need to take care to be more certain," she said, again her eyes beseeching the mage to understand. "The mind and the heart are not always of one accord." Her smile would melt the heart of a Balrogg, Sordaak decided. "One of us must remain sober."

"Damn! There you go, throwing bounds on me, already!" He smiled to ensure his words did no harm.

"It is my choice. I will measure the weight of this restriction, and ensure we do not cross the line."

"Damn! That line seemed to be getting closer." Again he smiled to remove offense from his words.

Cyrillis punched him in the arm. "Wait not, want not."

"Hell, I'll be wanting for years, I fear."

"Ha, ha!"

"Are you two decent?" The voice was Thrinndor's, but in the poor light of the bedchamber it was impossible to tell for sure.

"Of course," Sordaak said. "What can you possibly want at this early hour?"

"Early? It is nearing noon."

"Noon? How late did we tarry?"

"I do not know about you two, but I remained in the dining hall until well after midnight." Thrinndor made a show of putting his hand to his head. "Too much wine for me!"

"Wuss!" Sordaak said. "I'm *pretty* sure we were there until only a few hours ago." He looked over at the cleric and his smile straightened. "Pretty sure."

"Whatever," the paladin said. "We must prepare for the coming horde."

"Horde?"

"Minions," explained the paladin patiently. He obviously had not consumed the giant's wine to the excess he claimed.

"Minions? Even the whole lot of them at one hundred plus does not qualify as a 'horde.'"

Thrinndor stood at the entrance to the bedchamber, clearly uncomfortable at having to be there, and shrugged. "Still, we must prepare."

Sordaak glared at the paladin. "Give us a minute," he said.

Thrinndor shrugged, turned and walked away.

"What is to become of us?" Cyrillis asked.

"Good question," Sordaak replied. "One for which I don't currently have an answer. However, I'm one of those who believe that all good things come to those that wait." He smiled. "And I am willing to wait."

Cyrillis leaned in, closed her eyes and kissed the mage lightly on the lips. "As am I," she said as she pulled away. "Now, give me some privacy as I pull myself together."

"Got it," the mage said as he rolled off of his side of the bed. "Never let it be said that the all-powerful Sordaak didn't know when he was being dismissed." He smiled at the cleric as he followed in the paladin's footsteps. He discovered he had urgent matters to attend to himself when he had gotten to his feet.

Chapter Twenty

Minions, Part Two (Three?)

When Cyrillis finally made her way back to the dining hall, the rest of her companions were seated at the table.

"Always waiting on a woman," Sordaak said with a smile.

"Yes, and I am pleased to see that you are already accustomed to that," the cleric said sweetly as she brushed by him and climbed into a seat at the table.

There were steaming platters of eggs, breakfast meats, breads, cheeses and various accompaniments laid out on the table. Vorgath was already working on trimming down a plate laden with the above as the cleric settled in.

"Stormheart informs me that an advance contingent from Ice Homme will make a plateau not far from here by the end of the day," Thrinndor informed the companions as they attacked their plates, some more heartily than others.

"So much for three or four days," Savinhand complained as he eyed a piece of bacon, smoked with a wood he did not recognize. He made a mental note to ask about that.

"Yeah, well," Sordaak said as he applied some butter to his bread. His stomach couldn't handle the thought of the eggs after the amount of drink he had consumed the night before. Even the butter was a stretch. "It will be easier to deal with them in this fashion—assuming the minions continue to be stupid enough to come at us a few at a time."

"This particular contingent will likely have one, maybe two, High Lords among their ranks."

"Sweet!" Sordaak said around a mouthful of the bread. "If we can separate the upper holier-than-thous from the lesser holier-than-thous, this will get even easier!"

"Explain, please."

That damn paladin can be so formal even this early in the morning, Sordaak thought. "Dealing with a High Lord or two is bad enough, but when you surround them with a bunch of sword-toting, shield-wielding meat-shields, you can have a real mess on your hands." The mage bit off another hunk of bread. "These Lords obviously feel confident in their control of the giants, or they wouldn't take the chance of venturing out ahead of their support troops. That allows us to deal with these mental midgets without the encumbrance of the sword-slinging morons they would normally be dragging along."

"I see," Thrinndor said as he eyed the plate in front of him distastefully. Although he had partaken of the strong drink less than others had, his stomach was still doing flips when faced with the prospect of the greasy bacon and eggs that had somehow made their way onto his plate. "That is indeed good news, assuming it will hold to be correct."

Sordaak considered complaining with the "you dare to doubt me" train of thought, but decided against it, as it was just too damn early. Besides, as he had no proof of his wisdom to trot out in support of this particular matter; it was only too normal to doubt at this juncture. So, he spread some unknown fruit jelly on his next piece of bread and continued eating.

The day passed in relative boredom as the companions stored up some much needed rest and prepared for the upcoming action. Sordaak sent Fahlred to warn the dwarves and ask them to wait a few miles outside of Ardaagh. The mage would let them know when their force would be needed.

Stormheart and his wives led the companions out to meet the Minion High Lords. He assured Thrinndor the females of his kind were as adept in battle as the males, but the males tended not to want to risk the continuance of their kind by allowing the women to fight (or something like that—the paladin suspected the males feared these females might best them in battle, but wisely chose not to mention this suspicion). Thrinndor assured Stormheart that his wives were welcome, as long as he—their leader—did not feel special dispensation was warranted. The giant leader had scoffed at the suggestion, and so their grouping had four giants along.

Sordaak still had trouble telling the males from females but decided that could be more his fault than theirs and said nothing.

Per plan, the giants walked out to meet the Minion High Lords, with the giants leading the Lords through a narrow ravine from which the companions would head up their attack.

Everything was going according to plan, until as the Lords entered the ravine, a shadow floated across the ground in front of the troupe, followed by the loud scream of a dragon.

Shit! The High Lords of Set had a dragon overhead keeping watch on their movement.

Thrinndor silently signaled for the others to join him against the face of a large boulder that would provide some cover, provided they had not already been spotted.

Vorgath was the first to speak. "That damned winged rodent makes no difference! We still have the Lords to deal with. If the dragon choses to join the fracas, so be it." He brandished *Flinthgoor* just in case his friends were unsure what he meant. "The dragon can't stop our attack on the Lords, nor can it bring backup any quicker."

Thrinndor pondered the words of the barbarian for just a moment. While he pondered, Sordaak spoke. "For once, I agree with our diminutive friend. Either way, nothing can be done about it now."

Thrinndor nodded. "Agreed." He looked around at his party. "Back to your places, then. On my signal."

The companions returned to their places and waited. The giants, the two lords and a small contingent of minions continued to approach their trap.

Thrinndor was within moments of signaling the attack when the dragon screeched again and the Minion Lords stopped the procession. Sordaak waited, holding his breath when the Lords pointed at the crevice and shouted. The minions all broke for cover, two stepping in front of their Lords and escorted them toward safety.

Even though their prey had scattered, Thrinndor gave the signal. He knew the surprise had been lost, but also that their side still had strength in numbers.

Sordaak stepped from behind his rock and sprayed the entire ravine with his web spell. Vorgath yelled one of his battle cries, leapt from behind his rock and raced down the narrow path he had selected to best get him to the bottom. Breunne loosed a barrage of arrows, each finding their mark not in a Lord, but in one of the protective minions. Savinhand sprinted up from well behind, hacking and slashing with both hands at any target that presented itself. And Thrinndor stepped out from behind a bush directly in the path of where the Lords were *supposed* to be—but this ambush was going anyway but as it had been planned.

As such, the paladin had no one within immediate reach of his sword.

The dragon screeched from high overhead again, and suddenly the floor of the ravine was clear. All the minions had scattered for cover.

"Damn!" spat the paladin as his eyes searched the sky for the dragon. He dove hard to his left as the sky above him erupted in a gout of flame. His quick actions allowed him to escape the brunt of the strike, but still he felt the effects as he tumbled twice and surged to his feet.

Sordaak was not so lucky. The flame spell that blasted him from above caught him by surprise and he was knocked to the ground by the force of the blast, his face and hands badly burnt and his robe smoldering. Still, he knew better than to remain where he was and rolled hard to his left until he came up against a large rock. He struggled to his hands and knees, shaking the cobwebs from his head as he did so.

Breunne continued to loose arrows at any target that presented itself. He dove to the ground when out of the corner of his eye he saw a shadow speeding toward him. He almost escaped, but a single talon from the dragon was enough to ensnare him as it dug mercilessly into his shoulder. Through his pain, the ranger heard the beat of the massive wings as the monster struggled to drag the additional weight skyward.

Savinhand, having slain one of the Lords protectors, followed another into the brush at the base of a cliff face and immediately went into hide mode when he discovered he was alone. The rogue heard footsteps close by but never saw who those footsteps belonged to. He slowly worked his way around the bush and was knocked a wicked blow to the head from behind as he tried to stand to see over it. Savin fell more than dove to the ground, his reflexes taking over so that he rolled to his right as quickly as the pain in his head would allow. He ended up under another bush where he lay still, afraid to even breathe. *There was someone skilled in the arts with the Minions! Perhaps even an assassin.*

Vorgath finished his battle cry and charged into the clear area at the base of the ravine to find…nothing. He searched right and left, seeing no one! The magicuser's web spell was spread across the path on both sides, but, as far as he could tell, there was nothing trapped within it. Certainly nothing was moving within the sticky sinews.

He picked a direction—left—and charged ahead, only to be slammed on the head by a staff from one of the Minion Lords. Only his Mithryl helm kept him from being knocked senseless. As it was, he was stunned and stumbled a few steps to his right before he got his footing under him again. The barbarian shook his head to clear his vision, but could find no sign of his assailant.

Wary now, he began to search in a much more controlled fashion.

Cyrillis, who was without attack duties on purpose, was at a loss to figure out what had happened to her companions. Breunne she saw carried off, but there was nothing she could do for him at the moment. She felt the mage's burns and threw a healing spell his direction and sensed that she had connected as the burning sensation went away. She maintained her vantage point on the rim of the ravine, relying on her senses to guide her, waiting.

Breunne sensed the dragon was only carrying him off of the ground to drop him from a deadly height, but he was not afraid. He knew his boots would keep him from harm in that regard. So he focused instead on what could he do to neutralize the dragon.

The ranger reached up and grasped the creature's leg just above the claw as the dragon opened its talons. Instead of dropping like a rock, Breunne swung his body weight up and over, at the same time pulling the dragon down hard. The resultant change in momentum flipped the fighter high over the dragon, and with some judicious effort on his part, he was able to land on the monster's back between its wings. Immediately the ranger jumped toward the neck, where he grabbed the leading edge of the wings as the dragon screamed in fury and dove toward the ground, spinning as it went.

With all his strength the fighter hung on through twists and turns; some coming within inches of the ground. The longer he was able to hold on, the more confidence Breunne gained in his ability to do so. Soon he sat astride the beast's neck, his legs doing most of the work keeping him there. "You're not going to be rid of me so easily, *wurm*!" he shouted, using the slang that he knew all dragons hated.

"You underestimate my determination, human," the dragon hissed back.

Damn, Breunne thought, yet another hyper-intelligent dragon. *Was there no end to these creatures?*

"I think I'll take you to my lair where my young can feast on a *live* meal for a change." The dragon chuckled as it banked toward the mountains not far to the west.

Breunne waited until they got closer. "As much fun as that sounds to be, I think I'll decline." As they passed what for most would have been uncomfortably close to a peak, the ranger activated his boots and kicked free of the dragon. Clear, he dove for a nearby copse of trees, knowing the monster would not give up easily.

Indeed, the dragon roared its displeasure and dove after the rapidly receding human. The beast had to pull up as the trees approached for fear of impaling itself on one of the taller evergreens. Breunne continued his dive, swerving around and through the branches until he slowed and came to a rest about halfway up a massive pine.

The dragon roared in frustration as it circled the small grouping of trees. "Your respite is only temporary," shouted the dragon. "I will destroy the trees one at a time until I find you!"

That was not something the ranger had considered. He was sure the dragon capable of carrying out this threat. Indeed, as he sat in his perch, he heard one of the trees shatter under the force of a blow from the monster, and then a crash as it fell to the ground.

Shit! Breunne glanced around quickly. There were perhaps only twenty or twenty-five trees in this copse, and as another crashed to the ground he figured he had only a few minutes before the tree in which he was hiding was discovered. And then he would be in a world of hurt.

An idea came to him, and he began to work his way down his tree until he neared the ground. Keeping the trunk of the tree between him and the dragon, he was able to remain out of the beast's sight.

As the dragon leapt into the air on the far side of the trees to bring down another, Breunne made his move. He jumped from his perch on the lowest branch to the ground where he used his tumbling skills to break his fall. Then, as low to the ground as he could, he ran the short distance to a felled tree and dove into the mass of twisted branches that covered the ground. There, he hid and waited.

The dragon did as promised, felling all the trees but one. Figuring the ranger to be hiding there, the creature circled the tree, confident it had its prey trapped. "Come on out, little man. I will take mercy on you and make your death a quick one." When

Breunne didn't answer, the dragon screeched and crashed into the tree, sending it toppling with the sheer mass of its body. It fell toward where Breunne hid.

At the last second, the ranger saw the tree coming, and tried to scramble out of its path. He almost made it.

The falling tree landed on the one under which he was hiding, and that pushed the first tree closer to the ground.

A blinding flash of pain coursed through the ranger's back as the tree trunk pinned him to the ground, forcing the air from his lungs. He scratched and clawed at the earth, trying to pull himself free. But there was nothing to grab.

As the darkness of unconsciousness washed over him, a stark realization came with it: No one knew where he was.

*

Back in the ravine, the remaining companions were having their own troubles. Sensing that the dragon had departed, the giants were beating the bushes with clubs, looking for the Minions. Vorgath had reunited with Thrinndor, and together they searched for their prey.

Savinhand heard them moving about and wanted to warn them of the assassin, but he dared not expose himself. Besides, he was confident he could neutralize that threat *if* he could find it. Silently, he slid his ring of invisibility onto his finger and only then did he begin to move.

Sordaak knew that he needed to get back to higher ground and began working his way up the ravine wall. He went as silently as he could, but knew he had not the skill in that regard of either the ranger or the thief. Briefly, he wondered what had become of them as he had seen neither since the melee began, but he hadn't time to ponder that for long.

He gained the rim of the small canyon and spotted Cyrillis crouched next to a rock about a hundred feet away. Sordaak stood and was about to call to her when he saw one of the minions sneaking up behind her. He was out of range for his spells and knew that if he shouted he would alert both of them.

So, instead, he crouched low and ran toward the minion. Intent on the cleric, the minion didn't see or hear the magicuser until it was too late.

The man raised up knife in hand, intent only on plunging his blade into the cleric's back. Sordaak got within range before he could strike, however. The mage pointed his finger and released the spell he had prepared.

The lightning bolt hit the minion in the side and knocked him reeling. Sordaak jerked a dagger from the belt at his waist and followed his spell in, jumping on the staggering robed figure.

Too late the minion saw the blade coming, allowing the mage to bury it deep into the man's neck. Sordaak jerked his dagger free and plunged it this time to the hilt into his adversary's chest.

The minion's eyes opened wide in surprise and then glazed over even before he fell to the ground.

Startled by the sound of the lightning bolt, Cyrillis stood and turned in time to see the mage in action with his dagger. Seeing the wicked-looking blade the minion had held lying on the ground caused her to put her hand to her mouth as she realized how close she had come.

"Watch your back," Sordaak said between heavy breaths.

The healer's eyes went wide and the mage realized she was looking past him. Sordaak dropped to a knee as he spun, again readying and releasing a spell even before he had a target.

The force darts found their target unerringly, hitting the High Lord square in the chest who had swung his staff at where the sorcerer's head had been.

The darts did little damage, but they always hit and almost always surprised who or whatever they hit. This was no exception.

The High Lord took a step back, found his footing and then he pointed his finger at the mage and said his word of power. Sordaak dove behind a rock, with Cyrillis diving the other way as a column of flame crashed from the sky, hit the ground and spread rapidly.

Although both his and the cleric's actions had been quick, they weren't quick enough. Both caught the full force of the spell on their backs and were knocked face-first into the rocky surface of the ravine's rim.

Stunned, Sordaak rolled over and tried to regain the breath that had been knocked from him by the force of the spell as he also tried to rise. He almost made it. The Minion Lord swung his staff at the prone mage, hitting him in the forehead as he came up.

Sordaak's head was enveloped in in pain and light as yet another spell—or perhaps an ability of the staff—released on impact. The mage fell back to the ground and did not move.

The High Lord smiled as he raised his staff for a killing blow. However, Cyrillis had other ideas. Jumping to her feet she saw the Minion knock the sorcerer out and raise his staff.

"Leave him alone, asshole!" she shouted as she took the one step necessary to reach the Lord, swinging *Kurri* with both hands and all her might. The Minion Lord raised an arm to ward off the staff at the last second, but was too late.

Cyrillis' staff crashed into the Lord's head and a brilliant flash of light erupted at the point of impact. The man's head snapped over, his neck broken. And then something else happened—something the cleric hadn't seen before: The Minion Lord simply disintegrated. There was nothing left but a small pile of ash and his staff, which clattered to the ground.

"Impressive," Vorgath said as he walked up behind the cleric. He and Thrinndor had come up to see what all the commotion was about.

Cyrillis ignored them and knelt beside the sorcerer. The skin on his forehead was charred and black. Already a large knot was growing there. She used her health sense to determine that he was badly hurt.

The cleric closed her eyes, placed both hands on the wound and silently mouthed the words to her most potent healing spell. She felt the energy pour through her hands and into the sorcerer's unconscious body.

At first nothing happened, but then Sordaak's eyes fluttered and opened. His eyes darted back and forth as he tried to place his surroundings. Finally settling on Cyrillis he said, "A man could get used to waking up like this." He smiled.

The healer returned the smile and then stood. "Enough lying around," she said. "I believe there are still minions about."

Vorgath shook his head. "I think between the two you killed, the one Savinhand got, the two the giants chased down and this guy," he threw the body he had been dragging around to the ground in front of him, "I think we got them all."

"Not all."

Everyone on the rim turned to see Savinhand stumble into sight not far away.

"How do you know?" Vorgath demanded.

"Because—" The thief's eyes rolled back in his head and he pitched forward to land face first onto the ground at his feet. There was a nasty looking dagger protruding from his back with a wide blood stain circling it.

"Shit!" Vorgath spat as he stepped closer. "Damn thief *always* has to be right!"

"No!" Cyrillis moaned as she pushed her way past the barbarian and rushed to the Savinhand's side and knelt there. She again closed her eyes, dipped her head and quickly whispered the words to her healing spell, allowing the power to pour through her hands and into her patient.

Next, she checked for a pulse and found it to be very weak. "Damn, the blade must be poisoned!" She gripped the handle of the knife with both hands and ripped it clear. Cyrillis pitched the blade aside and cast a spell to neutralize the poison she suspected was coursing through the rogue's veins, and then she poured more healing into him.

Even before she checked his pulse again she could see that he was doing better. His breathing, which had become shallow and ragged, now eased. Color was returned to his skin and the muscles in his neck no longer twitched uncontrollably.

Cyrillis sat back, brushed a stray lock of hair from her face and breathed a sigh of relief. "Anyone else require attention?"

"Where's Breunne?" Sordaak asked.

"What?" The healer's eyes flashed back open and her head spun to look in the direction she had last seen the ranger and the dragon. "Oh, no!"

Now it was Vorgath's turn. "What?"

Cyrillis pointed toward the mountains to the west. "When last I saw him, the dragon was carrying Breunne that way."

Chapter Twenty-One

IcyBitch

"OK, that's not good." Leave it to Vorgath to state the obvious. "How long ago was that?"

"Right after the action began," the cleric replied. She couldn't take her eyes off the horizon where she had last seen the dragon.

The four giants walked up and Thrinndor explained to them the situation.

When Cyrillis pointed the direction they had gone, Stormheart said, "That is who we call IcyBitch. She, too, serves Ice Homme." He paused as he studied the horizon. "She is very old and has a lair in those mountains."

"Where?" Thrinndor asked.

"It is not far," the giant replied. "I can take you there."

"I'm not sure that's going to be necessary," Marna said. All eyes turned to the giant as she pointed. "IcyBitch returns."

Heads turned to see where Stormheart's mate pointed. At first nothing could be seen. But before the dwarf could say so he saw a faint spot moving toward them.

"Spread out," commanded Thrinndor. "We take her alive, if possible."

"Have you lost your mind?" the barbarian roared.

The paladin slowly turned to face his friend. "That dragon may be our only hope to find Breunne." His tone was even and insistent. "We will take her alive. Now, spread out."

Vorgath considered arguing further, but knew that wouldn't even make *him* feel better. He hated it when that happened. There was nothing like a good argument. He stomped off to the other side of the ravine and stood with his arms crossed.

"I'm going to try to bring her to the ground with a web if she gets close enough," Sordaak said. "It won't hold her long, so you had better be ready to subdue her."

"Blunt weapons!" Thrinndor shouted. He could clearly see the dragon now. She was coming fast. "I have an idea. Cyrillis, put on a robe from one of the High Lords. The rest of us will hide. Let's see if we can get her to come to you."

Cyrillis rushed to the dead priest, and with Sordaak's help removed his robe.

"Damn," the sorcerer said, "you'd think these guys would wear something under these robes as cold as it is where they're from!" When the body rolled over as a result of jerking on the robe, they could all see he had no genitalia. Sordaak made a low whistle. "Must be a rough life being a priest of Set."

"Some gods—and religions—require castration as a means to ensure the priest remains focused," Thrinndor said.

"I knew there was a reason I chose to avoid such service," Savinhand said as he looked upon the body.

"If you guys are done ogling a dead priest," Vorgath shouted, "you should probably take your places."

Thrinndor turned to see the dragon was getting close. Cyrillis threw on the robe and covered her head. The rest of the party—including the giants—dove for whatever cover they could find.

Cyrillis alone stood on the rim of the ravine, exposed for all to see. She held her staff off to one side, defiant.

The dragon circled once and then came lower, eventually landing not far from the cleric. Something clearly bothered the creature, perhaps Cyrillis was shorter than expected, or maybe her stance was wrong. The dragon snorted a couple of times and moved slowly moved toward the cleric anyway.

"Where are the rest of your people?" the dragon asked, her eyes swiveling.

Cyrillis didn't say anything. Instead she raised her staff and pointed down the ravine. Instantly, she realized her mistake. She had pointed with *her* staff!

The dragon's eyes went wide and she leapt into the sky, her wings clawing for air.

Sordaak stepped from beneath a small tree and fired his web spell multiple times.

At first the webs had little or no effect. And then one captured a wing and the dragon came crashing back to earth from a height of about twenty feet.

Sordaak continued to pour out the spells, and the dragon continued to shred them. But that shredding took time. The giants rushed in first, their clubs raised for attack.

In panic, the dragon tried to jump into the air even though her wings remained fouled, and so she again crashed to earth.

Stormheart was the first to reach her, and he dealt the dragon a mighty blow to the head. Then the other giants were on her, with the remaining companions up next.

Sordaak continued to cast his webs and they continued to be effective. Occasionally the dragon would work her tail or a claw free and she would knock one or another of her assailants senseless, but Cyrillis was there to heal any damage done. Twice, the dragon shot out her breath weapon, which succeeded in freezing both web and man—but the sorcerer was ready with more web spells and Cyrillis had made sure the companions were prepared for her icy blast with resist cold blessings.

Slowly—mostly because the clubs didn't do the damage against the scales that a sharp weapon could—the attack had the desired effect. IcyBitch was slowing down.

Finally, Stormheart swung his club with both hands and dealt the dragon a mighty blow to the head. Icy's eyes glazed over, and she slumped to the ground.

"Quick," Thrinndor shouted, "bind her wings, claws and mouth shut. She must not be allowed to be able to move when she awakens!" He had been on the receiving end of one of her icy blasts. "Especially her mouth!" He shivered with the memory.

The companions breathed a sigh of relief as Cyrillis tended to wounds and buoyed spirits. The dragon was a sight to see: Her white scaly skin was black and blue in places, in others scales were missing completely. She was bound completely by a prodigious amount of rope.

Thrinndor gathered the companions and the giants.

Stormheart stood before Cyrillis and bowed low at the waist. "Thank you for healing me and mine during battle. It has been a long time since someone took the time to do that for us."

Cyrillis blushed slightly at the compliment. "I only did what I was trained to do: my duty." Still, one could easily see the appreciation was appreciated.

The paladin cleared his throat. "All right, everyone, take your places around the dragon. I will ask our healer to revive her, and we must be ready in the event she manages to free herself." He got nods from everyone as they spaced themselves evenly around the monster.

Thrinndor nodded to Cyrillis, who stood at the head. The healer returned the nod, closed her eyes and bowed her head. Next she reached out and gently stroked the nose of the great beast.

Instantly, the enormous eyes opened, each as big as a dinner plate. Cyrillis hadn't noticed before, but the eyes were a beautiful blue—as deep as the azure of a bitter cold cloudless morning sky. The eyes registered surprise, fear, hatred and, finally, curiosity.

Thrinndor stepped into the creature's line of sight, his flaming bastard sword in his right hand for all to see. "I am gratified you yet live," the paladin said formally. The dragon stared back with unblinking eyes. Thrinndor got the feeling she was amused. "It seems you took something—someone—who I would like to have back."

Thrinndor was fairly certain she tried to move her head side-to-side, but she was bound so tight he couldn't be sure.

"I am going to loosen the ropes that bind your mouth shut," the paladin continued. "Realize that we are prepared for your icy breath and it will do little or no harm should you unwisely try to use it." He waited for a reaction but got none. "I am going to trust you so that you can speak. If you try to do anything other than speak, you will be killed. If you choose to cooperate, I will instruct the healer to tend to your injuries." He paused. "Do you understand? If so, and you will comply, blink your eyes twice."

Cyrillis found she was holding her breath as she waited for the dragon to respond. An eternity seemed to pass before the dragon blinked once. Twice. The cleric exhaled.

Thrinndor reached forward and slipped the two knots that had been fixed for the purpose and stepped back.

At first nothing happened. Then the dragon slowly opened her mouth and closed it a couple of times. When she opened it next, a puff of icy air came out.

Thrinndor was ready to retighten the knots, but then he thought he noticed the dragon was smiling.

"Just kidding," the dragon said softly. "I've always wanted to do that, but this is my first opportunity." Now he knew the dragon was smiling.

"Where is our companion?"

"Good question." Thrinndor raised his sword. "Wait!" the dragon said hurriedly. "That time I wasn't being funny. I picked up your friend with the intent to drop him from up high. But he had different ideas. Somehow he managed to get on top—I *hate* it when the man climbs on top," the beast chuckled at her own joke, "and I flew all over trying to get him off, to no avail. So, I informed him I would take him back to my lair and we'd discuss the matter there. He didn't like that plan, either, and jumped off before we got there. I chased your man into a small copse of trees but was unable to find him."

The dragon paused, and Thrinndor feared she had said all she was going to on the matter. "I was a little pissed, so I knocked down the trees Still unable to find him, I blasted the landscape with ice. If he's still there, he's probably pretty cold by now."

Now Thrinndor was certain the damn dragon was smiling.

"Are you going to turn me loose now?"

"I do not think that would be in our best interest," answered the paladin.

"But I told you everything you asked, and I even told you the truth! What more can you ask of me?"

Now Thrinndor was sure she was pouting. Damn, she's good.

"You can take us back to the copse of trees." This came from Vorgath, who remained behind the dragon, *Flinthgoor* at the ready.

"I'm not sure who said that," the dragon said, "but you can tell him that that might be a bit hard under current circumstances."

"A real wise ass," muttered the barbarian.

"I heard that!" said the dragon. "For your information both my wisdom and intelligence scores are off the charts!"

"What charts?"

Thrinndor watched the dragon roll her eyes. "If I have to explain, then it is of no use. Never mind!"

The paladin was starting to like this dragon. "If we untie you," he heard the barbarian gasp, "how do we know you will not simply fly away?"

"You don't."

"Ha!" Vorgath said.

"Unless I give you my word."

Thrinndor waited, but no more was forthcoming. "Will you?"

"Will I what?"

It was the paladin's turn to roll his eyes. "Will you give me your word that if I untie you, you will not simply fly away? *And* that you will take us to where you last saw our companion."

"Yes."

"Not good enough."

"For what?"

"Tell me that you will not attempt to fly away if we release you and that you will take us to our companion."

"Very good," the dragon said. "I believe I can safely assume that your cerebral scores were pretty good, as well. It is nice to be dealing with humans that are actually smarter than the average rock." The dragon laughed. Vorgath snorted. "Very well. I give you my word that I will not simply fly away if you release me. *And* that I will take you to where I last saw your companion."

Still Thrinndor hesitated.

"You don't trust me?"

"No," Vorgath said.

"Ouch! That hurts coming from a dwarf barbarian! What is your name, little man?" Savinhand chuckled at this.

The barbarian hesitated. He wanted to know how the dragon knew he was a dwarf barbarian. "Vorgath. What's yours?" he said belligerently.

"I have many names—"

"More than you know," the dwarf muttered.

"Really? What do they call me now?"

Vorgath hesitated. "To the giants you're known as 'IcyBitch.'"

The dragon laughed. "I kinda like that one. Over the years I have been called far worse." She chuckled deep in her chest. "You may call me Pantorra."

"Is that your name?" Cyrillis asked.

"It is one I've been called for many hundreds of years, dear. What's yours?"

"I am Cyrillis."

"Very pretty name. Perhaps you can convince these lame-brains that my word is good, and that you may trust me once it's given."

"Well," the cleric began. "I am not sure I have that kind of influence, at the moment."

"Good, safe answer," the dragon laughed. "However, you underestimate yourself, dear. You have but to ask, and your will shall be done."

"Very well," Thrinndor said. "You have convinced me. I am going to release you. However, should you decide to go back on your word—and I do not believe you will—that dwarf barbarian behind you will hunt you down if for no other reason to make you number three on the wall in his study."

"Number three? Really? Who were numbers one and two?"

Vorgath hesitated and stole a covert glance at Cyrillis. He still had not discussed with her his reasoning on having the dragon heads stuffed and mounted.

"Melundiir and Theremault." Cyrillis answered for him.

The dragon's voice took on a sorrowful note. "So it was you who bagged my friends." A silence settled on the group. "I must certainly stand by my word, then. While I am certainly old, I am not ready to be gathering dust in some hero's study!" Her voice took on a chill. "One last pitch: Doubting the word of a dragon can be compared to doing the same of a paladin." Pantorra leveled her gaze at Thrinndor, who, with Cyrillis, remained the only figures visible to her.

"That does it!" Vorgath grumbled as he walked around to where he could also be seen. "After that I'll release you myself." He lowered his voice to make it more menacing. "However, if you even think of double-crossing us, what pretty boy here said is only the beginning of what I'll do to you."

The two locked eyes for a moment, measuring one another's will. "Very well," the dragon said. "You may release me."

Vorgath nodded and stepped forward to begin untying the multiple of knots that kept the dragon from moving. Savinhand and Thrinndor moved in to help.

The giants stood back and watched with rocks and clubs at the ready in the event the dragon was less than truthful. Sordaak stood with them, and Cyrillis walked up and stood in front of the dragon's face. "You knew Melundiir?"

Startled at the question, the dragon drew back. When she moved back in, her eyes showed she understood. "Yes dear, I did. Did you know her as well?"

Cyrillis nodded, biting her lip to hold back the tears. "She was a friend." Her voice faltered. The cleric lifter her chin defiantly. "She let me ride her."

"Then she must have considered you a true friend." Pantorra was silent for a moment. "And you must have known her during one of her few happy times."

"What do you mean?"

"Well," the dragon said, looking over at the barbarian who was in a deep, animated conversation with the paladin, "suffice it to say that your barbarian friend did her a favor. She was miserable trapped in that protection chamber for the Library of Antiquity. Yet she had given her word, and the only way to release her from that vow was how she finally did get released—by her death."

A tear coursed down the cleric's cheek. "Why must these things be so regimented? So final?"

"Because, without law and rules there would be nothing but Chaos—and that would be a terrible way to live."

Cyrillis nodded.

"You know that your friend Melundiir had many names, also?"

The cleric looked up, her face clouded in doubt as she shook her head. "No, I did not."

"One of those names you may remember." Pantorra's voice got very quiet. "Jacinth."

Stunned, Cyrillis took a step back. She almost tripped over a rock. Sordaak noted her distress and walked over to take her elbow. "Is everything all right?"

The cleric nodded as she stepped closer to the dragon. "You are certain?"

Pantorra nodded. "Search your heart and memories, dear. You will then know it to be true."

Cyrillis' eyes widened as the memories came flooding back. Jacinth had been sent to be her nanny. But after Cyrillis' parents died, Jacinth had raised her as her own. Until the day she walked away. It was after that when Ytharra brought Melundiir around.

It was *true*! Cyrillis rushed forward and threw her arms around the dragon's neck, tears flowing freely down her cheeks.

"Easy, dear—there are several sore spots where you are squeezing so tightly."

Cyrillis stepped back, instantly contrite. "I am *so* sorry! Here, allow me to help you."

"That's not necessary, young lady. I'll be fine."

"No, I insist." Cyrillis bowed her head and mumbled the words to a prayer of healing and then she stepped in and released that healing into the neck of the dragon. Instantly wounds healed over and stopped bleeding. Bruises faded and strained ligaments were repaired.

"Well, if you insist." Pantorra smiled.

"OK, enough of this mushy shit." Vorgath and Thrinndor had walked up as the conversation ended. "We have a ranger to find."

"How do you intend to show us where he is?" Thrinndor asked.

"That is also a good question," Pantorra said.

"Take me to him," the paladin said.

"No."

"Why not?" Concern instantly returned to the paladin's voice.

"Remember the 'man on top' thing? That's not something I made up. Men rely too heavily on their sharp weapons to hang on, or to force their will on whoever or whatever." Pantorra hesitated for a moment. "I'll take Cyrillis. Your ranger will probably need her ministrations, anyway. Yes, I'll take Cyrillis."

Thrinndor could not find fault in her logic, yet he could not in good conscience allow the cleric to go where he—the leader—should go.

"I have skills as a healer, as well. And, my strength might be necessary to free him."

"I know that you are the leader of this group of adventurers," Pantorra answered, "but in this you should relinquish. Your healing powers as a paladin are indeed not inconsiderable. Yet, what if they prove insufficient? Your healer is the logical choice. And where matters of strength are concerned, I think I can handle anything that comes along."

Thrinndor was running out of arguments. "Very well," he said. "But know this: that staff our healer carries would be sufficient to knock some sense into your head should you wander from the assigned path."

Pantorra chuckled. "I am certain that *Kurril* is indeed sufficient, and that your cleric is up to the task. Rest assured, o Paladin of Valdaar, I will take her to this companion of yours, and I will find a way to return them to you should he yet live."

Thrinndor wanted to know how she knew whom he served, but decided they had wasted enough time while Breunne could be seriously injured or worse. "Very well," he said again. "Go with speed. We will await your return at a camp down in the ravine."

The dragon nodded and turned back to Cyrillis. "If you will climb aboard, my dear, we'll go see if we can find this companion of yours."

"Yes, of course." The cleric took the offered boost from the paladin and climbed the rest of the way up to the dragon's neck.

"Hang on if you wish," Pantorra said, "but I've never lost a rider I didn't want to lose, and I do not plan to do so now." With that she leapt into the air and spread her wings. Soon she was gaining altitude and headed west.

"I hope you know what you're doing," Vorgath grumbled as he started down the wall of the ravine toward the floor. He wanted to get a fire going before it got dark.

"So do I, old friend. So do I." Thrinndor watched the dragon fade into the distance and then turned to follow the dwarf down.

Chapter Twenty-Two

Pantorra

Breunne's eyes fluttered open and the first thing he saw was Cyrillis' face. "Damn, a guy could get used to seeing you the first thing in the morning." He smiled.

"Yeah, well," the healer said sternly, "first of all, it is late afternoon. And second, I have heard that line before." She returned his smile. "I am glad to see you yet remain among the living."

"Me, too." The ranger's brow's knitted in concentration. "The last thing I remember was being trapped under a tree..."

"Yes you were. And a tough time we had of finding you under there! I had to use my health sense to find you. It is a good thing you remained alive, even if just barely."

Breunne tried to look around, but he couldn't see much. "Where are the others?"

"Back at the ravine," Cyrillis answered.

The ranger was confused. "How did you get me out from under the tree?" But, before she could answer, he thought of another question. "And how did you find me here in the first place?"

Cyrillis took a deep breath. "Pantorra brought me here. It was she that lifted the tree off of you."

"Who?" As he asked the question, the dragon stepped into his view. Ignoring the pain in his side, he rolled quickly to his left, drew his bow and notched an arrow, all before the cleric could blink, let alone answer his question.

"*STOP!*" Cyrillis shouted.

Breunne didn't release the arrow, but he didn't lower the bow, either. From this range, he was fairly certain he could put the arrow through either eye of the dragon, and maybe even score a death blow.

"Pantorra brought me here to rescue you."

"That dragon is the reason I was buried under the tree in the first place." He talked without lowering the bow.

"Sorry about that," Pantorra spoke. "But in my defense, you kind of provoked me."

The ranger eased his draw on the arrow but maintained the bow ready to shoot. "*You* carried me aloft!"

"And you did the unthinkable! You climbed on top!"

"Dropping me from a thousand feet up was not what I'd usually call being friendly!"

"*All right!*" Cyrillis shouted. She looked from one to the other. "Breunne, allow me to explain. When we discovered you missing—I saw Pantorra carry you away, by the way—and then saw her returning, we decided to capture her and find out what she had done with you." She took a ragged breath. "Long story short: We did so, and have become friends."

"*Friends?*" Breunne was incredulous. "With a *dragon?*"

"Easy there, little man. I haven't had anything to eat in several days, and you are starting to look appealing. Rest assured, friendship with the likes of you is not very high on my list of fun things to do, either."

The ranger lowered his weapon. "You sure about this?"

"Sure? Of course not," responded the cleric. "However, she did bring me to you and helped me to get you from under the tree. So I think we can trust her."

"Yes, you can," Pantorra said. "For now."

"What do you mean by that?" Breunne considered raising his bow, again, but decided against it.

"It means that I have given my word to your paladin leader to return the two of you to the ravine." The dragon appeared to shrug. "After that, we will see."

The ranger eyed the dragon suspiciously. "How do you plan on doing that?"

"Get you back to the ravine? Fly you back, of course. I can carry the two of you for that short distance, but I'm glad that it is not further than that."

Breunne looked at the western sky. The sun was nearing the horizon; he had been out for several hours, he figured. "Very well, let's get moving then."

"You don't have to sound so *happy* about it!" Pantorra said, sarcasm dripping from her tone. "Believe me; playing transport for humans is more than a little demeaning. I hope none of my friends see me!"

"Friends?" Breunne was again concerned. "There are others of you around?"

"Of course," Pantorra said with a wink. "There are several in this region alone." Her eyes narrowed. "However, your dwarf companion informs me there are recently two less. That is distressing."

"Can we continue this conversation back at camp?" Both the dragon and ranger turned to look at Cyrillis. "I would like to get back before it gets dark."

Pantorra turned back to the ranger. "Is she always like this? I mean, she seems a bit pushy."

"You don't know the half of it!" Breunne winked at Cyrillis as both climbed aboard for the return flight. As he settled in he asked, "You will be a little more stable in your flight this time, I assume?"

The neck of the giant beast twisted around so she could look at both of her passengers. "Of course. I wouldn't want my new friend to fall off now, would I?"

Breunne nodded, and the dragon looked away. The ranger felt her muscles bunch beneath his legs as she prepared for flight. "Friend?" he whispered to Cyrillis. "I assume she means you?"

Cyrillis nodded as the dragon spread her wings and leapt clear of the ground. For a time conversation was not possible as the massive wings clawed for air. Breunne could tell she was struggling with the weight of both of them, but now was not a good time to bring it up, he surmised.

The flight back was uneventful and Breunne took the time to study the terrain from a vantage point until now he had not thought possible, and quite probably will not be again. He made some mental notes to make some changes to the small cadre of maps he'd collected over the years.

All too soon—for the both of them—the trip was over. They found the companions in a sheltered lee of the ravine, a fire blazing to ward off the chill that was rapidly descending on the heels of the departing sun.

Breunne jumped to the ground first and helped Cyrillis do the same. The healer briefly considered refusing the help, knowing she could just have as easily made the jump, but understood the manner in which the gesture was intended and smiled instead.

Three of the four men left the warmth of the fire to walk out to meet their returning companions, Sordaak remained behind. Pantorra had landed a sufficient distance away so as not to disturb the fire.

Thrinndor was the first to speak. "I see that you yet live." He directed this at the ranger.

"Yes, thanks to these two." Breunne waved a gracious arm at the cleric and dragon.

"Yeah well," Vorgath grumbled, "none of that would have been necessary if it weren't for that oversized windbag."

Pantorra's eyes narrowed. "Listen, little man, allegiances are sometimes made and broken based comments like that."

The barbarian stood and stretched himself to his full height. "Not a comment; merely a statement of fact. If you hadn't been taking orders from the *minions*, we wouldn't be having this—"

"*WHAT?* That band of miscreants couldn't command a bath water battle fleet! I take orders from *NO ONE!*"

The gathering suddenly got real quiet. So much so that when a loud *pop* came from the fire, several of the companions jumped.

It was Sordaak who broke the silence. "Just what were you doing traveling with them, then? Surely you don't expect us to believe you just so happened to be in the area?"

The dragon shifted her gaze to the sorcerer, who remained sitting on a log by the fire. "It's no concern of mine what you believe, magicuser."

"Oh?" Sordaak put his hands on his knees and pushed himself wearily to his feet. "Then why do you remain among us?" The mage arched an eyebrow. "We as a group have subdued you once, and certainly the thought process would follow that we could do so again."

"Easily," the dwarf interjected, "or we could make it more permanent, this time." He smiled, his teeth reflecting the light from the fire in a sinister fashion.

"Yet you did not flee once the opportunity presented itself," Sordaak finished. "Why?"

"You are very observant," Pantorra said quietly, her eyes not straying from those of the mage.

Sordaak shrugged. "That's been said of me a time or two."

Silence again blanketed the gathering. Finally, the dragon sighed and her demeanor changed. "Very well—you are correct. I have been working for the minions." Vorgath puffed up to interject, but Pantorra didn't let him. "But only under duress."

The dragon hesitated as she clearly was struggling with how much to reveal. "Go on," Sordaak urged.

"The minions stole my eggs!"

"*What?*"

Moisture welled up in the dragon's eyes. "Please! You *must* help me! I am the last of my kind in the land, and the minions are taking advantage of that. I serve them or they will destroy my eggs." She fought to regain composure. "Earlier this year, while I was away, the high lords entered my lair and stole my last three eggs." Her eyes took on a sorrowful tint. "The last male of my species was slain in the giant wars in a land far to the south."

"Good riddance, I say," Vorgath mused as he dug in his pack for his pipe.

Pantorra's eyes narrowed in a moment of rage and she took in a sharp breath. Sordaak feared she was about to strike with her frosty breath. But she let the breath out slowly instead. "Without dragons, little man, with what would you test your skill in battle?"

The dwarf sat upright and scratched his chin. "I vote we assist this overgrown lizard in any way we can!" His smile was twisted.

"Whatever!" Sordaak quickly wiped the smile off of his face as he again turned to face the dragon.

"Perhaps it will make negotiations easier if I do this," Pantorra suggested as her great bulk began to diminish in size rapidly. Soon, standing before them was an attractive middle-aged woman in white robes and with beautiful long white hair. Her eyes remained the same piercing blue, however.

"Yes, I like that *much* better," said the ranger appreciatively.

Pantorra bowed slightly at the waist in acknowledgement of the compliment.

"Me, too," said the barbarian. "I feel much less likely to be eaten."

The woman snorted. "I would have to be *very* hungry, indeed, to eat a tough old dwarf such as yourself."

"Bah!" Vorgath spat. "Who're you calling old? I'm not even in my prime yet!"

"Really? You look to have been ridden hard and put away wet by that prime." Pantorra smiled.

The barbarian snorted in return and looked over at the paladin. "Can I kill her now? Or should I wait until after she shows us where her lair is?" He winked as he too smiled.

"Bring it on, little man. It's been a hundred years or so since I last dined on a dwarf—perhaps my memory of such is a bit off. You look appropriately fatted to make a nice morsel."

Vorgath made a show of sucking in the bulge in his middle. "Fatted? There is nothing here but lean, mean, fighting machine!"

"Whatever!" Pantorra rolled her eyes. She turned her head to look at the paladin. "You keep him around for his jesting abilities, right?"

Thrinndor's eyes bulged as he choked back a laugh. "Actually, he does not get in the way all that much in battle."

"Oh?" Pantorra mused.

"Get in the way?" Now it was the dwarf's eyes that bulged.

"If you guys are done marking your territory," Sordaak interrupted, "perhaps we can get back the original discussion." He had everyone's attention. "How is it you think we can help you?"

Pantorra hesitated. "The Minions have the eggs hidden somewhere deep in their palace. They should hatch any day now. If allowed to hatch under Minion control, the young dragons will be subservient to them as long as they live."

The mage's gaze was unwavering. "What is it you would have us do?"

"You are going to the palace anyway. Find the eggs and return them to me."

Sordaak was startled. "How do you know we are going to the palace?"

Pantorra shrugged. "You seek the staff, do you not?"

The sorcerer did not react, although that took some doing. "What staff?"

"You do not need to feign ignorance with me, magicuser. I know that you seek *Pendromar, Dragon's Breath.*"

Sordaak again maintained his composure. "How is it you know this? And, what does the staff have to do with the palace?"

Pantorra measured the mage with her eyes, trying to gauge his thoughts. "What else could you and your companions possibly want from the Minions in this place? Although how you learned that the staff is there is a mystery to me. Until a century or so ago, it was in my possession."

"*What?*"

Pantorra nodded. "You heard correct. I took the staff from the dead body of a would-be powerful sorcerer such as yourself when he and his companions tried their hand against me." She shrugged again. "They were not successful."

"How did the Minions get the staff?"

Pantorra's expression turned grim. "A horde of at least a hundred Minion warriors, led by two high priests, approached me all those years ago and said they would allow me to live if I surrendered the staff." Her shoulders slumped. "I considered fighting, but knew in my heart I could not prevail against such a horde and the staff would be theirs anyway when I fell. Surviving was more important. Besides, I tried to wield the staff but could not. It was useless to me, so I gave it to them."

"Did they say why they wanted it? I know for a fact that they cannot use the staff, either."

Pantorra nodded slowly. "They said the staff must be kept from those such as you who would try to use it to return an ancient evil to the land. An evil that had been absent for countless millennia. That would not be allowed. They said they could ensure that never happened."

The staff *is* here! Sordaak could scarcely contain his elation. Outwardly, his emotions remained in check. "Assuming you are correct and we seek this staff, why should we help you by returning your eggs?"

"Two reasons," the dragon said as she squared her shoulders. "First, I will swear fealty to you and support your endeavors even unto my last breath."

"Why would you trade one subservience for another?" It was Thrinndor who interrupted this time.

Pantorra's gaze shifted to lock eyes with the paladin. "Because my kind must be allowed not to pass forever from the land. That alone provides reason enough for my servitude."

"And the second?" Sordaak's eyes had not left the dragon woman.

Pantorra's eyes stared intently into those of the paladin. "Second, I have knowledge concerning the sword you also seek."

Chapter Twenty-Three

Minion War

Thrinndor took two steps toward the woman. "Tell me what you know."

Pantorra didn't flinch. She shook her head. "Return to me my eggs. Only then will I give you the information you seek."

The paladin deliberately put his hand on the pommel of his sword. "I could make you talk."

The dragon woman again shook her head, her eyes never leaving those of the paladin. "No, you could not." She set her jaw in determination. "I would take the information with me to the afterlife ere I talked."

Thrinndor's eyes searched those of this woman who refused to give him what he so desperately needed. "Very well. At least tell me the name of this sword so that I may know you actually possess that which I require."

"*Valdaar's Fist.*"

The paladin's eyes continued to peer into those of Pantorra. Abruptly, he allowed his shoulders to sag. "Now please tell me how it is you know I seek this sword."

The dragon woman nodded. "Dragons live many hundreds of years—some even of the higher order may live many *thousands* of years. The wars and other goings-on of man are known to us. We choose not to participate—your business is generally not ours. But still we take notice, if for no other reason to *ensure* your business remains not ours." She hesitated.

"There is more," Thrinndor urged.

"There is more. Once a century, there is a gathering of all the dragons. During that time we share information such as the rise and fall of Valdaar—and other gods, if such comes to our notice." A tear appeared in an eye and made its way down her lovely cheek. "Theremault and Melundiir will be sorely missed at our next meeting." Another tear formed and followed the first. "Our numbers have steadily declined over the last millennia." She lifted her chin proudly. "Once we numbered in the thousands." Her shoulders sagged in defeat and her eyes fell to the ground at the paladin's feet. "At the last gathering there was barely two hundred of our kind remaining."

"Two hundred *dragons*?" Vorgath was mesmerized by the thought.

Pantorra nodded as she raised her head to stare at the dwarf. "There are very few remaining here in what you call the land. Those such as yourself have gotten too proficient at hunting my kind and hastening our trip to the afterlife."

In the silence that followed, a question popped into Cyrillis' head. "How long can you remain in human form?"

"And are all dragons capable of taking that form?" Sordaak asked before the dragon could answer.

Pantorra shook her head. "No. The shape-shifting is only available to those of us who possess the ability to cast spells, which is roughly only a fifth of our numbers." She turned to face the cleric. "Maintaining human form requires the use of energy. That energy can last several days—weeks, even for the highly skilled of my kind. But if the energy wanes, we revert back to dragon form. I can maintain this form for only a few days—a week at most."

"Where is this gathering held?" Vorgath was clearly more than a little interested.

"Surely you do not expect me to answer that." Pantorra shook her head. "Suffice it to say that we hold the gathering far from the reach of man. It is many days' travel, even for me."

Sordaak rubbed his chin. "When will the next gathering take place?"

Pantorra eyed the mage intently before answering. "I am going to decline to answer that question as well, on the grounds that I can think of no good reason for you to have that information."

"If we are to return your eggs to you, and you are to fulfill your required servitude, it would seem requisite that I—we—know when would be the gaps in said servitude." Sordaak crossed his arms on his chest and waited.

"Very good, I see that you are indeed smarter than you appear," the dragon woman smiled as she nodded. "Return my eggs to me and I will be certain to let you know prior to any lapses in my service."

The mage considered arguing further, but decided there would be no point. For now.

"Two hundred dragons?" Vorgath still had stars in his eyes.

"Somewhat less this gathering, I am certain." Pantorra's demeanor was again sad. "I know of at least three of my comrades that have fallen in this past year alone that will not be in attendance."

Thrinndor walked to where he had made his bed, irked that information on the sword was so close and yet he could not have it.

Sleep would surely elude him this night.

*

Morning found the companions, giants and the dragon—still in human form—gathered around a large boulder on which the paladin had drawn what they knew concerning the locations of both their allies and enemies.

At Thrinndor's request, Pantorra reverted back to dragon form and took flight to verify and update this information. The clouds remained low, but she assured the paladin that those would not affect her vision, as the heat-related component in her vision easily penetrated the mists.

Vorgath's eyes strained to see where she had gone but soon gave up. "Are you certain we can trust her?"

Sordaak's eyes too returned to the crude rendition of the surrounding land on the rock. "Yes. As long as she needs us to get her eggs we can."

"Agreed," the paladin said, eying the nearness of the two rocks that symbolized Minion armies on his "table," and their proximity to a pine cone being used to show their own current location. Only a few hours of travel separated the three markers. The dwarf contingent was considerably farther away—two days, at least.

The companions and guests silently cleaned up from breakfast as they awaited the dragon's return. Each was preoccupied in his or her own way with the challenge they faced.

More than a hundred Minions awaited them before this day would end. That was *a lot* of Minions, no matter how you sliced them. The barbarian chuckled at the pun.

The group had scarcely prepared for travel when Pantorra returned. She reverted to human form, and the companions again gathered around their makeshift battle plan.

The dragon reached out and moved the rock on the table that symbolized the Minion army from the southern region closer to the pine cone that was their present location. After surveying the table, she also moved the other rock, again closer.

"Those damn Minion Lords must have alerted the armies to our presence," grumbled the barbarian.

"Of course they did." Cyrillis shook her head at the obvious.

"The real question is," Breunne said as he eyed the narrowed distances between the groups, "why haven't they joined forces? Surely a contingent of their combined might could prove our undoing."

Thrinndor scratched what had over the past couple of weeks become a full beard. "Perhaps they hope to catch us in a scissor action—pinch us between the two armies." He pointed to the second rock. "See how the army from Ice Homme is moving parallel to the one from the south? I believe they mean to get behind us."

"A sound tactic, to be sure," agreed the ranger. "We can counter that by moving quickly and attacking the army from Ice Homme here." He pointed to an area on the map that had the rock denoting the local army between them and the rock denoting the army from the south.

The paladin nodded, then looked skyward at the still low clouds. "Weather report?" He looked over at the barbarian for his answer.

Vorgath arched an eyebrow. He then took in a deep breath and also looked skyward. "Weather should hold as-is for another day or two. I'm not sure past then, but I believe another cold stretch is due."

"*What?*" Pantorra was incredulous as she stared past the paladin at the barbarian. "On what can you possibly base those predictions?"

Thrinndor took a step back, giving his friend room. He kept the barbarian within arm's length should restraint become necessary.

Vorgath's demeanor remained aloof, but his tone was icy. "Look, you oversized keg cooler, I have been doing this adventuring thing for a long time. During that time I have picked up indicators as to tendencies in the weather patterns. While I could certainly explain to you the intricacies of this prognostication, I do not believe now would be the opportune time."

Thrinndor did a double-take at the barbarian, checking to make sure it was indeed his old friend talking. A quick glance at the dragon showed her only reaction was a raised eyebrow. "It would be unwise to doubt our diminutive companion," the paladin said hurriedly.

"Unwise or not," answered the woman, "I find it hard to believe that that old windbag is blowing more than hot air."

Vorgath's eyes narrowed. "Who're you calling *old?*" he growled, low and deep. "It seems to me *your* years far exceed mine!"

"That would be a correct assessment, oh miniature one," Pantorra snapped back. "However, I only got to these middle years in my life by not believing everything I hear—especially that which comes from a self-serving blowhard such as yourself." She gave him a smile, but it contained no warmth.

There was a sharp intake of breath from several of the companions as Vorgath stood to his full height. "*Blowhard?* That from a giant rodent that uses her *breath* as a weapon?" Now the barbarian also smiled.

It was the dragon lady's turn to rise to her full height. "Perhaps I should remind you just how well that weapon works?"

Vorgath stepped away from the boulder, giving himself room to work. "Bring it, dragon *bitch!*"

"*ENOUGH!*" Cyrillis shouted. Both the barbarian and Pantorra turned to look at the cleric, inquisitive eyebrows raised. "Could you *please* save some of that for our mutual enemies?"

Pantorra returned her eyes to the barbarian. "Your healer seems a bit tense."

Vorgath rolled his eyes. "You got that right!"

"Mayhap she merely needs to be serviced? Surely one of you virile males can handle the task?"

Thrinndor's eyes bulged as Vorgath continued with a straight face. "Nah," the barbarian waved a negligent hand and winked at the dragon. "Something about her being 'reserved.'"

"Oh, one of *those.*" Pantorra shook her head as she again faced a clearly perplexed cleric. "That certainly explains a lot." She shook her head again. "You know there are other ways, my dear?"

"*What?*" Cyrillis' face turned crimson. "*ENOUGH!*" She shouted again. "I will not have you—or *anyone*—discuss my sex life!"

"Or lack thereof," muttered the barbarian, still not looking at the cleric.

The cleric's eyes narrowed as she took the two steps necessary to stand in front of Vorgath. Sordaak thought for sure she was going to slap him, and edged that direction in the event an intervention was required, but when the healer lifted her right hand it was to jab a finger into the face of the diminutive fighter. "I will thank you for not bringing this subject up ever again."

Vorgath shrugged. "As you wish," he said with a straight face. "However, one last comment and I will say no more: Whoever this 'reservation' is for had better get on with his duties! You are starting to get on my nerves!" The barbarian spun on a heel and marched out of the clearing. "Can we please get on with the Minion beat-down?" he tossed over his shoulder as he disappeared from sight.

The others in the group waited as the healer clearly struggled to contain her ire. Saying nothing, she spun to lambaste the men with a withering stare.

Suddenly, everyone in the clearing had somewhere else to look.

After a few moments of uncomfortable silence where even the birds held their breath, the paladin cleared his throat noisily. "We need to be moving."

Now everyone had someplace else to be. Those not finished packing hurriedly stuffed their packs and slung them to their shoulders.

Cyrillis muttered under her breath angrily and the remaining companions gave her a wide berth as they went about their duties. Within minutes the grouping had gathered at the edge of the clearing, Vorgath staring off in the direction they were to take.

A few last-minute plans were made, and positions were taken for a fast march. With the giants along, the companions could afford to use both the ranger and the rogue as scouts, and as such both slipped past the barbarian, disappearing into the brush.

Pantorra reverted to dragon form and took to the skies, promising to monitor the movement of the Minions from the air and report if anything appeared different than discussed.

*

By noon the companions were in position behind the Minion army from the South, and Pantorra assured them the second army was at least two miles away on the other side.

They hurriedly grabbed a bite to eat, knowing it might be some time before they would again have the opportunity. While they ate, they went over their plans.

Pantorra was to lead the High Priests—she knew there to be two—and as many of their Minion Lords as she could into a trap.

"You are surrounded," a shout came from above them on the rim of the canyon they had planned to as the jaws for their trap. "Surrender the staff to us now and we may yet allow some of you to live.

"Trap!" Thrinndor shouted as he rolled off of the rock where he had been sitting. He continued rolling until he was under cover of some of the brush that surrounded where they had stopped.

Vorgath cast a withering glance at the dragon. "I knew we shouldn't have trusted that *bitch*!" Pantorra ignored the remark, melding into the brush and then disappearing. Shaking his head, the barbarian did as the paladin, quickly tumbling into the brush to his left.

In less than five seconds the clearing where the companions had stopped was empty, leaving little or no sign that it had ever been occupied.

"Very well," shouted the now amused voice, "we will do this the hard way! Kill them! Kill them *all*!" He waved his right arm and on all sides the hills above them erupted with men in black robes and armor, swarming down the hillsides at a full run.

"Spread out!" Thrinndor hissed, hoping the others heard him. "Use the brush for cover and fall back to the clearing when you are forced to move. Do not let them get behind you. Cyrillis, find a central point and heal as best you can. Stay out of sight. Sordaak, give me some crowd control, *now*!"

"Take out the High Priests first!" answered the magicuser from a bush not far away.

Thrinndor glanced at the rim of the canyon where one of the High Priests still stood. He had no idea where the other was, but the paladin was pretty sure the dozen or so Minions of Set between him and the Priest would have something to say about that particular maneuver. "I cannot get there," he hissed.

"Then we are destined to fall," replied the sorcerer.

"I'll take care of the High Priests," Savinhand said from somewhere off to their right. "You take care of the rest."

"Deal!" shouted the paladin as he jumped from his hiding place and clove a robed Minion nearly in two with his flaming sword.

Sordaak stood, stepped away from the bush to give him room and pointed his finger at a group of Minions rapidly approaching to his right. A sinewy strand shot from his finger and instantly the Minions were entangled in the sticky strands of a web. Briefly he considered following that up with a fire ball, but he decided slowing more of the charging attackers was more important than harming those already ensnared.

He was right.

Slowly he turned in small increments, alternating between web, darkness, Ice Storms and clouds of nauseous gas spells. Occasionally he threw a fireball or wall of fire spell up on the rim when he spotted a High Priest. He didn't want those guys to think he had forgotten about them.

He needn't have worried. Between his attacks on the priests and the crowd control spells, he had far more attention than he wanted. "All yours," he said, not really caring if he was heard. "I'm going incognito for a few." With that, he went invisible and quickly ran to his left to get clear of the area.

Thrinndor heard the mage, but was too busy to even acknowledge. After his initial kill, surprise was no longer his and he was quickly surrounded. The paladin slashed at the Minion trying to get behind him, causing the man to give way. The big fighter worked his way in such that the prickly bush was at his back, giving him a modicum of protection—or at least warning—from that side.

In his usual display of tact, Vorgath howled a battle cry to build his rage and charged the largest grouping of Minions in his vicinity. Startled, the Minions broke formation and scattered, but not before two of their number lay dead on the floor of the canyon. Not one to put his back to a wall, the barbarian instead preferred charging forward to protect his flank. As such, he kept moving, conscious only of chasing the largest grouping of the enemy in his line of sight.

Breunne deployed *Xenotath*, launching arrows at any and all available targets, taking special note of the ranking Minions, much to their annoyance. Having loosed more than thirty arrows, he was confident in several kills, including at least one—and possibly two—Minion Lords. However, as the Minion army pressed his location, he too put his back to a bush and waited with his longsword in his right fist and a specially enchanted dagger in his left.

The ranger didn't have long to wait, as his arrows and marksmanship attracted plenty of company. He set his feet at shoulder width and met the onslaught with grim determination.

At first, Cyrillis was merely frustrated. The brush hid her companions and any potential injuries from her. She too put her back to a bush, facing as best she could the last known positions of her companions. But her line of sight was too limited by the scrub brush. Although it was scarcely higher than the top of her head, it effectively hid her friends from her.

Calming herself, the cleric closed her eyes and shifted her focus from her eyes to her health-sense. As she stretched forth her power, soon she was able to locate her friends and also to determine their status; health-wise, anyway.

Knowing that using her healing powers at this distance consumed additional spell energy and that this battle could go on for hours, Cyrillis healed only when the situation dictated—meaning she bit her tongue and merely monitored minor injuries instead of her usual ministrations at the first hint of damage.

As such she had little to do, at least initially. Instead, the cleric took the time to ready additional reserves, placing wands and potions that might be of use at her fingertips. And she gripped *Kurril* tightly in her right hand, ready to loose the power contained within at the slightest need.

Unlike their new friends, the giants formed a four-sided box, allowing ample room to swing enormous clubs or massive swords as need dictated, thus preventing Minion access to their backs. They moved as one when the situation dictated, and thus had little trouble with the smaller, weaker humans.

The spells cast by the High Priests were another matter. Battered by columns of flame and other offensive spells, Stormheart finally decided he'd had enough. The giant pointed to a rise where two of the Priests were readying another spell, spoke a word of power and a single bolt of lightning shot from his finger. The crackling energy split as it approached the two High Priests and then split again. The bolt danced all along the crest of the hill, striking no less than ten of the servants of Set. The two Priests, however, took the brunt of the electric storm.

The giant leader smiled as the two lords quickly retreated over the crest of the hill and out of his sight. He continued smiling as he returned his attention to the small army of Minions that had the misguided conception that by sheer numbers they could challenge the giants. Already their bodies littered the canyon bottom around him and his companions.

Savinhand, following his discussion with the paladin had gone into stealth mode and, careful to avoid contact with the charging army, quickly made his way up to the rim of the canyon where he had last seen one of the Minion High Priests.

Peering out from behind a small tree/large bush, Savin spotted his adversary not far from where he expected him to be. It was what he saw on the other side that concerned him even more: At least a hundred Minions of Set were waiting for the command to strike, hidden from his companions by the crest. Most of them were astride horses, explaining how they had gotten here so quickly.

But how had they known *where* to be? It made no sense. Damn! Briefly the thief's eyes scanned the sky, but he could find no sign of the dragon. He considered returning to inform the paladin, but decided his first priority should be to take out this High Priest, who was casting spells and directing the movements of a cadre of his troops.

Silently he worked his way around the tree/bush and got into position behind the priest. Checking his surroundings one more time, he crouched low and sprinted the final few steps, his vorpal sword in his right hand and a trusty dagger in his left.

Savinhand jumped the last few feet, intending to stab hard with both weapons at the exposed back of his adversary as he crashed into him. However, instead of the resistance of flesh and bone, his blades clove nothing but air! They passed right through the priest!

Shit! Illusion!

The rogue twisted in midair, landing awkwardly on his feet and then pitched forward in a cloud of dust. He allowed his momentum to carry him, rolling twice before attempting to stand. That proved to be a bad idea as arrows rained down all around him, two finding their mark.

He felt the sharp pain as first one arrow penetrated the thick leather jerkin that covered his upper thigh in his left leg, the other lodging deep into the fleshy part of his side, below his rib cage on the right side. He winced in pain, but again bolted into motion, bounding down the ravine side, using as much cover as was possible while he sheathed his weapons.

Arrows continued to whip past him as he weaved back and forth, trying to throw off the aim of these persistent archers. Apparently this worked, because he didn't feel the pain of any more arrows.

Where was the paladin? Vorgath was easy to spot; at least a dozen bodies lay scattered around the barbarian. The dwarf was breathing heavily and bleeding from several open wounds on his arms and torso. As Savin rounded a bend, the dwarf dispatched the last Minion in front of him with a tremendous slash from *Flinthgoor* that cut the man in two at the waist. The barbarian glared about wildly, a deep rage burning in his eyes.

"Over the hill!" Savinhand shouted. "There are more than a hundred more preparing to attack!" The dwarf's eyes followed the fast-moving rogue for a moment, Savin's words not penetrating the mist of rage that enveloped him. But slowly he nodded, released another howl of rage and launched himself up the hill.

"Wait!" Thrinndor called after the rapidly disappearing dwarf, but it was to no avail. Vorgath quickly disappeared over the crest of the hill.

The paladin shook his head and looked quickly around for others in his party. He spotted the giants, still in formation, not far off. "Stormheart!"

The giant bashed the Minion he was engaged with over the head with his massive club and looked the paladin's way.

"Another wave waits over the hill!" Thrinndor pointed up the slope the dwarf had recently ascended.

The giant leader nodded his understanding and barked a word of command. Together he and his fellow giants moved that way, fighting as they went. Stormheart found he had no adversary for a few moments, and used the time to begin a spell. He began waving his arms over his head in an ever-tightening circle.

Thrinndor turned his attention to the rogue's wounds and was about to remove one of the arrows, but he was roughly shoved aside. "Move," Cyrillis said as she studied Savin's injuries. "I will take care of this," she said without looking up. "Tend to your duties."

The paladin knew better than to argue, and he turned his attention back to the giants. As he watched, the clouds overhead began to darken and swirl in the same motion as the massive arms of the Storm Giant. Another command and Stormheart's mates ceased their fighting and joined their leader. Soon all four sets of arms were waving overhead, and the clouds swirled darker still—now almost black. An occasional bolt of lightning lashed out from the maelstrom, striking an unsuspecting Minion every time one did.

The Minions in the vicinity, seeing an opening, renewed their attack on the formation of giants. Thus they began to wreak unimpeded damage on the four. Still, the giants continued to weave their spell.

Breunne, seeing the giants were in trouble, dropped his swords and *Xenotath* leapt into his hands. In groups of three, arrows sped toward their targets, none missing their mark. In moments the area around the giants was clear.

But the ranger too had had a couple of Minions close aboard, and they took the opportunity to attack the distracted fighter.

Thrinndor, seeing them move in, ran the short distance to the ranger's aid, his flaming bastard sword nearly decapitating the nearest adversary as the man raised his staff to attack.

The paladin took a step to get between the other Minion and Breunne, but hesitated when he saw the priest was a young woman.

The woman used Thrinndor's hesitation to her advantage. She whipped the end of her staff up in a vicious blow that caught the unsuspecting paladin squarely in the groin. Although he was wearing his codpiece, the ferocity of the blow stunned him. A searing pain blinded the fighter as he doubled over. His left hand—shield still in place—moved instinctively to cover his genitals.

But his foe was finished with that area of his body. Instead, she swung her staff with both hands and the paladin's head filled with bright lights and more pain as the heavy end of the woman's staff connected with his temple. Thrinndor pitched forward into the dirt, his face breaking his fall and there he did not move.

The Minion priest raised the staff high over her head, intending to finish her work with one blow. But suddenly she found breathing difficult as an arrow, fired at close range, penetrated her heart. A second arrow pierced her throat.

She looked up at the ranger, yet another arrow drawn back ready to loose, her face mottled in rage. The woman tried to speak, but when her mouth opened, crimson blood bubbled out and down her thin features to flow off her chin.

Her eyes went wide in surprise and then rolled back into her head as she slumped to the ground beside the paladin and lay still.

"Paladin down!" Breunne shouted as he knelt to verify his friend still breathed. Satisfied, he turned his attention back to the giants. Thrinndor was sure going to be sore when he awakened.

"On it," he heard Cyrillis reply from across the clearing where she had been tending to the rogue. Breunne didn't turn to acknowledge as the massive storm the giants were brewing caught and held his attention. As the ranger watched, the swirling clouds began a rapid descent toward the crest of the canyon.

Tornado! The giants had called into existence a tornado! Breunne had not even been aware that was possible!

But suddenly the downward motion slowed. The tornado writhed in midair, unable to either continue its descent or climb back to the heavens. The ranger glanced around and quickly spotted the problem: A Minion High Priest stood on the hill and held his staff aloft, pointing it at the twisting mass of wind. Breunne could feel the power being exerted by both the priest and the giants.

The ranger again raised *Xenotath* and loosed three arrows in rapid succession at the priest. Although all three found their mark, Breunne was certain the resulting damage was slight. Yet, the arrows had the desired effect—the High Priest got distracted as he raised his guard, thereby losing his concentration on stopping the tornado.

Satisfaction showed on Stormheart's face as he lowered his concoction the rest of the way to the ground, instantly sucking up at least a dozen Minions that had failed to scatter in time.

Frustrated, the High Priest of Set looked around wildly for the source of the distraction and spotting the ranger a short distance away, pointed his staff at the offending human.

Breunne dove to his right, taking cover behind an outcropping of rock as a lightning bolt blasted the earth where he had been standing, showering the immediate vicinity with dirt. The ranger rolled twice more and surged back to his feet, another arrow notched on *Xenotath*'s powerful string.

The High Priest had started down the hill after his adversary. The ranger loosed three more arrows, but the Minion Lord easily knocked them from their path with a wave of his hand.

Ugh-oh, Breunne thought as he again threw himself to the ground, when another blast shook the place where he had been. White-hot pain shot up his leg from his left foot as he had not quite cleared the area. He continued tumbling away from the blast as he applied one of his limited healing spells to his foot. Instantly his appendage felt better, but he knew his foot was far from 100 percent.

He jumped back to his feet, his bow again at the ready when another lightning bolt hit him square in the chest. The explosion of pain and energy sent him reeling backward, knocking the breath from him.

Breunne tried to roll to his right, but his movements felt sluggish, and he knew he was badly hurt. He felt another blast wrack his body with searing pain, and then everything went black. He thought he heard "ranger down" over the ringing in his ears as consciousness left him.

"Son of a bitch!" Cyrillis muttered as she brushed back a lock of hair that had escaped its binds. "Cannot any of these men use a damned shield?" She ducked low and took a circuitous route to the fallen Breunne. Her senses told her that he yet lived and that his various maladies were not immediately life-threatening.

Thrinndor, feeling somewhat better for having had his turn with their cleric, was still hobbled by his recent close encounter with the Minion priestess. He dodged from bush to tree as he made his way up the steep slope toward the Minion Lord. The paladin could see the black robed human was taking time to heal his wounds, and he decided that an interruption was warranted.

Thrinndor flipped his shield sideways and released the bolt he had notched in his crossbow. His aim was true; the projectile caught the Priest square in the chest.

The Lord howled in either rage or pain. It didn't matter; the effect was what the fighter had intended, disruption of the man's healing.

The paladin raised the shield as he ducked behind a large boulder, the combination serving to deflect the majority of the lightning bolt's energy that flashed his way. Most. His shield arm boiled in pain and then went numb from the damage absorbed through the shield.

Deciding to attack while the Priest had to reload, Thrinndor kept moving around the rock and launched himself up the slope at what he hoped to be a confused Minion. He held his shield loosely in front of him as a battering ram, his flaming sword high over his head in anticipation of action.

As the paladin approached the Priest, however, Savinhand materialized behind the man and suddenly the surprised Minion Lord's head landed in the path of the charging fighter.

Thrinndor came to a skidding halt beside a grinning Savinhand. "Damn, I love this sword!" The rogue reached out with the aforementioned weapon and gently pushed the still standing, but headless, body of the priest. The torso toppled forward, landing next to the head in the dusty, dead grass atop the knoll.

Both turned to look at the carnage on the mesa when Vorgath screamed another of his battle cries. He was surrounded by four of the Minions. As Thrinndor quickly moved to help, the barbarian lowered his greataxe and pirouetted, swinging *Flinthgoor* in a broad arc that did varying amounts of damage to his adversaries.

One such enemy looked down as his intestines spilled from the gash at his waist. The creature's eyes rolled back in his head and he crumpled to the ground.

Another lost his right hand just above the wrist as he tried in vain to block the flashing instrument of death. The Minion screamed and backed up a couple of steps, staring at the stump that had been his hand.

A third tried to duck the weapon as it flashed her way, but the blade glanced off the female Minion's head with a dull *thunk*, taking most of her hair and a significant portion of her scalp with it. She screamed in pain, dropped her staff, put her hand to her bloodied head and stumbled away.

The woman's lowered head deflected the axe upward, where it lodged deep into the neck of the fourth Minion. Its momentum finally spent, *Flinthgoor* remained there until Vorgath wrenched it free. The Minion's hands went to his throat and he tried to speak, but only blood came from his lips. The man's eyes glazed over and he pitched forward to land at the barbarian's feet.

The dwarf glared about wildly, searching for other adversaries, but none stood nearby. He stumbled forward and then dropped to one knee, spent. Blood seeped from several open wounds on his face, neck and upper torso. There were also mottled bruises beginning to show in various places.

Scattered around the barbarian were more than a dozen of his enemy. Yet his eyes searched for the one who got away—the female Minion now far out of his reach. He considered going after her, but knew she would not make it far. Her wounds were mortal.

Vorgath also knew he was not going far. He was light-headed from loss of blood, and repeated use of his battle rage had left him in a weakened state, unable to pursue.

Thrinndor slowed to a walk and surveyed the carnage around the dwarf, checking to ensure none of the Minions showed signs of resisting further. None did.

The paladin reached down, hooked a hand under the barbarian's armor and helped him to his feet. As he did so, Thrinndor used the contact to pour some of his paladin healing benefits into his friend.

Vorgath's bent back straightened, his shoulders squared and a glint returned to his dulled eyes. "Thanks." He too glared at the dark-robe-clad bodies scattered around them, daring any to move.

Savinhand joined the two and together the three of them surveyed the carnage that had become the mesa. The tornado, its malevolence controlled by the giants, had cut a wide swath through the Minion army. Twenty or thirty of their number could be seen swirling high overhead, caught up in the maelstrom.

As the trio watched, Stormheart ceased whirling his arms and brought them down to his waist. Slowly, he lifted them skyward and the tornado followed suit, its broad base lifting free of the ground and headed for the clouds. Within seconds, the three were forced to take shelter under a scrub oak as minion bodies began to rain from the sky.

From there, they watched as Sordaak stood atop an outcropping of rocks, his attention focused on the large force of Minion soldiers he had trapped in a box canyon. The mage waved his arms overhead and blasted a group of them with a fireball. Two or three walls of fire blocked the Minion warrior escape, and it was obvious they were helpless.

Then several of the fighters got in formation and rushed the walls of flames between them and the magicuser, only to be thwarted by something within the flames. The Minions came up against a different wall, through which they could not pass. In panic, they turned to retrace their steps, but they were too late. The flames claimed the soldiers, and to a man and woman they collapsed in heaps, their robes flaring briefly as they burned in the intense heat.

Sordaak sent yet another ball of fire into a grouping of the hapless Minions. When the smoke cleared, none were standing. The mage stood sentinel over the opening until his last wall of flame burned itself out and then a little longer, verifying none had survived. Again, none had. The caster finally turned away from what he had done, looking around for somewhere else to direct his power.

"Do any Lords yet live?" Thrinndor asked of his two companions.

"I don't think so," Savin replied. "I killed two and Sordaak slew a third." The rogue shrugged. "If there were more than three, they have fled and escaped."

"Three holds with the information we were provided."

"Agreed," said Breunne as he approached the group, the cleric right behind him.

"Glad to see you are feeling better," Thrinndor said with a deferring nod.

"Yeah, me, too," the ranger replied with a wry smile. "Anything left to do here?"

Vorgath shook his head and was about to speak when a dark-robed figure broke free of some nearby shadows and bolted for the far side of the mesa.

Breunne raised *Xenotath* and loosed a volley of arrows, each finding their mark. The figure stumbled and pitched forward onto the bare ground. The Minion tried to push himself back up, then collapsed and lay still.

"Was that necessary?" All eyes turned to the cleric, who posed the question. "He was clearly trying to escape."

Breunne raised an eyebrow. "Either we kill them now, or wait to meet them again at Ice Homme." He waited for an answer, but none was forthcoming. "For one, I'd prefer to keep as many as possible from gathering to oppose us in masse."

Thrinndor nodded his agreement. "Spread out. We must check the mesa for others who would escape to fight another day."

Chapter Twenty-Four

Aftermath

"One hundred and seventeen," Savinhand answered the unasked question as the companions gathered around a fire built by Vorgath. The companions had briefly considered trying to make it back to Mioria and the warmth of the giant caves, but Thrinndor put a halt to that speculation. The party was too tired to march quickly, and getting there well after dark was not an option.

Breunne raised an eyebrow but said nothing as he glanced quickly at Cyrillis. The cleric pretended not to hear the body count as she warmed her hands in the growing blaze. Her lips pressed together in a fine line spoke volumes, however.

"Sounds about right." The barbarian squinted past the flames at his friend the paladin seated on the other side. His shoulders slumped suddenly as he lowered his eyes to look deep into the fire. "I have to admit I lost count at twenty or so, right after charging over that hill."

Thrinndor smiled and his eyes twinkled. "Twenty seems to be about right for the limited intellect of your over-the-hill mind."

Vorgath puffed up as he glared at the paladin. Finally, he too smiled as he let the air noisily out of his chest. "Well, even at only twenty I'm certain to have doubled your measly total!"

"Whatever," the paladin said flippantly. He then made a show of counting on his fingers. Eventually he nodded begrudgingly. "I am certain I got at least ten—possibly more."

"Ha!" snorted the barbarian. "I knew it!"

The thief cleared his throat and all eyes turned to him. "There were thirteen dead Minions surrounding your position on the mesa," he told Vorgath.

"And I got two getting to that position," the barbarian said.

A hush fell over the grouping. "That's thirty-five," the ranger said solemnly.

"Your legend grows, old one." Thrinndor shook his head slowly. "I believe I am going to have to cease with our wager. The church is going to complain!"

Vorgath chuckled. "Very well," he said as he shook his head. "I'll let you out of your wager—for the sake of your poor church!"

"Oh, no. I will not have my good name smeared with welching on a wager entered into by myself willingly!"

The barbarian shrugged. "As you wish!" He smiled and winked. "It seems your church gets a large portion of my take, regardless!"

The paladin returned the wink. "Yes. It seems we do, at that!"

"I would remind you that you are discussing a wager over who killed the most out of *more than a hundred* human beings." Cyrillis' tone was edged with ice that was mirrored in her eyes. Evidently she tired of the discussion.

"Those were Minions of Set," the paladin said evenly, frost tainted his words as well. "They are hardly worthy of being called human." The cleric glared at Thrinndor, her eyes lances of anger. "Their propensity for human sacrifice puts them beneath my concern for their mortality." His glare matched that of their healer. "It also seems to me they had you on their altar, and only my hand stayed theirs from making you one their sacrifices."

Cyrillis' lips became non-existent as crimson worked its way up her neck.

"Not all of them were human." Sordaak stood, his eyes holding those of the cleric as he walked up to stand before her. Slowly his right hand reached up, grasped her tunic and pulled at it, exposing the still fresh scar on her neck. "I *enjoyed* watching every Minion die within the flames of my spells." His eyes held hers for a moment longer, and then he turned on the ball of his foot and stalked into the night, quickly out of the influence of the fire.

Silence hung over the party, only broken only by the occasional popping of a sap pocket within the wood on the fire.

"He's correct." It was Savinhand who finally spoke. "I counted seven Drow and three half-orcs among their ranks."

"Damn Minions will take anyone!" Vorgath said, poking the fire with a branch in his right hand.

Again the silence took the night.

Cyrillis stood after a few moments. "It appears my ire was misguided." She looked from one to another ringing the fire. "For that I apologize. However, I will not apologize for speaking out against levity as it pertains to a contest which counts the dead as a wager—even the dead of our enemies." She too turned on a heel and strode from the clearing.

After a few more minutes of silence, Thrinndor spoke. "There will be no more wagers." His demeanor left no room for discussion. "And we will each tend to a meal on our own—no prepared meal this night."

Savinhand nodded as he stood.

"What happened to the dragon?" All heads turned to fix on Breunne.

Vorgath stood. "Yeah, where is that traitorous bitch?"

"That traitorous bitch is right here." Pantorra in human form stepped into the firelight.

Weapons were drawn and quickly the dragon woman was surrounded. She made no further move.

The flames from Thrinndor's sword were mirrored in Pantorra's impassive eyes as the paladin stepped in front of her and placed his face within inches of hers. "Where have you been?"

"Around."

"You lied to us!" Thrinndor pressed his face even closer.

"Worse, you led them *to* us," Vorgath spat.

"I did no such thing!" Pantorra answered. She didn't flinch.

"Explain yourself, then." The paladin took a step back and folded his arms on his chest.

"First of all, I do not need to explain my actions to you—any of you." She returned the paladin's glare. "My pact to you was only *if* you return my eggs to me. Second, I must look to my own devices."

"Explain," Thrinndor repeated.

"There was a good chance, possibly better than half such, that you would fall to the Minions. I could not take that chance that you would fail and my service to you become known. So I took to the skies and remained high above the action until a few minutes ago."

"Yet you told us after recon that they remained over a mile from our location." Breunne, sensing no malice, sheathed his weapon but did not move. He, too, crossed his arms on his chest.

"That I did," Pantorra nodded as she acknowledged the ranger. "I must have misjudged the distance and, as you have seen, a large portion of their force was mounted. They must have ridden hard to get to you as quick as they did."

"How did they know our location?" Sordaak walked back into the influence of the fire's light as he spoke.

The dragon-lady turned her head to eye the mage. "You are clearly making the assumption that they did."

"What?" Vorgath alone had failed to stand down. He held *Flinthgoor* tightly in both hands, as if daring the woman to make a move.

Pantorra rolled her eyes. "Their scouts must have known of your previous location, and they made an assumption as to where you would stop. Either that or they merely happened upon your camp moving to get behind you."

"While what you say *could* be one explanation as to their movement, another could be that you told them where to find us." Thrinndor was not convinced. "Why should we believe what you say?"

It was Pantorra's turn to fold her arms on her chest. "I am here."

"What?" the barbarian repeated.

The woman turned to face the dwarf. "Look, little man. This might hurt a little, but think about it. If I had betrayed you to the Minions, would I stand here now of my own accord?"

Vorgath fought back a sharp reply as he used the time to do as she asked. "You would if you wanted us to *think* you didn't betray us!" Finally, he sat *Flinthgoor* aside and crossed his arms on his chest, satisfied he had made his point.

Pantorra glared at the dwarf for a moment, then turned back to face Thrinndor. "Did you understand any of that?"

The paladin hesitated. "He makes a point. Your deception could be two-fold."

An incredulous Pantorra allowed her mouth to slack. "Not you, too?"

Sordaak pushed his way past the paladin to confront the dragon. "This is how I see it. You fly off to verify position of the Minion armies and within a few minutes of your return, we are attacked. You disappear and only return after we destroyed both armies. You were not seen at any point during the battle. Now you want us to believe that you merely stayed neutral until the fight was decided."

Pantorra returned the mage's glare. "That pretty much sums it up." When no one moved and none immediately responded, she continued, "Look, I could not let the Minions know I had allied myself with you in the event they were victorious. Certainly you must realize this. It should also be noted that I did not at any time fight *for* the Minions. I remained high above the battle, staying out of it until decided. Even then I had to wait until darkness hid my movements. I could not take the chance that any of those who yet live report my presence here."

After a few moments' silence, Breunne asked, "How many survived?"

"Finally, a good question! About twenty or so are currently making their way back to Ice Homme. Some will not make it, so severe are their wounds."

Sordaak looked up from the coals he was playing with. "How many Minions are already at Ice Homme?"

"Also a good question," Pantorra said. "This is really not much more than an educated guess, but I believe they left about fifty Minions behind to guard the palace."

"Damn," muttered the rogue. He had had just about enough of these Minions.

"Of course, the High Lord awaits you there, as well."

"Us," corrected the cleric.

"What?"

"You said 'you.' Surely you now realize that we will prevail, and that you must aid us?"

Pantorra shook her head slowly. "No, that cannot be. Until you and your companions take Ice Homme and secure my eggs, I cannot take the chance of being seen with you. I will fly recon and do what I can from afar. But in the end, the attack will fall to you and your companions."

"I was afraid you'd say that," replied a morose Savinhand as he too stared into the fire. "Haven't we seen enough of these maggots?"

"Bah!" spat the dwarf. "What's another seventy or so of these lower life forms known as Minions?"

Cyrillis stared at the barbarian. "Did you not hear what she said about there being a High Lord? He is undoubtedly very powerful."

"She," corrected Pantorra.

"What?"

"You said 'he.' High Lord Kiarrah is a she."

Cyrillis' face went white and she took a stunned step backward, where she tripped over a rock and landed on her backside. Instantly, Sordaak was by her side, but she ignored him. "*Who?*" The healer's voice was barely above a whisper.

"Kiarrah," Pantorra repeated. "Do you know her?"

A distraught cleric shook her head. "Yes! I mean no! I do not know *what* I mean! It cannot be the same person!"

"What vexes thee so, dear one?" Pantorra was almost purring.

Cyrillis accepted Sordaak's hand and allowed him to pull her to her feet. That act gave her time to compose herself, and think.

"I know—knew—a young woman that went by that name. Surely the leader of the Minions of Set cannot be so young."

"The leader of the Minions of Set can be any age he or she wishes. The leader can become almost anyone they wish, dear. However, it just so happens that the current leader is indeed a very young woman."

"Impossible!" snorted the barbarian.

Pantorra fixed the dwarf with a glare. When Vorgath shifted uncomfortably under the gaze, she pursed her lips tightly. "I should think that one of your advanced years would know better than to speak of that which they know little or nothing."

Vorgath puffed up, but just as quickly he deflated. "I know that the leader of the Minions is usually a very powerful priest. No young'uns need apply," he said, lifting his chin defiantly.

"You mistakenly assume that advanced years are requisite for power. Therein lies your folly, old one." Pantorra shook her head sadly as she turned her eyes back to Cyrillis. "Kiarrah reportedly was identified as a potential for leadership while yet a toddler. She was admitted to the University before her teen years. Her acumen for the lore of Set was so advanced that she completed the six-year program in two." The dragon-woman was silent for a minute. All eyes were on her as she continued. "Within a year of her graduation, she challenged the then leader and tore out his heart in three minutes. That was four years ago." Pantorra turned her unblinking eyes on the dwarf. "She has yet to see her twentieth birthday."

Cyrillis absently brushed herself off and slipped her hand into that of the magicuser at her side. Her eyes took on a haunting look as she raised them to peer into those of the dragon-woman. "She *must* be the same Kiarrah—that would explain *so much*!"

Thrinndor spoke for the first time. "How so?"

The healer blinked twice as she acknowledged the paladin with her eyes. Cyrillis licked her lips. "Remember when I introduced you to the young woman back at the temple? That was Kiarrah." The paladin nodded. "If she was—as I suspected at the time—a spy; that would explain our expulsion from the temple, and maybe even the disappearance of Correlle, Brequarre and even Kridmaar!"

Thrinndor nodded as he realized she was correct. "But she *is* just a child!"

"She is no child!" Cyrillis and Pantorra said in unison. The two looked at one another and smiled.

"It is said," Pantorra continued, "that *this child* not only ripped out the previous leader's still beating heart with her bare hands, but that she *ate* it while the High Priests watched."

"*What?*" Savinhand was incredulous. "Why would she do *that?*"

It was Thrinndor who answered. "In some cultures there are those that believe eating the heart of your adversary grants you the powers of that adversary. The Minions of Set are one such culture."

"What you say is sooth," answered Pantorra. "Except that you sound as if you doubt such a ritual provides the results indicated." Her eyes locked with those of the paladin. "I assure you that Kiarrah consumed the powers of her predecessor in that moment."

Sap popped in the fire several times before anyone spoke. Vorgath stood with *Flinthgoor* gripped tightly in his right fist. "Then she will undoubtedly prove to be a worthy adversary." His demeanor said he was not boasting. "When do we get started?"

Thrinndor took in a deep breath and let it out slowly. "Sit down. This may take a while." Vorgath complied, and the others who had not found a seat did so as well. The giants could be heard doing the same just beyond the reach of the fire's light.

The paladin stood and eyed Pantorra, trying to decide whether she needed to hear what was about to be said. In the end, the comfort taken from knowing *where she was* won out.

"I think the 'when' of the matter will become known when we figure out 'how' we want to handle this." As he talked, Thrinndor rotated his head and body as necessary to make eye contact with each in the party. Pantorra, he ignored. "Our information indicates that we will have sixty to seventy Minions, with a High Lord and probably at least one High Priest among their number." He paused as he collected his thoughts. "They will be well-armed and well-protected within the walls of their fortress. An all-out assault would certainly prove our undoing." He paused again, not sure how he was going to present this.

"I have a plan," the paladin continued, "but first, I want to hear ideas from the group so that I can gauge its worthiness.

Vorgath was first. "Bah! We don't need a plan! We go up, knock the door down, walk in and kick some Minion ass! A tried and true—by us—method of dealing with their kind." He glared around, daring any to counter.

Thrinndor coughed into his left hand. "While that is certainly one possibility—"

"One possibility likely to get us all killed!" Sordaak said, not looking up from the fire.

"You have a better plan?" growled the barbarian.

"Of course—"

"*Bullshit!*"

The magicuser raised his eyes slowly and turned his head until his eyes bored into those of the dwarf. "I listened to your lame-brained plan! Now you will listen to one less so."

No one said anything. Eventually Vorgath shifted uncomfortably under the penetrating stare of the sorcerer. "Go on," the dwarf growled as he lifted his chin. "I'm listening."

Sordaak nodded slowly. "Thank you," he said evenly. "I think we should fly in—"

"*Seriously?*" Vorgath interrupted. "That's your plan? *Fly in?*"

The sorcerer turned back to stare down the dwarf. Only when Vorgath surrendered by looking down at his boots did Sordaak continue. "Breunne has the boots. One or two more can be dropped off by the dragon, and I can use the 'Fly' spell to get another two or three over the walls. We 'fly' over an unprotected portion of their fortress/palace/keep, surprise them and—as you say—kick minion ass once we're inside."

The dwarf looked up. "I'm not being 'dropped off' by no stinking dragon!" Quickly he glanced at the seated Pantorra. "No offence."

"None taken." The dragon woman dipped her head in deference. "One can certainly take your chosen profession into account as to your taste." She shrugged.

"Profession?"

"Barbarian, of course."

"Oh." Vorgath blinked twice. "I suppose that should be taken into consideration."

Thrinndor hid a smile. "Any other suggestions?"

"What about the dwarves?" All eyes turned to Cyrillis.

"What about them?" Vorgath asked guardedly.

"Twenty-five hundred dwarves should prove sufficient to both breach the walls and subdue whatever is left inside." Cyrillis smiled sweetly as the others continued to stare.

"We cannot chance losing those that would surely fall in such an attempt," Sordaak protested.

"Perhaps that can be avoided." The eyes rotated back to the paladin as Vorgath put some more wood on the fire and made the necessary adjustments to keep it burning hot. "First, are there any other thoughts as to how we should approach Ice Homme?"

Thrinndor used his eyes to check with each of his companions, in each case securing either a shake of the head or shrugged shoulders. "Very well. While each of the proposals submitted have merit, perhaps a combination of all three would serve our purpose."

The paladin shifted his weight to a more comfortable position upon the rock on which he sat. This allowed the final pieces to his plan to come together in his head. "First, we call the dwarves." He held up his hands to block the protest that Sordaak took in a sharp breath for. "However, it is not my intent for them to see battle—rather, I want to use them as a show of force. A decoy."

Guardedly the mage exhaled and remained silent.

Thrinndor continued. "I have never actually been to Ice Homme, but I have seen paintings depicting it and the surrounding area." He looked over at Pantorra. "Correct me if such is required." The dragon-lady nodded. "There is a large, open, ice-covered plateau that fronts the keep. In fact, the keep is the only thing on the plateau of ice that spans several square miles, making it hard to approach unseen."

Pantorra again nodded so the paladin continued, "Twenty-five hundred dwarves is a very large force—one that cannot be ignored. We will have them spread out and set up camp across the road that leads from the south to their main gate. Done properly, they could easily block the entire southern access. We'll include in their number the horses captured from the Minion cavalry, which I believe number more than a hundred." A nod from Breunne confirmed this. "While I know dwarves revile riding—"

"Not *all* dwarves feel that way." Pantorra looked down her nose at Vorgath. "Just those who lack enough common sense to get their feet off of the ground!"

"Bah!" spat the barbarian. He didn't elaborate.

"Even better!" Thrinndor was careful not to make eye contact with his friend. "If they can make use of the horses to patrol the entire plateau, we can give credence to the fact we mean to place them under siege and possibly wait them out."

"We're not?" Savinhand asked.

"Of course not. We have a temple to build! Besides," the paladin smiled, "I want to be out of there before winter truly sets in."

"Here, here!" agreed the dwarf. "The worst winter of my life was spent holed up in a cave not far from there."

Thrinndor lifted an eyebrow but decided that story would have to wait for another time. "While the denizens of Ice Homme are distracted with the dwarves, we will select a dark night and have Savin and Breunne fly in unnoticed." He paused to obtain assenting nods from both men. "Once inside, they will make their way to the main gate, neutralizing any guards encountered on the way."

"That sounds more like my line of work," Vorgath protested.

"Silence is required," Thrinndor countered. "Remaining undetected is imperative."

"*That* certainly does not fit your line of work," Pantorra said with a wry twist to her lips.

"Whatever!" The barbarian crossed his arms on his chest and scowled at the fire.

"Rest assured, old friend, that there will be adequate action to sate even you!" Thrinndor winked at the dwarf.

"There'd better be!"

The paladin stifled a smile as he continued. "Besides, you said something about wanting to kick in the front door. I propose something along those lines. Sort of. Breunne and Savinhand will open the main gates—quietly—letting the rest of us and the giants inside. We will get as close as we dare under the cover of darkness, waiting for the signal.

"From there we will maintain the surprise as long as we are able, neutralizing as many of the Minions as possible before we are discovered. That is when the general melee will commence, and if done properly, we should be done by the time the sun rises." He looked around the group, seeking comment. "The dwarves will then come in and help with cleanup duty, making sure none escape."

Sordaak looked up from the ember he had been studying. "I still don't like it. This jaunt north for the dwarves will cost me at least a week when they could be building."

Pantorra pondered the question for a moment. "Perhaps not." Sordaak raised an eyebrow. "Ice Homme is less than a day's march to the beachhead due west of there. We can have your ships pick them up there instead of in Ardaagh as originally planned. That will cut the required time away from your precious temple in half."

Slowly Sordaak bobbed his head in agreement. Then he stopped and his eyes narrowed. "Kiarrah?"

Thrinndor hesitated. "I am certain she will prove a troublesome adversary."

The sorcerer looked deep into the paladin's eyes. "I am certain you are correct." He pursed his lips into a thin line. "Leave her to me."

"No," moaned the cleric.

Sordaak reached out a hand and grasped hers tightly. "It must be that way," he chided gently. "Oh, rest assured I have no intention of going at her *alone*! But, if she's as powerful as we've been led to believe," at this he stole a quick look at

Pantorra, "she will be prepared for the fighters." Now he looked at Thrinndor, who waited to hear what the mage had in mind. "I will go in first, alone, to get her attention. Once I do, then the rest of you will come in and try to take her attention away from me. I doubt you'll be able to do so, but it should be fun trying!" Sordaak winked at the barbarian.

Vorgath winked back. "You can have all the attention she has to offer! I'm kind of attached to my heart, and if she were to try to remove it…" He shook his head. "Well, that might piss me off!"

Sordaak laughed. "I'm sure we'll have to tweak the plan as we go along."

"Yeah, like she might not sit and wait for us to come for her." Breunne's tone was ominous.

The mage looked over at the ranger. "Right."

"Sounds like a plan!" Savinhand said. Anything was better than the all-out war they had experienced earlier that day.

"We need to get word to the dwarves." Thrinndor raised an eyebrow in the direction of the mage.

Sordaak nodded and closed his eyes. Fahlred appeared on his shoulder, winding his tail around the mage's neck in his usual fashion.

Pantorra gasped, stood quickly and took a step back, her eyes never leaving the creature on Sordaak's shoulder. "What is *that*!"

"Fahlred?" Savinhand asked, "That's a quasit."

The dragon woman scowled at the rogue. "I *know* what a quasit is! What is it doing *here*?"

"It is a 'he,' and he is my familiar." Sordaak's eyes were again open and his face was impassive.

"But—" Pantorra stammered. "Familiar? I have not heard of a quasit as a familiar to a human in all my years!"

"Indeed," Sordaak replied evenly. "My research shows the last recorded such event occurred more than a millennia ago." Now he smiled. "You might be interested to know that when I look at you through his eyes, I see you as the dragon."

"Really?" Pantorra said as she took her seat. "Most interesting. Wait, you can look through his eyes while yours are still open?"

Sordaak nodded. "Yes. That took quite some time to get used to, but it comes in handy, on occasion."

"I bet it does!" Pantorra murmured. "Why did you call him?"

The mage scowled. "I was going to send him to speak with the dwarves, but I just realized that they have not met him, and that might not go so well."

"Ya think?" Vorgath asked sarcastically.

"Shut it, midget!" Sordaak snapped without looking over at the barbarian. "I need some quiet to think!"

"Can't you just teleport to them?" Thrinndor asked.

"No," the magicuser mumbled. "It doesn't work that way. I have to have been to the place I want to teleport to—I must be able to visualize the place before I can go there." He put his chin in his hand as he considered his options. Finally he looked up at the paladin and shrugged. "Sorry, boss. I can't help with this one."

Thrinndor's eyebrow's knitted together as silence overtook the gathering.

"I can." Heads turned as attention focused on Pantorra. "I will need help from one of you, however." She smiled. "After all, I doubt a dragon would be well received by the dwarves of the Silver Hills. Someone is going to have to explain me to them so they will not try to turn my scales into a set of armor."

The paladin raised an eyebrow in Vorgath's direction.

"Don't look at me, pretty boy! I don't like horses. I'm sure as the Seven Hells not going to climb aboard no high flying dragon!"

Thrinndor turned his raised brow next to the sorcerer.

Sordaak looked from the dwarf to the paladin to Pantorra and then back to the paladin. "Aw, hell! I don't seem to have a choice, do I? The dwarf clan won't recognize anyone else!" He then turned his distraught face to the dragon. "Tell me you at least have a saddle I can strap myself in to?"

"I most certainly do not! I have not lost a rider, yet!" Pantorra smiled as she stole a sheepish look at the ranger. "At least not one I was not *trying* to lose!"

"Ha, ha!" Breunne said. When Sordaak raised a questioning eyebrow, the ranger added, "Long story. I'll explain some other time."

Pantorra snickered as she turned her attention back to the mage. "Rest assured, magicuser, if I want you to stay aboard, you will not fall!"

"Comforting."

There followed a lively discussion about going back to Mioria to rest to wait for the dwarves there in relative comfort or press on to Ice Homme. In the end Thrinndor's desire to get a better feel for what they were up against won out, so following a hastily prepared meal and more discussion on tactics, body count and the such, they all turned in.

The giants, knowing they would not immediately be needed in battle, asked to return to Mioria, promising to catch up with the group down the road with enough supplies to take them through at least a week.

Thrinndor agreed, and they departed immediately.

Pantorra reverted to dragon form, Sordaak climbed aboard and in a cloud of dust they were airborne.

Chapter Twenty-Five

Travel Plans

Morning dawned, finding most of the battle-weary companions loath to leave the comfort of their blankets. Only Savinhand could be heard rattling pans and stirring the fire as he prepared breakfast.

One by one the members of the party approached the fire to warm their hands and pour cups of coffee. It had been a particularly cold night, and more than one of them had lamented the choice to not accompany the giants back to their caves.

The wind had picked up during the night and the temperature had fallen as the wind speed had risen. The dawn eased slowly into being as the clouds overhead hung low and sullen, blocking out the majority of the sun's light and warmth. It appeared the dwarf's weather forecast was going to prove correct. By now most of the companions knew how to recognize the scent of snow riding the will of the wind.

"Damn, I hate being right all the time," grumbled the dwarf as he wrapped both hands around the cup he held, both to warm them and to shield the vessel from the cooling effects of the sub-freezing air.

Thrinndor thought a snide remark was indicated at this point, but couldn't muster the effort necessary to do so. Since leaving his blankets the wind had sucked not only most of the warmth from his bones, but also any levity from the air.

Savinhand had put extra wood on the fire so that now it blazed with an intense fury as he prepared breakfast. Fortunately Vorgath had had the foresight to build the fire in the lee of a large boulder, keeping most of the bitter wind off of the companions as they ate a silent meal.

"Where is Pantorra?" Cyrillis asked.

Without looking up from his plate Vorgath said, "She didn't return last night."

"I did so." Heads turned to see Pantorra standing at the edge of the bush, smiling. "What a *beautiful* morning!" She seemed unaffected by the cold; in fact, she stood wearing no more than what she had when she first changed into human form—an icy white raiment, sleeveless and gathered at the waist by a glittering belt.

"*What a beautiful morning!*" mimicked the dwarf. "Icy bitch!" he added, sotto voce.

"Thank you," Pantorra said pleasantly.

"Any word on the movement of our enemies?" Thrinndor asked.

Pantorra shook her head. "Nothing has changed. They remain scattered and are moving north. It appears they have no leader."

"Good," Breunne said. "That part of our plan was successful, anyway."

"Speaking of plan ... do we have one?" Sordaak asked.

The paladin turned away from the fire, attempting to warm his backside. "We travel north to Ice Homme as fast as the weather allows. I want at least a full day to scout the area before we enact our assault."

"And if the Minions refuse to cooperate?" It was Savinhand who raised the question.

The paladin's right eyebrow ventured higher on his forehead. "Please explain."

Savinhand finished drying the pan he had in his hands before responding. "If you were the leader of the Minions, were as smart as we have been led to believe and knew your armies have been decimated by your enemies," the rogue looked up and locked eyes with the paladin, "would you sit and wait for those same enemies to come and knock on your front door?"

The party leader blinked twice as he pondered the question. "That is a question that bears thought. Please continue."

Savin shrugged. "I'm not sure what I would do in that situation. However, I'm sure *I* wouldn't sit and wait for us to come to my home."

As the companions finished packing, the wind eased and snow began to fall.

"Great," muttered the barbarian, "three days north in this?"

"Four if we do not get moving," Thrinndor said.

The dwarf glared at his friend, but uncharacteristically no words came to mind.

"Let's go then," Sordaak said as he brushed the wet snow from the saddle and pulled himself up onto the back of his mount. "Our destiny awaits."

Thrinndor lifted an eyebrow as he too climbed stiffly onto his horse and took up the reins.

Savinhand led his mount over to Sordaak, handed him the reins and turned to face the paladin. "I will scout ahead on foot." He looked over at the paladin. "I'll see you at camp this night, unless something happens before then."

Thrinndor nodded as the rogue turned and strode into the brush. In seconds he was out of sight.

"I'll take the point," Breunne said, "and search for good footing for our animals."

Again the paladin nodded. He and the others took up a loose formation with the barbarian afoot at the end of the single-file column.

*

Throughout the day the companions trudged through the increasing snow-fall slightly west of due north, angling their way back toward the coast. Soon after breaking camp they found themselves climbing the flanks of the Westron Mountains, the range that ran all along the coast north of Ardaagh. Their destination was on a flat plateau high up in that range.

On this side of the mountains the sun set early. As dusk approached, unwilling to risk harm to their animals, Thrinndor called the ranger back to the formation and ordered him to move ahead and find a suitable place to make camp.

Breunne nodded and still on foot he jogged ahead, slowly at first, and then with ever increasing speed as his legs warmed to the task.

After the companions had gone perhaps a half-hour further and it was becoming difficult to see, the paladin spotted Breunne standing in the path not far ahead. Silently the ranger turned and walked into a copse of trees in the deep shadows of a high peak.

Breunne led the party a few hundred yards off of the faint trail they had been following, down a glade through which ran a small stream. The ranger turned north and soon the companions found themselves at a cliff face.

There they saw an opening in the cliff that promised shelter within. It had snowed steadily all day, so that now there was six or seven inches in the spaces between trees.

Lying next to the cave opening was a large bear. There were three arrows protruding from the beast's chest. Breunne noted his companions' questioning glances. "We needed shelter. He objected."

Vorgath nodded approvingly. "At least we'll have fresh meat for a few days." He grasped a fistful of bear fur and twisted. "This hide will make a fine cloak—assuming I have time to work and cure it."

Breunne walked to his pack animal and removed a bundle of torches. These he lit and handed all around. "The cavern is large enough to accommodate us and our animals. I didn't take time to explore the cave fully—it goes back into the mountain quite far."

Thrinndor nodded. "I will do so once we are settled for the night. Is there a place where we can safely set a fire?"

"I believe so," answered the ranger. "With what little investigating I did, I smelled old, dry ashes. This shelter has been used before by humans, I'm fairly certain."

"All right, leave the animals here for now," the paladin said. "Sordaak, Cyrillis, please gather wood for a fire and get one going." He looked over at the barbarian, who had drug the bear off a ways and was busy gutting it. "Vorgath is busy. Breunne and I will see how far the cavern goes back."

The paladin got nods all around as the companions set about their assigned tasks.

"What about Savin?" Cyrillis asked.

"He'll find us," the ranger said. "I doubt he is far off."

Breunne and Thrinndor each took a torch and walked to the cave entrance.

"Be wary in there," Sordaak said suddenly. Thrinndor turned to peer at the mage with a questioning look. "I don't know what's back there, but Fahlred is skittish. Something's bothering him about what lies inside the cave."

"Perhaps the bear?"

The sorcerer shook his head. "No. Something deeper in the mountain."

The ranger and paladin looked at one another, shrugged, shifted the torches to their left hands and drew swords with their right.

"Should I come with you?" the cleric asked.

"I do not think that necessary," Thrinndor answered. "We will call if assistance is required." Side by side they entered the opening.

Cyrillis bit her lip and nodded as she watched the light from their torches fade from view.

"Come on," the mage said as he grasped her hand, "Let's do as told and gather some wood." Cyrillis looked up and tried to peer into the eyes of the mage, but the darkness was now almost complete and she could see nothing but deep pools of shadow. She nodded and sighed as he led her away from the opening in the direction of some nearby trees.

*

By the time the paladin and ranger returned, Sordaak had a nice fire going in a hearth they had found far back in the cavern. There were now torches inserted into holders obviously set in the walls for the purpose, and the dank chill was beginning to leave the chamber.

There was another chamber past the main one. Sordaak and Cyrillis led the animals in a few at a time and stripped saddles and gear from them. There was even some dried out long grass back there, indicating this chamber had been used for this purpose more than once. In the back was a small pool of water that was clearly fed from somewhere. The horses and mules munched contentedly on the grass and drank greedily from the pool, happy to be out of the wind and snow.

Sordaak had resigned himself to having to prepare something to eat and was as such rattling pots and searching for something to cook when Savinhand appeared at his elbow. "I'll take over here, if you don't mind."

The mage didn't even jump. "Please," he said as he stepped aside. He bent to pick up some almost empty skins. "I'll go refill these."

The rogue nodded absently as he set his cooking implements in order and figured out the support system for his pot. He went back to the packs and removed his largest frying pan. On second thought, he grabbed the smaller one, as well.

Into the now boiling pot hanging over the fire he cut up some tubers he pulled from a bag at his feet. He added a few pinches of dried, crumbled leaves and some salt. As he stirred the concoction, Vorgath walked up, bloodied from his work with the bear, and deposited some thickly cut steaks onto the rock next to the thief.

"That was an old bear, so these will probably be a little tough. But the fresh meat will be a good change."

"Agreed," Savin said as he eyed the steaks. "I believe I have something that will make those easier to chew."

The barbarian shrugged and stomped back out into the night to continue work on the carcass.

The smell of frying meat filled the air and the chamber had warmed considerably as Cyrillis began to worry about the continued absence of the two scouts. She was about to say as much when both emerged from the tunnel that led to the chamber where they had tied the animals.

"Where have you two been?" she asked crossly.

Thrinndor lifted a brow. "Seeing where that tunnel led, of course."

"Did you find anything?" Sordaak asked.

"No." It was Breunne that answered. "We followed the tunnel for more than a mile, passing several intersections of other tunnels along the way. Generally the passage led to the west, deeper into the mountain."

"I still don't like it," Sordaak said as he got up from where he had been sitting and walked over to the opening. "I can't even get Fahlred to come into *this* chamber, let alone that one."

"You cannot tell what is bothering him?"

"No," replied the mage. "And I don't think he knows, either. But *something* sure has him on edge."

"Hmmm. Well, keep him nearby, please. He will certainly be our best indication that something is amiss." The paladin thought for a moment. "Is there any way we can block that back opening?"

"Maybe," the sorcerer said thoughtfully. "Savinhand and I will take a look after we've had something to eat." The smell of food only served to increase his hunger. The party had not stopped for any reason on their trek north, and his stomach was grumbling in anticipation.

The meal complete, Cyrillis volunteered to clean up as the rogue and mage left the main chamber to go see to the back entrance. Thrinndor and Breunne built a door out of blankets to keep out most of the cold, and Vorgath went back outside to continue work on what remained of the bear.

An hour or so later found the party gathered around the fire, tired yet restless after an extended day of travel.

"Were you able to secure the back entrance?" Thrinndor asked the mage, who had settled into a niche in the wall with Cyrillis curled up at his side, her head resting on his shoulder.

Sordaak nodded. "I put up a wall of stone that should at a minimum slow down any who wish to enter that way."

"And I set a few surprises in the event anything gets past his wall," Savinhand said.

"Good." The paladin turned his attention to the way they had come in. "Now we'll just need to watch this opening."

"Fahlred will keep watch outside," Sordaak said. "Nothing can approach from that direction without my knowing about it."

"Even better."

"I would have thought the Storm Giants would have caught up to us by now," Cyrillis said as she stifled a yawn.

Breunne shook his head. "No, their caves were quite a bit out of the way. I figure they probably didn't get started until late morning, at best."

Thrinndor nodded. "They might catch up to us tomorrow, late. But best not count on them until the day following."

"Oh."

"Even with the weather we made good time," the paladin continued. "If we are able to maintain this pace, we should make Ice Homme by the end of that third day."

"Do we have a plan once we get there?" Sordaak asked. "Or are we just going to do this 'recon' shit until the dwarves arrive?" He glanced down at the top of the woman's head that rested on his shoulder. "Sorry," he murmured as he stroked her hair, lightly.

"Ummm hmmm." Cyrillis was getting cozy and appeared to have not heard.

Thrinndor's right eyebrow worked its way up his forehead until it was flirting with his hairline.

"No, that recon *stuff* about has it covered. I do not want any more surprises."

"So," Savinhand too found it hard to take his eyes off of the new couple, "do you still think she will be waiting for us when we get there?"

"That remains a good question." Thrinndor tore his eyes away from the cleric and shook his head. "One I cannot answer. I feel she would wait until the remnants of her army join her before she would make a move, however."

"And if she moves south to hasten that joining?" Savinhand persisted.

Thrinndor shrugged. "In that event, we will have to be even more vigilant to ensure she does not surprise us."

"Now we're on the same page." The rogue smiled.

The paladin stretched and yawned. "I want to get an early start in the morning. We had all best turn in and get some rest."

Sordaak didn't move, but he nodded to indicate he at least heard the request. Cyrillis was fast asleep, a contented smile on her face.

Breunne followed Thrinndor to where he had set up his bedding not far from the entrance to the cavern. Vorgath and Savinhand soon joined them. All eyes turned back to the mage and his companion.

"That is an interesting turn of events," the paladin said quietly.

"It appears our cleric might have found her 'reservation,'" Vorgath agreed, doing his best to whisper. It was not something he was particularly good at, but somehow he managed to avoid being heard by the pair.

"I doubt that," the paladin snorted derisively. "I am certain Valdaar has not made his will known to her as of yet."

"Well, she certainly seems to be content to branch out on her own then," Savinhand said.

"That is what concerns me," Thrinndor said softly, his eyes not leaving the couple. "I feel—as does she—that it is her destiny to remain chaste for the return of our god. Although neither of us can explain why that is."

"And if she does not?"

"I cannot answer that question," the paladin said. "I can only monitor the situation and interject my beliefs should that become necessary. In the end, however, I am going to have to trust her." He sighed as his shoulders slumped. "It is not my place to intercede."

"Perhaps she knows what she's doing," Breunne whispered, "and she's just getting cozy."

"Perhaps," replied the paladin. "Perhaps."

The men doused the torches, leaving one in the chamber with their horses so they wouldn't spook easily. They then went to their bedrolls and crawled in. Except Savinhand, he went to the fire and built it such that several logs would fall into the pit in succession as the one before it burned low, ensuring the fire would stay burning for several hours. It would get cold in the cavern without it.

The companions were startled awake by a shrill squeal, followed immediately by the sounds of galloping animals.

"The horses!" shouted the ranger as he lunged to his feet.

"Shit!" shouted Sordaak as he stood upright, eliciting a surprised yelp from Cyrillis as she was dumped onto the floor.

The fire had burned down and was but a dull glow in the pit. Other than that, the chamber was pitch dark. The sorcerer said a word of command and all the torches lit at once.

The sound of weapons being drawn filled the air as blankets were cast aside and fighters lunged to their feet.

Savinhand was leading the way when he hit something in the opening leading back to the pack animals. Hard.

He was repelled back into their own chamber, and only quick action by the paladin kept him from falling to the stone floor.

"What the—?"

Thrinndor set the rogue back on his feet as he slowed to a halt where he had seen Savin contact the unseen wall.

"Move!" Sordaak pushed the mildly surprised paladin aside roughly and stepped up to investigate. "Just as I thought, Force Wall." He turned and looked at the paladin, a concerned look on his face.

"Can you take it down?"

A disgusted look crossed the mage's face. "Of course I can take it down!" He waved a negligent hand toward the opening. "Down," he said. "But, before you go charging in, know that that is a fairly powerful spell. One which I only recently learned myself."

Thrinndor hesitated. "What do you suggest?"

Sordaak glared at the paladin. "Aw hell! Go charging in! I'll hang back in the event their spell-slinger elected to stick around. But, I doubt he has."

Thrinndor nodded and turned back to the opening, but was again roughly shoved aside. "Move, pretty boy," Vorgath said, "let those who hesitate less through!" With that, the barbarian was through the opening and quickly out of sight around the bend.

Breunne glanced at the paladin, shrugged and followed the barbarian more slowly, Savinhand right behind him. Thrinndor shook his head and then stepped through the opening.

Sordaak moved to follow, but spotting something on the floor, he bent and picked it up. Scroll ends—that explained the Force Wall spell. It took more than a novice to cast that powerful of a spell even from a scroll. The caster had to be at least close in ability. No doubt about it, there was a fairly powerful sorcerer working with the enemy.

"Sordaak!" A shout came from the animal chamber. "Get up here!"

The mage dutifully picked up the pace. What he saw as he rounded the last corner was a chamber empty except for his friends. They all stood next to the exit he and Savinhand had secured earlier. "Where are the animals?"

Exasperated, Vorgath rolled his eyes. However, instead of shouting, he just pointed down the tunnel.

"Well, go get them!" Sordaak said. "I'll stay closer this time."

Without even looking at the opening, Vorgath raised *Flinthgoor* and lightly swung at the opening. The greataxe was repelled by some invisible force.

"Damn!" muttered the sorcerer as he raised a hand toward the opening and spoke a word of power. He lowered his hand. "Clear."

The barbarian turned and started down the passage, and Savinhand stepped in and inspected a trap he had set. There was blood on the floor near one.

"Wait!" commanded the paladin. Vorgath obediently came to a halt and waited without turning. "We must stay together. Those passages twist, turn and have several intersections with other passages. It would be easy to get separated and lost."

Still perched over his trap, Savin said, "I got one of them," pointing to the pooled and smeared blood on the floor of the passage.

Breunne walked up behind to him to investigate. He stooped and ran his finger through the blood, sniffed it and wiped his finger on the wall distastefully. "Goblin," he spat.

"Goblins?" Thrinndor protested. "They are not smart enough to stage something like this."

"They are if properly led." Sordaak knelt and retrieved another set of scroll ends.

"Are we through talking?" grated the dwarf, still without turning.

"No," the mage said, inspecting the remaining scroll parts. "I believe these walls were but a delaying tactic." He looked up.

"They worked!" Vorgath turned at last to face the others and folded his arms across his chest expectantly.

"Patience, Old One," Sordaak beamed at the dwarf. Vorgath didn't rise to the bait. Instead the barbarian scowled back from beneath his bushy eyebrows and the mage knew he was on thin ice. He cleared his throat. "These are scroll ends," he held them high so all could see. "They match the two I picked up from back there." He pointed the way they had come.

"So?" Thrinndor was beginning to feel his friend's impatience. Their animals were undoubtedly moving farther away with each passing moment.

"So?" Sordaak mimicked. "These scrolls were fairly high up on the food chain of spells! As such, they would have been *very* expensive—far more expensive than our animals!" He waited.

"What are you trying so hard not to tell us?" Breunne was just as impatient, but something the caster said piqued his curiosity.

Sordaak made a show of rolling his eyes. "This theft of our animals was not because whoever stole them needed them for food or recreation!" He purposely drew out a pause, but no one stepped up. Disappointed, he continued. "They were taken to slow us down."

"*What?*"

"Who would want to slow us down?" Cyrillis had walked up behind them.

Sordaak turned to face her. "Who, indeed?" He waited for her to come up with it on her own.

Suddenly the cleric's eyes opened wide. "*Kiarrah!*" The magicuser nodded.

A silence filled the camber, broken only by the sound of flickering torches.

"That means she knows where we are." Breunne was the first to voice what was going through everyone's mind.

It was not a question.

Chapter Twenty-Six

Complications

Although sunrise was still more than an hour off, none of the companions felt like returning to their bedrolls.

Savinhand puttered about with making breakfast while the others packed up. The goblins had not taken the time to reload the pack animals, so their gear was intact.

But the companions now had no way to carry everything.

Thrinndor took charge of dragging the packs back into the main chamber and began redistributing what was necessary and what would have to be abandoned.

"Take only what you can carry," he said. "I will build a sled that we can take turns pulling for the food items."

"But, that will leave a trail easy to follow," Cyrillis protested.

"Our location is already known," Sordaak said gloomily. "As is our destination." He locked eyes with the paladin, who nodded. "Attempting to remain hidden will only slow us further."

"Agreed," Thrinndor said. "As soon as we eat, we break camp." He paused, looking into the eyes of each of his companions. "We will move fast—faster than we did *with* the animals. We must get ahead of where she expects us to be."

Sordaak thought for a moment. "Since we don't really need to get there for two or three more days, maybe we should change directions? Come at her from a different location?"

Savinhand turned from the fire. "Maybe we could even go back and join forces with the giants and the dwarves?"

Thrinndor took in the suggestions and pondered. "I believe a change in direction is indeed warranted. However, I do not want to meet up with the dwarves at this point. That would unnecessarily imperil them as well as slow us greatly," he explained. "We would be at least five days from Ice Homme were we to do that. That delay is unacceptable."

There was silence among the group again, marred only by the sizzle of frying meat in the pan and the occasional pop from a pocket of sap in the fire.

"What I do not understand," Cyrillis said, sitting on her pack, "is why did she not attack us while we slept?" All eyes rotated to the cleric. "If she is as powerful as thought, and she had a pack of goblins at her disposal, surely we would have been easily overwhelmed and defeated."

Sordaak shook his head. "I don't think she was actually present." He looked down at the scroll ends sitting on top of his bag. "There was rumored to be a wizard in these parts who tried a few years ago to unite the goblins." He looked up at Thrinndor, who listened with a cocked eyebrow.

"Pradopharr?" Breunne asked, turning from the fire. He had his plate in hand as he was about to get his portion of breakfast.

"The one and same. However, he was only partially successful. The goblins are fiercely tribal, and Pradopharr met resistance at every turn. Still, after many battles he reportedly managed to put together quite an army of the vile little creatures."

"To what end?" Thrinndor was intrigued. He had never heard of such an undertaking. "Surely a wizard capable of such power as you describe could put his talents to a more productive use."

Sordaak shrugged. "Pradopharr was reported to be more than a little crazy."

"Even more than you?" Vorgath asked with a straight face.

The sorcerer scowled at the dwarf. "Yes, even more so than me." He smiled. "He was originally a student of Quozak—my mentor of old—and was said to also covet *Pendromar*. His plan must have been to take Ice Homme with his army. It's the only thing that makes sense." He shook his head slowly.

"But now he's sided with *Ice Homme*?" Cyrillis said doubtfully. "That seems a bit odd."

Sordaak looked over at the cleric, who was seated not far away. "Unless he was promised the staff in exchange for service or services."

Thrinndor stopped with this spoon halfway to his mouth. "That means this Pradopharr could hold the staff?"

Sordaak stood with his plate in hand and headed over to the fire. "Possible, but I don't think likely," he said as the rogue ladled a mixture of tuber, corn and leftover bear meat onto his plate. "Otherwise I would have insisted we go after our animals." He shook his head again. "No, I believe our young Kiarrah has the staff, but she is unable to use it—or she would have certainly attacked by now."

The mage again took his seat and spooned some of the concoction into his mouth and nodded. "Pradopharr is simply an unknowing lackey. She sent him to slow us down."

"And when she discovers he was unsuccessful?" Breunne asked.

Sordaak stared at the ranger, his mind considering the question. "I'm only guessing here, I don't know the bitch, but surely she will be displeased. I'd assume she'll order him to attack."

"Why?" Heads turned to the barbarian as he had finally decided to join the conversation. After a moment of silence, he rolled his eyes. "I can see no advantage to slowing us down. Actually, that would seem counterproductive, assuming she knows of the dwarf army behind us."

Sordaak nodded his head slowly, taking another bite while he thought about it. "We must assume she has spies all over the northern lands, and is therefore aware of all we do. It's the only thing that explains how she knows where we are."

"Not the only thing," Vorgath countered. "Icy Bitch."

"But she is an unwilling servant of theirs," Cyrillis protested.

Sordaak set his plate aside. "She *told* us she is an unwilling servant." He waved his spoon for emphasis. "It's possible she made up the story of the eggs to gain our trust and spy on us."

"I sensed no such complicity in her!" The cleric's tone indicated there was doubt in her mind, however.

Thrinndor ignored the healer. "That would certainly explain a lot of what has happened since we first came upon her. It is possible she has been lying all along."

"It certainly would."

At the sound of the dragon's voice in human form, Thrinndor and Vorgath dove from their seats in opposite directions. Breunne spun and drew his bow in the same instant, an arrow already notched and ready to loose by the time he reached his feet. Savinhand simply vanished. Cyrillis too stood and turned to face the new occupant, but her face was a mixture of distrust and wanting to believe.

Sordaak alone remained seated. His perch conveniently faced the opening that led back out to the open air, and he took on a mien of indifference as he spooned some gravy mixture into his mouth and chewed silently.

"I see that distrust rules the day," Pantorra said lightly. "Does no one remember that I assisted you in rescuing the ranger when his life hung in the balance?"

Breunne did not ease his stance; his arrow remained ready to fly. Vorgath and Thrinndor remained in battle stance, weapons drawn and ready to attack. Cyrillis crossed her arms and waited.

Sordaak finished chewing what was in his mouth, set his plate aside and made a show of wiping his mouth with a convenient piece of cloth. This complete, he finally looked up and acknowledged the visitor.

"Ease up," he said as he waved an arm to his companions. "She knows that we have subdued her once and could do so again should we so choose."

"Yet she shows up right after our mounts are stolen," Vorgath grated, not lowering *Flinthgoor* one inch. "Coincidence?"

"Oh." Pantorra put her hand to her chest dramatically. "Am I too late? Have the goblins already stolen your horses?"

"You knew they were coming," Sordaak said tiredly.

"Of course," the dragon-woman said evenly. "Your adversary trusts me implicitly—as long as she holds my eggs."

"Then why are you here?" Thrinndor asked. He, too, kept his flaming bastard sword and shield at the ready.

"Now," finished the cleric. Her suspicions had gotten the better of her. Too much required explanation. "Why are you here now?"

Pantorra shrugged. "That bitch has no intention of *ever* returning my eggs to me. In fact, it is my belief she plans to raise them as her pets after she disposes of her remaining obstacle." She paused for a moment and then waved an arm encompassing the companions.

"OK, I'll bite," Breunne said, an arrow at the ready. "What obstacle?"

The dragon woman looked surprised at the question. "Why, all of you, of course."

The fire crackled and popped a couple of times before anyone spoke. In small increments, weapons were lowered.

It was Sordaak who broke the silence. "Obstacle to what?"

Pantorra blinked a couple of times before answering. "You really do not know, do you?"

"Let's just pretend for argument's sake that we don't."

"Very well." The dragon-woman lowered her hands to her side and her eyes locked with those of the sorcerer. "She means to unite and rule all the land—"

"Preposterous!" bellowed the barbarian. He lowered his greataxe and now leaned on his weapon, openly inviting the dragon to make an aggressive move.

"How does she plan on doing that after we've decimated her armies and scattered them to the wind?" Breunne kept *Xenotath* in his left fist, but he lowered the weapon and allowed the string pressure to ease.

Pantorra ignored the interruptions.

"Please explain." Sordaak remained still, not allowing his eyes to stray from the dragon-woman's as he motioned for her to sit opposite him. She did so, but sufficiently far from the blazing fire that she wouldn't be too uncomfortable.

"Thank you," she said as she took the proffered seat. Once settled in, she again locked gazes with the mage. "Surely you know by now that she wields the staff you seek."

Sordaak's lips formed a fine line as he shook his head. "*Pendromar?* That's not possible. No Minion of Set can even hold that staff—let alone wield it."

Pantorra shook her head. "You underestimate her. That is unfortunate. She is no normal Minion of Set. Rather, with the staff in hand, her powers far exceed those of any previous High Commander of Set." She looked over at Cyrillis,

Kurril cradled in the crook of her arm, "You have done exactly what she has wanted all along. You have brought the second staff to her."

"Now I *know* you are full of shit!" Vorgath stormed.

"Shut up!" both Thrinndor and Sordaak shouted at once. The paladin didn't like where this was going. "Go on," he at last said quietly.

Pantorra nodded, also ignoring the barbarian. "Once she gets her hands on *Valdaar's Fist*, she means to use the *Artifacts of Power* to raise this dead god of yours."

The stunned silence that followed filled the chamber for several moments. "How does she plan to get the sword?" Sordaak demanded.

The dragon-woman shook her head. "I do not believe she has figured that out yet." She raised a hand to forestall the coming protests. "Rest assured, however, that she is both working on it and capable of doing so."

"But she cannot even make the attempt to raise Valdaar without those of the proper lineage present," Thrinndor protested.

Pantorra shrugged. "I do not pretend to know the intricacies of either her plans or of the ceremony required." The fire popped a couple more times before she continued. "Continue to underestimate her at your own peril. What I speak here is sooth. She plans to rule all the land, and she desires to raise your god in the process."

Thrinndor shook his head. "That is the part that makes no sense. How does raising Valdaar help her? They would not be allies."

Pantorra acknowledged the paladin with a raised eyebrow. "What makes you think that?"

"Valdaar is a servant of Law. By definition, Minions are servants of Chaos."

"That is valid," the dragon-woman said. "But I see you are missing one thing: Kiarrah has no intention of allowing your god to live. Once Valdaar is out of the way, Set can be brought to prominence as the premier god in the land."

"Even assuming she is successful in slaying our lord, surely his brother Praxaar would not allow Set and his Minions to rule!" Cyrillis pointed out.

"Following the war to end all wars, Praxaar vowed to never again meddle in the affairs of man." Thrinndor's tone was subdued.

The sorcerer and paladin exchanged glances. "Damn!" muttered the spell-caster, "this complicates matters somewhat."

"No it doesn't!" Vorgath said stubbornly. "We continue as planned: March in there, kick her scrawny little ass, take this damn staff and get on with life!" He folded his arms on his chest as if that were the end of the conversation.

Sordaak glared at the barbarian. "While that may in the end be the action we take, there are other considerations to be taken into account before we do. Now, please sit down and allow us to plan accordingly."

Vorgath glowered from under his bushy eyebrows but said nothing more along those lines.

"I do not understand something." All eyes moved to the cleric, and she shifted uncomfortably in her seat. "Kiarrah is *so young*! I mean, she is in her late teens, at best!"

Pantorra nodded. "That she is, dear. However, it is also my belief that hers is an old soul."

"Reincarnation?" Thrinndor was dubious.

Pantorra nodded. "No proof, mind you, but it all fits. Her powers are far too extensive for one so young."

"But reincarnation has not been attempted for many a millennia!" Cyrillis protested.

"Not true, dear," Pantorra smiled at the cleric. "It has been *attempted* many times over that span, but seldom has the result been *successful*."

"Who was she in her former life, then?" Cyrillis continued the argument. She had heard of no such attempt, successful or otherwise.

"That I cannot answer, child," replied the dragon-woman. "Although it was reported that a priest of the highest order of Set made the attempt decades ago. Nothing was ever heard from him again."

"But you said *decades* ago!" Cyrillis refused to let it go. "Kiarrah is not old enough!"

"Reincarnation is not an exact science," refuted Pantorra. "It is said that sometimes it can be several decades before a suitable vassal is located."

"Ha!" snorted the cleric. "From what little I know of reincarnation, a suitable vassal is found and prepared *before* the attempt is even made!" Her eyes flashed as she crossed her arms on her chest.

"That is true, my dear. However, one of the reasons an attempt may become *unsuccessful* is that the new host sometimes rejects the old soul. Often that would be the end of said attempt—and the end of the soul making the attempt. But there have been documented occurrences when an especially powerful soul may wander the land in search of an acceptable host. Sometimes even for *decades*."

Vorgath got up and added another piece of wood to the fire, shaking his head as he did. All this talk of spooks and hosts made him nervous. While he'd aided more than one ghost, shade, and/or other less-than-living denizen of the underworld on their journey to the afterlife, he'd never encountered one looking to do more than scare or harm the living. None of this "looking for a new host" shit, and he didn't *want* to encounter such a creature. He shivered at the thought as he returned to his seat.

"All right," Sordaak said, "let's summarize. We have a young, powerful new leader of the Minions that also now wields *Pendromar*, plans on raising your dead god, only to later slay him. In so doing, she plans on making Set a premier god and put the Minions in control of the land." He glanced around. "I miss anything?"

"Perhaps," mused the paladin, quietly. All eyes focused on their leader as he scratched the ever-lengthening hairs on his chin. He brought his eyes down from some spot on the roof of the cavern to lock with those of the caster. "This

Kiarrah is clearly well-versed in the lore that surrounds the raising of our lord. As such, she must certainly be aware that only those who are direct descendants of Valdaar's High Council may use the artifacts of power to return him to this realm." His eyes traveled to lock with those of Pantorra. "Surely she cannot believe we will willingly assist her in this endeavor?"

Pantorra blinked twice. "I know not her plans for you. However, she must have something figured out. Originally she asked for the three of you to be brought in alive." Her eyes shifted from Sordaak, to Thrinndor and finally rested on Cyrillis. "However, now she no longer cares." She shrugged. "Dead or alive— it matters not. She has pledged a million plat for *each* of your heads. As such she has many ready to do he will."

Chapter Twenty-Seven

Quick March

A surprised silence fell over the companions.

"Leave us," Sordaak ordered, drawing a raised eyebrow from the paladin. Pantorra stood stiffly. "You do not trust me?"

"Of course not!" the mage said with a dismissive wave. "What you have told us is unverifiable, at best. You're asking us to believe you are not our enemy by telling us supposed secrets to gain our trust." Sordaak shook his head. "No, too much has happened that could easily be explained by your duplicity. At a minimum, I believe you would play both sides against one another if it works to your advantage."

Pantorra dipped her head in a short bow. "Well said, young sorcerer. I would indeed—if doing so would return my eggs to me."

"There's the rub," Sordaak said, turning on the dragon-woman and jabbing a finger in her direction, "we have only your word that there even are these eggs!"

Pantorra's eyes opened wide. "I assure you there are." With that, she spun on a heel and marched from the gathering. "I will await your instructions down by the creek."

Thrinndor watched her walk away, her back ramrod straight.

"What—?" Vorgath began.

Sordaak stopped him with a raised hand as he also closed his eyes, clearly communicating with his familiar. After a few moments, he nodded and opened them. "She has done as she said. She has reverted to dragon form and waits down by the creek in the basin."

"What's the plan?"

Thrinndor took in a deep breath as he thought. "I believe a variation on our earlier discussion is in order. We pack up and leave immediately. I now want to lose both whoever is watching us and the dragon, so we will only take what we can carry. Initially we will continue on the path north, but by midday we will turn east and cross the mountains." The party leader paused. "Once we turn east, we will pick up the pace—I want to be several miles from the path before it is discovered we are not where we are supposed to be. We will march through the night."

Vorgath started to protest, but the paladin continued before he could. "We make camp at daybreak tomorrow. We will only travel by night after this day is through."

Quickly final preparations were made as Savinhand put out the fire.

Clear of the cave opening, Sordaak called his familiar, signaled for the others to wait for him there and strode down the hill to the dragon.

Seeing her in this form made the mage slightly uncomfortable. Her ponderous bulk towered over him. "I think it best if we continued alone."

The dragon's eyes narrowed until they were mere slits. "Surely you must realize that if it is my desire to maintain contact with you, I can do so from afar?"

"Of course," the mage said dismissively. "However, I don't think we should be seen together." The dragon waited patiently for an explanation. "Kiarrah must not suspect that you aid us. In fact, you should probably go to her and report our progress." Pantorra nodded. "Maybe you should wait for us there."

The dragon stared into the eyes of the mage, trying to read whether there was more.

"Very well," she said. "I will see you in two days."

"Or so," corrected the sorcerer.

The dragon nodded, spread her wings and launched herself into the pre-dawn sky.

Sordaak was still brushing the dust kicked up by the dragon's departure from his cloak when the others walked up.

"What did you tell her?" Vorgath asked as his eyes tried in vain to see where the dragon had gone.

"To get lost," the mage replied as he shouldered his pack and started back the way they had come the night before.

Thrinndor motioned for the others to gather around. He looked over at Breunne. "Do you know of the pass I intend for us to use?"

"Yes."

"Very well, scout far ahead. Let us know if you encounter anyone." The ranger nodded as the paladin turned his attention to the thief. "Savin, I want you not as far ahead and more to the east of our intended path." Savin nodded as the paladin continued. "We will set a leisurely pace until we turn east. At that point we will double our speed."

Savin and Breunne exchanged glances and disappeared into the dark. Thrinndor gave them a few minutes to get into position and then led the way back toward the main path.

Morning came slowly, the clouds seemingly unwilling to let the sun's warmth through to the people far below. Not long after that it began to get noticeably colder.

"Snow by midday," announced the barbarian.

"Great!" mumbled the sorcerer.

The snow had just begun to fall when the giants caught up with them. Thrinndor filled them in on what had transpired, telling of their meeting with the dragon at the last.

Stormheart nodded his agreement to their suspicions. "We do not trust her, either. She is too secretive to be of use as a companion."

Thrinndor nodded and pointed off to the east. "Now we must pick up the pace. I want to be in the foothills at the base of that mountain in an hour."

Stormheart looked to where the paladin pointed. "So you intend to cross at Yarmlyth's Pass?"

Thrinndor hesitated but ultimately nodded. He should have known the giants knew the area well.

"We can travel much faster if you allow us to carry you," Stormheart suggested as the humans broke into a slow jog, while the giants merely lengthened their stride.

Again Thrinndor hesitated. It went against his usual code to be carried. However, one look at the tips of the mountains shrouded in the snow and clouds, and his reticence faded. He glanced at his companions, currently warmed from the effort of the march, but he knew that was going to change.

"Very well," he said, "but only until under the cover of darkness."

Stormheart nodded and gave the orders for his "wives" to select a companion. The giant leader selected Thrinndor and unceremoniously picked him up and slung the paladin into the cradle position. "Sorry," the giant grinned, "but this is the most efficient way to carry you."

The paladin bit back his pride, knowing the giant spoke the truth. The party leader waited for the outburst he assumed to be coming from the barbarian. However, one was not forthcoming. Thrinndor craned his neck to get a good look at his friend, but Vorgath was studiously ignoring everyone as he settled into the arms of his giant.

The giants were obviously well rested as Stormheart set a pace that the humans would not have been able to keep up with, even for a short time. The giants' body heat soon began to radiate as they warmed to their task, carrying the humans and moving at a steady jog.

The miles flew by as the snow thickened. Soon even the bases of the big mountains were not visible. Thrinndor had to rely on the giants as the darkness began to move in. Occasionally they passed a landmark, and he was sure that the giant leader passed close enough to several to assure Thrinndor that they were on the desired path.

The paladin pulled his cloak about his shoulders, trying to keep out the bulk of the snow, which had increasingly thickened as the evening progressed. A couple of times he looked behind to verify that the other giants were keeping pace. He needn't have bothered—only the coalescing breath coming out of their mouths in labored fashion showed any kind of strain as they followed their leader.

Finally gray faded until only the snow from the sky provided any light at all and Thrinndor signaled for the giants to stop. Obediently, Stormheart slowed and came to a halt as his companions gathered around him. Their breaths came in billowing clouds of vapor as aching lungs fought for oxygen. But, looking around, the paladin had the feeling that the giants had not exerted themselves all that much.

"We will walk from here," the paladin said. The giant leader set the paladin down and Thrinndor stomped feeling back into his stiff joints, waving his arms around to get circulation back.

Stormheart unslung a fluid-filled skin from his shoulder. Removing the stopper, he pressed the skin to his lips and drank deeply. Finished, he passed the skin to the other giants, who each drank greedily.

"If you would allow us to continue to carry you and your companions, we can more than double the pace we would set with you moving afoot." Stormheart's voice did not show the slightest hint of strain from the past four or five hours of not only carrying a heavy burden but also moving at a pace that the humans could not have matched.

"That will not be necessary."

"It is if we are to gain a place where we can all rest in comparative warmth by dawn. It will not be easy, but we can make it if we pick up the pace a bit."

Thrinndor tried in vain to penetrate the gloom surrounding the giant's eyes, but he had to give up. "If you can do so safely, we would be in your debt. I would like to gain Ice Homme ere dawn of the day following the morrow. I am working on a plan, and speed is required—as is stealth."

"But—" Cyrillis started to protest.

"We had best be going then," Stormheart interrupted. "Take care of any personal business you might have and get something out to eat. You can have your meal while we run. We leave in five minutes."

The paladin cast a "ask no questions" glance at the cleric while he stepped back into the nearby brush to relieve himself. The others did likewise, the barbarian rubbing his eyes as he stumbled along.

Breunne and Savinhand joined the group as they gathered to once again leave. Both were obviously winded from trying to keep pace. Thrinndor made a quick change in plans. "We will have to alternate time in the arms of the giants if we are to keep up the pace."

"I am fine," protested the ranger between breaths.

"No you are not. We must travel even faster if my plan is to work." The paladin rested an unwavering glare on the ranger. "Stormheart, please carry Breunne and instruct whichever of your companions that was carrying the dwarf to carry Savinhand, instead."

Neither Breunne nor the rogue complained further as the giants stepped forward to claim their cargo. Quickly, the paladin removed the bulk of his armor, tied it together and handed it to the giant leader. While the armor was made of the lightest possible materials and enchanted to further enhance that effect, it would still prove cumbersome to wear while running for extended periods.

"We will trade out at two-hour intervals. As speed and darkness would preclude efficient scouting, Vorgath and I will follow the group. Using the path you cut through the snow will ease our travel greatly."

Stormheart nodded. "Let us know if we set too ambitious a pace."

"We'll keep up," the barbarian said around a bite of biscuit. "If the paladin falters, I'll carry him!"

"Ha!" snorted Thrinndor, "I was about to say the same."

The dwarf made a show of rolling his eyes. "I'll wager you dinner at the best restaurant in Farreach that you falter first!"

The paladin smiled and winked at the barbarian. "No way! You eat too much! Besides, I have seen you run down mounted parties, and they with what should have been an insurmountable lead!"

Vorgath puffed his chest out. "Chicken!"

"No," laughed the paladin. "Just smart." He tapped the side of his head and winked again as he turned to face Stormheart. "All right, let us move out."

The giant leader turned without a word and strode purposefully along the path. He sped up, frequently checking back to ensure he had not lost those following. Satisfied, he continued to speed up until they were indeed moving faster than before.

Thrinndor, in very good shape and still very young and the barbarian kept up, but just barely.

When finally they again stopped, the paladin had been on the verge of halting the column. His reserve of strength was nearly exhausted. His hands on his knees, he puffed and panted while the switch was made. Again, the giants passed around a skin.

"What is that drink?" Thrinndor asked. He was again nestled comfortably in the arms of the giant leader and the column had returned to full speed.

"An elixir that restores our strength and stamina somewhat."

"Would that be of any use to us?" the paladin asked, intrigued.

"No," the giant said, his breath coming evenly following the brief rest. "Your hearts are not strong enough to withstand what it would do to them." He glanced back over his shoulder at the ranger and rogue. "Rest now, or those two will require relief before you are ready."

Thrinndor nodded and leaned his head back against the upper arm of the giant. The muscle there was as hard as a rock, and therefore not of much comfort.

Thus the night passed. By the time the giants slowed for the last time the group approached a small cabin nestled up against the base of a high cliff and dawn was making itself known along the eastern horizon. The four men had had to trade out more often as the night wore on and their stamina waned.

The cabin was much larger than it appeared from the outside, as it was built such that it hid an opening in the cliff face. There were bunks aplenty as this must have once been either a hostelry or a bunkhouse for some base of operation.

Vorgath, having pulled a double shift in the wake of the giants to allow an exhausted Savinhand more rest, stumbled through the door and immediately fell into one of the bunks.

A fire was already set in the huge hearth, which Sordaak soon had blazing. Savinhand, somewhat rested from his double shift in the arms of a giant, put together a meal for everyone.

The giants went back deeper into the cavern, sat on the floor and began to talk among themselves as they wound down from their ordeal.

"What is this place?" Thrinndor asked as he watched the rogue work.

"It's an old mining weigh station for a shaft that used to penetrate deep into these mountains," Stormheart answered. "It has long been abandoned, but sees occasional use by those that know of it." He turned and pointed to a boarded-up section of an interior wall. "That shaft goes back and down for several miles."

"Not again!" moaned the magicuser as he walked up to inspect the boards. The wood was old and some was rotten. This shaft had clearly not been used in *many* years.

"Rest assured," Stormheart said as he noted the uneasy look on the mage's face, "nothing can approach us from those depths." Sordaak turned and raised a questioning eyebrow but said nothing. "Long ago the miners hit an underground reservoir and the mines have been flooded since."

Sordaak returned his attention to the portal. "Just the same, I'll make sure we are not disturbed." He closed his eyes and called for Fahlred, who appeared instantly. "At least, not from this direction."

After a few moments of silent communication with the familiar, the quasit nodded and winked out of existence. Sordaak again closed his eyes and concentrated, following the progress of his familiar.

Presently he opened his eyes and Fahlred reappeared on his shoulder. The mage nodded and turned to peer through a small opening in the wood. He mumbled the words to a spell, pointed his finger through the crack in the portal bindings and released the energy. He repeated this process four times before he nodded and returned to the fire, apparently satisfied.

"Did you put up another wall?" Cyrillis asked.

Sordaak shook his head. "Walls have proved ineffective. I set several traps that will warn us if we are approached from that direction."

Thrinndor nodded his approval. "That is good. We must rest until dusk."

The mage turned and leveled a stare at the paladin. "You do realize that the heat portion of the dragon's sight would be able to find us, day or night?"

Thrinndor's eyes widened. "I had not considered that."

Savinhand turned from the fire, spoon in hand. "So our efforts to throw her off may have been a waste of time?"

"No," the mage shook his head as he got up to look through a window at the snow-covered landscape on the other side. "At least I don't think so. The clouds—and even the thick snow—should have provided an adequate blanket and hidden our movement from her." He turned back to the room. "She would have had to been flying very low to see us through that," he jerked a thumb over his shoulder.

"It is not only her from whom we seek to remain hidden." All eyes shifted to the paladin, who was seated wearily at a table set in the middle of the room. "Kiarrah could have spies all over this land. We still yet may also encounter her minions as they attempt to make their way back to Ice Homme."

Sordaak nodded. "We stay put during the day, then." He turned to again stare out the window at the heavily falling snow. The tracks they had made to get to this point were almost covered already.

A good development, that.

*

Sordaak slept fitfully. He had been well-rested when they got to the cabin, and his body ached with the nearness of the staff. Several times he got to his feet and paced silently through the darkened retreat. They had covered the windows with blankets, effectively blocking out the cloud-filtered light beyond.

Once he even slipped unheard out through the door into the cold beyond, seeking to walk off some of his excess energy. But the cold chased him back inside after only a few minutes. The snow had continued to fall, and now there was at least a foot-and-a-half of the stuff covering the ground and bending trees to the breaking point—and past, in some cases.

Finally, as the cloud shrouded sun dipped behind a mountain to the east and the cabin began to darken, he could stand it no more. The mage went to stand next to where the paladin slept.

"Yes?" came the muffled question from beneath the blankets.

"The sun is almost gone. We should be moving."

Nothing happened for a few moments, and Sordaak feared the paladin had gone back to sleep. But, with a groan, a pair of bare feet appeared from under the blankets, followed immediately by the attached legs. The blanket was cast aside, and the tousled head of their leader appeared.

Thrinndor stretched and yawned deeply. "Already?" He searched around for his socks and, finding them, he pulled them on, noting several holes in both with a frown. "Coffee on?" he said as he groaned again and pushed himself to his feet.

"Yes," Sordaak said as he followed the big man to the hearth.

Steaming mug in hand, the paladin turned to face the room. "All right people, rise and shine! We have another long night ahead."

Blankets moved and were cast aside, except for one. That one emitted the snore of a still slumbering dwarf. With a sigh, Thrinndor walked over and prodded the mound of covers with his toe. "Come on, old one. We depart in thirty minutes."

Getting no response from the mound, the paladin raised his foot up and again prodded the dwarf, more roughly this time.

A hand shot out from under the covers, grabbed the plant leg of the fighter and jerked that leg out from under the surprised paladin. Thrinndor landed on his ass with a crash, spilling hot coffee all over the floor as he did.

The paladin frowned at the smiling face that appeared when the blankets were tossed aside. "Was that necessary?"

Vorgath sat up, his eyes going from the paladin to the spilt coffee. "You're going to have to work on your dexterity," he said with a shake of the head as he swung his still booted feet out from under the blankets. "I hope there's more coffee." The dwarf pushed himself to his feet, ignoring the astonished look from his leader and shambled over to the hearth.

Stifling a smile, Sordaak poured a cup for the barbarian and handed it to him. "I'll put on another pot."

The others made their way through the gloom to stand next to the big fireplace and absorb some warmth from it as the water for the coffee heated.

Sordaak started to remove the blanket from a window, but Thrinndor stopped him. "Leave the windows covered." The mage raised an eyebrow as he turned to face the paladin. "Light from the windows can be seen for many miles on a dark night."

"Not through that mess," the sorcerer said, pointing out a window. "It's still snowing hard out there."

"Just the same, I would rather not chance it. How much snow has fallen?"

"Three feet, if there's an inch," replied the caster. "More where it has drifted."

"Damn," muttered the dwarf as he took a sip of the scalding coffee. "That sucks!"

"It's bitterly cold out there, too. I don't think I've seen it that cold before."

"Damn," repeated the dwarf. Abruptly he turned and pointed the finger from his empty hand at the paladin. "What's this plan that has us in such an all-fired hurry?"

Thrinndor waved a hand at the table but looked over at Savinhand, who was still stretching next to his recently abandoned bed. "Savin, if you will begin a quick, hot meal, I will share my plan with everyone."

The rogue nodded and stumbled over to the fire as the giants walked up. The ceiling was high for the humans, more than ten feet above their heads, but the giants had to duck under the beams. They seated themselves on the cold floor next to the table, obviously wanting to hear this plan as well.

Deciding the coffee had had long enough on the fire, the paladin refilled his cup and took a seat at the table. He brought the pot with him and set it in the center.

Cyrillis was the last to join them, having recently returned from the detached privy area. She shivered as she reached for the pot. "One of these days, some enterprising young man—or woman—is going to figure out a way to attach the toilet to the main chamber, AND find a way for it not to stink so much!" She wrinkled her nose distastefully.

Thrinndor grinned as he put his cup back on the table. "My plan is to make our move on Ice Homme before daybreak tomorrow."

A stunned silence fell on the cabin.

Savinhand was to speak as he turned to face the table. "But Ice Homme is still two days north and much higher in the mountains, isn't it?"

Thrinndor shook his head. "I do not think so. We climbed steadily through the night and made very good time." He turned to look at Stormheart. "I believe we are about a hundred miles from where we camped yesterday."

"Closer to one hundred and twenty."

The paladin's right eyebrow lifted slightly and he turned back to the group. "Even with the detour—we would have had to climb into the mountains, eventually, as Ice Homme is on a massive plateau high in these same mountains—we should be no more than fifty or sixty miles from the minion stronghold."

The paladin again turned to look at the giant leader. "If we can set a similar pace as last evening, we should be able to cover the remaining distance with several hours to spare." The giant nodded, and Thrinndor turned back to the table. "That will allow us a brief time to rest and prepare so that we can enter the palace just before dawn."

"But the dwarves will not get there for another two days," protested the cleric.

"At least," agreed the rogue, still working a pan at the hearth.

"My plan does not require their assistance."

Sordaak cocked his head, interested in this change in plans. "Should I send word to have them turn around and head back to Ardaagh?"

Thrinndor shook his head. "No. I want Kiarrah to *think* we are waiting for the dwarves. I want her to *think* she still has two days to prepare."

Sordaak nodded, liking where this was headed.

"How are we going in?" It was Breunne who voiced what had crossed more than one mind.

"Same as we discussed, with a few notable changes. The giants were not in our original plan. Cyrillis, Sordaak, Vorgath, one of the giants and I will walk up to the front gate and attempt to gain admittance. Breunne, Savinhand and the remaining giants will go over a rear wall and make their way to meet with the rest of us, wherever that might be."

The companions ate a quick meal and packed what remained of their food and equipment. Before the light had faded from the sky, they were again on the trail. As before, Thrinndor and Vorgath started on foot.

The snow was still falling but had eased somewhat. A chill wind had picked up out of the north, and occasionally stars could be seen through breaks in the clouds.

The worst part: It was getting cold. Fast.

Chapter Twenty-Eight

Welcoming Committee

Sordaak, Cyrillis, Thrinndor, Vorgath and Stormheart rested in the lee of an overhang of rock southwest of Ice Homme. The remainder of the companions remained on the move, attempting to gain the northern perimeter of the Minion University without being detected, and before dawn broke.

Fahlred stood watch while they slept fitfully. They were too close to risk a fire. An hour before sunrise the quasit roused his master, and soon all had eaten a cold meal of biscuits and dried meats, washed down by fortified wine—anti-freeze, as Vorgath called it.

With more than a half-hour of darkness remaining, the band stepped from their hiding place into the open and set foot on the road to the palace supposedly containing the last vestiges of Minions in the land.

Ice Homme was situated on a vast flat plateau and surrounded by the craggy peaks of the Northron Mountains. It was said that long ago the plateau was a lake, but it had frozen over many centuries ago—never again to thaw in these most frigid northern reaches of the land. It was said that temperatures in this region had not risen above freezing in recorded history.

If there was ice below the multiple layers of packed snow, none that now lived had ever seen it.

Stormheart walked hunched over to disguise his size, and the companions stayed close to disguise their numbers. They walked quickly, both because it helped warm their limbs and to not give the inhabitants of the palace too much time to look elsewhere.

"If Pantorra has been reporting to Kiarrah our movements and plans," Sordaak asked as they approached the sealed gate in the outer wall, "why is it we think she has not told her of our plans for a split attack?"

Thrinndor lifted an eyebrow as he turned to look at the sorcerer. "I am counting on it. If you remember, however, our original plan was to sneak in and do the bulk of our damage from the back. We are now flipping the plan. Our presence at the front gate, and subsequent attack, is to cover the rear approach."

Sordaak shrugged. "I hope you're right."

The paladin turned back to the path ahead. "Me, too."

The party stopped a few feet short of the enormous gates inset in the outer wall. The gates were lit by two large sconces on either side of the wooden doors. Thrinndor could hear voices on the other side. Clearly their approach had not gone unnoticed.

Vorgath stepped forward and used the head of *Flinthgoor* to pound on the wood of the massive portal. More voices were heard and they were more excited this time. Those voices were followed by the sound of a bolt being pulled back. A previously unnoticed section of the door swung outward on noiseless hinges, about a foot square. A face appeared in the opening. "What do you want?"

Thrinndor stepped forward. "An audience with Lord Kiarrah."

"*High* Lord Kiarrah is away on business. Go away." The face withdrew, and the portal started to close.

Thrinndor grabbed the door and easily pulled it back open. "Wait. We are cold and hungry. Surely you can provide us shelter until she returns?"

There was some insistent whispering on the other side of the gates and then the face reappeared. "Put down your weapons and you will be granted admittance."

"That is acceptable." Thrinndor had anticipated this, and the companions had brought along extra weapons to be discarded in the event. He nodded to his companions, who made a show of complaining but cast aside these weapons nonetheless.

The paladin, having dropped a longsword, turned back to face the opening.

"*All* of your weapons."

Thrinndor stared at the hooded figure, his face masked by darkness. "Very well." He had anticipated this, too. He again nodded to his companions.

Now the complaining began in earnest—also part of the plan. A staged argument between Vorgath and his leader even ensued. Finally, more weapons clanged into the pile off to the side. There was no way to disguise or otherwise hide *Flinthgoor*, so reluctantly the barbarian tossed his greataxe onto the pile. However, the handle of the weapon spun such that it was only a few feet from him.

Cyrillis had wrapped *Kurril* and it was tied on her back and under her cloak, effectively hidden. It was also not within easy reach, and that bothered her. This was the first time since the incursion into Dragma's Keep that she did not have the staff readily at hand.

Clearly seeing the monstrous axe get added to the pile was a tipping point, indicating the party had been expected. The face disappeared again, and the portal swung shut, this time unimpeded by the paladin. Voices were audible and the companions could hear the sound of a massive bolt sliding aside, followed by a second. Thrinndor also heard footsteps on top of the wall, so he knew they were still being watched. This had also been anticipated. Timing was going to be crucial.

But the awaited signal—the opening of one of both gates—was for some reason delayed. Vorgath was getting edgy, and had inched slowly toward his beloved axe. And Thrinndor was getting a bad feeling and was just about to share this information when both doors flew open with unbelievable speed, arrows rained down from above and dozens of hooded figures surged from the open portal. A column of flame blasted from high over their heads, blinding the companions and knocking Vorgath, Cyrillis and Sordaak to the ground. Only Stormheart and Thrinndor remained standing, but they were stunned and blinded.

Trap!

Vorgath alone escaped being blinded, and only because he dove for *Flinthgoor* the instant the gates moved, and thus his face was to the ground when the Flamestrike hit. However, he took the brunt of the spell along his back and was smashed to the ground short of his objective. Two of the arrows also found their mark though the protective leather covering his back. Several others bounced harmlessly off of that same armor.

Ignoring the pain in his back, the barbarian howled in rage and lunged toward the handle of his axe. Just as his fist was about to close on the shaft, the weapon was kicked out of his reach and he landed awkwardly on his chest, his arms outstretched.

Knowing he was in trouble, he rolled hard to his right, gritting his teeth as both arrows snapped off, leaving their heads in his body. Vorgath surged to his feet and planted his fist into the first face that presented itself. It was the Minion who had kicked his axe.

Blood showered the front of the man's tunic as his nose was instantly shattered and his head snapped back. He was unconscious before his shoulders hit the ground.

Spotting his greataxe a few feet away, Vorgath took a step that direction and was confronted by a pole-axe wielding Minion, with another of the hooded warriors standing menacingly to the right of the first.

The barbarian didn't hesitate, instead lowering his shoulder and slamming into the first Minion. The man's air left his lungs in a *whoosh* as the diminutive fighter used his forward momentum to flip the suddenly breathless Minion over his back and into the second man.

A general melee ensued as other Minions stepped in to stop the barbarian. But Vorgath was not to be denied. He knocked two more Minions to the ground and bent to wrap his hands on his prize. As he stood, victorious, another column of flames blasted the ground in front of him, knocking him on his ass.

At the first sign of trouble, Thrinndor threw back his cloak and yanked this flaming sword from its sheath at his belt. But the Flamestrike effectively blinded the paladin and knocked him back a step. His hearing recovered quicker, and he heard shuffling of feet to his right. So he whipped his sword around in an arc that buried the blade deep into the shoulder of a Minion. The man yelled in pain and lunged clear of the paladin's reach.

Assuming the direction the man had come from, Thrinndor lunged that way and swung his blade wildly. This time he connected with an unfortunate woman seeking to get behind the paladin. She screamed as his blade carved a gouge from her right shoulder down to her waist. She fell back, clutching the two sides of the wound, trying to keep the skin from separating.

Thrinndor was beginning to be able to discern shapes when the second column of flames blasted the ground behind him, knocking him forward onto his knees. When he managed to stand upright again, he found himself surrounded by robed figures.

Sordaak and Cyrillis had been standing side-by-side when knocked to the ground by the impact of the flame spell. His eyes streaming tears, he crawled on hands and knees toward where they had been standing. He called the cleric's name softly as he crawled, waving an arm wildly out in front of him, hoping to find her that way, if necessary.

"Here!" Cyrillis replied, not far to the mage's left. The healer was struggling to free *Kurril* from her cloak when an arrow hit the back of her thigh. She bit her lip to keep from screaming, drawing blood. "I am trying to free my staff!"

Sordaak turned that direction. "Never mind that! Remove Blindness! Quickly."

"But—"

"*Now!*" An arrow easily penetrated the billowy robe of the mage and pierced his left side from behind. "Aagh!"

"*What?*"

"Never mind!" Sordaak discovered it was possible to shout from between clenched teeth. "Remove my blindness!"

The intensity in his voice caused her to stop struggling with her staff, even though she almost had it free, and cast the required spell.

"Thanks," Sordaak said as he pushed himself to his feet.

Without hesitation, the healer removed her own blindness, making the task of removing *Kurril* from its binding much easier. She used the staff to push herself to her feet just as the second column of flame hit right in front of her. Fortunately she was inspecting the arrow protruding from the back of her leg, so her eyes were averted and she was not again blinded. She was, however, again knocked to the ground.

Anticipating the second Flamestrike, Sordaak was able to close his eyes and turn away in time. As a result, he took only minor damage to his back and legs. Opening his eyes, he looked around quickly for the source of the spells while he prepared one of his own. Spying a young woman motioning her arms as if preparing a spell, he quickly pointed his finger at her and released his spell. Fireball. The blast knocked her back a step and interrupted her spell. "Game on, bitch!" he shouted.

A roar from behind the mage caused him to turn and see Stormheart with a Minion in each hand, swinging them like weapons. He was working his way over to the pile of weapons and his sword, ignoring the occasional arrow that penetrated his tough skin.

Sordaak looked up and placed two walls of flames upon the parapets where the archers were loosing arrows at a frenetic pace. Too many were finding their target to ignore them. He smiled at the yelps of pain that accompanied the firewalls.

These actions, however, allowed the enemy spellcaster to cast more magic. Flame Strike. Again. Apparently clerics had limited access to offensive spells.

This one knocked Sordaak to the ground. Again. He was getting annoyed with this woman. He rolled to his right, coming up short mid-roll as the arrow protruding from his right side came in contact with the ground. The resultant stabbing pain nearly took his consciousness. He fought the blackness that threatened to overwhelm him and lined up another spell at the young woman trying to slow roast him into oblivion.

He spat the words to another spell and again pointed his finger. An icy cone shot forth and encompassed his adversary. She shrieked and ducked back inside the gates.

Sordaak tried to stand to give chase, but he found he was unable push himself to his feet. His teeth clenched as he sagged back to a sitting position. "Help," he called out.

Cyrillis, only a few steps away administering to Vorgath, heard the feeble cry. She turned and involuntarily her hand went to her mouth. She took two steps toward the magicuser, the words to her most powerful healing spell coming to her mouth of their own volition.

Sordaak was a sight to see. His robe was pinned to his side by the arrow and the lower part of his raiment was soaked in blood. It was also charred and torn in several places.

Cyrillis released the energy as she touched the mage's shoulder. Instantly, she felt his pain ease. Sordaak started to rise. "Hold still," she said as she pushed gently on his shoulder, keeping him from rising.

"I must go after her."

"After I remove that arrow, you can." Knowing the sorcerer's determination, the healer worked quickly. "This might hurt a bit." Cyrillis could see that the arrow was not lodged deeply, but the head was larger than most. This was indeed going to hurt.

The cleric mumbled the words to a prayer, placed her left hand on Sordaak's side around the arrow and with her right she got a firm grip on the arrow shaft. She released the words to the spell as she yanked hard on the arrow.

A moan escaped the sorcerer's lips as his eyes threatened to roll back in his head. Then the spell kicked in and his shoulders squared. "Thank you," he said as he stood and strode purposefully in the direction of the gate.

Thrinndor turned in time to see the mage pass through the gates. "Sordaak, wait!" The sorcerer paused and turned look at the paladin. "Take Stormheart with you for muscle!"

Sordaak glanced around the area in front of the gates. Already there were the bodies of more than twenty scattered about, with at least that number still standing. In the brief time he hesitated, the giant slew two more.

"Muscle is not required where I go." Sordaak glanced into the alley on the other side of the gates. "Do not follow me until I summon you." The mage stepped inside before the paladin could say more.

"No," Cyrillis moaned, and she took a step to follow the sorcerer.

Thrinndor grabbed her by the arm, forcing her to turn and look into his eyes. "He knows what he is doing."

"But—" Cyrillis' eyes went back to the gates, now devoid of activity.

"We have to trust him." The paladin released the cleric's arm as they were approached by a Minion intent on more than conversation.

Cyrillis was distracted from Sordaak's plight by a shout from Stormheart. He had been beset by five Minions, each armed with halberds, and they had succeeded in taking down the giant. He was bleeding badly from a wound in the back of his leg. One of the enemy had hamstrung him, and was stepping in, halberd held high, to finish the giant.

The healer leapt into action, swinging *Kurril* with all her strength at the attacker. The head of the staff hit the man in the back of his head and then something unusual happened. A bright flash erupted at the contact point and the man's head and shoulders disintegrated in the blast. The remainder of his body collapsed to the frozen ground.

Cyrillis did not have time to be amazed by what she had done, but rather spoke a prayer of healing and touched the giant near the wound on his leg. On contact her healing power poured into the wounded warrior, and the wound closed. But a cursory glance showed the healer that the giant had sustained many other wounds at the hands of the Minions.

She was preparing yet another healing spell when she felt blinding pain in her back. Cyrillis spun to confront her attacker, only to see a woman not much older than herself raise her halberd for a killing blow. The healer tried to raise her staff to block the blow, but her arms felt as if they were made of lead and she could not.

As the blade began its inexorable descent toward her neck, Cyrillis closed her eyes, waiting for the end to come.

It never arrived. She felt a heavy object hit her chest, causing her to open her eyes and widen in horror at the head that lay in her lap. A woman's head with no torso and her eye's still open. She tried to bring her hands around to push the grotesque thing away, but quickly discovered that her arms were the only thing holding her up. When she moved them, she slipped to the ground. She tried without any success to rise, and then Cyrillis' eyes rolled back in her head and darkness overtook her.

"Thrinndor!" Stormheart bellowed. It was his blade that had separated the Minion's head from her shoulders. "Tend to your cleric." He pointed with the blade in his fist at the prone healer. Then he turned to confront two more Minions trying to sneak up on him.

"Shit!" Thrinndor muttered as he dispatched the Minion standing in his way. He ran to the cleric's side and could see her that wounds were mortal. "No!" the paladin shouted as he dropped to his knees and skidded to a halt next to her severely damaged body.

The fighter dropped his sword and shield on the way down and placed both hands on the wound that had split her from shoulder to waist. He then poured every ounce of healing energy he had into her supine form.

The cleric's bleeding stopped and her skin knitted together before his eyes. However, her eyes did not open. The paladin glanced around to ensure he was not about to be disturbed. They were not; Stormheart and Vorgath each had two or three Minions, and there seemed to be no others.

Thrinndor reached down and forced the cleric's right eye open. Her eyes were still rolled back, and this worried him greatly. His healing percipience was nowhere near as good as an actual healer's, but he generally knew what to check for and how to interpret what he found. The paladin leaned in and put both his hands on Cyrillis' shoulders and closed his own eyes in concentration.

He could tell she had lost too much blood, but could discern nothing else that ailed her. So he quickly pulled a water skin from his shoulder harness, jerked the stopper from the bag with his teeth and allowed a small amount to trickle into her mouth. He repeated this a couple of times until her eyes fluttered open.

Thrinndor again used his healing ability—his last for the day, at least until he could rest.

Color returned to Cyrillis' cheeks, and she smiled her thanks until realization as to where she was came flooding back to her. The cleric glanced around quickly as the paladin helped her to her feet.

A once-over revealed to her that both the barbarian and the giant were still fighting, but she was unsure *how* they were able to do so; both were in a bad way. The healer brushed a lock of wayward hair out of the way and threw a spell of healing at the closer giant first, followed immediately by a spell for the dwarf.

That by no means brought the two back to full health, but it treated their immediate needs, and both stood taller for her effort.

Next she checked the paladin, who had moved to assist Vorgath as he was struggling to keep up with the three Minions busy trying to undo the cleric's efforts, but she discovered he was relatively unscathed.

A quick check of her own status caused her to nod approvingly at the job done by the paladin. She was indeed thirsty, but that would have to wait. The barbarian and giant were both still bleeding from several wounds, and Vorgath had a deep purple knot growing on the side of his head where his helm used to cover. Cyrillis used her staff to release more healing energy into the barbarian, paying special heed to the damage done to his head.

She alternated back and forth, applying her healing skills to first one and then the other until she was certain they were going to survive, a fact she felt better about as the last of the Minions succumbed to the ministrations of Thrinndor's sword.

Noting quickly that the four of them were in relatively good shape, the healer turned toward the main gate and closed her eyes. She reached out with her percipience but was thwarted by the thickness of the walls. Cyrillis couldn't sense any of her companions. Of special concern was Sordaak. She bit her lip in frustration and worry.

Thrinndor and Vorgath did a quick count and came up with forty-nine. The paladin stared at the open gates and pondered. That still left twenty-five or thirty unaccounted for.

That was too many.

*

Sordaak stopped once inside the main gates to allow his eyes to adjust. There was no sense getting his brains knocked out by someone he couldn't see. He summoned Fahlred and sent the familiar ahead to scout.

As part of his studies back in the Library of Antiquity, he had examined the layout of the University and committed it to memory. In the event memory failed him, he had also committed it to paper. Sordaak smiled as he pulled the image up in his mind. While he couldn't be sure where the priest had gone, he had a pretty good idea and headed that way by continuing down the alley to the right of the main gates.

Pulling a ring of invisibility he had purchased for such situations from a small pouch at his side, he quickly slipped it on and ducked into another alley that had branched off to his left. In the event he encountered an unfriendly, the mage prepared a spell.

Not wanting his attention to waver, whenever he needed to check on what his familiar was seeing the sorcerer ducked into a dark place and paused. He was beginning to get concerned as neither of them had encountered anyone when an image of what he was certain were the doors to the main temple formed in his mind. He bade Fahlred to wait for him there and got an acknowledgment before the mage continued.

Sordaak rounded a corner and came to an abrupt halt when he discovered two Minion guards standing at attention blocking the passage. Glancing around quickly, he ducked into the entrance to a building and briefly considered his options. He smiled as he settled on one and changed spells.

Removing a different component from his pouch, he focused his attention on the larger guard to the left and weaved his spell. Abruptly the guard stiffened and then turned to glare at his companion. He then pulled back his fist and punched the man hard in the side of his head.

"Hey!" shouted the unknowing Minion. "What the hell was that for?"

The first guard lowered his pole-axe to a fighting stance and snarled something unintelligible as he jabbed it at the other man, clearly trying to run him through.

Sordaak snickered silently as he used the distraction to slip past the two. The mage made sure to check on them until they were out of sight behind yet another twist in the alley, but he needn't have bothered. The two could be heard arguing and fighting long after he had passed.

A couple more twists in the path and he found where his familiar patiently waited. Sordaak lifted an eyebrow as he lifted the pull ring only to discover the ornate double doors before him were locked. He waved his hand dismissively and the doors blasted open in a thunderous crash.

The sorcerer sauntered slowly through the opening created as though strolling through a park. His mind was racing though, hoping the High Lord didn't have many companions.

"Was that necessary?" Kiarrah stood on a dais, next to the raised altar. She held *Pendromar, Dragon's Breath* nonchalantly in her right hand.

Sordaak glanced left and right but saw no one else in the chamber. "I believe you have something that belongs to me." He could see through Fahlred's eyes that there were two bodies concealed behind a set of draperies at the back of the raised dais. Silently, the magicuser asked his familiar to look for another entrance.

"What, this old thing?" Kiarrah shifted the staff to her left hand, flaunting the artifact as she did.

Fahlred showed his master a hidden door situated between the two men hidden behind the draperies. Sordaak had suspected as much. The mage stepped around the end of a rear bench and slowly began walking down the center aisle. This, the main temple, was quite large, with seating for easily a couple hundred Minions.

"Yes, that old thing," Sordaak replied, his tone mocking. "Hand it over, and I may yet allow you to live." He didn't like this; she should have more protection than two. The High Priest was far too confident. The mage silently directed his familiar to continue looking around.

Kiarrah tipped her head back and laughed. Sordaak decided he didn't care much for that. There was something familiar about the young woman, though; he was certain he had seen her somewhere before. He shook his head, unable to place her. "Surely you do not believe it will be that easy?"

Even the voice was familiar. "You can't even begin to use its powers." The fleeting look of frustration that crossed the priest's face was enough to tell Sordaak he'd guessed correctly.

"Oh, no?" Kiarrah slammed the heel of the staff to the stone floor of the dais and leaned it toward the still approaching mage. "See what I have *not* begun to use," she shouted as a gout of flames shot from the head of the staff.

Sordaak had expected the flames, however. Quickly he brought both arms up, crossed them in front of his face and muttered a word of warding. The flames parted as they got to the mage's arms and went around him without any damage.

"That's it?" Sordaak sneered. "A novice could have called forth that paltry spell." He was getting worried; he was certain there were more Minions in the chamber, but Fahlred couldn't find them. But he knew he couldn't wait any longer. The magicuser uncrossed his arms and pointed the index finger on each hand at the points where his familiar had shown the hidden adversaries. Lightning bolts shot from his fingertips, and the electricity danced at the indicated points. Sordaak gritted his teeth as he continued to pour energy into the spell, holding the blinding bolts on the bodies now wriggling in pain behind the curtains.

Releasing the spell suddenly, he shouted a word of force and waved his hands over his head. As the two bodies sagged to the floor, the doors Sordaak had entered through slammed shut and the bolt slid into place. A click was heard as the hidden door also latched shut.

Kiarrah's eyes opened wide. This had not gone as she had planned. Quickly, those same eyes narrowed to slits as she gripped *Pendromar* tightly with her left hand, tilting the staff slightly so that the head was toward her adversary. Next she raised her right hand, extending it toward the caster and her fingers flexed as she allowed her eyes to roll back into her head as she concentrated on a new spell.

Sordaak stopped in his tracks as he felt his heart begin to pound. It was his turn for his eyes to open wide as he realized what she was doing. Quickly he shouted the words to his fireball spell and launched it at the priest.

The detonation of flames was on target but other than a singed robe and a red face and hands she showed no outward signs of damage. Kiarrah's chanting grew louder as the magicuser felt the pressure in his chest also increase. The blood was pounding in his ears as he shouted the words to his cone of ice spell and quickly released the energy.

The ferocity of the resulting blast of ice particles actually knocked the High Priest back a step, but her concentration never wavered.

Now Sordaak was seeing spots from the increased pressure in his head, and he was certain his chest was about to burst. "Get Thrinndor!" he shouted at his familiar, not even bothering to verify the quasit was still in the room. Involuntarily, he took a step forward, fighting the urge to do so, but needing to do something that might reduce the pain he felt.

Frost still coated the priest's eyebrows when Sordaak pointed his finger again. This time he chose lightning bolt and released the energy, again knocking Kiarrah back a step. Still, she continued to chant, although her smoldering robe hung in tatters from her shoulders and her skin was charred in several places.

Sordaak felt the panic rise in his throat as he was now almost completely blind and could hear nothing over the pounding of blood in his ears. Surely his chest would soon explode and his journey to the afterlife would begin.

In a final effort he stopped fighting the urge to approach the cleric; instead, he stumbled forward as fast as he could, tripping over the unseen raised edge of the dais. With his final conscious thought the words to another spell tumbled from his froth-covered lips and he used the energy of his falling to launch himself at Kiarrah, her chanting now at a feverish pitch. Sordaak released the energy to the spell he had prepared through his hands as they clasped around the cleric's throat.

Electrical energy surged through his hands and blackened what was once lovely skin, sending her crashing backward with the magicuser landing on top. Then everything went dark for the sorcerer as consciousness faded.

Chapter Twenty-Nine

Kiarrah & Shaarna

As the adrenaline from the battle subsided, Cyrillis made the rounds to find her companions had weathered the storm relatively well, yet her ministrations were necessary to some extent for each of them.

She clucked her tongue in mock fashion as she bandaged the barbarian. "You really should consider a shield."

Vorgath shrugged. "Not gonna happen."

The healer smiled and nodded. "I know."

Thrinndor watched the interchange with amusement and was startled by the sudden appearance of Fahlred two feet away.

"Master dying," the quasit spoke in guttural common. "Says you should come, now."

"*What?*" Thrinndor surged to his feet, yanking his sword from his belt as he did. "*Where?*"

"Follow." Fahlred turned and ran surprisingly fast on his short legs toward the gates.

The paladin glanced around, noting the others had neither seen nor heard the encounter. "Sordaak is down," he shouted. He then turned and sprinted after the mage's familiar, knowing the others would follow.

They did, grabbing weapons and surging into action.

Cyrillis, a look of grim determination on her face, grasped *Kurril* in her right hand and fell in step behind the paladin.

Thrinndor rounded a corner into an alley and came across a confused Minion standing over the fallen body of one of his companions. The paladin didn't ask questions. He made a quick thrust with his sword as he ran past, knocking the man into a wall. He didn't bother to turn to see if his efforts were effective, knowing if the man yet lived, Vorgath would take care of that.

The barbarian did so without breaking stride.

Thrinndor skidded to a halt behind the quasit, who was staring at a pair of ornate doors.

"Here," the quasit said and winked out of sight.

As the rest of the companions joined him, the paladin tested the doors, finding them locked. In exasperation, he rattled the doors to gauge their strength.

Abruptly Stormheart stepped forward, pushed the paladin aside and kicked the doors open with a crash. The giant glanced over at Thrinndor and shrugged. "I thought we were in a hurry."

"Indeed," the paladin said as he rushed into the room, followed immediately by Cyrillis.

Thrinndor went directly to the dais, but stopped short; staring at the grisly scene before him. Sordaak remained on top of the High Priest, his hands still wrapped around her blackened neck. Neither moved. Fahlred lay on his back next to his master, his unseeing eyes staring at the high ceiling.

"Move!" Cyrillis said through clinched teeth as she shoved the paladin out of the way and rushed to the magicuser's side.

"I am going to have to find better places to stand."

"What happened to him?" Vorgath asked, pointing to the quasit.

Thrinndor looked where the barbarian pointed. "If a familiar's master dies, they die as well."

"Oh."

"He is not dead," Cyrillis said as she rolled Sordaak over onto his back. She didn't sound all that convinced. "He will not die." The healer put both hands on the mage's chest and closed her eyes. Her percipience told her that the heart itself had been damaged.

Cyrillis quickly spoke the words to a spell and reached inside the sorcerer with her power. She broke into a sweat as the effort required strained her abilities. Satisfied, she pushed back, opened her eyes and spoke the words of healing.

Sordaak's eyes sprang open and his back arched as he took in a gasping breath. The healer repeated the healing spell, the sorcerer's posture eased and he sat up. "Thank you." His voice was coarse. "Some weirdo kept trying to get me to come toward the light." He shook his head. "The light didn't appear all that attractive and," he looked into the cleric's eyes, "I'm pretty sure I'm still needed here." Sordaak smiled.

Cyrillis flung her arms around the mage's neck. "Damn straight!" Tears were running down her cheeks. She pushed back and wiped the tears away with the back of her hand. "You are not permitted to go into battle without a healer—me—ever again."

Sordaak considered arguing that point, but one look at the cleric's face and he decided that would not be in his best interest. The mage cleared his throat and averted his eyes. That's when he saw his prone familiar for the first time. "No!" Quickly he looked back to Cyrillis. "Heal him! He must not be permitted to die!"

Startled, the cleric checked the quasit. "I am not sure I can."

"You must try!"

Uncertain, Cyrillis turned back to the quasit. Hesitantly, she placed a hand on the chest of the creature. She found that touching the demon-spawn made her skin crawl. But Sordaak's insistence made her continue. The healer took in a deep breath, closed her eyes and whispered the words to her spell. Gently she again reached out with her health-sense, looking for any sign of damage.

Confused, she opened her eyes and pushed back. "He is not damaged that I can tell. His heart just stopped." Quickly she spoke the words of healing and touched her hand to the creature's bare shoulder.

Fahlred winked out and back in again, this time on Sordaak's shoulder. Quickly he wrapped his tail around the sorcerer's neck and hissed at the cleric.

"Fahlred says thank you," Sordaak said with a smile.

"That did not sound like thank you to me!"

"I assure you it was."

"What happened here?" Thrinndor demanded. He stood over the dead High Priest.

Sordaak stood and dusted himself off. "That bitch tried to remove my heart." He walked over and kicked the young woman in the head. "She damn near succeeded." He put his hand over his heart and rubbed his chest.

"Where's that damn thief?" Vorgath demanded.

"I am sure he and his company are fine and will join us shortly." Thrinndor looked around. Something was bothering him.

"Finally!" Sordaak bent and pulled the staff from the dead High Priest's fingers. "*Pendromar!*" He held the staff at arm's length and admired the intricate runes carved in the ancient wood.

"Give me that!" A young woman ran out from behind the draperies, ripped the staff out of Sordaak's hands and sprinted for the entrance doors.

"*Stop her!*" Sordaak shouted.

The young woman looked neither right nor left in her haste. Thrinndor reached out to grab her arm as she passed, but she evaded his grasp, hitting him with the staff. An explosion rocked the room, and the paladin was thrown back.

Sordaak waved his hand and for the second time the entrance doors slammed shut. This time, however, the bolt was unable to slide into place as it had been broken by the giant's entry.

The young woman stopped at the doors, initially frustrated by their closing. Quickly she reached for a pull ring and heaved with all her strength. The door swung easily inward, and she was about to step through when it slammed shut again. She looked up to see the giant standing over her, holding the door shut.

"Let me pass!" she shouted as she swung the staff at the giant, connecting with his right hip. Another explosion occurred and Stormheart was flung backward.

In triumph, the young woman again reached for the pull ring, but by this time Sordaak had recovered. He reached into his component pouch as he stepped off the dais. He strode down the aisle and cast his spell.

The young woman's hand stopped short of the ring. She tried again, but some unseen force prevented her. She spun, placing her back against the unseen force. Her eyes darted around, alighting on the approaching mage. "Release me."

"Hand over the staff, explain why it is you took it from me, how it is that you are able to hold it and I may yet let you live."

The young woman looked around fervently and bolted to her right, skirting the benches to a side aisle, running back toward the dais.

"Stop her! There's a door behind the drapes!"

Vorgath was closest and managed to get to the door first.

The woman raised the staff to strike.

"If you try to hit me with that staff, I won't hesitate to take your head off with this." Vorgath brandished *Flinthgoor* with both hands to show he meant business.

The woman didn't even hesitate. Without slowing, she whipped the staff around and in a flash slammed the barbarian in the groin with it. The usual explosion was heard and Vorgath crossed his eyes and crumbled to the ground, his hands clutching his groin.

The woman was by him and out the door before anyone else could get close. Sordaak hadn't enough energy left for another wall. "Stop her!" He was already at a dead run, trying to catch her.

Cyrillis squatted by the barbarian's side, and she had to stifle a smile. "Now where have I seen that maneuver before?" However, she could see the dwarf was in agony, so she dispensed with further discussion on the matter and eased his pain with her healing magic. She went light, however, as she too was running low on energy.

Color returned to the barbarian's face. "Thanks," he mumbled as he sat up. With the cleric's assistance, he climbed unsteadily to his feet.

"I thought you were wearing a codpiece?" Cyrillis asked as politely as she could.

"I *am*!" protested the barbarian as he resisted the urge to reach down and rub the affected area. "I don't know what the hell that staff does to people but, when I catch her, we won't have to worry about an attack from *her* anymore!"

That said, he leaned toward the door and hoped his wobbly legs would keep him upright as he began his pursuit. They did.

Sordaak had been gone for only a moment—with Thrinndor having exited right behind him—when much cursing and no small scuffle could be heard approaching from the other direction.

Vorgath stopped short when one of the female giants came through the door with the scratching, clawing and cursing woman held at arm's length. Savinhand, Breunne and one of the other giants soon followed.

"Anyone lose a human female?" the giant asked.

Vorgath checked to ensure the struggling woman didn't have the staff. "Put her down, and I'll lose her permanently!"

Sordaak and Thrinndor burst back into the temple. "Where's the staff?" the mage demanded immediately.

"Here," replied the ranger. He unwrapped a blanket-covered parcel he held in his left hand, being careful not to touch the wood.

"Where is the other giant?" Cyrillis asked, noting one was missing.

"Back there," replied the giant not carrying the woman. The woman held at arm's length was silent now as she stared at the barbarian, who was approaching with malice in his eyes. The giant looked over at the cleric. "She was unable to stop this woman and her staff. She may require your assistance."

"I'll show you where," Savinhand said.

Cyrillis followed the rogue at a run.

Sordaak rushed over to retrieve the staff. *Pendromar* in hand, he stepped in front of Vorgath, who growled from deep in his chest. "Get out of my way, trickster."

"Not yet," replied the mage, his voice placating. "There are a few questions she must answer for me first. *Then* she's all yours."

The barbarian mulled it over, clearly wanting to argue. Finally he set the head of *Flinthgoor* on the stone floor and leaned on it. "Go on. Ask your questions." His lips twitched. "I'll wait."

The mage nodded. "Thank you. I'll be brief." He turned back to face the giant, who still held the young woman's feet clear of the floor. "Put her down. If she tries to escape, hit her with that club. Hard. I don't need the answers *that* bad."

The giant nodded and set the woman down. Her eyes darted around, but she could see she was surrounded and chose to stand still. She crossed her arms on her chest, flipped her head to get her long dark hair out of her face and let out a breath noisily in the age-old fashion indicating she intended to say nothing.

Sordaak rolled his eyes. "You'll talk, or Vorgy gets to have his way with you; and I will not guarantee his intentions."

It was the woman's turn to roll her eyes. "Your intention is to let him have his way with me whether I talk or not. Remember?"

Sordaak cocked his head to the right. "There is that, I admit." He thought for a minute. "Well, if you provide the answers I am looking for, I will see what I can do about commuting your sentence."

Vorgath growled again.

The sorcerer turned, faced the barbarian and winked. The big fighter considered arguing, but changed his mind. He nodded slightly.

"Yeah, right," the woman said, sarcasm dripping from her voice. "You will get *nothing* from me!"

Sordaak ignored the woman's outburst. "Tell me how it is that you can use this staff." He held *Pendromar* up for her to see. "Only those of the proper lineage may use it."

The woman sighed deeply and made a show of inspecting a chipped fingernail, but she said nothing.

The sorcerer also sighed as he looked over her shoulder and nodded at the giant behind her.

The female giant returned the nod, raised her club and swung it, connecting with the woman's shoulder and knocking her to the floor.

"I'll start with a simpler question: What is your name?"

The woman rubbed her shoulder while glaring at the giant, who showed exactly zero emotion in return. She climbed back to her feet, favoring her shoulder as she did, but remained silent.

Sordaak nodded to the giant again.

"Wait!" The woman rubbed her shoulder some more, but she continued to glare at the giant. Slowly she turned her glare on the magicuser. "Shaarna. My name is Shaarna."

Stunned, Sordaak took two steps back, stumbled and sat down hard on a first row bench. He swallowed hard a couple of times, trying to find his voice.

Shaarna raised an eyebrow. "You did not know?"

The mage shook his head. "Spell it," he was finally able to get out.

Shaarna briefly considered not answering, but a glance behind her revealed the giant smacking her club into her free hand. She continued to glare at the giant as she spelled it out. "S-H-A-A-R-N-A." Finished, she turned to see Sordaak's reaction.

The mage's mouth moved a couple of times with nothing coming out. "It can't be." He stood and walked slowly to stand before the woman. "Leave us," he said, his eyes never leaving those of Shaarna. When no one moved, he turned and shouted, "*LEAVE US!*"

Feet shifted, but no one made a move to leave. Thrinndor spoke first. "Explain."

Sordaak glared at the paladin and he opened his mouth to shout again. Abruptly, he dropped his eyes to the stone at his feet and clenched his teeth. When he looked back up, the mage was much calmer. "She is my sister. What we must discuss is for my ears only. For now."

Thrinndor's eyes opened wide in surprise. His gaze shifted to the woman. "If she tries to escape?"

"If she tries, she will be prevented," Sordaak replied. His eyes moved to his sister and held hers. "But she won't."

Shaarna crossed her arms on her chest non-committedly.

"Leave us."

Thrinndor looked around the room at his companions, his eyes winding up back on the sorcerer. "Very well. We will await you out in the alley."

Vorgath stepped up and put his face in Shaarna's. "*Please* attempt to escape." He then turned on a heel and strode from the room.

When everyone but Sordaak and his sister had left, Sordaak walked over and closed the main entrance double doors and then walked quickly to the hidden door and closed it as well.

When the magicuser came out from behind the curtain, he saw his sister standing on the dais staring down at the dead woman that lay there.

Shaarna looked up at the sorcerer's approach. "You must be more powerful than I was told to be able to kill her by yourself. She was *very* powerful. I underestimated you."

"She did as well." Sordaak looked down at the High Priest and then back up at his sister, stunned yet again. The resemblance between the two was unmistakable.

Before he could get his voice going again, Shaarna spoke. "You didn't know she was our sister, either?" Sordaak shook his head. "We were twins."

It was too much for the sorcerer to digest. He stumbled over to a throne-like chair on the dais, sat down and put his face in his hands. When he finally looked up he asked, "Why was I not told?"

Shaarna met his gaze, her face grim. "It was not something you brought up when anyone who hinted that the local lord might be promiscuous suddenly disappeared."

"Lord Faantlaw? My *father*?" Sordaak was too stunned to put the incredulity he felt into the statement.

Shaarna nodded. "It was widely known—although seldom spoken of aloud—that more than your father's eyes wandered." She hesitated, not sure how far she could take this conversation. "*Our father's.*" The young woman licked her lips. "Although in the case of my mother, it may have not been entirely his fault."

A befuddled magicuser shook his head in an attempt to rattle his thoughts into some semblance of order. "Not his fault? How so?"

Shaarna took in a deep breath; she had gone too far now to stop. Her brother deserved the truth, *needed* the truth. "My mother was a beautiful woman and fairly young when she seduced your father."

"Wait. *Seduced?*"

Shaarna nodded, giving her time to piece together what she needed to say, and figure out in what order to say it. "I know this must all come as a shock to you—"

"Damn right! I was told I was an only child."

"Understood." Shaarna's pretty face showed a deep determination that hadn't been there moments ago. "This next piece of information is not going to help matters: It is rumored that Lord Faantlaw fathered at least a half-dozen children in Nomarr and possibly others in neighboring villages."

Sordaak stared at his sister, his lips moving without a sound. Finally he was able to mutter. "Horny old bastard! That certainly complicates things somewhat."

"You have no idea," Shaarna said softly.

"What do you mean by that?" Sordaak was suddenly belligerent.

His sister returned that belligerence. "Your ignorance of your siblings has greatly complicated the matter of the lineage of Dragma."

That little explosion almost did the spellcaster in. "What? How does my connection to that ancient sorcerer concern you?"

"Because that makes me—and every other bastard child of our father—of that same lineage."

The sorcerer's mouth dropped open. Somehow that little fact had evaded him. Until now. Sordaak rubbed his temples. Damn! Now his head was beginning to hurt. Abruptly he held out his hand to the side and called forth a flame, allowing a portion of that flame to sear his hand. He recognized the onset of his mind wandering to another reality, and knew by experience that pain would ward him of that impending transference. He shook his hand, dousing the flames.

Curiosity got the better of Shaarna. "What was that about?"

Sordaak looked at his reddened hand. "That's a long story, and I'd rather not get into it right now."

Shaarna looked from his hand and back to his eyes. "Very well, perhaps some other time." She hesitated again, sneaking a peek at her brother. "There's more."

"Of course there is! Now what?"

Shaarna bit her lip. "It's about my mother."

Sordaak lifted an eyebrow and waited.

"And why she seduced our father." It was her turn to wait. She was disappointed. Sigh. "She seduced him because of her lineage." Sordaak's eyes opened wide, but he still said nothing. "My mother is the product of a planned combination of lineages." She looked over at her sister. "As are—were—my sister and I."

Sordaak stared at his sibling, his mind whirling. "I'm sure you think what you leading up to is obvious. But please spell it out for me."

Shaarna nodded. "My mother was of the direct lineage of the line of Angra-Khan—"

"WHAT?"

"—and Valdaar."

*

Sordaak used what remained of his strength to pull open the right door that led back out to the alley and his friends. He stepped through slowly, using *Pendromar* as a crutch.

Cyrillis jumped down from the barrel she had been sitting on and rushed to his side. The cleric put her arm around his waist and supported him from his other side. It was all she could do; she had used up her energy reserves on the giant. "Are you all right?"

Sordaak nodded as he continued down the alley, headed for the main gate.

Vorgath pushed his helm back up to the top of his head and looked up from his resting place in a doorway. "Where's the girl?"

"I let her go."

"You *what*?"

The sorcerer straightened his stance and pushed his shoulders back. "I let her go."

"Explain yourself."

Sordaak turned to stare at the paladin. He had expected this reaction—it was one of the reasons he had sent Shaarna out the back door more than a half-hour ago. He'd waited in the chair on the dais, using the time to figure out how much he needed to tell his companions. And how to say that which needed to be said. None of that helped much now that he was face to face with them, his *friends*. He knew that lying to them was no longer an option.

The spellcaster allowed his shoulders to sag. "I can't—at least not now." He looked up and into the paladin's eyes, silently begging him to not press the issue. "All I will say for now is that we may yet need her. Please trust me on this."

After a few moments the paladin nodded. "Very well. We will trust your judgment in this matter for the time being." He looked around at the others. "We must rest."

Sordaak shook his head. "Not here."

Thrinndor's right eyebrow arched.

The mage continued down the alley toward the main gate. He waved an arm for them to follow him. "We can't stay here—not even to rest. This place is built to diminish energy such as mine."

"Like in the chambers preceding The Library?" Breunne asked.

"Similar." Sordaak nodded. "I don't have time to explain." He had almost waited too long in the temple, and now he was feeling it.

The companions were silent as they fell in step. Breunne and Savinhand took the lead, with Vorgath bringing up the rear. Thrinndor didn't expect much more in the way of trouble, but it was best to be prepared. There were still too many Minions missing.

Outside the gates Sordaak was able to square his shoulders. Clearly, he felt better having exited the palace.

"What about Pantorra?" Cyrillis asked suddenly.

Savinhand looked over at the healer. "She's been here and gone. We—Breunne, the giants and I—ran into her while diminishing the resistance." He smiled, flashing his white, even teeth. "She was in human form and she was carrying a large bag with three eggs inside."

"Huh," Vorgath grunted. "I guess she wasn't lying after all."

Breunne shook his head slowly. "No, I believe she was sincere in her efforts to aid us. She told us that she understood our distrust of her, and that she owed us." The ranger turned to face Sordaak. "She said she owed you most of all, and that she would keep her vow. She is your servant, and yours to call." His eyes glistened as he turned and looked at the others. "She said to thank all of you for her and that she will remain forever indebted to us."

Cyrillis stood tall. "I am glad she got her eggs. Hers will be such a great tale to hear!"

Sordaak looked over at the healer and smiled a broad smile. He then turned to Thrinndor. "We must be moving."

"You are in no shape to travel," the paladin replied.

"I'll make it." The mage looked up at the sky to gauge the time. "If we leave now we can make the cabin before night falls."

"That will be a hard trip, and we are without healing and magic until we rest." Thrinndor clearly wanted to stay.

Suddenly, Sordaak understood why. His demeanor softened as he put a hand on the fighter's shoulder. "Your sword is not here, and I doubt you will glean any information from within these walls." The paladin's shoulders sagged, and he nodded. The magicuser continued. "Theremault told us what we needed to know, and that was later supported by Pantorra: Bahamut has your blade. To get *Valdaar's Fist*, we must either convince the king of all dragons surrender it to us, or wrench it from his cold, dead hands."

This ends *Ice Homme*, Book Three in the Valdaar's Fist saga.
Please join me, Sordaak, Thrinndor, Cyrillis, Vorgath, Savinhand, and Breunne
as this epic tale concludes in *The Platinum Dragon*.
There are yet many surprises to spring.

Thanks for reading.

Forthcoming in 2015...
The Valdaar's Fist Saga Continues!

Valdaar's Fist Book One – *Dragma's Keep*

Valdaar's Fist Book Two – *The Library of Antiquity*

Valdaar's Fist Book Three – *Ice Homme*

Valdaar's Fist Book Four – *The Platinum Dragon*

Acknowledgements

I'd like to thank my beta readers. There is a core group of three people who have urged, guided, and cajoled me into continuing these adventures that are my books.

Robert Lewis was the first person to lay eyes on *Dragma's Keep*, and he continues to get first dibs on subsequent books. His kind words and genuine support help to keep me moving forward—as do his own works, for he is a musician and as such has written several songs about my books and the characters therein. I hope that one day we can work together to produce those songs for they are truly beautiful!

Todd Rindlisbacher is a reader of all things fantasy. He asked to read my first book and continues to ask for more. He has a keen mind and I value his input on my character development and many other aspects of these books.

Kellie Sands is an avid reader and quick to give appropriate criticism whether good or bad. She has had several insights that have made these books decidedly better.

Thank you all and I hope we'll continue this relationship for many books to come.

About the Author

Vance Pumphrey traces the evolution of his high fantasy novels from his Nuclear Engineering career in the U.S. Navy—not an obvious leap. He started playing Dungeons and Dragons while in the Navy, though, and the inspiration for the Valdaar's Fist series was born.

Ice Homme is the third book in the Valdaar's Fist quartet. A fourth book in the series follows soon.

Retired from the Navy, Vance lives in Seattle with his wife of thirty-plus years.

To find out when the next Valdaar's Fist book will be released, check out VancePumphrey.com.